T0359195

NO.1 *NEW YORK TIMES* BESTSELLING AUTHOR

DEBBIE MACOMBER

WITH

REBECCA WINTERS   KIM FINDLAY

Midnight Wishes

MILLS & BOON

CONTENTS

SAME TIME, NEXT YEAR   5
Debbie Macomber

THE PRINCESS'S NEW YEAR WEDDING   177
Rebecca Winters

A NEW YEAR'S EVE PROPOSAL   311
Kim Findlay

Same Time, Next Year

Debbie Macomber

The
ESSENTIAL COLLECTION

Shipment One

A Little Bit Country
Country Bride
Wanted: Perfect Partner
Cindy and the Prince
Some Kind of Wonderful
The Courtship of Carol Sommars

Shipment Two

Navy Wife
Navy Blues
Navy Brat
Navy Woman
Navy Baby
Navy Husband

Shipment Three

Yours and Mine
The Bachelor Prince
Denim and Diamonds
The Wyoming Kid
The Man You'll Marry
Marriage Wanted
Laughter in the Rain

Shipment Four

The Cowboy's Lady
The Sheriff Takes a Wife
Marriage of Inconvenience
Stand-In Wife
Bride on the Loose
Same Time, Next Year

Shipment Five

Rainy Day Kisses
Mail-Order Bride
The Matchmakers
Father's Day
A Friend or Two
No Competition

Shipment Six

First Comes Marriage
White Lace and Promises
Friends—and Then Some
The Way to a Man's Heart
Hasty Wedding
That Wintry Feeling
Those Christmas Angels

Shipment Seven

Borrowed Dreams
Starlight
Promise Me Forever
Shadow Chasing
For All My Tomorrows
The Playboy and the Widow

Shipment Eight

Fallen Angel
Yesterday's Hero
Reflections of Yesterday
All Things Considered
The Trouble With Caasi
Almost Paradise

DEBBIE MACOMBER

is a number one *New York Times* and *USA TODAY* best-selling author. Her books include *1225 Christmas Tree Lane, 1105 Yakima Street, A Turn in the Road, Hannah's List* and *Debbie Macomber's Christmas Cookbook,* as well as *Twenty Wishes, Summer on Blossom Street* and *Call Me Mrs. Miracle.* She has become a leading voice in women's fiction worldwide and her work has appeared on every major bestseller list, including those of the *New York Times, USA TODAY, Publishers Weekly* and *Entertainment Weekly.* She is a multiple award winner, and won the 2005 Quill Award for Best Romance. There are more than one hundred million copies of her books in print. Two of her Harlequin MIRA Christmas titles have been made into Hallmark Channel Original Movies, and the Hallmark Channel has launched a series based on her bestselling Cedar Cove series. For more information on Debbie and her books, visit her website, www.debbiemacomber.com.

To Beth Huizenga, my friend.
I admire your strength, your romantic heart
and your love of life.

PROLOGUE

New Year's Eve—Las Vegas, Nevada

JAMES HAD BEEN WARNED. Ryan Kilpatrick, a longtime friend and fellow attorney, had advised him to stay clear of the downtown area tonight. The crowd that gathered on Fremont Street between Main and Las Vegas Boulevard was said to be close to twenty thousand.

But James couldn't resist. Although he had a perfectly good view of the festivities from his hotel room window, he found the enthusiasm of the crowd contagious. For reasons he didn't care to examine, he wanted to be part of all this craziness.

The noise on the street was earsplitting. Everyone seemed to be shouting at once. The fireworks display wasn't scheduled to begin for another thirty minutes, and James couldn't see how there was room for a single other person.

A large number of law-enforcement officers roamed the area, confiscating beer bottles and handing out paper cups. A series of discordant blasts from two-foot-long horns made James cringe. Many of the participants wore decorative hats handed out by the casinos and blew paper noisemakers that uncurled with each whistle.

James remained on the outskirts of the throng, silently enjoying himself despite the noise and confusion. If he were younger, he might have joined in the festivities.

Thirty-six wasn't old, he reminded himself, but he looked and felt closer to forty. Partners in prestigious law firms didn't wear dunce caps and blow noisemakers. He was too conservative—some might say stodgy—for such nonsense, but it was New Year's Eve and staying in his room alone held little appeal.

Impatient for the fireworks display, the crowd started chanting. James couldn't make out the words, but the message was easy enough to understand. It amused him that the New Year's celebration would be taking place three hours early in order to coordinate with the one in New York's Times Square. Apparently no one seemed to care about the time difference.

As if in response to the demand, a rocket shot into the air from the roof of the Plaza Hotel. The night sky brightened as a starburst exploded. The crowd cheered wildly.

Although he'd intended to stand on the sidelines, James found himself unwillingly thrust deeper and deeper into the crowd. Luckily he wasn't prone to claustrophobia. People crushed him from all sides. At another time, in another place, he might have objected, but the joy of the celebration overrode any real complaint.

It was then that he saw her.

She was struggling to move away from the crowd, with little success. James wasn't sure what had originally attracted his attention, but once he noticed her, he couldn't stop watching. Joyous shouts and cheers rose in the tightly packed crowd, but the young woman didn't share the excitement. She looked as if she'd rather be anywhere else in the world.

She was fragile, petite and delicate in build. He saw that she fought against the crowd but was trapped despite her best efforts.

James soon found himself gravitating in her direction. Within minutes she was pressed up against him, chin tucked into her neck as she tried to avoid eye contact.

"Excuse me," he said.

She glanced up at him and attempted a smile. "I was the one who bumped into you."

He was struck by how beautiful she was. Her soft brown hair curved gently at her shoulders, and he was sure he'd never seen eyes more dark or soulful. He was mesmerized by her eyes—and by the pain he read in their depths.

"Are you all right?" he felt obliged to ask.

She nodded and bit her lip. He realized how pale she was and wondered if she was about to faint.

"Let me help." He wasn't some knight who rescued damsels in distress. Life was filled with enough difficulties without taking on another person's troubles. Yet he couldn't resist helping her.

She answered him with a quick nod of her head.

"Let's get out of here," he suggested.

"I've been trying to do exactly that for the last twenty minutes." Her voice was tight.

James wasn't sure he could do any better, but he planned to try. Taking her by the hand, he slipped around a couple kissing passionately, then past a group of teens with dueling horns, the discordant sound piercing the night. Others appeared more concerned with catching the ashes raining down from the fireworks display than with where they stood.

Perhaps it was his age or the fact that he sounded authoritative, but James managed to maneuver them through the crush. Once they were off Fremont Street, the crowd thinned considerably.

James led her to a small park with a gazebo that afforded them some privacy. She sank onto the bench as if her legs had suddenly given out from under her. He saw that she was trembling and sat next to her, hoping his presence would offer her some solace.

The fireworks burst to life overhead.

"Thank you," she whispered. She stood, teetered, then abruptly sat back down.

"You want to talk about it?" he asked.

"Not really." Having said that, she promptly burst into tears. Covering her face with both hands, she gently rocked back and forth.

Not knowing what to do, James put his arms around her and held her against him. She felt warm and soft in his embrace.

"I feel like such a fool," she said between sobs. "How could I have been so stupid?"

"We're often blind to what we don't want to see."

"Yes, but… Oh, I should've known. I should've guessed there was someone else. Everything makes sense now… I couldn't have been any blinder."

He shrugged, murmuring something noncommittal.

She straightened, and James gave her his pressed handkerchief. She unfolded it, wiped away the tears and then clutched it in both hands.

"I'm sorry," she choked out.

"Talking might help," he said.

She took several moments to mull this over. "I found him with another woman," she finally said. "He wanted me to come to Vegas with him after Christmas, and I couldn't get time off from work. So I said he should go and have fun with his friends. Then...then I was able to leave early this afternoon. I wanted to surprise him on New Year's Eve and I drove straight here. I surprised him, all right."

And got the shock of her life, too, James mused.

"They were in bed together." Her words were barely audible, as if the pain was so intense she found it difficult to speak. "I ran away and he came after me and...and tried to explain. He's been seeing her for some time.... He didn't mean to fall in love with her, or so he claims." She laughed and hiccuped simultaneously.

"You were engaged?" he asked, noting the diamond on her left hand.

She nodded, and her gaze fell to her left hand. She suddenly jerked off the diamond ring and shoved it into her purse. "Brett seemed distant in the last few months, but we've both been busy with the holidays. I noticed he didn't seem too disappointed when I couldn't get time off from work. Now I know why."

It was preferable to learn about her fiancé's roving eye before she married him, but James didn't offer platitudes. He hadn't wanted to hear them himself.

"The problem is, I really love him." She shook almost uncontrollably. "I want to claw his eyes out, and yet I know I'll always love him."

"Are you hoping to patch things up?"

She raised her head. "No. It's over. I told him that and I meant it. I could never trust him again, but you know what?" She hesitated and drew in a deep breath. "I think he was grateful when I broke the engagement. He doesn't want me back—he wants *her*." She stiffened, as if bracing herself against an attack.

"It hurts right now, but it'll get better in time," James said, squeezing her hand.

"No, it won't," she whispered. "It'll never get better. I know it won't."

James partially agreed with her. Part of him would always belong to Christy Manning. Even now, he had trouble remembering her married name. She wasn't Christy Manning anymore, but Christy Franklin, and her husband was the sheriff of Custer County, Montana.

"Yes, it will, but it'll take a year," James said briskly.

"Not with me. I'll never get over Brett."

"You believe that right now, because the pain's so bad you can't imagine it'll ever go away, but it does, I promise you."

Slowly she turned to study him. "You know? It sounds as if you're talking from experience."

He nodded. "Five years ago the woman I loved broke off our engagement." He laughed derisively. "You see, there was a small problem. She married someone else while she was engaged to me."

"That's terrible," she said with a sigh of righteous indignation. "What kind of woman would do that?"

"It's not as bad as it sounds. You see, her parents are good friends of mine, and I realize now they pressured Christy into accepting my engagement ring. She was fond of me and agreed because she wanted to make her family happy. I don't think she ever realized how much I loved her."

"Do you still love her?"

It might have been a kindness to lie, but James found he couldn't. "Yes, but not in the same way."

"Despite what I know, I can't picture myself not loving Brett." She straightened and wiped the tears from her cheeks. "I suppose I should introduce myself since I've cried all over your shoulder. I'm Summer Lawton. From Anaheim."

"James Wilkens. Seattle."

They exchanged brief handshakes. Summer lowered her gaze. "I wish I could believe you."

"Believe me?"

"That it'll take a year to get over Brett. It doesn't seem possible. We've been dating for nearly five years and got engaged six months ago. My whole life revolved around him."

At one time James's life had revolved around Christy.

"We were apart for less than a week," Summer continued, "and I was so lonely, I practically went through contortions to get to Vegas just so we could be together tonight."

"The first three months are the most difficult," he told her, remembering the weeks after the breakup with Christy. "Keep busy. The worst thing to do is stay at home and mope, although that's exactly what you'll want to do."

"You don't understand," she insisted. "I really love Brett."

"I really love Christy."

"It's different for a man," she said.

"Is it really?" he countered. "A year," he reiterated. "It'll take a year, but by then you'll have worked through the pain."

Her look revealed her doubt.

"You don't believe me?"

"I just don't think it's possible. Not for me. You see, I'm not the type who falls in love at the drop of a hat. I gave everything I had to Brett. It's like my whole world caved in and there's nothing left to live for."

"Shall we test my theory?" he asked.

"How?"

"Meet me back here on New Year's Eve, one year from tonight."

"Here? In this gazebo?"

"That's right," he said. "Right here."

"Same time, same place, next year."

"Same time, same place, next year," he echoed.

CHAPTER ONE

SUMMER PICKED UP the mail on the way into her apartment and shuffled through the usual bills and sales flyers. The envelope was there, just as it had been on the first of the month for the past eleven months. A letter from James.

He couldn't possibly have any idea how much she looked forward to hearing from him. The first letter had come shortly after they'd met on New Year's Eve and had been little more than a polite inquiry. She hadn't written him back mainly because she was embarrassed about spilling her heart out to a complete stranger.

His second letter had arrived February first. He told her about the weeks immediately after his breakup with Christy, how the pain had intensified when he'd expected it to lessen. His honesty and generosity touched her heart. It seemed uncanny that her anguish mirrored his so completely. She wrote back then, just a short note to tell him how she was doing, to thank him for writing.

That was how it had started. James would write at the beginning of every month and she'd answer. Gradually their letters grew in length, but were never any more frequent. She liked the formality of exchanging letters, preferring that to the quick and casual convenience of email.

In the year since Summer had met James Wilkens, she'd been tempted to phone him only once. That was the day Brett got married. Ironically, his wife wasn't the girl he'd brought to Las Vegas, but someone he'd met recently. Summer had felt wretched and holed herself up in her apartment with a quart of gourmet ice cream and three rented movies. She'd made it through the day with a little fudge swirl and a lot of grit.

Holding James's letter in her hand, Summer tore open the envelope and started reading on her way into the apartment.

"That's from your lawyer friend, isn't it?" Julie, her roommate, asked. Wearing shorts and a halter top, Julie wandered barefoot through the apartment, munching on a carrot.

Summer nodded, kicked off her shoes and lowered herself onto a padded wicker chair. Her eyes never wavered from the page.

"He wants to remind me of our agreement," Summer said, pleased he hadn't forgotten.

"Agreement?"

"To meet him in Vegas on New Year's Eve."

"Are you going?"

Summer had always planned to follow through on her promise, although she probably should've thought twice about meeting a stranger. But he wasn't *really* a stranger. She felt she knew James, was comfortable with him. He was a friend, that was all, someone who'd been there when she needed him.

"Are you going?" Julie repeated.

Summer looked up and nodded.

"What's James like?" Julie asked, sitting across from her. The two of them had been close ever since high school and both of them were in the production at Disneyland. Summer had been especially grateful for Julie's unwavering friendship in the past year.

"He's older," Summer said, chewing the corner of her mouth as she tried to recall everything she could about him. "I'd guess he's at least forty. Kind of a stuffed shirt, to tell you the truth. He's about six feet tall and he must work out or something because I remember being surprised by how strong he was."

"Is he handsome?"

Summer had to smile. "You know, I don't actually remember."

"You don't *remember?*" Julie was incredulous. "I realize you were upset, but surely you noticed."

"He has very nice brown eyes and brown hair with some gray in it." She raised her hand to her own hair and wove a strand around her finger. "I'd say he's more distinguished-looking than handsome."

"Is there something romantic going on between the two of you?"

Summer did care for James, but not in the romantic sense. He'd helped her through the most difficult night of her life. Not only had she clung to him and cried on his shoulder, but he'd stayed with her until the early hours of the morning, listening to her pain, comforting and reassuring her.

"We have a lot in common," was all she'd say to Julie's question about a romance.

"I have a feeling about you and the mysterious James," Julie said, her forehead creased in a frown. "I think you're falling in love."

Love? Not Summer. She'd decided last New Year's Eve that she was finished with love. It sounded melodramatic and a bit ridiculous to be so confident that she'd never love again, but she'd come to that conclusion the minute she found Brett with his girlfriend. Her feelings hadn't changed in the past eleven months.

Although he'd never said as much, she was sure James felt the same way after losing Christy. It'd been six years, and from what she knew about him, there wasn't a woman in his life even now. There wouldn't be a man in hers, either.

This didn't mean that Summer never intended to date again. She'd started going out with other men almost immediately. Pride had prompted her actions in the beginning. Later, she wanted to be able to write James and tell him she was back in the swing of things. He'd applauded her efforts and recounted his own endeavors in that area after Christy had broken off the engagement. As she read his account of various disastrous dates, she'd laughed, truly laughed, for the first time in months.

"You're going to meet James on New Year's Eve, and everything will change," Julie said with a knowing smile.

"What do you mean, everything will change?"

"You won't see him as just a friend anymore," Julie predicted. "You might be surprised to discover there's more to him than you suspect."

"Julie, I told you he's got to be forty years old."

"You're sure of this?"

"No," she said reluctantly. "But… I don't know. I picture James sitting in front of a fireplace, smoking a pipe, with his faithful dog sprawled at his side."

"A basset hound, no doubt."

"No doubt," Summer agreed with a laugh. James was wonderful—no argument about that—but she could never see herself falling for him. Nor would he be interested in someone like her. The man was a distinguished attorney, while she starred in a musical version of *Beauty and the Beast* at Disneyland. Working in the theater wasn't an easy way to make a living, but Summer loved the challenge and the excitement.

"You might be surprised," Julie said again. The tone of her voice suggested that great things were going to happen for her friend this New Year's Eve.

New Year's Eve

Summer freely admitted she was nervous about the rendezvous with James. She got to the gazebo nearly fifteen minutes early and was astonished to find him already there. He was sitting on the bench, the one they'd shared a year earlier. In that moment Summer had a chance to study him with fresh eyes.

The first thing that struck her was that Julie was right.

He was nothing like she remembered. Dignified and proper to the very back of his teeth, but there was something compelling about him. She recalled how Julie had wanted to know if James was handsome. If Summer were to answer that question now, she'd give an unequivocal *yes.* But he wasn't handsome in a Hollywood sense. He certainly wasn't boyishly good-looking like Brett, with his sun-streaked blond hair. But James Wilkens was appealing in a way that spoke directly to her heart. She knew from his letters that this was a man of conscience, a man of integrity, a man of honor. All at once Summer felt as if the oxygen had flown from her lungs.

He saw her then and slowly stood. "Summer?" He sounded equally surprised. His eyes widened briefly.

"Hello, James. I'm early," she said, feeling guilty at being caught staring so blatantly. "I'm always early…it's a family trait."

"I am, too." He grinned. "Usually early, I mean."

Summer had been looking forward to this evening for weeks. There was so much she wanted to say, so much she had to tell him. All at once she couldn't think of a single thing. "The streets are crazy," she said in a hurried effort to make conversation. "I didn't want to risk being late."

"Me, neither," he said. "I hope you don't mind, but I made dinner reservations."

"Thank you." She stepped into the gazebo and sat down next to him.

"So," he said, as if he wasn't sure where to start. "How are you?"

Summer laughed lightly. "A lot better than I was last year at this time. I told you Brett got married, didn't I?"

"You wrote about it."

Summer rarely felt shy, but she did now. She owed James more than she could possibly repay. "Your letters were a godsend," she said, "especially during the first few months. I don't know what I would've done without you."

"You would've done just fine." How confident he sounded, as if there was never a doubt that she'd get over her fiancé's betrayal.

"The first of every month, I'd run to the mailbox. Your letters were regular as clockwork and I counted on them." It had become a ritual for her, an important part of her recovery.

"I enjoyed your letters, too," he said. Fireworks splashed across the night sky, momentarily diverting their attention. "Do you want to join in the festivities?" he asked.

Summer shook her head. "Do you mind?"

He smiled. "Actually I'm just as glad. The crowd got to be a bit much last year."

"I'm so glad you were there," Summer said fervently. "You were like a guardian angel. You helped me so much that night."

"You helped me, too."

"Me? How?" Summer could hardly believe that.

"It's true," James assured her. "Seeing your pain reminded me how far I'd come in the years since losing Christy."

"Was it worse knowing she'd married that sheriff?" Summer asked tentatively. For her, learning about Brett's wedding hurt the most. Friends, under the guise of being kind, were more than happy to relate the details and what they knew about his bride. Every piece of information had cut like a knife.

"Yes."

"Weren't you angry?" she asked. How anyone could treat James in such a shabby manner was beyond her. To be engaged to a man as wonderful as James and then to secretly marry someone else was the most underhanded thing Summer had ever heard of.

"I wasn't angry at first, so much as depressed," he said thoughtfully. "Anger came later. It's the reason I took up squash. I worked out my aggression on the court. It helped."

Summer figured that was a sport an attorney would enjoy.

"It must've been hard finding out Brett was married."

She lowered her gaze and nodded. "Other than the first few weeks after he broke our engagement, the day of his wedding was the worst. It seemed so completely unfair that he should be happy while I was hurting so terribly. If it was ever in me to hate him, it would've been then."

"And now?"

"Now," she repeated. "I certainly don't hate Brett, but I don't love him like I did a year ago. He was a big part of my life, and for a long time my world felt empty without him."

"Does it feel empty now?"

"Not in the least. I'm happy, James, and I didn't believe that would ever be possible."

"Then I was right. It took you a year."

She laughed. "I'm over him and happy to be with you tonight."

"There isn't anyone I'd rather be with on New Year's Eve." He glanced at his watch and stood. "I hope you haven't eaten."

"I didn't. I only arrived a little over an hour ago, and I'm starved." She'd been anxious about their meeting, so her appetite had been nil all day. Her stomach wanted to make up for lost time now.

James led her into the Four Queens Hotel, weaving through the crowds gathered around slot machines and gaming tables. With several thousand people milling around outside, she'd assumed the casinos would be less crowded, but she was wrong.

James took her hand then, gripping it firmly in his own. Summer was surprised by how good that felt. By the time they walked down the stairs to Hugo's Cellar, an elegant, romantically lit restaurant, Summer felt as if she'd survived a riot. So much for all the effort she'd taken with her appearance. She thought she was fortunate to be in one piece.

After a five-minute wait, they were escorted to a booth and presented with elaborate menus. Candles flickered gently, casting dancing shadows on the walls. The noise and bustle upstairs and on the street outside the casino were blessedly absent.

They dined in leisure, shared a bottle of white wine and a calorie-rich dessert. They had so much to talk about—books, movies, world events, their families and more. James asked about her job at Disneyland and seemed genuinely interested in her budding career as an actress.

When she learned he'd recently been appointed a superior court judge to the King County bench, she insisted on ordering champagne to celebrate.

"You should've told me sooner," she said. "It's such wonderful news—so well-deserved."

"It's just temporary," James explained, looking uncomfortable. "I've been appointed to serve out the term of Judge Killmar, who had to retire for medical reasons."

Summer wasn't sure he would've told her if she hadn't asked him about his own hopes and dreams. Only then did he mention it was one of his lifetime goals to serve as a superior court judge.

"You intend on running for the position yourself, don't you?"

"Yes," he said. "But the primary isn't until September, and the election's in November. There're no guarantees."

"You'll win," Summer told him with supreme confidence. Wagging her finger at him, she added, "And don't give me that look. I can't imagine anyone *not* voting for you."

James's eyes met hers. "You're good for my ego," he said. She thought she heard him mutter "too good" under his breath but decided to ignore that.

By the time they'd finished dinner, it was close to twelve. As they made their way out of the casino, someone handed Summer a foil crown and a noisemaker. She donned the hat and handed James the whistle.

The New Year was fast approaching, which meant that her night with James was nearly over. She didn't want it to be.

The crowds had thinned out considerably after the fireworks display. They were standing on the sidewalk outside the Golden Nugget casino when a cheer rose from inside.

"It must be midnight," James commented and ceremoniously blew the noisemaker. "Happy New Year, Summer," he said in a voice so low it was almost a whisper.

"Happy New Year, James."

They stood facing each other, and then, as if this were the moment they'd anticipated all evening, slowly moved toward each other. Summer saw how James's eyes darkened as her own fluttered closed. She wanted this. Needed it.

She sighed audibly as his mouth settled over hers.

CHAPTER TWO

SUMMER WAS NO novice when it came to kissing, but James left her breathless and clinging to him for support. She hadn't expected anything like this. She'd expected them to lightly brush lips and then laugh and wish each other a happy New Year.

It hadn't happened like that.

The instant James's mouth was on hers, she'd gone languid. She was immobile, her arms locked around his neck and her body pressed intimately to his, her lips seeking more.

Summer would've liked James to kiss her again. And again. She didn't want it to end. But she didn't know how to ask him to continue.

Slowly, with what she thought might be reluctance, he released her. She stood there looking at him, arms dangling stiffly at her sides while her face reddened with embarrassment. She considered telling him she wasn't usually this blatant.

"Happy New Year," James said. He didn't sound like himself at all. He cleared his throat and swallowed visibly.

"Happy New Year," she whispered, and stepped away from him.

James reached for her hand and held it in his own. Summer was grateful for his touch. They started walking, with no destination in mind, or none that Summer was aware of. She looked at James, wondering if he felt as confused and uncertain as she did. Apparently he did, because he grew quiet and introspective.

"I believe I'll call it a night," he announced unexpectedly. He checked his watch and frowned. Summer suspected it had been a year since he'd last stayed up past midnight. He was so proper, so serious and sober. Yet she'd enjoyed every minute of her evening with him. They'd talked and laughed, or at least she'd laughed. James had smiled, and she had the impression he didn't do that often, either. Every time he'd grinned, Summer had felt rewarded.

Now she'd ruined everything. She couldn't bear to know what he thought of her. An apology, words of explanation, stumbled over themselves, but she couldn't make herself say them—because she *wasn't* sorry about their kiss. She'd savored it, relished it, and hoped he had, as well.

"I'll call it a night, too," Summer said. She waited, hoping he'd suggest they meet the following day. He didn't.

By the time they returned to the Four Queens, where they were both booked for the week, Summer was miserable.

"James," she said as they walked across the lobby. Either she apologized now or regretted saying nothing. "I'm sorry. I...don't know what came over me. I don't generally... I can only guess what you must think of me and..."

"You?" He hesitated in front of the elevator. "I was wondering what you thought of *me*. I can only beg your indulgence."

The security guard asked to see their room keys before calling for the elevator. James easily produced his while Summer sifted through the contents of her oversize purse before finding hers.

The elevator arrived, and they both entered. There was no one else inside. Still, James didn't ask to see her again, and Summer's heart grew heavier as they ascended. Her room was on the tenth floor, and his was on the fifteenth.

The silence closed in on them. When the elevator stopped at her floor, the doors slid open, and James moved aside.

Summer glanced at him expectantly. Okay, so he didn't intend to see her again. It made sense, she supposed. A superior court judge wouldn't be interested in dating an actress.

"Good night," she said brightly as she walked out of the elevator.

"Good night, Summer," James said softly.

She hesitated, hoping he'd ask her at the last minute, but he didn't. Discouraged, Summer trudged to her room, unlocked the

door and went in. She sat on the edge of her bed, trying to sort
out her muddled thoughts.

When Summer had requested a week's vacation, she hadn't
planned to spend every available second with James. She knew
he'd taken the same length of time, and he'd probably been thinking the same thing.

She slipped off her shoes and wiggled her toes in the thick carpet. If it wasn't so late, she'd call Julie and tell her friend she was
right. One evening with James, and she saw him in a completely
different light. The moment she'd seen him in the gazebo that
evening, she dismissed the father-figure image she'd had in her
mind all these months. More than anything, that kiss convinced
her James was more than a friend. What became of their relationship would depend on several factors, the most important of which
was James himself.

The phone on the nightstand rang, and Summer groped for it.
"Hello?"

"Summer, I'm sorry to bother you."

Her heart gave a sigh of relief. "Hello, James."

"I've got a rental car," he said. "I know it might not be something you'd consider fun, but I thought I'd drive over to Hoover
Dam in the morning. Would you care to join me?"

"Why wouldn't I consider that fun?" she asked.

"I'm sure there are friends here your own age you'd prefer to
spend time with and—"

"Friends? I thought you were my friend."

"Yes, but I was thinking of friends closer to your own age."

His answer irritated her. "I'm not exactly sure what you're insinuating, but if it is what I think it is, you're wrong, James."

"Listen, Summer, all I want to know is if you'd like to join me
in the morning."

That might have been his original question, but she wasn't finished with what she had to say. "I took a week's vacation, and I
know you have several days. I don't expect you to entertain me,
if that's what you're worried about, because I can find plenty to
do on my own."

"I see."

"And yes, there are any number of people my age in Vegas.

There would be in any city. If you want my company, fine, but if you'd rather not see me again, I can accept that, too." Not easily, but she'd do it and have a perfectly good week without him.

He was strangely silent.

"James? Are you still there?"

"Yes. Are you always this direct?"

"No, but I didn't want there to be any misunderstanding between us. I value your friendship, and I don't want it ruined because of something silly."

"Nor do I." A short pause followed. "Forgive me for being dense, but I'm not sure I understood your answer. Are you going to Hoover Dam with me or not?"

Summer had waited all evening for this kind of invitation, and now the words were almost anticlimactic. "Would you like me to come?"

"Attorneys do this all the time, you know," he said with a chuckle.

"Do what?"

"Answer a question with one of their own. Yes, Summer, I'd very much enjoy your company."

"Great. When do you want to leave in the morning?"

James told her, and they set a time to meet in the lobby. Summer replaced the receiver and lay back on the bed. She smiled to herself, eager for morning.

James hadn't thought of himself as all that old, since at thirty-seven he was the youngest superior court judge in Washington State. Being with Summer, however, made him feel downright ancient.

She was perfectly named. Being with her was like walking along Green Lake in the middle of August, when the air carried the scent of blooming flowers and sunshine warmed the afternoon. She shone with a summery brightness that made him feel content. More than content. Happy.

James couldn't remember any time he'd smiled more than during their dinner together. She'd told him about playing her role at Disneyland. Her joy and enthusiasm for her job bubbled over like champagne. He could have listened to her all night.

She certainly hadn't done all the talking, however, and to his surprise he'd found himself telling her about the ins and outs of his own position with the court and the upcoming election, which was vital to his career.

His life was very different from hers. While Summer worked in the delightful world of fantasy, he struggled with the often cruel, unjust world of reality.

Naturally he couldn't give her any details about the cases he'd heard, but just talking about his short time on the bench had lifted his spirits considerably. It felt good to share his thoughts with her and he'd enjoyed her opinions and her sometimes unpredictable views.

Then they'd kissed. Talk about sexual chemistry! For the life of him, James couldn't explain what had happened when she'd slipped into his arms. He'd never intended the kiss to become that intense, but once he'd started, nothing could have stopped him.

He'd been afraid his reaction had shocked Summer, but apparently that wasn't the case. Later she'd apologized to him and James hadn't known what to say. She seemed to think she'd done something wrong. She hadn't. The truth was, she'd done everything right.

The next morning James sat down in the lobby to wait for Summer. He was excited about this outing. He'd decided earlier not to invite her, feeling it would be unfair to dominate her time. She was young and beautiful, and he doubted she wanted to spend her vacation with a staid older guy like him.

He'd gone to his hotel room and congratulated himself on not mentioning the trip to Hoover Dam. Ten minutes later he'd talked himself into calling her on the off chance she might be interested.

Well, she'd told him. A smile pulled at the edges of his mouth. Summer had seemed downright angry when he suggested she'd prefer to be with friends her own age.

James liked the idea of being her friend. The operative word being *friend*. He wasn't going to kiss her again—that was for sure.

First, he was afraid of a repeat performance of that kiss in the street. Secondly, he was way too old for her. He enjoyed her company tremendously, but then any man would. He wasn't going to ruin the bond they'd created; becoming romantically involved, if she even wanted to, would do exactly that.

Summer stepped off the elevator, and James watched as every eye in the place seemed to gravitate toward her. She was stunning. It wasn't the clothes she wore, although the pretty pink pants and matching sweater flattered her. It was Summer herself.

She searched the lobby until she saw him, and then she smiled. James felt as though the sun was beaming directly down on him.

He stood and waited for her to join him. "Did you have breakfast?" he asked.

She nodded. "Hours ago."

"Me, too."

"If you're ready, we can be on our way." All he had to do now was stop staring at her....

A few minutes later, the valet took his ticket for his rental car, and they waited for him to drive the luxury sedan to the back of the hotel. When the car arrived, the young man opened the car door and helped Summer inside. James was almost jealous to have been denied the privilege.

They drove out of Las Vegas in companionable silence. James had studied the map so he knew which freeway to take.

"Do you ever think about her?" Summer asked.

James had no idea what she was talking about. "Who?"

She laughed. "That's answer enough. Christy. Your ex-fiancée."

"Ah yes, Christy." James mulled over Summer's question. "Sometimes. Generally when I'm feeling especially lonely or when I see a couple with kids. That's when I wonder what Christy's and my children would have looked like.

"Do you still think about Brett?" he asked.

She lifted one shoulder in a halfhearted shrug. "Sometimes. It's different with me, though."

"Different?"

"From what you told me about Christy, she went to Montana to help her sister and met someone there."

"She would've broken the engagement right away, but it seemed like a heartless thing to do over the phone." Despite everything James felt a need to defend her. "When she did get back, her mother had arranged for a huge engagement party and I was extremely busy with an important lawsuit. I never blamed Christy for not telling me about Cody right away. She had her reasons."

"*I* blame her," Summer said stiffly. "It was a rotten thing to do."

"You blame Brett, too, don't you?" This was what their conversation was really about, James suspected. Something had happened recently that had hurt her all over again.

"Right before I left," she said in a small voice, "a friend called to tell me Brett and his wife are expecting a baby."

"A friend?" James wondered about that. There seemed to be a certain type of person who delighted in being the first to deliver bad news.

"I'm going to be twenty-eight next month," she told him.

He smiled. "From the way you said that, one would think you're ready to apply for your retirement benefits."

Summer smiled back. "I suppose I sound ridiculous."

"No, you sound hurt. It's only natural, but that pain will fade in time, as well, especially if you meet someone else and get involved in another relationship."

"You didn't."

James couldn't argue. "It wasn't because I'd dedicated myself to loving Christy for the rest of my life. To be fair, I'm not sure why I never got involved again. It's not like I made the decision not to."

"Do you date?"

"Occasionally." A few months ago, two women had let him know that they'd welcome his attentions. James was flattered and he did enjoy a night out now and then, but he could never seem to dredge up much enthusiasm for either woman.

"What about you?" he asked, then mentally kicked himself. The answer was obvious. Someone like Summer had a long line of men waiting to ask her out.

"I don't date all that often," Summer surprised him by saying. "It's funny, when Brett and I first broke up I saw a different man every night. Within a month I was sick of it, sick of pretending I didn't care, sick of telling everyone about all the fun I was having."

"And now?"

"I haven't been out all month. December is crazy, anyway, with Christmas and family obligations and everything else. In November, I went to a dinner party with a member of the cast, but it was as friends, and it was more a favor to Steve than anything."

Silly as it seemed, James was offended that she didn't count their dinner the night before as a date. He certainly had. Their time together had been the highlight of the year for him.

"My parents want me married," she murmured thoughtfully. "They hinted at it over Christmas."

Now, that was something James could identify with. "My father's a longtime widower and I don't have any siblings. He's been hounding me for years to marry, but his real interest lies in grandchildren."

"I'm not willing to marry just anyone," she insisted.

"I feel the same way."

They glanced at each other and then immediately looked away. Silence again filled the car. James didn't know what Summer was thinking, but he knew where his thoughts were taking him and it spelled trouble.

As they neared the outskirts of Boulder City, James mentioned some of the local facts he'd read. "This is the only city in Nevada that doesn't allow gambling."

"Why?"

"It was built for the men who worked on the construction of the dam. I'd guess it has something to do with making sure the workers wouldn't squander their hard-earned cash on the gaming tables. If that happened, their families would see none of it."

"I wonder if it helped," Summer mused aloud.

The next hour and a half was spent driving over Hoover Dam. They didn't take the tour. The day was windy, and James was afraid Summer's sweater wouldn't be enough protection against the cold.

Once they were back on the Nevada side, they stopped long enough for pictures. James felt the wind as he took several scenic photos of the dam with the digital camera he'd bought last year.

Far more of his shots were aimed at Summer. She was a natural ham and struck a variety of poses for him. He wanted a keepsake of his time with her.

James asked another tourist to get a picture of the two of them together. He placed his arm around her shoulder and smiled into the camera.

"Can you send them to me?" she asked, rubbing her arms in an effort to warm herself.

"Of course," James agreed, pleased that she'd asked.

He turned up the heater when they returned to the car. He noticed that Summer's eyes were drooping about ten miles outside Boulder City. He located a classical-music station on the radio, and the soft strains of Mozart lulled her to sleep.

She woke when they were on the Las Vegas freeway. Startled, she sat up and looked around. "Wow, I must be stimulating company," she said, and smiled.

"I'm accustomed to quiet. Don't worry about it."

"James," she began, then yawned, covering her mouth. "What do you think of women who ask men out on dates?"

"What do I think?" He repeated her question, never having given the subject much thought. "Well, it seems fine in theory but I can't really say since it's never happened to me."

"Do you view them as aggressive?"

"Not necessarily. I know women invite men out all the time these days."

She smiled, and her eyes fairly danced with excitement. "I'm glad to hear you say so, because I bought two tickets to a magic show. It's this evening at one of the other downtown hotels. I'd enjoy it very much if you went with me."

James had walked into that one with his eyes wide-open. "A magic show," he murmured with pleasure. He hadn't even dropped her off at the hotel yet and already he was looking for an excuse to see her again.

"It's the late show, as it happens, which doesn't start until eleven. You'll come with me, won't you?"

"Of course," he said. If he wasn't driving, James would have pumped his fist in the air.

Although she'd spent nearly the entire day with James, including lunch and a light dinner on the road, Summer counted the hours until they met for the magic show. She was dressing when the phone rang.

"Hello," she said, thinking it could only be James. Her heart began to beat faster.

"Summer, it's Julie."

"Julie!" Summer had tried to call her friend earlier that evening, but she hadn't answered either her cell or the apartment phone. "Happy New Year!"

"Same to you. How's it going with the distinguished attorney?"

Summer sank onto the edge of the bed. "Really well. By the way, he's a superior court judge now."

"Wow. That's great. So you're getting along well," her friend echoed in knowing tones. "Do you still see him as a father figure?"

"No way," Summer said, and laughed. "There's less than ten years between us."

"So." Her friend's voice fell. "Tell me what's been happening."

"Well." Summer wasn't sure where to start, then decided to plunge right in. "He kissed me last night, and Julie, it was incredible. I don't ever remember feeling like this in my life."

"So you'd say there's electricity between you?"

That was putting it mildly. Hoover Dam should produce that much electricity. "You could put it that way."

"This is just great!"

"We went to see Hoover Dam this morning, and tonight we're going to a magic show."

"This sounds promising."

That was how it felt to Summer, as well. "James invited me to drive to Red Rock Canyon with him tomorrow to feed the burros."

"Are you?"

"Of course." It had never occurred to Summer to refuse. She didn't care if he asked her to study goat dung; she would gladly have gone along just to be with him.

"Julie…"

"Yeah?"

"Would you laugh at me if I told you I'm falling in love with this guy?"

"Nope. I've seen it coming for months. You pored over his letters, and for days after you got one, it was James this and James that. I'm not the least bit surprised. This guy must really be something."

Summer's heart sank as she confronted the facts. "He's a judge, Julie. A superior court judge. I'm an actress. We're too different. I live in Anaheim and he's in Seattle. Oh, it's fine here in Vegas, but once we leave, everything will go back to the way it was before."

"You don't want that?"

"No," Summer admitted after some hesitation.

"Then you need to ask yourself exactly what it is you *do* want," Julie said.

Her roommate's words rang in her mind all through the magician's performance. Summer sat beside James and was far more aware of him than the talented performer onstage. There was magic in the air, all right. It sizzled and sparked, but it didn't have a thing to do with what was happening onstage.

After the show, James escorted her to his car, which was parked in a lot outside the casino.

"You've been quiet this evening," James commented.

"I talked to my roommate earlier," she told him when he slid into the driver's seat.

"Does it have something to do with Brett?"

"No," she said, shaking her head for emphasis. When James inserted the key to start the car, she placed her hand on his forearm to stop him. "James," she said softly, "I know this is an unusual request, and I'm sorry if it embarrasses you, but would you mind kissing me again?"

He didn't look at her. "I don't think it's a good idea."

"Why not?"

"Considering what happened the first time, it seems unnecessarily risky."

"I see," she murmured, disappointed.

"Summer, listen," he said impatiently. "You're beautiful and very sweet, but I'm too old for you."

"If you're looking for an excuse, James, you're going to need something better than that." This was the second time he'd brought up their age difference, and it made her mad. "Forget I asked," she said heatedly. "It was a stupid idea."

"That's exactly what I said." He turned the ignition switch, and the engine fired to life.

"You're probably going to tell me you didn't feel anything. Go ahead and lie, but we both know that's exactly what it is—a lie."

James expelled a labored sigh. "I didn't say anything of the sort."

"Then you're afraid."

Summer noticed the way his hands tightened around the steering wheel.

"I prefer to think of myself as cautious."

"Naturally," she mumbled.

What surprised Summer was how much his rejection hurt. No doubt James viewed her as immature and naive. Pushy, as well. She was probably the first woman who'd ever asked him out and the only one who'd sought a kiss.

Shame burned in her cheeks. The sooner they were back at the hotel and she could escape, the better.

The engine revved, but they weren't going anywhere. In fact, James had pulled the car onto the side of the road.

"You might as well know," he muttered, turning off the car. "I've had one hell of a time keeping my hands off you as it is. It doesn't help that you're asking me to kiss you again."

Having said that, he drew her into his arms. His lips were hungry and hard, his kiss long and deep. He broke it off abruptly.

"There," he whispered. "Satisfied now?"

"No," she whispered back, and directed his mouth back to hers.

This time the kiss was slow and sweet. Her mouth nibbled his, and she was completely and utterly amazed by how good it was.

"Summer," he said, "we're going to have to stop."

"Why?" she asked, and her tongue outlined his lips.

James groaned, and she experienced an intense sense of power.

"I don't have a lot of control when it comes to you," he admitted.

"I don't mind."

"I wish you hadn't said that." He kissed her again, deeply, and when the kiss ended, she was clinging to James, mindless of anything but what was happening between them.

James rested his forehead against hers, his breathing uneven. After he'd regained some control, he locked his arms around her and drew her close. For the longest time all he did was hold her.

It felt like heaven to be in James's arms. Summer felt cherished, protected...*loved.*

"I was afraid of something like this," he said quietly.

"Something like what?"

He groaned. "Think about it, would you?"

"I *am* thinking about it. I don't understand the problem. I like it when you kiss me and touch me. I assumed you liked it, too."

"I do," he said. "That's the problem."

"If you say you're too old for me, I won't be held responsible for my actions."

He chuckled at that. "All right," he said, brushing the hair away from her face. "I'm not too old for you in years, but in attitude."

"Well, that's easy enough to change. We'll start first thing in the morning."

"Start what?" he asked, clearly confused.

She kissed him, letting her lips play over his. "You'll see."

CHAPTER THREE

JAMES WAS WAITING in the lobby early the following morning. Summer's face broke into a disgruntled look when she saw him. Hands braced on her hips, shaking her head, she walked around him.

"What?" he asked, thinking he might have left part of his shirttail out.

"Where did you say we were going?" she asked.

"Red Rock Canyon."

"Do you always wear a shirt and tie to feed wild burros?"

James wore a shirt and tie to everything. "Yes," he answered.

"That's what I thought. Then I'd like to suggest we stop at a mall first."

"A mall? Whatever for?"

She looked at him as if she questioned his intelligence. "I'm taking you shopping," she announced. "If you have any objections, you'd better voice them now."

"Shopping," James repeated slowly. That was probably his least favorite thing to do. He avoided malls whenever possible. "But why?" he asked innocently. He wasn't giving in without a fight.

"Clothes," she informed him, then added in case he hadn't figured it out, "for you."

He frowned.

"You don't have to do this," Summer said. "I think you look

wonderful in a suit and tie, but you'd be far more comfortable in jeans and a T-shirt."

So this was what she meant about altering his attitude. She hadn't mentioned that it involved torturing him by dragging him in and out of stores.

"James?" She gazed up at him with wide eyes. "Are we going to the mall or not?"

It was on the tip of his tongue to tell her he felt perfectly relaxed in what he was wearing. He would've said it, too, if she hadn't blinked just then and her long, silky lashes fanned her cheek. Without much effort this woman was going to wrap him around her little finger. James could see it coming, but he lacked the strength to offer even token resistance.

"How long will it take?" he asked, and glanced at his watch, trying to give the impression that the burros only made their appearance at certain times. They did, but not in the way he was hoping to imply. The minute they suspected visitors had something edible, they appeared.

"We won't be more than an hour," she promised. "Two at most."

He was being fed a line, and he knew it. They'd be lucky to make Red Rock Canyon before nightfall.

"All right," he said with a sigh, wondering how a mature, reasonable male would allow a woman he'd barely met to dictate his wardrobe.

A relationship between them was unrealistic for so many reasons. The age factor, for one. And then she lived and worked in southern California, while his life was in Seattle. He didn't know much about acting, but it seemed to him that if she was serious about her career, California was the place to be. Long-distance relationships rarely survived.

"You won't regret this," she said with a smile.

She was wrong. James already regretted it.

The only shopping mall he knew of in Vegas was the one located on the Strip between two of the largest casino hotels. He drove there and pulled into the underground parking.

When he turned off the ignition, Summer leaned over and kissed him.

"What was that for?" he asked, although he realized he should be counting his blessings instead of questioning them.

"To thank you for being such a good sport."

Little did she know.

To his surprise, Summer stuck to her word. It took less than two hours for her to locate everything she felt he needed. James followed her around like a dutiful child—and discovered he was actually enjoying himself. He let her choose for him, and she did well, generally picking styles he might have picked himself.

"I feel like I squeak when I walk," he said as he led the way back into the underground garage. Almost everything he had on was new. Right down to the running shoes and socks. He'd changed in a washroom at the mall.

"You look twenty years younger," Summer told him.

"In which case, you could be accused of cradle-robbing."

She laughed and slipped her arm through his. She pressed her head against his shoulder, and James derived a good deal of pleasure from having her so close. He was still trying to figure out how he was going to keep his hands off her.

"Sometimes it feels like I've known you forever," she whispered.

James felt the same way. It was as if she'd been part of his life for a very long time. "I have the feeling I'm going to have a huge long-distance phone bill once I get back to Seattle."

Summer closed her eyes and sighed deeply.

"What was that about?" He unlocked the car door and loaded the shopping bags into the backseat.

"I'm grateful, that's all," Summer told him.

"Grateful?" James asked, joining her inside the car.

She was quiet for a moment. "I don't respond to other men this way—the way I have with you. I can't give you a reason or a logical explanation. In the last year, since we've been writing, I've felt close to you. It's as if you know all there is to know about me. My secrets, my faults, everything.

"That night a year ago, when we met, was probably the most devastating of my life. I don't know what I would've done if it hadn't been for you. Generally I'm the first person to dismiss this sort of thing, but I believe we were destined to meet."

James had wondered about that himself, although he'd always seen himself as a rational man. Of all the people in that massive New Year's crowd, they'd found each other. It had to mean *something*. He didn't doubt that fate, kismet or whatever you wanted to call it, had brought them together.

"I've never experienced the things I do when you kiss me," she confided.

She wasn't alone in that, either. He started the engine and pulled into the traffic that continuously flowed along the Strip. Concentrating on his driving rather than looking at Summer helped him restrain his emotions—and his impulses.

If they'd stayed in the parking garage much longer, James knew they'd have had a repeat performance of the night before.

Kissing her again had been a big mistake. He'd spent half the night fighting off the image of her in bed with him. If he took any more cold showers, the hotel was going to complain about the amount of water he used.

Summer's voice was unsure when she spoke. "I thought that after last evening you wouldn't want to see me again."

James nearly drove the car off the road. "Why would you think that?"

She lowered her gaze to her hands, which were folded primly in her lap. "Well, I behaved so…brazenly."

"You?" She obviously didn't know how close he'd come to losing control. Superior court judges weren't supposed to lose control. James couldn't remember the last time something like this had happened. Probably because it never had…

"It's good to know I'm not in this alone. I don't think I could stand that."

"Trust me, I'm experiencing the same feelings you are," he told her in what had to be the understatement of the century.

"We'll both be going our separate ways in the next few days. Until just now, I didn't know if I'd ever hear from you again."

"We've been in touch all year—why would that end?" He didn't expect anything permanent to develop between them, though; that would be asking too much.

"We can take turns calling each other," she offered. "Maybe exchanging emails."

"All right," he agreed.

Summer was silent following that, and he was beginning to recognize quiet moments as a warning. "What's wrong?"

She glanced at him and smiled softly. "I was thinking it would be nice to see each other every once in a while. I hope I don't seem pushy."

Seeing her on a regular basis suited him just fine. They hadn't even gone their separate ways yet, and James was already starting to feel withdrawal symptoms.

"I could fly up and visit you one month, and you could fly down and visit me the next," she suggested, again sounding uncertain.

James's hands tightened around the steering wheel. He suspected that the more often he saw her, the harder it would be to let her go.

"You're not saying anything."

"I was thinking."

"What?"

The complete truth would have embarrassed them both. "I was reviewing my schedule." The primary wasn't until September, but Ralph Southworth, a businessman and longtime friend who'd agreed to head James's campaign, had made it clear long ago: From here on out, James's life wasn't his own. Every place he went, every civic event he attended, would be a campaign opportunity.

"And?"

"February might be difficult for me to get away." His workload had suffered because of this vacation, and another trip, however brief, so soon afterward could cause additional problems.

"That's okay, I can come to you. In fact, I've probably got enough frequent-flyer miles to make the trip free."

"Great. Then I'll try to come to Anaheim in March."

"Wonderful." She lit up like a sparkler on the Fourth of July. Then she hesitated and bit her lower lip. "April might be difficult. Disneyland stays open until midnight during spring break, and we add a second *Beauty and the Beast* show in the evenings. It's hard to get a free weekend then."

"We can work around it." He didn't want to mention that from June onward, his schedule would be impossible. There was no hope of visiting California, and even if she was able to come to Seattle, he couldn't guarantee he'd be able to spend any time with her.

"Yes, we can work around any obstacle," she agreed. But she didn't sound optimistic.

They were outside the city now, driving on a two-lane highway that led to Red Rock Canyon. "I'll be very involved in my campaign this summer." He didn't feel he could be less than honest.

"Summer's the busiest time of year for me, too," she said with an air of defeat. "But we can make this work, James, if we both want it badly enough."

It frightened him how much he wanted Summer, but he was a realist, so he pointed out the obvious. "Long-distance relationships hardly ever work."

"How do you know? You've had several and you speak from experience?"

James resisted the urge to laugh at her prim tone. If memory served him, his first-grade teacher, Mrs. Bondi, had used precisely that voice. Come to think of it, he'd been in love with her, too.

"You'd be shocked by how few relationships I've had," he confessed.

"Do we have a relationship?" Summer asked softly.

James certainly hoped so. "Yes," he answered. And then, because she seemed to need convincing, he pulled onto a dirt road, behind a ten-foot rock. A trail of red dust plumed behind them.

"Why are you stopping?" she asked.

James wore a wide grin and held out his arms. "It appears to me you need a little reminder of how involved we are." James knew he was asking for trouble. Trouble with a capital *T*. His resistance was about as weak as it could get.

"Oh, James."

"A few kisses is all, understand? I don't have much willpower when it comes to you."

"You don't?" The words were whispered. "That's probably the most beautiful thing you've said to me."

"Has anyone ever told you that you talk too much?" James asked as his mouth swooped down on hers. He kissed her the way he'd been wanting to all morning. No, from the moment he'd watched her approach him in the gazebo.

He kissed her again and again, unable to get his fill. He demanded and she gave. Then she demanded and he gave. He moaned and she sighed. Then and there, James decided he'd do whatever he had to—move heaven and earth, take a red-eye flight—to be with her. He doubted once a month would be enough.

He plowed his hands into her hair and sifted the long strands through his fingers. With their mouths still joined, he lowered one hand to her throat. Her pulse beat savagely against his fingertips.

James had never thought of himself as a weak man. But with Summer he felt as hot and out of control as a seventeen-year-old in his dad's car.

Reluctantly he dragged his mouth from hers and trailed moist kisses along the side of her neck.

"James."

"Hmm?" He brought his mouth back to hers, kissing her slow and easy. Talking was the last thing on his mind.

She pulled slightly away. "James."

"Yes?" he asked, distracted.

"We seem—" she whispered breathlessly.

His lips returned to her face, lighting on her forehead, her nose, her chin.

"—to have company."

James went still. When he'd left the road, he'd made sure they were out of sight of other drivers. "Company?" he repeated. He could already imagine the headlines. King County Superior Court Judge Caught in Compromising Position in Las Vegas.

"They look hungry."

James's gaze followed Summer's. Burros, five of them, stood outside the car, studying them intently. They were waiting for a handout.

James grinned. At least the burros didn't carry a camera.

Summer smiled, too.

"I brought along a loaf of bread," he said, and reached into the seat behind him.

"Should we get out of the car?" she asked.

"I don't think that's a good idea." He'd read about the burros, but wasn't sure how tame they were. "Perhaps we should lower the window a bit and feed them that way."

Summer opened her window a couple of inches, far enough to ease a slice of bread out to the eager mouths. Just how eager was something they were to quickly learn.

"Oh!" Summer backed away from the window as a large tongue poked through the small opening.

Soon they were both laughing and handing out the bread as fast as they could. James was going to be sorry when it ran out. Summer certainly seemed to be enjoying herself, and so was he.

When the loaf was finished, they raised the windows. It took the burros a while to realize their food supply had come to an end.

When the burros finally left, James started the engine and pulled back onto the road. They drove for another hour, stopped and toured a visitors' center, taking in the beauty of the countryside.

James felt Summer staring at him as he drove back to the city.

"Now what?" he asked.

"I can't get over the change in you."

"You mean the clothes?"

"Yes. You look like a Jim instead of a James."

James grinned. "There's a difference?"

"Oh, yes, a big one."

"Which do you prefer?" he asked, studying her from the corner of his eye.

His question made her hesitate. "I'm not sure. I like the way Jim dresses, but I like the way James kisses."

"What about how Jim kisses?" The conversation was getting ridiculous.

"Too impatient, I think."

"Really?" He couldn't help feeling a bit miffed. "What's so wonderful about James?"

"His restraint. When James kisses me, it's as if he's holding back part of himself. I have the feeling he's afraid to let go, and it drives me crazy. I want to discover what he's hiding from me. I know this probably sounds a little crazy, but I find James intriguing."

"And Jim?"

She giggled. "Don't tell him, but he's sexy as hell."

"Really?" James was beginning to feel downright cocky.

"He's got that devil-may-care attitude. I have a strong feeling we should be grateful to those burros, because there's no telling what could've happened between us in the canyon."

She was right about that.

"It's those shoes you made me buy," James told her. "The minute I put them on, I had this incredible urge to look for a basketball court and do slam dunks." James loved the sound of Summer's laugher. He'd never been one to tease and joke, but he reveled in her appreciation of his wit.

It was midafternoon when they arrived back at the hotel. After showing the security guard their keys, they stepped into the elevator.

"How about dinner?" he asked, hoping he sounded casual when in reality he felt anything but.

"Sure. What time?"

"Six," he said. Three hours, and he'd be more than ready to see her again. He wanted to suggest they do something until then, but didn't feel he should monopolize her time, although he'd pretty much succeeded in doing that anyway.

"Six o'clock. In the lobby?"

"The lobby," he agreed.

The elevator stopped at her floor, and Summer stared down at her room key. "I'll see you at six."

"Six." They sounded like a couple of parrots.

"Thanks for taking me this morning," she said, easing toward the door. "And for coming to the mall."

"Thank you." He bounced an imaginary basketball and pretended to make a hoop shot.

She smiled, and acting on pure instinct, James lowered his mouth to hers. The kiss was gentle, and when they broke apart, it was all James could do not to follow her to her room.

Summer sat on the end of her bed, trembling. She closed her eyes and tried to relive those last seconds with James and couldn't. Being in his arms was the only possible way to recapture the sensation she experienced each time she was with him.

Julie, her roommate, had known long before Summer had realized it herself. When James had asked her how often she dated, she'd invented an excuse to explain why her social life was non-existent of late.

But it was really because of his letters.

Hearing from James had become an important part of her life. On the first day of every month she rushed to the mailbox, knowing there'd be a letter from him, each longer than the one before. She'd fallen in love with the man who'd written her those beautiful letters.

Unfortunately she hadn't realized it until she'd seen James. She was worried that she alone experienced all this feeling, all this awareness. But after he'd kissed her, she knew that couldn't be true. He felt it, too.

She smiled to herself, remembering how flustered he'd looked when she'd said they had an audience.

Summer smiled at the memory.

Lying down on the bed, she stared up at the ceiling and soon found herself giggling. She was in love with James. She didn't feel a second's doubt, not the slightest qualm or uncertainty. To think she'd actually believed she'd never love another man after Brett.

She might have drowned in a pool of self-pity if it hadn't been for James. She owed him so much.

As she considered their plans to continue seeing each other, she knew it would be difficult to maintain the relationship, especially since they lived such separate lives.

It would require effort and commitment on both their parts. Summer was willing. She could tell that James wasn't as convinced as she was that they could make this work, but she didn't harbor a single doubt.

Summer dressed carefully for her dinner date with James. She chose a simple sundress with a lacy shawl and pretty sandals.

He was waiting at the same place in the lobby, but he surprised her by not wearing a suit and tie. He'd worn one of the short-sleeved shirts they'd bought that day and a pair of khaki pants. For a moment she barely recognized him. He looked relaxed, as though he hadn't a care in the world.

"James," she whispered when she joined him.

"Jim," he corrected, and grinned. He placed his hand inside his pant pocket and struck a catalog pose.

Summer laughed delightedly.

"I hope you're hungry," James said. He tucked her hand in the crook of his arm and guided her toward the door.

"I'm starved."

"Great. We're about to indulge ourselves in a feast fit for the gods." When they reached the sidewalk of Glitter Gulch, the lights made it as bright as the noonday sun.

"I thought about the conversation we had this afternoon," he announced out of the blue.

"About keeping in touch?"

He nodded. "I'm not sure what we have, the two of us, but whatever it is, I don't want to lose it."

"I don't, either."

"I've only felt this strongly about one other woman in my life."

"I've only felt this way about one other man."

"If I was going to put a name on this…this thing between us…"

"Yes?" she asked when he hesitated. James was a thoughtful man. She didn't mean to rush him, but she wanted him to say what was already on the tip of *her* tongue. Consequently, she had no qualms about leaping in. "I love you, James Wilkens. I want to throw my arms in the air and sing."

He looked at her as if he were actually afraid she'd do exactly that. "What you feel is just gratitude."

"Gratitude," she repeated scornfully. "*Just* gratitude." She shook her head. "I'm capable of knowing my own mind, thank you kindly, and when I say I love you, I mean it."

"I see," James said, and his voice fell.

"You don't have to worry about telling me how you feel, either," she was quick to assure him. It wasn't necessary; his kiss told her everything she needed to know.

"But…"

She stopped in the middle of the crowded sidewalk and pressed her finger to his lips.

"I'm too old for you," he muttered.

She narrowed her eyes.

"But I'm crazy about you, Summer. Call me the biggest fool that ever lived, but it's true."

"Thank you very much."

James chuckled. "I haven't been doing a very good job of hiding how I feel. Maybe that's because I didn't expect to feel like *this*." He splayed his fingers through his hair. "In retrospect, I wonder what I did expect."

"I assumed we'd have dinner that first night and we'd talk about what we said in our letters, and then we'd more or less go our separate ways, me back to my life in California, you back to yours…"

"Really." He arched his eyebrows.

"I wanted Julie to fly in for the weekend, but she refused and I couldn't get her to give me a reason. I know now. She realized what I hadn't—that I'm in love with you. My feelings developed slowly over the past year, and Julie saw it happening." She inhaled a deep breath. "I don't want to lose you, James. We can make this work if we try."

"It's not going to be easy."

As his words faded an idea struck Summer. "Oh, my goodness." James stopped abruptly. "What is it?"

"James." She clasped his arm as she stared up at him. With every passing second the idea gained momentum. "I just thought of something…wonderful," she said urgently.

"What is it?" His arm circled her waist.

"Oh, James. Kiss me, please, just kiss me."

"Kiss you *here?*" James asked, appalled.

"Never mind." She laughed and, throwing her arms around his neck, she stood on the tips of her toes and kissed him, a deep, lingering kiss that communicated her feelings to him—and his to her.

He stared down at her dumbstruck when she stepped away.

"James," she said breathlessly, "I think we should get married."

"Married." The word was barely audible.

"It makes sense, don't you agree? I know how I feel about you, and you've admitted your feelings for me. Here we are, both worried about the most ridiculous things, when we already have what's most important. Each other."

Still James didn't say anything. He looked around, and his expression seemed slightly desperate, but that could have been her imagination.

"I can guess what you're thinking," she said with a laugh, "but I've got an answer for every one of your arguments."

"We hardly know each other."

That was a pretty weak argument. "Is that so? You know me better than friends I've had all my life. You've seen me at my worst. You've listened to my pain and my frustrations. There isn't a thing I can't talk about with you."

He frowned, and Summer longed to smooth the lines from his brow and kiss away his doubts.

"Don't look so worried! Honestly, James, anyone would think you were in a state of shock."

"I am." This came through loud and clear.

"But why?" His hesitation took her by surprise. She knew the idea would take some getting used to on James's part. He didn't leap into projects and ideas the way she did. He was methodical and thoughtful and carefully weighed every decision.

"Perhaps I'm assuming something here that I shouldn't," she said slowly. "You don't want to marry me, do you, James?"

CHAPTER FOUR

SUMMER WAS MORTIFIED to the very marrow of her bones. Without even trying, she'd managed to make a complete fool of herself. James had never come right out and *said* he was in love with her. But with all their talk about how important they were to each other, she'd naturally assumed he cared as deeply for her as she did for him. She'd assumed he'd want to marry her.

"James, I'm sorry," she said in a weak voice. Past experience had taught her to right wrongs as quickly as possible.

"Summer..."

"Of course you don't want to marry me. I understand. Really, I do," she said and pretended to laugh, but it sounded more like a muffled sob. "Now I've embarrassed us both. I don't know why I say the ridiculous things I do." She tried to make light of it by gesturing with her hands. "I guess I should've warned you that I blurt out the most incredibly awkward stuff. Forget I said anything about marriage, please—otherwise it'll ruin our evening."

James was silent, which made everything ten times worse. She'd rather he ranted and raved than said nothing.

In an effort to fill the terrible silence, she started chattering, talking fast, jumping from one subject to another.

She commented on how busy the casinos were. She talked about the big-name stars performing in town. She mentioned a friend of a friend who'd won the California State lottery, and then brought up air pollution problems in Los Angeles.

"Summer, stop," James finally told her. "It's fine."

She snapped her mouth shut. How she was going to get through the evening without humiliating herself further, she didn't know.

Her stomach was in such a knot that by the time they reached the hotel where the restaurant was located, she felt sure she'd only be able to make a pretense of eating.

The hostess seated them, but Summer got up as soon as the hostess left them.

"If you'll excuse me," she said.

James looked up from his menu.

"I'll be right back." She was hoping that a few minutes alone in the ladies' room would help her regain her composure.

"Summer, wait," James said. "I don't want you to feel bad about this."

She nodded, determined to drop the subject entirely. "Did you notice they had lobster on the menu?" She didn't actually know if this was true or not.

"It's just that most men prefer to do the asking."

"Of course." And it went without saying that the very proper King County Superior Court Judge James Wilkens wouldn't want an empty-headed actress for a wife.

Summer asked a passing waiter directions for the ladies' room. As she walked across the restaurant, weaving around tables, she felt James's eyes following her.

Once inside the restroom, Summer sat on the pink velvet sofa and closed her eyes. After a number of deep, calming breaths, she waited for the acute embarrassment to pass.

It didn't.

Briefly she toyed with the idea of slipping away, but that would've been childish and unfair to James. His only crime had been his silence, and he'd already explained that was simply his way. Just like making a world-class fool of herself seemed to be hers.

Five minutes later she rejoined him.

He looked up, almost as if he was surprised to see her. "I wasn't sure you'd be back."

"I wouldn't be that rude. It isn't your fault I'm an idiot."

"Stop," he said sharply. "Don't say such things about yourself."

"I can't believe I thought you'd marry someone like me," she said, poking fun at herself. "The girl who always speaks before she thinks and leaps before she looks."

"As a matter of fact, I do plan to marry you." He announced this while scanning the menu, which he then set aside. He watched her as if he expected some kind of argument. Summer might have offered him one if her throat hadn't closed up, making talking impossible.

The menu slid from her fingers and fell onto the table. Nervously she groped for it.

"Have you decided?" James asked.

She stared at him blankly.

"What would you like to order for dinner?"

"Oh." She hadn't even glanced at the menu. Frazzled as she was, she chose the first thing she saw. "Chicken Dijon," she said.

"Not lobster? It isn't every day one becomes engaged. I think we should celebrate, don't you?"

Somehow she managed a nod.

The waiter came, and James ordered for them both, requesting lobster and champagne. Their server nodded approvingly and disappeared. A moment later he returned with a champagne bottle for James's inspection.

"We'll need to see about an engagement ring," James said as though they were discussing something as mundane as the weather. "I imagine Las Vegas has quite a few good jewelers."

The waiter opened the champagne bottle with a loud pop and poured a small amount into the fluted glass for James to sample. He tasted it and nodded. Soon both their glasses were filled.

Summer breathed easier once they were alone. "James," she whispered, leaning forward. "Are you sure you want to marry me?"

He leaned toward her, too, and a grin slowly formed. "Yes."

"All at once I'm not convinced I'm the right person for you."

"Shouldn't I be the one to decide that?"

"Yes, but... I'd hate to think we're reacting to circumstances that wouldn't repeat themselves in a hundred years."

"Then we'll have a long engagement. We'll both be positive before we take that final step."

"All right." Summer felt only mildly reassured.

"We'll continue to see each other on a regular basis," James told her.

"Yes...we'll need that." She didn't like the idea of being apart so much, but that couldn't be helped.

"I wouldn't want the engagement to be *too* long," Summer said. "I dated Brett for five years, and we were unofficially and then officially engaged almost that whole time. We both know where that ended up."

"Do you wish you'd married him?"

"No," she answered emphatically. "I don't have a single regret. I know you'd never do the things Brett did."

James's eyes brightened with intensity. "It isn't in me to hurt you."

"And I'd never knowingly hurt you," she promised.

"In light of what happened between Christy and me, I'm not fond of long engagements, either."

"Do you regret not marrying her sooner? That way she would've gone to visit her sister as a married woman."

"I've thought about that," James said. "Christy would never have allowed anything to develop between her and Cody if we'd been married. Getting involved with him behind my back was almost more than she could bear."

"I see." Summer figured she could read the writing on the wall. "You wish you'd married her, don't you?"

"No."

His quick response surprised her. "Why not?"

"Christy Manning didn't love me as much as I loved her. I'm sure she would have done her best to be a good wife, and we probably would have grown close over the years, but she would've married me for the wrong reasons."

"The wrong reasons? What reasons?"

"She was trying to make her parents happy."

"Okay," Summer said slowly, still feeling her way carefully around the subject. "So neither of us wants a long engagement. How long is long? A year?"

"That's too long," James said with feeling.

"Six months?"

He hesitated. "That'll make it June."

"June's a nice month," Summer said without any real enthusiasm. "Will you want me to live with you in Seattle?"

"Yes. Is that going to be possible?"

"Of course." She nodded vigorously.

"What about your career?"

She lifted one shoulder. "To tell you the truth, I was getting a little tired of playing Belle anyway. From what I understand, theater in Seattle is thriving. There wouldn't be any problem with me being your wife and an actress, would there? You being a judge and all."

"None that I can think of."

"Good." Summer picked up her fork and ran her fingers along the smooth tines. "My current contract expires in April."

"April," James said. "Can you arrange a wedding on such short notice?"

"You bet I can," she said, grinning. "Oh, James, I can't believe this is happening."

"To be honest, neither can I," he admitted.

Summer had never seen him smile as brightly.

The waiter brought their dinner, and James looked at the man who was a complete stranger and said, "The young lady and I have just become engaged."

Their server smiled broadly. "Congratulations."

"Thank you."

Summer would have added her thanks, but James had shocked her speechless. He wasn't joking; he really meant to follow through with their wedding and he was excited about it. Excited enough to announce their plans to a stranger.

"This hotel has an excellent wedding chapel," the waiter continued. "I gather that more than one celebrity has been married in our chapel."

"Right here in the hotel?" James asked.

"Many of the larger hotels provide wedding services for their guests."

"Don't arrangements have to be made weeks in advance?"

"Not always," the waiter explained. "A lot of people don't decide which chapel to use until after they arrive. Apparently you can get married with a few hours' notice—if the chapel's available, of course."

"Of course," James murmured.

A look came over him, one she'd seen before. "Our wedding will be in April," she said hastily.

"My very best to both of you." The waiter refilled their flutes with champagne.

"James," Summer said after the server had left their table, "is something wrong?"

"Nothing. What makes you ask?"

"You're wearing an odd look."

"What do you mean?"

"It's a look that says you're not sure you like what you're thinking. Or hearing or seeing. The same one you got when I said we had company in Red Rock Canyon the other day."

"In this case, it's what I'm thinking," he muttered.

"You want to call off the wedding?" She should've realized that when James said he wanted to marry her, it was too good to be true. This had to be the shortest engagement in history.

"I don't know where you get the idea that I'm looking for a way out when I'm thinking exactly the opposite. I can only assume impulsive thoughts must be transmitted from one brain to another." He drew in a deep breath and seemed to hold it for a long time. "Would you be willing to marry me now?"

"Now? You mean tomorrow?"

"Yes. Then we'll repeat the ceremony later with family and friends in April."

Speechlessness happened rarely with Summer, and yet James had managed to cause it twice in the same evening. Her mouth dropped open, but no words came out.

"Summer, have I utterly shocked you?"

"Yes," she admitted in a squeaky voice.

James grinned. "I'll admit this is the first impulsive thought I've entertained in years. If you can propose marriage at the drop of a hat, then I should be able to come up with something equally thrilling."

Summer knew she was going to cry now. She could feel the tears welling up in her eyes. She used her linen napkin to dab them away.

"Just remember when we tell the children about this night. You're the one who proposed to me."

"Children." Summer blew her nose. "Oh, James, I'm looking forward to being a mother."

"Then you agree to my plan?"

"Married twice?" Everything was going too fast for her. "I'd want Julie here as my maid of honor."

"Of course. We'll phone her as soon as we're finished dinner. I'll be happy to pay for her airfare."

The tears were back, filling her eyes. These were tears of happiness and relief; she loved him so much. "James, we're doing the right thing, aren't we?"

He didn't hesitate. "Yes. It's what we both want."

"You love me?" He'd never said the words.

His look softened. "Very much."

Her mind whirled with everything they'd need to do. "I'll have to tell my parents. You didn't intend to keep our marriage a secret from our families, did you?"

"No. I'll call my father, as well."

Already Summer could hear her mother's arguments "They're going to think we're crazy."

James grinned again. "Probably."

"What should we do first?" Summer asked as they left the restaurant after dinner.

"I suppose we should find an available wedding chapel."

"Shouldn't we contact our families before we do that?" This was the part Summer dreaded most, and she wanted it over with as quickly as possible.

"But if we have the chapel booked, we'll be able to tell them the time and place," James said.

"Oh, yes." Trust him to be so logical even when he was acting impulsive.

"The ring." James snapped his fingers. "I almost forgot."

"Don't look so concerned. We can pick something out later. A plain gold band is perfect for now. In April we can exchange those for a diamond if you want."

"I'd like you to have my mother's ring."

"I'd be honored to wear it," she said quietly.

He kissed her, and Summer blinked in surprise. It was the first time he'd ever initiated a kiss in public.

Since the waiter had mentioned the wedding chapel at this particular hotel, they tried there first. Summer hadn't expected it to be so easy, but booking their wedding took only a few minutes. The hotel would see to everything, from obtaining the license to the music and flowers. They'd be getting married at seven the next night.

"If I'd known it was this simple," James said as they walked back to the Four Queens, "I might have suggested it sooner."

Summer pressed her head against his shoulder. They stopped at a crosswalk and waited for the red light.

"I wish you'd kiss me again," she breathed close to his ear.

His gaze found her lips, and he cleared his throat. "I don't think that would be a good idea."

"I suppose you're right," she murmured, but disappointment underscored her words.

"You can call your family from my room."

"Okay," she said, but her mind wasn't on making the dreaded phone call as much as it was on being alone with James.

His thoughts must have been the same because their pace quickened as they hurried across the street and into the hotel.

The elevator ride seemed to take an eternity. As if James couldn't keep himself from touching her in some way, he reached out and brushed a stray curl from her cheek. His knuckle grazed her skin.

"I can't believe you're willing to marry me," he said.

"I feel like the luckiest woman alive."

"You?" He held his hand to his brow. "I want you so much I think I'm running a fever."

"I've got a fever, too. Oh, James, we're going to be so good for each other."

"Don't," he growled.

"Don't?"

"Don't look at me like that, Summer. I'm weak enough where

you're concerned. Much more of this, and I'm going to make love to you right in this elevator."

Summer smiled and moved against the back wall. "You're so romantic, James—and I mean that."

"You're doing it again."

"Doing what?"

"Looking at me like you know exactly what I want. Your eyes are telling me you want it as much as I do."

The elevator eased to a stop, and the doors slid open. Summer's heart pounded fast as neither of them made the slightest effort to leave.

"We were going to call our families," she reminded him just as the doors started to close.

James swallowed hard. "Yes, of course."

With precise movements he led the way out of the elevator and down the hallway to his room. She noticed that when he inserted the key his hand trembled slightly, and she loved him all the more for it.

"The phone's over by the—"

"Bed." She completed his sentence, and the word seemed to stick in her throat. She walked across the room and sat on the edge of the mattres, then picked up the phone to dial the familiar number.

It might've helped if she'd taken the time to figure out what to tell her parents. But she was afraid she'd lose her nerve.

She couldn't put into words what she felt for James. She'd never loved anyone this way, this much, and she believed he hadn't, either. They'd each been in love with someone else, and that other person had caused deep pain. This time was different.

She knew, even before they answered the phone, what her mother and father were going to say.

"James," she said, in a panic, banging down the telephone receiver and holding out her arms. "Please, could you kiss me first?"

She glanced over at the man she'd marry in less than twenty-four hours, and his face was a study in raw sexual need. He walked across the room. The bed dipped as his weight joined hers. With loving care he gathered her in his arms and claimed her mouth. The kiss was slow and sensual.

He broke away, and his breath was hard and labored. Eager for the taste of him, the touch and feel of him, she brushed her lips over the curve of his jaw, then brought her mouth back to his.

"Maybe you should call your father first," she whispered when she pulled away.

"All right," he agreed. Reluctantly he sat up and reached for the bedside phone. Summer knelt behind him, wrapping her arms around his waist and pressing her head against his shoulder.

"Dad, it's James," she heard him say.

"Fine...yes, Vegas is just fine." Summer could hear a voice on the other end of the line, but she couldn't make out what was being said.

"I'm calling to let you know I'm getting married."

The voice went silent.

"Dad? Are you still there?"

The faraway voice returned, this time speaking very fast.

"Dad... Dad... Dad." Each time James tried to cut in, he was prevented from saying anything.

In frustration, he held the phone away from his ear. "I think you'd better talk to him."

"Me?" Summer cried. "What do you want *me* to say?"

"Anything."

Summer took the receiver and covered it with her hand. "Just remember this when we talk to my parents."

"I will." He kissed her briefly.

"Mr. Wilkens," Summer said. It sounded as if the line had suddenly gone dead. "My name's Summer Lawton. James and I have known each other a year. I love him very, very much."

"If you've known my son for a year, how is it we've never met?"

"I live in California."

"California?"

"Anaheim. I'm an actress." She might as well give him all the bad news at once. She didn't dare look at James.

"An actress?"

"That's correct."

"You're sure you've got the right James Wilkens? My son's the superior court judge."

"Yes, I know. James and I are going to be married tomorrow

evening at seven but we're planning a larger ceremony in April. We felt it was only right to tell you about our plans." Convinced she'd done a miserable job, Summer handed the telephone back to James.

Father and son talked a few moments more, and the conversation ended with James abruptly replacing the receiver. He looked at Summer, but she had the strangest feeling he wasn't seeing her.

"James?"

"He's decided to fly in for the ceremony."

"That's great. I'll look forward to meeting him."

"He's anxious to meet you, as well. He hasn't set eyes on you and already he thinks you're the best thing that's ever happened to me."

Summer laughed and slipped her arms around James's neck. "He could be right."

James grinned up at her. "I know he is."

"I love you, James."

"I know. I love you, too. Now it's time to make that call."

Summer had been delaying the inevitable and knew it. She stared at the phone, expelled a heavy sigh and said, "All right, I'll call my parents. Be prepared, James. They're going to have a lot of questions."

"They couldn't be any worse than my father," he muttered.

"Wanna bet?" Summer punched out the number to the family home a second time and waited. It was the decent thing to do, call her family with the news of her marriage, but if they just happened to be away, out of town themselves, no one would blame her and James for going ahead with the ceremony.

Four rings. Summer was about to hang up.

"Hello," her mother answered cheerfully.

"Mom," Summer said. "It's me."

"I thought you were in Vegas this week with Julie."

"Julie couldn't come."

"You went alone?" Summer could hear the disapproval in her mother's voice.

"I met a friend here. That's the reason I'm calling."

"Your friend is the reason? What's the matter? You don't sound right. You're gambling and you've lost everything? Is that it?"

"Mom, it's nothing like that."

"I never did understand why you'd go back to Vegas after what happened there last year."

"Mom, can I explain?"

"All right, all right."

"I'm calling to tell you—"

"Don't beat around the bush. Just say it."

Summer rolled her eyes. She knew where her flair for drama had come from. "I'm getting married."

Her mother screamed, and the next thing Summer heard was the phone hitting the floor. Her father's voice could be heard in the background, followed by moaning and crying.

"What the hell's going on?" It was her father on the line.

"Hi, Dad," Summer said casually, as if nothing was out of the ordinary. "I called to tell you and Mom that I'm getting married tomorrow evening."

Summer's father said nothing for several seconds. "Do we know this young man?"

"No. But he's wonderful, Dad, really wonderful."

"Like Brett was wonderful?" her mother shouted into the extension.

"Helen, get off the phone. You're too emotional to talk any sense."

"Don't tell me what to do, Hank Lawton. This is our little girl who's marrying some stranger."

"His name's James Wilkens. He's from Seattle and, Daddy, I'm crazy about him."

"He's an actor, isn't he?" her mother demanded. "What did I tell you over and over again? Stay away from actors. But do you listen to me?"

"Mom, James is a judge."

Silence.

"Mom, Dad, did you hear me?"

"What kind of judge? Beauty pageants?" This came from her mother.

Summer almost groaned out loud. "No. Superior court. He was recently appointed to the bench and he'll run for election to his first full term this November."

"A judge, Hank," Helen said softly. "Abby's daughter married that attorney, and we never heard the end of it. Summer's got herself a judge."

"Would you like to talk to James?" Summer offered. It only seemed fair that he talk to her family, since he'd put her on the phone with his father.

"No," her father surprised her by saying. "When I talk to him, it'll be face-to-face. Pack our bags, Helen. We're headed for Vegas."

hat started, and we never heard the end of it. Summer's got her self a...

"Would you like to talk to James," Summer interrupted, only connecting half of what he was saying, about her family, but...

"No," her father surprised her by saying. "When I talk to him, I'll be...

CHAPTER FIVE

"SUMMER," JAMES SAID patiently when he saw her distress, "what did you expect your family to do?"

"I didn't think they'd insist on coming here," Summer answered. "I wanted it to be just you and me. We can involve our families later, in April. I felt obliged to let my parents know what we were doing—but I didn't expect anything like *this*."

"You don't want them to come?"

"No," she said quickly.

In some ways James could understand her regret. If truth be known, he would've preferred his father to stay in Seattle. As it was, James's time with Summer was already limited, and he didn't want to share with family the precious few days they had left.

"I'm afraid once you meet my mother, you'll change your mind about marrying me," she moaned.

"Honey, it isn't possible."

"My mother—she sometimes doesn't think before she speaks."

"I see." James felt he was being diplomatic by not mentioning that Summer possessed the same trait.

"My dad's really great… You'll like him, but probably not at first." She gazed at James with large, imploring eyes. "Oh, James, he's going to give you the third degree. I'll bet he's having a back-ground check done on you this very minute."

"I don't have anything to hide."

"See, Dad's been working with the seamy side of life for so many years, he suspects everyone."

"He's a policeman?"

Summer nodded. "I don't think he trusts anyone."

"Summer, if twenty-odd years down the road our daughter phones to tell us she's marrying a man neither of us has ever met before, you can bet I'll have a background check done, too."

"You know what this means, don't you?" she said, biting her lip. "We aren't going to have much of a honeymoon."

James chuckled. "Wanna bet?"

Summer grinned.

If this woman's smile could be bottled, James thought, it would be the most potent aphrodisiac ever made. He couldn't look at Summer and not want to make love to her.

"What about Julie?" James said in an effort to get Summer's mind off her parents' imminent arrival.

"Oh—I nearly forgot my best friend." She reached for the phone and called Julie's cell.

Since there were a number of things to do before the actual ceremony, James walked over to the desk and sat down to write out a list, not wanting to forget anything.

He was only half listening to the conversation between Summer and her roommate when he heard Summer's soft gasp and the mention of Brett, the man she'd once loved. James's ears perked up, and his fingers tightened around the pen.

"What did you tell him?" Summer asked in low tones. This was followed by "Good. Then you're coming? Great. You might want to talk to my parents and see if you can fly in with them. I'm sure they'll be eager to pump you for whatever you can tell them about James." After a few words of farewell, Summer replaced the receiver.

James turned around in his chair, wondering if she'd volunteer the information about Brett.

"Julie's flying in, too. I suggested she catch the same flight as my parents." She seemed self-conscious all at once.

Her eyes avoided his.

"So I heard." James waited, not wanting to approach the subject of her ex-fiancé, hoping she'd save him the trouble.

After an awkward moment, she blurted out, "Julie... Julie said Brett phoned."

James relaxed, grateful she chose not to hide it from him. "Did she find out what he wanted?"

"No. She hung up on him before he got a chance to say."

James had the distinct feeling he was going to like Summer's roommate.

Summer's shoulders moved in an expressive sigh. "I don't think either of us is going to be nearly as happy once our families arrive."

"How bad can it be?" he asked. All he cared about, all that was important, was marrying the woman he loved.

"My mother's going to insist we follow tradition and not see each other all day."

James frowned. He wasn't keen on that idea.

"My dad will keep you occupied with a whole bunch of questions. If you've got the slightest blemish on your record, he'll find it."

"I don't. Trust me, sweetheart, my background's been scrutinized by the very best. Your father isn't going to find anything."

She laughed softly. "In which case, Dad will probably thank you repeatedly for taking me off his hands."

James laughed, too. "Never mind. By this time tomorrow, we'll be husband and wife."

Summer's parents arrived early the following morning with Julie in tow. By chance Summer met them in the lobby on her way down for breakfast. James had called her room an hour earlier, before she was dressed, to tell her he was headed for the coffee shop. Summer had been too nervous to eat then, but had developed a healthy appetite since. She'd need fortification in order to deal with her parents.

"Mom! Dad! Julie!"

They threw their arms around her as if the separation had been ten years instead of a few days.

"I called Adam and told him his little sister's getting married," were the first words out of her mother's mouth. "He's taking time off work and he and Denise are driving in for the wedding."

"Mom," Summer protested, "James and I are having another ceremony later."

"Fine," Helen Lawton said briskly, "Adam will be there, too. Now stop fussing. It isn't like I held a gun to his head and told him he had to come. Your brother *wants* to be here."

"Daddy." Summer hugged her father. Stepping back, she placed her hands on her hips. "James is squeaky-clean, right?"

"How'd you know I had him checked out?"

"You're my father, aren't you?" She slipped her arm around his waist.

"How'd you ever meet a man like this?" Hank Lawton wanted to know. "He's as good as gold."

"Yes, I know. He's wonderful."

James appeared then, coming from the direction of the coffee shop, a newspaper under his arm.

Summer made the introductions, and while Julie and her family checked in to their rooms, Summer and James reserved a table at the coffee shop. They sat next to each other, holding hands.

"Are you ready for all this?" he asked her.

"I don't know." She sighed. "My brother's taking the day off and driving in for the ceremony. I thought we'd have a small, intimate wedding."

"It is small and intimate."

"My brother and his wife have three little kids, who'll probably cry through the entire ceremony."

"I don't mind if you don't," James said and gently squeezed her hand. "I suspect folks will talk about us the same way when we drag our children to family get-togethers."

"Our children," Summer repeated. She felt weak with pleasure at the thought of having a family with James. "I know I've said it before, but I'm looking forward to being a mother."

"Not nearly as much as I am to making you one," he said in a low voice. The teasing light left his eyes. "If you have no objections, I'd like a large family. Maybe four kids?"

"Four." She nodded. "I'd love to have four children. We're going to have a good life, James. I can feel it in my heart. We're going to be so happy."

"I feel that way, too. Being an only child, I was always drawn to large families. I suspect that's why I've been such good friends with the Mannings over the years."

"Christy's family?"

He nodded. "She's the youngest of five."

Her parents and Julie appeared just then, and ever the gentleman, James stood until the ladies were seated.

"I hope you don't mind if we steal Summer away from you for the day," Helen said even before she looked at the menu. "We have a million and one things to do before the wedding."

"We do?" Summer didn't know why she bothered to protest. She'd realized this would happen the moment her parents announced they were coming.

"First, we need to buy you a dress."

Silly as it seemed, Summer hadn't given much thought to her attire. A nice suit would do, she supposed, something flattering and stylish. The elaborate gown and veil could wait for the April ceremony.

"Then there's the matter of finding a preacher."

"The hotel provides a justice of the peace," James said.

"Do you object to a man of the cloth?" Hank asked sternly.

Summer wanted to leap to her feet and tell James this was a test, but she bit her tongue. Sooner or later her soon-to-be husband would have to sink or swim on his own with her family.

"Not at all. I'd prefer one myself."

Summer had to restrain herself from cheering. James had passed with flying colors.

"I've got the names of several ministers from our pastor in Anaheim." Her father patted his shirt pocket. "We'll leave the women to do their thing, and you and I can find us a proper preacher." His tone implied that his little girl wasn't being married by any justice of the peace.

"What about rings?" Helen asked.

"I thought I'd pick up a couple of plain gold bands for now," James explained. "I'd like Summer to wear my mother's diamond. She can choose the setting at a later date, and it'll be ready before the April ceremony."

Breakfast wasn't the ordeal Summer had expected. Julie sent

her curious looks now and then, and Summer knew her friend was waiting for an opportune moment so they could talk.

"We'll meet again at what time?" Helen asked, glancing at her watch.

Summer's father studied his, while Summer and James gazed longingly at each other.

"Six," Helen suggested.

"That late?" Summer protested. They were being cheated out of an entire day. No one seemed to appreciate that her time with James was already limited.

"I'll see to everything," her mother assured everyone. "Hank, all you need to do is get James to the chapel on time."

"Don't worry about my not showing up," James said. "I'm deeply in love with your daughter."

Julie's elbow connected with Summer's ribs. "What did I tell you?" she whispered out of the corner of her mouth.

Julie had more than gloating on her mind, and so did Summer's mother. When they'd finished their coffee, Helen organized a shopping expedition. She made it clear that a suitable wedding dress wasn't the only thing on her list. If her daughter was about to marry a superior court judge, she'd go to him with a complete trousseau.

The minute Summer and Julie were alone in the store, her roommate grabbed Summer's arm. "I heard from Brett again," she whispered.

"Did he phone?"

"No. This time he stopped by the apartment, right before I left for the airport."

"No." Summer closed her eyes, not because she had any regrets or because she harbored any doubts about James.

It was as if Brett possessed some kind of radar that told him when he could cause her the most trouble.

"He's been asking about you. Apparently he talked with a couple of the cast members at Disneyland. Steve and Karen? Do those names sound familiar?"

"Yes." Summer clenched her fists. "I can't tell you how much this irritates me."

"You? The man's been making a pest of himself all week. According to Brett, you're pining away for him." Julie made a melodramatic gesture, bringing the back of one hand to her forehead. "You've been unhappy ever since the two of you split up—he says."

"Oh, puhleese."

"That's what I told him."

"If I was pining for anyone," Summer said, "it was for James."

"Exactly. I told Brett that, too."

"Thanks."

"I explained, with a great deal of satisfaction, that you're involved with someone else now, and he should stay out of your life."

"Good grief, he's married and about to become a father. The man has no principles." The thought of Brett trying to reestablish their relationship while his wife was pregnant with their child made Summer sick to her stomach. "I'm glad to be rid of him."

"You couldn't be getting married at a more opportune time. I'm telling you, Summer, from the way Brett argued with me, your marriage is about the only thing that'll convince him it's over."

"You did tell him I'm getting married, didn't you?"

"Yes, but he wouldn't believe me. He accused me of fabricating the whole thing."

"Girls, girls." Helen returned with a salesclerk.

"I wonder how long it'll be before she considers us women?" Summer asked her friend under her breath.

By evening Summer felt more like a French poodle than a bride. She'd been shampooed, her nails polished, her hair curled, her body massaged and moisturized. She'd been in and out of more clothes than a New York fashion model. And she was exhausted.

The idea of a white suit for the wedding was one of the first ideas to go. Before Summer could argue, she was draped in satin and silk from head to toe.

"You look absolutely stunning," Helen said.

Summer wasn't sure she could trust her mother's assessment. Her eyes went to Julie.

"She's right."

"But what about April?"

"What about it?" Helen's hands flew into the air. "You'll wear the dress twice. Big deal. No one needs to know."

She tried another arguement. "It's so much money."

"My baby girl only gets married once."

Well, no. She'd be getting married twice—to the same man, but still, there were going to be two ceremonies.

Julie arranged the veil and the long train for the photographer who was on his way, then handed Summer the intricate gardenia bouquet. "If you're going to throw that, just be sure and aim it my way."

Summer smiled. "You got it."

"Not yet, I haven't," Julie reminded her.

A knock sounded at the door, and Helen answered it. Summer didn't pay any attention, assuming it was the photographer her father had hired.

A few minutes later, Helen introduced the tall, balding man. "Summer, this is James's father, Walter. You should've told me he was a retired superior court judge himself."

Summer would have been happy to, had she known.

"My, oh, my," Walter said as he entered the room. He stood in front of Summer, hands on his hips, and he slowly shook his head. "And where did my son meet such a beauty?"

"Here in Vegas," Summer said. "A year ago."

"I was about to give up hope for that son of mine. It seemed to me he'd settled a little too comfortably into bachelorhood. This comes as a very pleasant surprise."

"I'm so glad you came to meet me and my family, especially on such short notice."

Walter withdrew a thick cigar from the inside of his suit pocket and examined the end of it. "Wouldn't have missed it for the world."

Walter sat down and made himself comfortable. After a moment he returned the cigar to his inside pocket. "I quit smoking five years ago and I still miss it. Every now and then I take one out and look at it, just for the thrill."

Summer could see she was going to like James's father.

"To be frank, I didn't think that boy of mine possessed this much common sense."

"He's a judge," Summer said, eager to defend her husband-to-be.

"When it comes to the law, James is one of the finest men on the bench. He seems to be worried about the November election, but as far as I can see, he won't have a problem. No, what I'm talking about is something else entirely."

Summer felt like sitting down, too. Both her mother and Julie had mysteriously disappeared, and since the photographer had yet to show up, she decided to relax.

"Have you seen James?" she asked, missing him dreadfully.

"Oh, yes."

"How is he?" She folded her hands, wondering what James was thinking and if he was sorry he'd gotten involved in all this. Everything had seemed so uncomplicated when they discussed it the night before.

"He's pacing in his room."

"Pacing," she repeated, certain this was a bad sign.

"It's just as well this wedding's going to happen less than an hour from now. I don't think your father and brother could keep James away from you much longer than that."

Summer smiled in relief.

"Never thought I'd see the day my boy would fall head over heels in love like this."

"But he was engaged before. I know about Christy Manning."

"Ah, yes, Christy. She's a dear girl, and James had strong feelings for her, but deep down I believe what he found so attractive about Christy was her family. There's quite a difference between the love James has for you and what he felt for Christy Manning. As you'll recall, he was content to stay engaged to Christy for a good long while. But you... He's marrying you so fast, my head's spinning. His, too, from the looks of him. You've thrown him for quite a loop."

"I love James, too," Summer said with feeling, "very much."

"Good. I hope the two of you will seriously consider making me a grandfather soon. I'm hoping for a grandchild or two to spoil."

"We'd like to have four."

"Four." Walter nodded, looking pleased. "But you're worried about something."

"Yes," she said softly, wondering how he knew. "My biggest fear is that I'm not the right kind of wife for James. I'm afraid I might inadvertently harm his career."

"What makes you think that?"

"I have this tendency to speak my mind."

"I find that refreshing."

"You will until I put my foot in my mouth and embarrass James. To give you an example…" She hesitated, not sure she should continue, then realized she couldn't very well stop now. "I'm the one who suggested we get married."

"Really?"

"It just…came out. It seemed like a brilliant idea at the time… you know how good things can sound until you've thought them through. Well, anyway, James stared at me like he'd swallowed his tongue."

Walter burst out laughing. "Forgive me, my dear. Continue, please."

"Naturally I felt like a fool. Mainly because James didn't say anything and didn't say anything and didn't say anything, and I was convinced I'd ruined everything."

"He said nothing, did he?"

"Well, he did mumble something about preferring to do the asking himself."

"And you clammed up."

"Oh, quite the opposite. I started talking at hurricane speed until he told me it was fine and I needn't worry. And then, after I'd fallen all over myself telling him how sorry I was, he said he thought it was a good idea. James came up with the idea of a ceremony now and then one in April."

"He did?" Clearly this was news to his father.

"Yes." Summer grinned sheepishly. "He said something about impulsive thoughts being contagious."

"There's more to the boy than I assumed."

There was another knock at the door, and the photographer let himself inside.

"I'd better get back to James," Walter said. "It's been a delight meeting you, Summer. I don't have a shred of doubt that you're the best thing to come into my son's life for a very long time. Make him happy, Summer, make him very happy."

"I intend to do my best."

"And while you're at it, teach him how to laugh."

Summer nodded. "I'll try." She had a sneaking suspicion they had plenty to teach one another.

James looked at his watch for the third time that minute. No one seemed to understand that he *needed* to see Summer. Needed to talk to her, find out about her day, tell her about his.

If he'd had even an inkling that their wedding was going to cause such a big commotion, he would never have agreed to contact their families.

James liked Summer's parents, but he'd prefer to spend his time with her. Alone.

"We can go into the chapel now," Hank Lawton said.

James was so grateful he felt like cheering. According to his calculations, the ceremony would take approximately twenty minutes, thirty at most. They'd sign the marriage certificate, and the rest of the night would be theirs. He couldn't tolerate any more of these separations, however brief. The next time Summer left his sight would be at the airport.

He saw her family in the small chapel, her brother's children wide-eyed and excited as the organ music rose triumphantly. He noticed that the wedding chapel was almost full and wondered for just a moment who the other guests were.

James went to stand in front with the minister, Reverend Floyd Wilson. James had rented the tuxedo because it seemed odd for the father of the bride to be wearing one and not the groom. Now, however, the shirt seemed too tight around the collar. He resisted the urge to insert his finger and give himself a little extra breathing space.

It was then that Summer appeared.

James felt as if someone had smashed him in the knees with a bat. Never in all his life had he seen anyone more beautiful. His heart beat so hard he thought it might pound straight through his chest.

Her dress was silk and lace with pearls, as traditional a wedding gown as any he'd seen. One would think Summer was a debutante and this a society wedding.

When she joined him at the altar and placed her arm in his, James felt this was the proudest moment of his life. He knew they'd repeat the ceremony in a few months, but nothing would match the blend of humility and pride he experienced right then.

Her brother, Adam, was kind enough to serve as his best man, while Julie, of course, was the maid of honor.

The ceremony itself was a blur. James's full concentration was on the woman at his side. He knew she was feeling the same emotions he was when she began to repeat her vows.

Summer's voice shook slightly, and she sounded close to tears. His arm tightened around hers as the minister said, "I now pronounce you husband and wife. You may kiss your bride."

James didn't need to hear that twice. Carefully he gathered Summer close, sighing when their lips met in the tenderest, sweetest kiss of his life.

She clung to him. "Oh, James, how soon can we get rid of everyone?"

He'd entertained that very question from the moment Summer's mother had taken her away that morning.

"Soon," he promised. Heaven only knew how they were going to cope with being separated for the next four months. "After dinner."

They were hit with a barrage of birdseed on their way out the door. They laughed and tried to catch it in their outstretched hands.

"Pictures," Helen insisted, and when Summer groaned, she added, "Just a few more. That's all."

"Mother, you'll get plenty of pictures later."

"I want some now," her mother insisted. But "some" turned out to be at least a hundred by James's estimation.

They signed the marriage license, and James took the opportunity to kiss his bride. "I don't ever want to spend another day like this one," he whispered.

"Me, neither," she said, then giggled. "But you're going to get something out of it. Mother bought me this cute little black nightie."

James could feel the hot blood circle his ears and...other places. "Your mother bought you a nightie?"

"She said it's her wedding gift to you."

"I'll thank her later."

"Wait until you see what Julie got us," she whispered.

"I have the feeling it isn't a toaster," he said wryly.

Summer laughed. "No. She picked it out when Mom wasn't looking. You do like tassels, don't you?"

"Tassels?"

"Shh." Summer looked around to be sure no one was listening. "I'll save them for after the honeymoon."

"Why?"

"Because, my darling husband, they cover—" She stopped abruptly.

"Yes?" he coaxed.

"Husband," she said the word as if saying a prayer. "James, you're my *husband*."

"I know. And you're my wife." It hit him then, too. The beauty of it, of belonging to each other, of the word itself.

Their families all seemed to return at once.

"I don't know about anyone else," Helen Lawton was saying, "but I'm starved."

There was a chorus of agreement. They trooped into the hotel's elegant restaurant and ordered dinner and champagne, although Summer could barely eat and had trouble following the conversation.

"We'll say good-night, then," James announced the minute they could leave without being rude. "Thank you all for making this the most incredible day of my life."

"It's still early," Helen protested.

"Helen," Hank snapped. "Think about it."

"Oh, yes, sorry." Helen's face brightened, and she smiled apologetically at James.

"Will we see you in the morning?"

"Helen!" her husband growled.

"I'm just asking, Hank. What harm is there in asking?"

"I don't know, Mom. What time is your flight?"

James didn't listen to the answer, although he supposed he should have. As it was, he had a hard time hiding his impatience. He and his wife—his wife—would only have two more days together. Luckily that was two days and *three* nights. Their flights were leaving within a half hour of each other, and then it would be a whole month before he saw her again.

"All right, then, darling," Helen said, hugging Summer, "we'll see you both in the morning."

The entourage left, and James was alone with Summer at last.

"Are we going to my room or yours?" she asked, smiling up at him.

"Neither. I rented the honeymoon suite here for the rest of our stay. Your mother packed your suitcase and had it sent over."

"You think of everything." She reached up and removed the wedding veil and shook her head, freeing her curls. "I can't tell you how anxious I am to get out of this dress."

James chuckled as he led the way to the elevator. "Not nearly as anxious as I am to get you out of it."

"Who were all those guests?" she asked him when they stepped inside the elevator car.

"I thought they were friends of your family."

"I've never seen them before in my life."

James shrugged. "Me, neither."

"You know what? I'll bet my mother invited them. She couldn't bear to have us married in an empty chapel."

James fingered his room key. "Are you hungry?"

"No."

"Good. Let's go work up an appetite."

Summer smiled and moistened her lips with the tip of her tongue. "I have a feeling you aren't talking about racquetball."

James cleared his throat. He wanted her so much his body trembled with the strength of his need. "You're right about that."

CHAPTER SIX

JAMES ASTONISHED SUMMER. She didn't know what to expect from him as a lover, but it wasn't this. They'd made love no less than three times during their wedding night, and Summer woke the following morning to find him standing at the foot of their bed, fresh from the shower.

His nude body glistened in the early-morning light. Droplets of water dripped from his hair and onto the dark curls that covered his chest.

"Good morning, Mrs. Wilkens."

Summer smiled and stretched her arms high above her head, arching her back. The sheet slipped away, exposing her breasts.

"Good morning, James." She saw that he was fully aroused and slowly lifted her gaze to his. Already her body was responding to him, throbbing with readiness and need. James's eyes narrowed as they focused on her.

Wordlessly she knelt on the bed and held out her arms to him. She smiled, thinking someone should've warned her about this man before they were married. At this rate, they'd both be dead within a week.

He walked over to the side of the bed, kissed her once, twice, and then knelt beside it.

All her life Summer had never experienced such power. Or

such love. Her breathing grew slow and shallow. She half closed her eyes in pleasure at the simple touch of his hand.

James groaned, and Summer recognized his meaning. He couldn't wait any longer. Neither could she. She threw her arms around his neck and slowly lay back against the bed, bringing him with her.

She smiled contentedly as they began to make love. All of a sudden her eyes flew open. "James, you forgot—"

"It'll be all right," he assured her breathlessly. "Just this one time."

She didn't want him to stop. Not now. "Okay."

James reached his climax soon after she experienced hers. A harsh groan tore from his throat, and his powerful body shuddered.

His shoulders still heaving, he gathered her in his arms and spread soft, delicate kisses over her face. He started to move away from her, but she wouldn't let him.

"Not yet," she pleaded. "I want to be a part of you."

"You are. You always will be. You could travel to Mars, and my heart would be with you." He brushed the damp hair from her forehead. "I can't believe you love me."

"I do, so much my heart feels like it's about to burst wide open. Will it always be like this?" she asked. "Two weeks ago, you were someone whose letters I looked forward to. This week you're the most important person in my life."

James kissed the tip of her nose. "It's only going to get better from here on out."

"Better?" She laughed delightedly. "I can't imagine it."

In one uninterrupted movement James rolled onto his back, taking her with him so she was sprawled across his chest. Across his heart. "I can't, either. Summer, I love you."

"Good." She pressed her head against his shoulder. "But what about—"

"I'll remember next time," he promised. "The last thing we need now is an unplanned pregnancy."

"I'm pretty sure this is my safe time, so don't worry."

James kissed her neck. "I suppose we should get dressed and meet everyone for breakfast."

"I suppose," she agreed, but neither of them showed any signs of moving.

"It won't be so bad," James whispered.

They'd been married less than twenty-four hours and already Summer could read her husband's thoughts. "Being separated? It's going to be terrible. I don't know how I'll last four months without you."

"Four months." He made it sound like an eternity.

"James, where do you live?"

He gave her a puzzled look. "Seattle. You know my address."

"But is it an apartment? A condo? A town house or what?"

"A house."

Summer liked the idea of that.

A slow grin spread across his face. "I must've known I was going to meet you. This is a big house on Queen Anne Hill with seven bedrooms."

"James!"

"It's a lovely older home. I'm quite proud of the garden. I hope you'll like it."

"I love it already."

"You haven't seen it."

"No, but I saw the look on your face when you talked about it. The house is going to be perfect for us, just perfect."

His eyes grew dark. "*You're* perfect."

"I hope we'll always love each other as much as we do at this moment." Summer laid her head on his chest and sighed.

Time had never passed more quickly for James. He'd dreaded leaving Summer almost from the moment they'd met again on New Year's Eve. It was as though Seattle was another world, one he wasn't that eager to return to. Not when it meant having to say goodbye to Summer.

His wife of two days was unusually quiet as they packed their suitcases on Saturday morning, the day of their departure. When she found him watching her, she offered him a reassuring smile.

The bellboy carried their luggage to the lobby. While James was checking out of the hotel, he noticed Summer twisting the plain gold band around her finger. His own felt awkward and heavy, and he wondered if she was experiencing any regrets. For his own part, he didn't have a single one.

Having returned the rental car earlier, James ordered a car. He and Summer held hands as they rode silently to the airport.

He wanted to assure her it wouldn't be so bad, but that would've been a blatant lie. Every minute he was away from her was a minute too long. He wanted to be sure she understood how much he loved her, how crucial she was to him. But the backseat of a limo with a driver listening in didn't seem the most appropriate place to tell her those things.

Nothing would ever be the same for either of them, and they both knew it.

The car dropped them off, and since they were flying on different airlines, they separated to check in their luggage and receive their seat assignments.

James finished first and caught sight of Summer hurrying through the crowd toward him. Even from that distance he sensed her sadness. He met her halfway and they went through security together.

"My flight leaves from Concourse B," she said, looking down at her ticket. Her voice was small and tight.

"Mine's Concourse A."

"What time's your flight?"

She already knew, but apparently needed to hear it again. "Ten-thirty," James told her.

"My departure's at ten."

He was perfectly aware of what time her plane left. "I'll walk down to Concourse B with you."

"You can't, James, you might miss your own flight."

Frankly he didn't give a damn. "Then I'll catch the next one."

"I'll worry. James, really, I'm a big girl. I can find my way around the airport."

"I didn't say you couldn't," he snapped, surprising himself.

Summer looked up at him, her eyes brimming with tears. She turned and walked away from him and headed for Concourse B.

James followed and wanted to kick himself. He wouldn't see his wife for weeks and here he was, apparently doing his utmost to start an argument. No doubt there was some psychological reason for his attitude. He'd examine what was happening later, but at the moment he was more concerned about saying goodbye to her properly.

Summer arrived at her gate and walked over to the window. James could see her plane and knew it wouldn't be more than a few moments before the boarding call was announced.

"I'm sorry, sweetheart." He rested his hands on her shoulders and closed his eyes.

"Me, too."

He frowned. She'd done nothing wrong. "For what?"

"Oh, James," she whispered brokenly, slipping her arms around his waist. "I'm going to be so lost without you."

"It's going to be hard." He wasn't willing to pretend otherwise. "I'll phone as often as I can."

"Do you have my work schedule?" she asked.

"Yes. Do you have everything you need?" They'd gone over the details a dozen times.

"No. I need you, James."

His hold on her tightened. He wondered if they were afraid they'd lose the magic. Afraid that once they returned to their respective lives, everything would change.

Her flight number was announced, and James tensed. It wouldn't be long before he saw her, he promised himself. He'd try for a week, two at the most. A few minutes later her row was called.

"That's you," he said reluctantly.

"I know."

But neither of them made a move to break apart.

Summer was the last one to board the plane, and James had to tear through the airport in order to catch his own flight. If anyone had suggested even ten days ago that the dignified James Wilkens would race through an airport so he could spend a few extra minutes with a woman, he would have scoffed. He wasn't scoffing now.

He arrived in the nick of time and collapsed into his seat, his heart racing.

Between dashing through airports and hours spent making love, Summer would be the death of him yet. He smiled as he snapped his seat belt into place. If he was to die that very moment, he'd leave this earth a happy man.

* * *

James's house had never seemed so empty. By the time he got home, it was dark and shadowy. His first mistake had been stopping at the office on his way back from the airport. After he arrived in Seattle, he'd spent what remained of the day working through the memos, briefs and case histories. No one else was in, so he was able to accomplish quite a bit, catching up on some of his backlog. He'd do anything he had to so he could arrange time away as soon as possible.

Summer was never far from his thoughts.

Once he reached his house, suitcase in hand, he was exhausted. He switched on the light in the kitchen, put down his bags and set his briefcase on the walnut table in the breakfast nook.

He hadn't eaten since that morning, and a look inside the refrigerator reminded him he'd been away all week. He'd need to order out or microwave something from the freezer.

Deciding against both, he heated a can of soup, ate, then showered. He'd showered that morning, but Summer had been in the stall with him and neither one had seemed particularly concerned about washing.

James stood in front of the mirror in the steamy bathroom and wiped off some of the condensation, then stared at his reflection. He didn't look all that different from the man he'd been a week ago. But he *was* different.

Unable to delay talking to Summer, he dressed quickly and headed for his book-lined den.

Having memorized her apartment and cell phone numbers, James called her at home.

Summer answered on the first ring. "Hello."

"Hello, darling."

"James!"

"I would've called sooner, but I went to the office. I needed to clear off my desk."

"Did you check your calendar?"

"First thing. I can fly down on a Saturday morning in two weeks, but I'll need to be back Sunday afternoon. That doesn't give us much time."

"No," she agreed, "but we'll make the most of it." Her relief was evident. "I was afraid once you looked at your schedule you'd find it impossible to get away."

"I don't care what it takes, I'll be in California in two weeks."

"Wonderful. I traded weekends with a friend so I can come to you in February. My mother's already started to plan the wedding. She's left a message with the secretary at the Moose Hall. It's a very nice building."

"Your mother's enjoying every minute of this, isn't she?"

Summer laughed. "Yes. But the one who surprises me most is my dad. I don't know what you said or did, but my dad thinks you walk on water."

It was his turn to laugh.

Then they were both silent. They'd spent nearly every minute of the previous week together. They'd discussed everything there was to discuss. Yet neither was willing to break the connection.

An hour later they were still on the phone. They hadn't spoken more than a few words between whispered promises and deep sighs. They'd shared a few secrets and memories, some of them very private. Very intimate...

In their next conversation, he'd let Summer know he couldn't handle much more of that.

"I've gotten together with a group of businessmen and spread the word," Ralph Southworth was saying.

James sat in his office, gazing into the distance. As always, his thoughts were fifteen hundred miles to the south with Summer. He barely heard his campaign manager. In eight days he'd be with his wife. The last six had been the purest form of torture.

He lived for the times he could phone her. Because she performed in the last show of the night, he couldn't reach her until after ten, and more often than not they spoke until past midnight.

"There's a dinner party this Friday night at the Morrisons'," Ralph announced.

James didn't comment.

"You're going, aren't you?"

"You mean to the Morrisons'?"

Ralph Southworth looked at him oddly. "Who else do you think I mean?"

James shrugged. Ralph was a good man, a bit abrasive at times, but sincere and hardworking. According to people James trusted, Ralph Southworth was the best man for the job of getting James elected to the superior court.

"What's with you lately, James?" Ralph asked abruptly. He pulled out a chair and sat down across from James's desk.

Ralph was nothing if not direct. "What makes you ask?"

"Something's not right. Ever since you got back from vacation, you haven't been the same."

James considered telling Ralph the truth. Part of him was eager to share the news of his marriage. Marrying Summer was nothing to be ashamed of—the opposite, in fact—but arrangements for the second ceremony were already being made. If he was willing to face the truth, James would have to admit he wasn't keen on explaining his sudden marriage, especially to the man who'd frowned on his vacation in Vegas. He preferred to leave things as they were and invite Ralph to the wedding in April. So far, he'd told no one about Summer and for the time being even left his wedding band at home.

"Have you ever been in love?" he asked, unable to resist.

Ralph shook his head adamantly. "Never, and proud of it."

James's eyebrows shot to his hairline. "I see."

"Women have ruined more than one good man. Don't be a fool, James. Don't do anything stupid at this point. Unless it's with someone who can help you politically, of course. Now, if you told me you were seeing Mary Horton…"

"Who?"

"Mary Horton—never mind, she's not your type. All I can say is that if you're going to fall for someone now, just make sure it's a woman who can help you politically."

"She can't."

Ralph tossed his hands in the air. "Somehow, I knew you were going to say that. Listen. Keep your head screwed on tight and your pants zipped up. The last thing we need now is a scandal, understand?"

"Of course. Summer's not like—"

"Her name is *Summer?*" Ralph rolled his eyes expressively. "James, listen to me. You've asked me to run your campaign, and

I'm glad to do it, but I'm telling you right now, getting involved with a woman named Summer is asking for trouble."

"Don't you think you're being unfair?"

"No. Where'd you meet her?"

"Vegas."

Ralph's mouth thinned. "Don't tell me she's a show girl," he muttered.

"No—but she's an actress."

A muscle leapt in his friend's jaw. "Don't say anything more. Not a single word. I've got high blood pressure and don't want to know any more than you've already told me."

"Summer has nothing to do with you," James said, finding it difficult to quell his irritation. Ralph made Summer sound like... like a mistake.

"Don't you remember a certain congressman who got involved with a stripper a few years back?"

"Summer isn't a stripper!"

"It ruined him, James. Ruined him. I don't want the same thing to happen to you."

"It won't. Furthermore, I won't have you speaking about her in those terms." In light of Ralph's reaction, James didn't think now was the time to announce they were already married. "If you must know, I intend to marry her."

"Great. Do it after the election."

"We've decided on April."

"April!" Ralph barked. "That's much too soon. Listen, you're paying me big money to run this campaign. You want my advice, you've got it. What difference would a few months make?" He paused, waiting for James's response. "Will you do that one thing?"

"I don't know."

"Are you afraid you'll lose her?"

"No."

"Then put off the wedding until after the election. Is that so much to ask?"

"I'm not sure which is worse," Julie said, applying bright red polish to her toenails, "this year or last."

"What do you mean?" Summer asked.

"You." She swirled the brush in the red paint and started with the little toe on her left foot. "Last year, after you broke up with Brett, you moped around the apartment for months."

Summer laughed. "This year isn't much better, is it?"

"Not that I can see. Listen, I understand how much you miss James. The guy's hot. No wonder you fell for him. If the situation was reversed, you can bet I'd be just as miserable. The thing is, you won't be apart for long. April's right around the corner."

Summer folded her arms and leaned against the back of the sofa. "I didn't know it was possible to love someone as much as I love James."

"If the number of times he calls you is any indication, I'd say he feels the same about you."

"He works so hard." Summer knew that many of James's late-night calls came from his office. She also knew he was putting in extra-long hours in order to free up time he could spend with her.

"Summer, he'll be here in a few days."

"I know."

"You haven't told him about Brett?" Julie asked.

Summer's nails bit into her palms. "What good would it do? James is fifteen hundred miles away. Brett hasn't got a chance with me. Unfortunately he doesn't seem ready to accept that. But he's going to get the same message whenever he calls."

"By the way, when James visits, I'm out of here."

"Julie, you don't need to leave. We can get a hotel room—really, we don't mind."

"Don't be ridiculous. This is your home. You'd be more relaxed, and both of you have been through enough stress lately."

Summer was so grateful it was all she could do not to weep. It was the stress, she decided, this tendency to be over emotional. "Have I told you how glad I am that you're my friend?"

"Think nothing of it," Julie said airily.

"I mean it, Julie. I don't know what I would've done without you these last weeks. I feel like my whole world's been turned upside down."

"It has been. Who else goes away for a week and comes home married? Did you think James had lost his mind when he suggested it?"

"Yes," she admitted, remembering the most fabulous dinner of her life. "I don't think he's done anything that impulsive his whole life."

Julie grinned. "Until he met you."

"Funny, James made the same comment."

The phone rang just then, and Summer leapt up to answer it on the off chance it was James.

"Hello," she said breathlessly.

"Summer, don't hang up, please, I'm begging you."

"Brett." Her heart sank. "Please," she told him, "just leave me alone."

"Talk to me. That's all I'm asking."

"About what? We have absolutely nothing to say to each other."

"I made a mistake."

Summer closed her eyes, fighting the frustration. "It's too late. What do I have to say to convince you of that? You're married, I'm married."

"I don't believe it." His voice grew hoarse. "If you're married, then where's your husband?"

"I don't owe you any explanations. Don't phone me again. It's over and has been for more than a year."

"Summer, please…please."

She didn't wait to hear any more. His persistence astonished her. When she'd found him with another woman, he'd seemed almost glad, as though he was relieved to be free of the relationship. In retrospect, Summer realized that Brett had fallen out of love with her long before, but had lacked the courage to say anything. Later, when he'd married, and she learned it wasn't the same woman he'd been with in Vegas, she wondered about this man she thought she knew so well, and discovered she didn't know him at all.

His behavior mystified her. After loving Brett for six years, she expected to feel *something* for him, but all the feeling she could muster was pity. She wanted nothing to do with him. He'd made his choice and she'd made hers.

"Brett? Again?" Julie asked when Summer joined her in the living room.

Summer nodded. "I hope this is the end of it."

"Have you thought about having the phone number changed?"

"That's a good idea. And I'm going to get call display, too."

Julie studied her for a moment. "Are you going to tell James why we've got a new phone number?"

"No. It would only worry him, and there's nothing he can do so far away. Brett doesn't concern me."

"Maybe he should."

Summer arrived at the Orange County airport forty minutes before James's flight was due, in case it came in early. Every minute of their day and a half together was carefully planned.

The only negative for Summer was the brunch with her parents Sunday morning. Her mother had several questions about the wedding that she needed to discuss with James. Summer begrudged every minute she had to share James; she knew she was being selfish, but she didn't care.

Julie, true to her word, had made a weekend trip to visit a family member, an elderly aunt in Claremont.

By the time James's plane touched down, she was nearly sick to her stomach with anticipation. As soon as he stepped out of the secure area, he paused, searching for her.

Their eyes connected and in the second before he started toward her, her heart seemed to stop. Then it began to race.

When they'd parted in Las Vegas, it felt as if everything had come to an abrupt standstill. Now she could see him, could *feel* him, for the first time since they'd parted two weeks ago.

Dashing between the other passengers, she ran toward him. James caught her in his arms and crushed her against him. His hands were in her hair, and his mouth hungrily sought hers.

His embrace half lifted her from the ground. She clung to him, fighting back a flood of emotion. Unexpectedly tears filled her eyes, but she was too happy to care.

James broke off the kiss, and Summer stared up at him, smiling. It was so good to see him.

"What's this?" he asked, brushing his thumb across the moisture on her cheeks.

"I guess I missed you more than I realized."

"You're beautiful," he said in a low voice.

"I bet you tell all the women that," she joked.

"Nope, only the ones I marry."

Summer slipped her arm around his waist, and together they headed toward the luggage carousel. "I packed light."

"Good." Because it felt so good to be close to him, she stood on the tips of her toes and kissed his cheek. "You'll be glad to hear Julie's gone for the weekend."

"Remind me to thank her."

"She's been wonderful."

"Any more crank calls?"

Summer had almost forgotten that was the excuse she'd given him when she'd had her phone numbers changed. "None." And then, because she was eager to change the subject, she told him, "I've got every minute planned."

"Every minute?"

"Well, almost. Mom and Dad invited us over for brunch in the morning. I couldn't think of any way to get out of it."

"It might be a good idea to see them."

"Why?"

James frowned, and she noticed the dark circles under his eyes. He was working too hard, not sleeping enough, not eating properly. That would all change when she got to Seattle. The first thing she'd do was make sure he had three decent meals a day. As for time in bed, well, she didn't think that would be a problem.

"There might be a problem with the wedding date," he said reluctantly.

Summer halted midstep. "What do you mean?"

"April might not work, after all." He paused. "It doesn't matter, does it? We're already married."

"I know, but…"

"We can talk about it later, with your family. All right?"

She nodded, unwilling to waste even one precious minute arguing over a fancy wedding when she already wore his ring.

CHAPTER SEVEN

FOR YEARS JAMES had lived an impassive and sober life. He'd never considered himself a physical man. But three weeks after marrying Summer, making love occupied far more of his thoughts than it had in the previous thirty-odd years combined.

"How far is it to your apartment?" he asked, as they walked to her car.

Summer didn't immediately respond.

"Summer?"

"It seems to me we have a few things to discuss."

"All right," he said, forcing himself to stop staring at her. She had him at a distinct disadvantage. At the moment he would have agreed to just about anything, no matter where the discussion led—as long as they got to her place soon. As long as they could be alone…

"I want to know why there's a problem with the wedding date."

He should've realized. "Sweetheart, it has more to do with your parents than you and me. Let's not worry about it now."

"You want to delay the wedding, don't you?"

"No," he responded vehemently. "Do you honestly think I'm enjoying this separation? I couldn't be more miserable."

"Me, neither."

"Then you have to believe I wouldn't do anything that would keep us apart any longer than necessary." James glanced at her as she drove. He was telling the truth, although not, perhaps, the whole truth. Time enough for that later, he thought. He was worried about Summer. She seemed pale and drawn, as if she weren't sleeping well or eating right. This situation wasn't good for either of them.

After fifteen minutes they arrived at her apartment building. He carried in his suitcase and set it down in her small living room, gazing around.

Summer's personality seemed to mark each area. The apartment was bright and cheerful. The kitchen especially appealed to him; the cabinets had been painted a bold yellow with red knobs. Without asking, he knew this was her special touch.

She led him into her bedroom, and he stopped when he noticed the five-foot wall poster of her as Beauty posing with the Beast. She looked so beautiful he couldn't take his eyes off it. He felt a hint of jealousy of the man who was able to spend time with her every night, even if it was in costume.

His gaze moved from the picture to the bed. A single. He supposed it wouldn't matter. The way he felt just then, they'd spend the whole night making love anyway.

He turned toward his wife. She smiled softly, and in that instant James knew he couldn't wait any longer. His need was so great that his entire body seemed to throb with a need of its own.

He held out his hand, and she walked toward him.

If he had any regrets about their time in Vegas, it was that he'd been so eager for her, so awkward and clumsy. Tonight would be slow and easy, he'd promised himself. When they made love, it would be leisurely so she'd know how much he appreciated her. They'd savor each other without interruption.

"Summer, I love you." He lifted the shirt over her head and tossed it carelessly aside. His hands were at the snap of her jeans, trembling as he struggled to hold back the urgency of his need.

He kissed her with two weeks' worth of pent-up hunger, and all his accumulated frustration broke free.

He eased the jeans over her slender hips and let them fall to her feet, then released her long enough to remove his own clothes. As he was unbuttoning his shirt, he watched her slip out of her silky underwear. His breath caught in his throat.

When James finished undressing, they collapsed on the narrow bed together. And then he lost all sense of time....

Summer woke to the sound of James humming off-key in the kitchen. The man couldn't carry a tune in a bucket, as her dad liked to say. Smiling, she glanced at her clock radio—almost 6:00 p.m. She reached for her housecoat and entered the kitchen to find him examining the contents of her refrigerator.

"So you're one of those," she teased, tying the sash of her robe.

"One of what?" He reappeared brandishing a chicken leg.

"You get hungry after sex," she whispered.

"I didn't eat on the plane, and yes," he said, grinning shyly at her, "I suspect you're right."

She yawned and sat on the bar stool. "Anything interesting in there?"

"Leftover chicken, cottage cheese three weeks past its expiration date, Swiss cheese and an orange."

"I'll take the orange." She yawned again.

"Have you been getting enough sleep?" He peeled the orange and handed it to her, frowning. It wasn't his imagination; she was pale.

"More than ever. I seem to be exhausted lately. All I do is work and sleep."

"Have you seen a doctor?"

"No. I'm fine," she said, forcing a smile. She didn't want to waste their precious time together discussing her sleeping patterns. She ate a section of the rather dry orange. "I better shower and get dressed."

"For the show?"

She nodded, sad that part of her weekend with James would be spent on the job, but there was no help for it. It was difficult enough to trade schedules in order to fly up to Seattle.

"I'm looking forward to seeing what a talented woman I married."

"I hope I don't disappoint you."

"Not possible." He shook his head solemnly.

"James," she said, staring down at the orange. "Do you ever wonder what's really there between us?"

He tossed the chicken bone into the garbage. "What do you mean?"

"Sometimes I'm afraid all we share is a strong physical attraction. Is there more?"

He swallowed; the question seemed to make him uncomfortable. "What makes you ask that?"

"In case you haven't noticed, we can't keep our hands off each other."

"What's wrong with that?"

"I think about us making love—a lot. Probably more than I should. You're a brilliant man. I'm fairly sure you didn't marry me because I challenge you intellectually."

"I married you because I fell in love with you."

He made it sound so uncomplicated.

"I love the way a room lights up when you walk into it," he said. "When you laugh, I want to laugh, too. I've never heard you sing or seen you perform on stage, but there's music in you, Summer. I sensed it the first night we met.

"Just being with you makes me want to smile. Not that you're telling jokes or doing pratfalls or anything—it's your attitude. When I'm with you, the world's a better place."

Summer felt her throat tighten.

"Like your father, an attorney or a judge can develop a jaded perspective in life. It's difficult to trust when the world's filled with suspicion. It's difficult to love when you deal with the consequences of hate every day. Perhaps that's been my problem all along."

"Not trusting?"

"Yes. You came to me without defenses, devastated, vulnerable, broken. I'd been hurt, too, so I knew how you felt because I'd experienced those same emotions. I'd walk through the fires of hell before I'd allow anyone to do that to you again." He walked over and held out his hand. "It's more than just words when I say I love you, Summer. It's my heart, my whole heart."

She gripped his hand with both of hers.

"If you're afraid our relationship is too much about sexual attraction, then maybe we should put a hold on anything physical for the rest of the weekend. Instead, we'll concentrate on getting to know each other better."

"Do you think it's possible?" She gave him a knowing look, then leaned forward. The front of her robe gaped open, and Summer watched as he stared at her breasts, then carefully averted his eyes.

"It's possible," he said in a low voice. "Not easy, but possible."

"I need to take a shower before I leave for work." She slipped off the stool and started to walk away. Then she turned, looked over her shoulder and smiled seductively. "Remember what fun we had in the shower, James?"

James paled. "Summer," he warned through clenched teeth. "If we're going to stay out of the bedroom, I'll need your help."

She turned to face him full on. "The shower isn't in the bedroom."

"Go have your shower," he said stiffly. "I'll wait for you here."

"You're sure?" She released the sash and let the silk robe fall open.

He made a sound that could mean various things—but he didn't make a move. Feeling slightly disappointed, Summer walked slowly into the bathroom and turned on the shower.

She'd just stepped inside and adjusted the water when the shower door was pulled open.

Naked, James joined her there. "You know I can't resist you," he muttered.

"Yes," she said softly. "I can't resist you, either."

Summer and her mother were busy in the kitchen at the Lawton family home. James sat in the living room with his father-in-law, watching a Sunday-morning sports show.

James didn't have the heart to tell Hank that he didn't follow sports all that much. And he sure wasn't going to admit he found them boring.

"Helen's going to be talking to you later," Hank said, relaxing during a spell of uninterrupted beer commercials. "She's having trouble getting a decent hall for the wedding reception in April. The church is no problem, mind you, but finding a hall's become pretty complicated."

"Summer said something about the Moose Hall."

"That fell through. I'll let Helen do the explaining."

"Does Summer know this?"

"Not yet. Couldn't see upsetting her. The girl's been miserable ever since she got back from Vegas. You want my opinion?" He didn't wait for a response. "You should take her to Seattle with you now and be done with it. It's clear to me the two of you belong together."

James wished it was that easy.

"I know, I know," Hank said, scooting forward to the edge of his chair as some football players ran back onto a muddy field. "She has to fulfill her contract. Never understood where the girl got her singing talent."

"She's fabulous." Summer's performance had shocked James. Her singing had moved him deeply and her acting impressed him.

Hank beamed proudly. "She's good, isn't she? I'll never forget the night I first went to see her perform at Disneyland. It was all I could do not to stand up and yell out, 'Hey, that's my little girl up there.'"

"There's such power in her voice."

"Enough to crack crystal, isn't it? You'd never suspect it hearing her speak, but the minute she opens her mouth to sing, watch out. I've never heard anything like it."

James had come away awed by her talent. That she'd willingly walk away from her career to be his wife, willingly take her chances in a new city, humbled him.

"She could go all the way to the top."

Hank nodded. "I think so, too, if she wanted, but that's the thing. She loves singing, don't get me wrong, but Summer will be just as happy humming lullabies to her babies as she would be performing in some hit Broadway show."

James's heart clutched at the thought of Summer singing to their children.

"Helen's mother used to sing," Hank said, but his eyes didn't leave the television screen. He frowned when the sports highlights moved on to tennis. "Ruth didn't sing professionally, but she was a member of the church choir for years. Talent's a funny business. Summer was singing from the time she was two. Now, Adam, he sounds like a squeaky door."

"Me, too." All James could hope was that their children inherited their mother's singing ability.

"Don't worry about it. She loves you anyway."

James wasn't quite sure how to respond, but fortunately he didn't have to, because Helen poked her head in at that moment.

"Brunch is ready," she said. "Hank, turn off that blasted TV."

"But, Helen—"

"Hank!"

"All right, all right." Reluctantly Hank reached for the TV controller and muted the television. His wife didn't seem to notice, and Hank sent James a conspiratorial wink. "Compromise," he whispered. "She won't even know."

James sat next to Summer at the table. "This looks delicious," he said to Helen. His mother-in-law had obviously gone to a lot of trouble with this brunch. She'd prepared sausages and ham slices and bacon, along with some kind of egg casserole, fresh-baked sweet rolls, coffee and juice.

Helen waited until they'd all filled their plates before she mentioned the April wedding date. "The reason I wanted to talk to the two of you has to do with the wedding date." She paused, apparently unsure how to proceed. "I wasn't too involved with Adam's wedding when he married Denise. I had no idea we'd need to book the reception hall so far in advance."

"But I thought you already *had* the place," Summer wailed.

"Didn't happen, sweetheart," Hank said. "Trust me, your mother's done her best. I can't tell you how many phone calls she's made."

"If we're going to have the wedding you deserve," her mother said pointedly, "it'll need to be later than April. My goodness, it takes time just to get the invitations printed, and we can't order them until we have someplace *nice* for the reception."

"How much later?" was James's question.

Helen and Hank exchanged looks. "June might work, but September would be best."

"September," Summer cried.

"September's out of the question." With the primary in September, James couldn't manage time away for a wedding. "If we're going to wait that long, anyway, then let's do it after the election in November." The minute he made the suggestion, James realized he'd said the wrong thing.

"November." Summer's voice sagged with defeat. "So what am I supposed to do between April and November?"

"Move up to Seattle with James, of course," Hank said without a qualm.

"Absolutely not," Helen protested. "We can't have our daughter living with James before they're married."

"Helen, for the love of heaven, they're already married. Remember?"

"Yes, but no one knows that."

"James?"

Everyone turned to him. "Other than my dad, no one knows I'm married, either."

Summer seemed to wilt. "It sounds like what you're saying is that you don't want me with you."

"No!" James could hear the hurt and disappointment in her voice and wished he knew some way to solve the problem, but he didn't. "You know that isn't true."

"Why is everything suddenly so complicated?" Summer asked despondently. "It seemed so simple when James and I first decided to do things this way. Now I feel as if we're trapped."

James had the same reaction. "We'll talk about it and get back to you," he told his in-laws. Both were content to leave it at that.

After brunch he and Summer took a walk around her old neighborhood. Their pace was leisurely, and she didn't say anything for a couple of blocks. She clasped her hands behind her back as if she didn't want to be close to him just then. He gave her the space she needed, but longed to put his arm around her.

"I know you're disappointed, sweetheart. So am I," he began. "I—"

"This is what you meant about problems with the April date, isn't it? The election."

"Yes, but..."

"I feel like excess baggage in your life."

"Summer, you *are* my life."

"Oh, James, how did everything get so messed up?"

"It's my fault," he muttered, ramming his fingers through his hair. "I was the one who suggested we go ahead with the wedding right away."

"Thank heaven. I'd hate to think how long we'd have to wait if you hadn't."

"I was being purely selfish and only a little practical. I knew I wouldn't be able to keep from making love to you much longer."

"And you're traditional enough—*gentleman* enough—to prefer to marry me first," she suggested softly.

"Something like that." She made him sound nobler than he was. He'd married her because he wanted to. Because he couldn't imagine *not* marrying her.

"As you said, the problem is the election. I had no business marrying you when I did. Not when I knew very well what this year would be like."

"The campaign?"

He nodded. "I've never been a political person, but it's a real factor in this kind of situation."

"I thought judges were nonpartisan."

"They are, but trust me, sweetheart, there's plenty of politics involved. I want to be elected, Summer, but not enough to put you through this."

She was silent again for a long moment. "One question."

"Anything."

She lowered her head and increased her pace. "Why didn't you tell anyone we're married?"

"I told my campaign manager you and I were engaged." James hesitated, selecting his words carefully.

"And?"

"And he asked me to wait until after the election to go through with the wedding. He had a number of reasons, some valid, others not, but he did say one thing that made sense."

"What?"

"He reminded me that I'm paying him good money for his advice."

"I see." She gave a short laugh that revealed little amusement. "I don't even know your campaign manager and already I dislike him."

"Ralph. Ralph Southworth. He isn't so bad."

"What will we do, James?"

"I don't know."

"Do you want me to wait until after the election to move to Seattle?"

"No," he said vehemently.

"But you have to consider Ralph's advice."

"Something like that." They walked past a school yard with a battered chain-link fence. It looked as if every third-grade class for the past twenty years had made it his or her personal goal to climb that fence.

"I've been thinking about this constantly," James told her. It had weighed down his heart for nearly two weeks, ever since his talk with Ralph. "There are no easy solutions."

"We don't need to decide right now, do we?"

"No." Actually James was relieved. At the moment he was more than willing to say the heck with it and move Summer to Seattle in April.

"Then let's both give it some thought in the next few weeks."

"Good idea." He placed one arm around her shoulders. "I've worked hard for this opportunity to sit on the bench, Summer, but it's not worth losing you."

"Losing me?" She smiled up at him. "You'd have a very hard time getting rid of me, James Wilkens, and don't you forget it."

James chuckled and kissed her lightly. It was a bittersweet kiss, reminding him that in a matter of hours he'd be leaving her again. Only this time he didn't know exactly when he could be with her again.

Summer rubbed her face against the side of his. "Not so long ago, I had to practically beg you to kiss me in public."

"That was before you had me completely twisted around your little finger." The changes she'd already wrought in his life astonished him. "I don't know what I did to deserve you, but whatever it was I'm grateful."

"Your flight leaves in less than five hours."

"I know."

"I suppose we should go back to the apartment." She looked up at him and raised her delicate eyebrows. "That's plenty of time for what I have in mind."

"Summer..."

"Yes, James?" She batted her eyelashes at him. He grinned. She managed to be sexy and funny simultaneously, and he found that completely endearing.

They made their farewells to her family and were soon on their way back to the apartment. There was time to make love, he decided, shower and pack. Then he'd be gone again.

Summer must have been thinking the same thing because she said, "We always seem to be leaving each other."

James couldn't even tell her it wouldn't be for long. They parked in the lot outside her apartment, but as soon as they were out of the car James knew something wasn't right. Summer tensed, her gaze on the man climbing out of the car next to theirs.

"Summer?" James asked.

"It's Brett," she said in a low voice.

"Brett?" It took James a moment to make the connection. "*The* Brett?"

Her nod was almost imperceptible.

"What's he want?"

"I don't know."

Apparently they were about to find out. He was big—football-player size—and tanned. He wore faded cutoff jeans, a tank top and several gold chains around his neck.

"Hello, Brett," Summer said stiffly.

"Summer." He turned to James. "Who's this? A friend of your father's?"

"This is my husband. Kindly leave. We don't have anything to say to each other."

"Your husband?" Brett laughed mockingly. "You don't expect me to believe *that,* do you?"

"It's true," James answered. "Now I suggest you make yourself scarce like the lady asked."

Brett planted his muscular hands on lean hips. "Says you and what army? No way am I leaving Summer."

"As I recall, you already left her," James said smoothly, placing himself between Summer and the other man. "I also remember that you got married shortly afterward. And didn't I hear, just recently, that you and your wife are expecting a baby?"

"We're separated."

"I'm sorry to hear that. Unfortunately Summer and I are now married and she's not interested in starting anything with you."

"I don't believe that," he muttered stubbornly.

"Oh, honestly, Brett," Summer said, not concealing her impatience. "Are you such an egotist you actually think I'd want you back?"

"You love me."

"Loved," she said. "Past tense."

"Don't give me any bull about you and granddaddy here."

"Granddaddy?" she snapped. "James is ten times the man you'll ever be." She pushed in front of James and glared at her former fiancé. "You know what? Every day of my life I thank God we ended our engagement—otherwise I'd never have met James. He's taught me what loving someone really means. Which is something *you* don't have a clue about."

James had Summer by the shoulders. "It won't do any good to argue with him," he told her. He looked at Brett, who was red-faced and angry. "I think it would be best if you left."

"Stay out of this," Brett growled.

"We're married," James said, trying to add reason to a situation that was fast getting out of hand. "Nothing you say is going to change that."

Brett spit on the ground. "She's nothing but a whore anyway."

James would've walked away for almost anything. But he refused to allow anyone to speak in a derogatory way about Summer. He stepped toward Brett until they were face-to-face. "I suggest you apologize to the lady."

"Gonna make me?"

"Yes," James said. He'd been a schoolboy the last time he was in a fistfight, but he wasn't going to let this jaded, ugly man insult his wife.

Brett's hands went up first. He swung at James, who was quick enough to step aside. The second time James wasn't so fortunate. The punch hit him square in the eye, but he didn't pay attention to the pain since he was more intent on delivering his own.

"James!" Summer repeatedly screamed his name. James could

vaguely hear her in the background, pleading with him to stop, that Brett wasn't worth the trouble.

The two men wrestled to the ground, and James was able to level another couple of punches. "You'll apologize," he demanded from between clenched teeth when Brett showed signs of wanting to quit.

Blood drooled from Brett's mouth, and one eye was swollen. He nodded. "Sorry," he muttered.

James released him just as the police arrived.

CHAPTER EIGHT

SUMMER WOULDN'T HAVE believed James was capable of such anger or such violence. Part of her wanted to call him a fool, but another part wanted to tell him how grateful she was for his love and protection.

His left eye was badly swollen, even with the bag of ice she'd given him. James had refused to hold it to his face while he talked to the police.

His black eye wasn't the only damage. His mouth was cut, and an ugly bruise was beginning to form along his jaw. Brett was in much worse shape, with what looked to be a broken nose.

After talking to both Brett and James and a couple of witnesses, the police asked James if he wanted to press charges. James eyed Brett.

"I don't think that'll be necessary. I doubt this…gentleman will bother my wife again. Isn't that right?" he asked, turning to Brett.

Brett wiped the blood from the side of his mouth. "I didn't come here looking for trouble."

"Looks like that's what you got, though," the police officer told him. "I'd count my blessings and stay away." He studied him for a moment, then asked, "Want to go to the hospital?"

"Forget it. I'm out of here," Brett said with disgust. He climbed inside his car and slammed the door, then drove off as if he couldn't get away fast enough.

"He won't be back," Summer said confidently. She knew Brett's ego was fragile and he wouldn't return after being humiliated.

"You're right, he won't," James insisted darkly, "because you're filing a restraining order first thing tomorrow morning."

Summer nodded, wishing she'd thought of doing it earlier.

"This isn't the first time he's pestered you, is it?"

Summer lowered her gaze.

"He's the reason you had your phone number changed, isn't he?"

She gave a small nod.

"Why didn't you tell me?"

"What could you have done from Seattle?"

"You should have told me. I could at least have offered you some advice. For that matter, why didn't you tell your father?"

James was furious and she suspected she was about to receive the lecture of her life. When nothing more came, she raised her eyes to her husband—and wanted to weep.

His face was a mess. His eye was completely swollen now. It might have been better if she could've convinced him to apply the ice pack. Anyone looking at him would know instantly that her husband the judge had been involved in an altercation—and all because of her.

The police left soon afterward.

"Can I get you anything?" Summer asked guiltily as they entered the apartment.

"I'm fine," he said curtly.

But he wasn't fine. His hands were swollen, his knuckles scraped and bleeding. All at once he started to blur, and the room spun. Everything seemed to be closing in on her. Panic-stricken, Summer groped for the kitchen counter and held on until the waves of dizziness passed.

"Summer? What's wrong?"

"Nothing. I got a little light-headed, that's all." She didn't mention how close she'd come to passing out. Even now, she felt the force of her will was the only thing keeping her conscious.

James came to her and placed his arm around her waist, gently guiding her into the living room. They sat on the sofa, and Summer rested her head against his shoulder, wondering what was wrong with her.

"I'm so sorry," she whispered, fighting back tears.

"For what?"

"The fight."

"That wasn't your fault."

"But, James, you have a terrible black eye. What will people say?" She hated to think about the speculation he'd face when he returned to Seattle, and it was all on account of her. Perhaps she should've told him that Brett was bothering her, but she hadn't wanted to burden him with her troubles.

"Everyone will figure I was in a major fistfight," James teased. "It'll probably be the best thing to happen to my reputation in years. People will see me in an entirely new light."

"Everyone will wonder...."

"Of course they will, and I'll tell them they should see the other guy."

Summer made an effort to laugh but found she couldn't. She twisted her head a bit so she could look at him. The bruise on his jaw was a vivid purple. She raised tentative fingers to it and bit her lip when he winced.

"Oh, James." Gently she pressed her lips to the underside of his jaw.

"That helps." He laughed and groaned at the same time.

She kissed him again, easing her mouth toward his. He moaned and before long, they were exchanging deep, hungry kisses.

"I refuse," James said, unbuttoning her blouse but having difficulty with his swollen hands, "to allow Brett to ruin our last few hours together."

She smiled and slid her arms around his shoulders. "Want to have a shower?" she breathed.

"Yes, but do you have a large enough hot-water tank?"

Summer giggled, recalling their last experience in her compact shower stall and how the water had gone cold at precisely the wrong moment.

The sound of the key turning in the lock told Summer her roommate was home. She sat back abruptly and fastened her blouse.

"Hi, everyone." Julie stepped into the living room and set her suitcase on the floor. "I'm not interrupting anything, am I?" Her gaze narrowed. "James? What on earth happened to you?"

* * *

James didn't expect his black eye to go unnoticed, but he wasn't prepared for the amount of open curiosity it aroused.

"Morning, Judge Wilkens." Louise Jamison, the assistant he shared with two other judges, greeted him when he entered the office Monday morning. Then she dropped her pencil. "Judge Wilkens!" she said. "My goodness, what happened?"

He mumbled something about meeting the wrong end of a fist and hurried into his office. It was clear he'd need to come up with an explanation that would satisfy the curious.

Brad Williams knocked on his door five minutes later. His fellow judge let himself into James's office and stared. "So it's true?"

"What's true?"

"You tell me. Looks like you've been in a fight."

"It was a minor scuffle, and that's all I'm going to say about it." James stood and reached for his robe, eager to escape a series of prying questions he didn't want to answer. He had the distinct feeling the rest of the day was going to be like this.

And he was right.

By the time he pulled out of the parking garage that evening, he regretted that he hadn't called in sick. He might've done it if a black eye would disappear in a couple of days, but that wasn't likely, so there was no point in not going in. He checked his reflection in the rearview mirror. The eye looked worse than it had the previous day. He pressed his index finger against the swelling and was surprised by the pain it caused. Still, he could live with the discomfort; it was the unsightliness of the bruises and the questions and curious glances he could do without.

Irritated and not knowing exactly whom to blame, James drove to his father's house. He hadn't been to see Walter in a couple of weeks and wanted to discuss something with him.

His father was doing a *New York Times* crossword puzzle when James let himself into the house. He looked up from the folded newspaper and did a double take, but to his credit, Walter didn't mention the black eye. "Hello, James."

"Dad."

James walked over to the snifter of Scotch Walter kept on hand and poured himself a liberal quantity. He wasn't fond of hard liquor and rarely indulged, but he felt he needed something potent. And fast.

"It's been one of those days, has it?"

James's back was to his father. "You might say that." He took his first sip and the Scotch burned its way down his throat. "This stuff could rot a man's stomach."

"So I've heard."

Taking his glass, James sat in the leather chair next to his father. "I suppose you're wondering about the eye."

"I'll admit to being curious."

"You and everyone else I've seen today."

"I can imagine you've been the object of more than one inquisitive stare."

"I was in a fistfight."

"You?"

"Don't sound so surprised. You're the one who told me there'd be times in a man's life when he couldn't walk away from a fight. This happened to be one of those."

"Want to talk about it?" His father set aside the paper.

"Not particularly, but if you must know, it was over Summer."

"Ah, yes, Summer. How is she? I'm telling you, son, I like her. Couldn't have chosen a better mate for you if I'd gone looking myself."

James smiled for the first time that day. "She's doing well. I was with her this weekend." James raised the Scotch to his lips and grimaced. "We had brunch with her parents."

"Helen and Hank. Good people," Walter commented.

"There's a problem with the April wedding date—on their end and mine. Helen suggested we wait until September. I said November, because of the election."

"Do you want that?" Walter asked.

"No. Neither does Summer."

"Then the hell with it. Let her finish out her contract with Disneyland and join you after that. You've already had a wedding. I never could understand why you wanted two ceremonies, but then I'm an old man with little appreciation for fancy weddings. What I *would* appreciate is a couple of grandkids. I'm not getting any younger, you know, and neither are you."

"Do away with the second ceremony?"

"That's what I said," Walter muttered.

James closed his eyes in relief. Of course. It made perfect sense. He'd suggested a second wedding because he thought that was what Summer wanted, but if he asked her, James suspected he'd learn otherwise. The wedding was for her parents' sake.

"How'd you get so smart?" James asked his father.

"Don't know, but I must be very wise," Walter said, and chuckled. "I've got a superior court judge for a son."

James laughed, feeling comfortable for the first time all day.

"Stay for dinner," his father insisted. "It's been a while since we spent any real time together. Afterward you can let me beat you in a game of chess, and I'll go to bed a happy man."

"All right." It was an invitation too good to refuse.

When James got home after ten, the light on his phone was blinking. He was tempted to ignore his messages.

He felt tired but relaxed and not particularly interested in returning a long list of phone calls. Especially when he suspected most of his callers were trying to learn what they could about his mysterious black eye.

The only person he wanted to talk to was Summer. He reached for the phone, and she answered on the second ring.

"I just got in," he explained. "Dad and I had dinner."

"Did you give him my love?"

"I did better than that—I let him beat me at chess."

She laughed, and James closed his eyes, savouring the melodic sound. It was like a balm after the day he'd endured.

"How's the eye?" she asked next.

"Good." So he lied. "How was the show today?"

"I didn't go in. I seem to have come down with the flu, so my understudy played Belle. I felt crummy all day. When I woke up this morning, I just felt so nauseous. At first I thought it was nerves over what happened with Brett, but it didn't go away, so I had to call in sick."

"Have you been to a doctor?"

"No. Have you?"

She had him there. "No."

"I'll be fine. I just want to be sure I didn't give you my flu bug while you were here."

"There's no sign of it," he assured her.

They must have talked for another fifteen minutes, saying nothing outwardly significant yet sharing the most important details of their lives. Their conversation would have gone on a lot longer, had someone not rung his doorbell.

It was Ralph Southworth. His campaign manager took one look at James and threw his arms dramatically in the air. "What the hell happened to you?"

"Good evening to you, too," James said evenly.

Ralph rammed all ten fingers through his hair. "Don't you listen to your messages? I've left no fewer than five, and you haven't bothered to return one."

"Sit down," James said calmly. "Do you want a drink?"

Ralph's eyes narrowed as he studied James's face. "Am I going to need it?"

"That depends." James pointed to the recliner by the large brick fireplace. He'd tell Ralph the truth because it was necessary and, knowing his campaign manager's feelings about Summer, he suspected Ralph *would* need a stiff drink. "Make yourself at home."

Instead, Ralph followed him into the kitchen. "I got no less than ten phone calls this afternoon asking about your black eye. You can't show up and then say nothing about it."

"I can't?" This was news to James, since he'd done exactly that. "I thought you were here to discuss business."

"I am." Ralph frowned when James brought an unopened bottle of top-shelf bourbon out of a cabinet. "So I'm going to need that."

"Yes."

"I met with the League of Women Voters and I've arranged for you to speak at their luncheon in July. It's a real coup, James, and I hope you appreciate my efforts."

"Yes," he murmured. "Thanks."

"Now tell me about the eye. And the bruises."

"All right," James said, adding two ice cubes to the glass. He half filled it with bourbon and handed it to his friend. "I got hit in the face with a fist more than once."

"Whose fist?"

"Some beach bum by the name of Brett. I don't remember his last name if I ever heard it."

Ralph swallowed his first sip of liquor. "Does the beach bum have anything to do with the woman you mentioned?"

"Yeah."

The two men stared across the kitchen at each other.

"Were the police called?" Ralph demanded.

It took James a moment to own up to the truth. "Yes."

Ralph slammed his hand against the counter. "I should've known! James, what did I tell you? A woman's nothing but trouble. Mark my words, if you get involved any further with Spring..."

"Summer!"

"Whatever. It doesn't matter, because her name spells just one thing. Trouble. You've worked all your life for this opportunity. This is your one shot at the bench. We both know it. You asked me to manage your campaign and I agreed, but I thought it would be a team effort. The two of us."

"It is." James wanted to hold on to his seat on the bench more than he'd ever wanted anything—other than to marry Summer. He also felt he was the best man for the position. To get this close and lose it all would be agonizing.

"Then why," Ralph asked, palms out, "are you sabotaging your own campaign?"

"I'm not doing it on purpose."

"Stay away from this woman!"

"Ralph, I can't. I won't."

Ralph rubbed his face with both hands, clearly frustrated.

"Summer's in California, but I plan on bringing her to Seattle as soon as I can arrange it. Probably April."

"Tell me you're joking."

"I'm not." James figured he should admit the truth now and be done with it. "We're married."

"What?" Ralph pulled out a chair and sank into it. "When?"

"Over New Year's."

"Why?"

"It was just...one of those things. We fell in love and got married. We were hoping for a more elaborate ceremony later, but I can see that's going to be a problem."

"You want to know what's the real problem, James? It's the marriage. Why didn't you tell me right away?"

"I should have," James said, sorry now that he hadn't. "But when you told me you'd never been in love, I didn't think there was much of a chance you'd understand."

"What you've done is jeopardize your entire campaign."

Somehow he doubted that. "Aren't you overreacting?"

"Time will tell, won't it?" Ralph asked smugly.

James decided to ignore that. "If anything, Summer will be an asset. She's lovely and she's good at connecting with people. Unfortunately her contract with Disney doesn't expire until April."

"That's right," Ralph said sarcastically. "I forgot, she's a show-girl."

"A singer and an actress and a very talented one at that," James boasted.

"An actress, a showgirl, it's all the same."

"Once she's finished with her contract, I want her to move in with me."

"Here in Seattle?" Ralph made it sound like a world-class disaster.

"A wife belongs with her husband."

"What about the beach bum?"

James frowned. "We don't have to worry about him. He's gone for good."

"I certainly hope so. And while we're making out a wish list, let's add a couple of other things. Let's wish that your worthy opponent doesn't find out about this little skirmish between you and Summer's previous lover-boy. And let's make a great big wish that he doesn't learn that the police were called and a report filed."

"He won't," James said confidently, far more confidently than he felt.

"I hope you're right," Ralph said, and downed what was left of his bourbon in one gulp. The glass hit the counter when he put it down. "Now tell me, what kind of damage did you do to the beach bum?"

"You didn't tell him, did you?" Julie said when Summer set the telephone receiver back in place.

"No." She sighed reluctantly. She rested her hand protectively on her stomach.

"A man has the right to know he's going to be a father," Julie said righteously. She bit into an apple as she tucked her feet beneath her on the sofa.

Summer closed her eyes. Even the smell of food or the sound of someone eating made her sick to her stomach. In the past two months she'd seen parts of toilets that weren't meant to be examined at such close range. She hadn't kept down a single breakfast in weeks. The day before, she'd wondered why she even bothered to eat. Dumping it directly into the toilet would save time and trouble.

"How long do you think James is going to fall for this lie about having the flu?"

It had been more than a month since she'd last seen him, and in that time Summer had lost ten pounds. Her clothes hung on her, and she was as pale as death. She seemed to spend more time at the doctor's office than she did at her own apartment. Her biggest fear was that being so ill meant there was something wrong with the baby, although the doctor had attempted to reassure her on that score.

"Why haven't you told him?" Julie wanted to know.

"I just can't do it over the phone." Besides, she remembered James mentioning that a pregnancy now would be a mistake. Well, she hadn't gotten this way by herself!

She knew exactly when it had happened, too. There was only the one time they hadn't used protection.

"When are you going to see him again?"

Summer shook her head. "I don't know."

"You talk on the phone every night. He sends you gifts. I can't think of anyone else who got six dozen red roses for Valentine's Day."

"He's extravagant...."

"Extravagant with everything but his time."

"He's so busy, Julie. I never realized how much there was to being a judge, and he really cares about the people he works with. Not only the people who stand before him, but the attorneys and his staff, too. Then there's the election...."

"So, go to him. He's just as unhappy without you."

"I've got three weeks left on my contract, and—"

"Do you really suppose no one's figured out that you're pregnant? Think about it, Summer. You came back from Vegas all happy and in love, and two weeks later you're heaving your guts out after every meal. No one expects you to perform when you feel this crummy."

"But…"

"Do everyone a favor and—" Julie stopped when there was a knock at the door. "Is anyone coming over tonight?"

"No." Summer laid her head back against the sofa and drew in several deep breaths, hoping that would ease her nausea.

"It's for you," Julie said, looking over her shoulder as soon as she'd opened the door. "It's Walter Wilkens."

Summer threw aside the blanket and scurried off the sofa, anxious to see her father-in-law. "Walter?" What could he possibly be doing here? "Come inside, please."

The refined, older gentleman stepped into the apartment. "Summer?" He gazed at her, his expression concerned. "James said you'd been ill with the flu, but my dear…"

"She looks dreadful," Julie finished for him. Her roommate took another noisy bite of her apple. "I'm Julie. We met at the wedding. Summer's roommate and best friend."

Walter bowed slightly. "Hello, Julie. It's nice to see you again."

"Sit down, please," Summer said, motioning toward the only chair in the house without blankets or clean laundry stacked on it.

"Would you like something to drink?" Julie asked.

"No…no, thank you." He cleared his throat. "Summer, my dear." He frowned. "Have you been to a doctor?"

"Yup," Julie answered, chewing on her apple. "Three times this week, right, Summer?"

"Julie," she snapped.

"Are you going to tell him or not?"

Summer tossed the tangled curls over her shoulder and groaned inwardly. "I don't have much choice now, do I?" She met Walter's eyes and realized her lower lip was trembling. She was suddenly afraid she might burst into tears. Her emotions had been like a seesaw, veering from one extreme to another.

"Summer, what is it?" Walter prodded.

"I'm pregnant," she whispered. She smiled happily all the while tears streamed down her cheeks.

Walter bolted out of his chair. "Hot damn!"

"Other than me, you're the first person she's told," Julie felt obliged to inform him. "Not even her own family knows, although her mother would take one look at her and guess."

"James doesn't know?"

"Nope." Again it was Julie who answered.

"And why not?"

"A woman doesn't tell her husband that sort of thing over the phone," Summer insisted. "Or by email." She needed to see his face, to gauge James's reaction so she'd know what he was really thinking.

"She's been sicker than a dog."

"Thank you, Julie, but I can take it from here."

"I can see that," Walter said, ignoring Summer.

"What brings you to California?" Summer asked cordially, looking for a way to change the subject.

"A business trip. I thought James might have mentioned it."

If he had, Summer had missed it. She had a feeling she'd been doing a lot of that lately.

"Well, my dear," Walter said, sitting back in his chair and grinning broadly. "This is a pleasant surprise."

"It was for me, too."

"I can just see James's face when you tell him."

"He probably won't know what to do, laugh or cry."

"He'll probably do a little of both."

Walter himself was laughing, Summer noticed. He hadn't stopped smiling from the moment he'd heard the news.

"Everything's always been so carefully planned in James's life," Walter said, still grinning. "Then he met you and bingo. He's a husband, and now he's about to be a father. This is terrific news, just terrific."

"James might not find it all that wonderful," Summer said, voicing her fears for the first time. "He's in the middle of an important campaign."

"Don't you worry about a thing."

"I *am* worried. I can't help it."

"Then we're going to have to do something about that."

"We are?" Summer asked. "What?"

"If my son's going to become a father, you should tell him, and the sooner the better. Pack your bags, Summer. It's about time you moved to Seattle with your husband where you belong."

"But…"

"Don't argue with me, young lady. I'm an old man and I'm accustomed to having my own way. If you're worried about his campaign, this is how we fix that. You'll be introduced to the public as his wife and we're going to put an end to any speculation right now."

CHAPTER NINE

SOMETHING WAS WRONG with Summer. James had sensed it weeks ago. He would have confronted her and demanded answers if she hadn't sounded so fragile.

There was that business with the flu, but exactly how long was that going to last? When he asked her what the doctor said, she seemed vague.

Part of the problem was the length of time they'd been apart. He hadn't meant it to be so long. Summer had intended to come to Seattle, but that had fallen through, just as his last visit to California had. Neither of them was happy about it, but there was nothing James could have done on his end. He was sure that was the case with her, too.

James paced in his den, worrying. When he had to mull over a problem, that was what he did. Lately he'd practically worn a path in the carpet. He felt helpless and frustrated. Despite Ralph's dire warnings, he wished he'd brought Summer back to Seattle. This separation was hurting them both.

His greatest fear was that she regretted their marriage.

Their telephone conversations weren't the same anymore. He felt as if she was hiding something from him. They used to talk about everything but he noticed that she steered him away from certain topics now. She didn't want to talk about herself or her job or this flu that had hung on for a few weeks. They used to talk for hours; now he had the feeling she was eager to get off the line.

James wondered about Brett, but when he asked, Summer assured him she hadn't seen or heard from him since the fight.

The fight.

His black eye had caused a great deal of speculation among his peers. James had never offered any explanation. Via the grapevine, he'd heard Ralph's version and found it only distantly related to the truth. According to his campaign manager, James had been jumped by gang members and valiantly fought them off until the police arrived.

When James confronted Ralph with the story, the other man smiled and said he couldn't be held accountable for rumors. Right or wrong, James had let it drop. He was eager to put the incident behind him.

James certainly hadn't expected married life to be this lonely. He'd never felt this detached from the mainstream of everyday life, this isolated. Missing Summer was like a constant ache in his stomach. Except that a store-bought tablet wasn't going to cure what ailed him.

His desk was filled with demands. He felt weary. Unsure of his marriage. Unsure of himself.

He went into the kitchen to make a cup of instant coffee when he saw a car turn into his driveway and around to the backyard.

His father.

He wondered why Walter would stop by unannounced on a Sunday afternoon. James wasn't in the mood for company—but then again, maybe a sounding board was exactly what he needed. Other than his father, there was no one with whom he could discuss Summer.

The slam of a car door closing was followed almost immediately by another. James frowned. Dad had brought someone with him. Great. Just great.

He took the hot water out of the microwave, added the coffee granules and stirred briskly. There was a knock at the back door.

"Come in, the door's open," he called, not turning around. He didn't feel like being polite. Not today, when it felt as if the world was closing in around him.

He sipped his coffee and stared out the window. The daffodils were blooming and the—

"Hello, James."

James whirled around. "Summer?" He couldn't believe she was really there. It was impossible. A figment of his imagination. An apparition. Before another second passed, James walked across the kitchen and swept her into his arms.

Laughing and sobbing at once, Summer hugged him close.

Then they were kissing each other. Neither could give or get enough.

Walter stood in the background and cleared his throat. "I'll wait for the two of you in the living room," he said, loudly enough to be sure he was heard.

As far as James was concerned, his father might as well make himself comfortable. Or leave. This could take a while.

Summer in his arms was the closest thing to heaven James had ever found. Not for several minutes did he notice how thin and frail she was. The virus had ravaged her body.

"Sweetheart," he whispered between kisses. He paused and brushed back her hair to get a good look at her.

She was pale. Her once-pink cheeks were colorless, and her eyes appeared sunken. "Are you over the flu?"

She lowered her eyes and stepped away from him. "I...you'd better sit down, James."

"Sit down? Why?"

Her hands closed around the back of a kitchen chair. "I have something important to tell you."

He could see she was nervous and on the verge of tears. The worries that were nipping at his heels earlier returned with reinforcements. Summer had more than a common flu bug.

"Just tell me," he said. A knot was beginning to form in his stomach. Was she ill? Was it something life threatening? The knot twisted and tightened.

"I don't have the flu," she whispered.

Whatever it was, then, must be very bad if his father had brought her to Seattle.

"How serious is it?" he asked. He preferred to confront whatever they were dealing with head-on.

"It's serious, James, very serious." Slowly she raised her eyes to his. "We're going to have a baby."

His relief was so great that he nearly laughed. "A baby? You mean to tell me you're pregnant?"

She nodded. Her fingers had gone white, and she was watching him closely.

James took her in his arms. "I thought you were really sick."

"I have been really sick," she told him crisply. "Morning sickness. Afternoon sickness. Evening sickness. I... I can't seem to keep food down.... I've never been more miserable in my life."

"I suspect part of her problem has been psychological," Walter announced from the doorway. "The poor girl's been terribly worried about how you were going to take the news."

"Me?"

"My feelings exactly," Walter said. "The deed's done, what's there to think about? Besides, you've made me an extremely happy man."

"A baby." James remained awestruck at the thought.

"Now tell him your due date, Summer—he'll get a real kick out of that."

"September twenty-third," Summer announced.

Everyone seemed to be studying him, waiting for a reaction. James didn't know what to think. Then it hit him. "September twenty-third? That's the date of the primary."

"I know. Isn't it great?" Walter asked.

"How long can you stay?" James asked, taking Summer's hands in his own.

Summer looked at Walter.

"Stay?" his father barked. "My dear son, this is your wife. I brought her to Seattle to live with you. This is where she belongs."

"You can live with me?" A man could only take in so much news at one time. First, he'd learned that his wife didn't have some life-threatening disease. Then he discovered he was going to be a father. Even more important, he was going to have the opportunity to prove what kind of husband he could be.

"Yes. I got out of my contract for medical reasons, and Julie's getting a roommate. So...everything's settled."

James pulled out the chair and sat Summer down. Then he knelt in front of her and took her hands in his. "A baby."

"You're sure you don't mind?"

"Of course he doesn't mind," Walter said, "and if he does I'll set up an appointment with a good psychiatrist I know. This is the best news we've had in thirty years."

"When did it happen?" James asked.

Summer laughed at him. "You mean you don't remember?" She leaned toward him and whispered, reminding him of the one episode the morning after their honeymoon night.

"Ah, yes," James said, and chuckled. "As I recall, I was the one who said one time wouldn't matter."

"I don't suppose there's anything to eat in this house?" Walter asked, banging cupboard doors open and shut.

"Why have you been so ill?" James wanted to know. It worried him. "Is it routine?"

"My doctor says some women suffer from severe morning sickness for the first few months. He's been very reassuring. I try to remember that when I'm losing my latest meal."

"Is there anything that can help?"

"She's got what she needs now," Walter said.

Summer laid her head on his shoulder. "I was worried you'd be upset with me."

"Why would I be upset when the most beautiful woman in the world tells me she's having my baby?" He reached for her hand and pressed her palm over his heart. "Notice anything different?" he asked.

She shook her head, giving him a puzzled look.

"My heart's racing because I'm so excited. Because I'm so happy. We're going to have a baby, Summer! I feel like I could conquer the world."

He wanted his words to comfort her. The last thing he expected was that she'd burst into tears.

"But you said a baby would be a mistake right now," she reminded him between sobs.

"I said that?"

"He said that?" Walter glared at James.

"I don't remember saying it," James told him. "I'm sorry, my love. Just knowing we're going to have a baby makes me happier than I have any right to be."

"Damn straight he's happy," Walter tossed in, "or there'd be hell to pay. I should've been a grandfather two or three times over by now. As far as I'm concerned, James owes me."

"I'll try and make it up to you," James promised his father with a grin.

Summer couldn't remember ever being so hungry. She'd been with James a week and had settled so contentedly into her new life it was almost as if she'd always been there.

"Would you like another piece of apple pie?" James asked. "Better yet, why don't we buy the whole thing and take it home with us?"

"Can we do that?" Summer was sure her appetite must be a source of embarrassment to him. They were at a sidewalk restaurant on the Seattle waterfront. Summer couldn't decide between the French onion soup and the Cobb salad, so she'd ordered both. Then she'd topped off the meal with a huge slice of apple pie à la mode.

"I'll ask the waitress," James said as though it was perfectly normal to order a whole pie for later.

"Have I embarrassed you?" she asked, keeping her voice low.

James's mouth quivered. "No, but I will admit I've rarely seen anyone enjoy her food more."

"Oh, James, you have no idea how good it is to be able to eat and keep everything down. I felt a thousand times better this past week than I did the whole previous two months."

"Then Dad was right," he said.

"About what?"

"The psychological effects of the pregnancy were taking their toll along with the physical. In other words, you were worried and making yourself more ill. I could kick myself."

"Why?"

"For not guessing. You have to forgive me, sweetheart, I'm new to this husband business."

"You're forgiven."

"Just promise me one thing. Don't keep any more secrets from me, all right?"

She smiled. "You've got yourself a deal."

"James?" A striking-looking couple approached their table.

"Rich and Jamie Manning." Sounding genuinely pleased, James stood and exchanged handshakes with the man. Then he turned to Summer. "These are good friends of mine, Rich and Jamie Manning. This is my wife, Summer."

"Your wife?" Rich repeated, doing a poor job of hiding his surprise. "When did this happen?"

"Shortly after New Year's," James explained. "Would you care to join us?"

"Unfortunately, we can't," Rich said. "The babysitter's waiting. But this is great news. I hope there's a good reason I didn't get a wedding invitation."

"A very good one." James grinned. "I've been meaning to let everyone know. But Summer just moved here from California."

"Well, the word's out now," Jamie said, smiling at her. "Once Rich's mother hears about it, she'll want to throw a party in your honor." Jamie and her husband shared a private, happy look.

"I'd better call your parents before I alienate them completely," James said.

"I'll be seeing you soon," Rich said and patted James's shoulder as he passed by. "Bye, Summer."

James was silent for a moment, and Summer wasn't sure if he was glad or not that his friends had stopped to talk. She didn't think he intended to keep their marriage a secret, yet he hadn't made a point of introducing her around, either.

"Is there a problem?" she asked.

"No. It's just that I was hoping to give you some time to regain your strength before you met my friends."

Summer's gaze followed the couple as they made their way toward the front of the restaurant.

"They're happy, aren't they?"

"Rich and Jamie?"

Summer nodded.

"Yes." He relaxed in his chair. "They came to see me a few years back with perhaps the most unusual request of my career." He smiled, and Summer guessed he must've been amused at the time, as well.

"What did they want?"

"They asked me to draw up a paper for a marriage of convenience."

"Really." That seemed odd to Summer. Although she'd just met the couple, it was clear to her that they were in love.

"They'd come up with some harebrained scheme to have a baby together—by artificial insemination. Rich would be the sperm donor."

"Did they have a baby?"

"Yes, but Bethany was conceived the old-fashioned way without a single visit to a fertility clinic."

Summer shook her head. "This doesn't make any sense to me. Why would two healthy people go to such lengths to have a child? Especially when they're perfectly capable of doing things…the usual way?"

"It does sound silly, doesn't it?"

"Frankly, yes."

James leaned forward and placed his elbows on the table. "Jamie and Rich had been friends for years. Since their high school days, if I recall correctly. Jamie couldn't seem to fall in love with the right kind of man and, after a couple of disastrous relationships, she decided she was giving up dating altogether."

"I love the tricks life plays on people," Summer said, licking melted ice cream off her spoon. She looked across the table at the remnants on James's plate. "Are you going to eat that?" she asked.

He pushed the plate toward her.

"Thanks," she said, and blew him a kiss. "Go on," she encouraged, scooping up the last bits of pie and ice cream. "What happened?"

"Apparently Jamie was comfortable with her decision, except that she wanted a child. That's when she approached Rich about being the sperm donor."

"Just between friends, that sort of thing?"

"Exactly. At any rate, Rich didn't think it was such a bad idea himself, the not-marrying part. He'd had his own ups and downs in the relationship department. But the more he thought about her suggestion, the more problems he had with being nothing more than a sperm donor. He suggested they get married so their child could have his name. He also wanted a say in the baby's upbringing."

"And Jamie agreed to all this?"

"She wanted a child."

"So they asked you to draw up a contract or something?"

"Yes, but I have to tell you I had my reservations."

"I can imagine."

"They have two children now."

"Well, this so-called marriage of convenience certainly worked out," Summer told him.

"It sure did."

While she was looking around the table for anything left to eat, she noticed that James was studying her. "How are you feeling?" he asked.

"A thousand times better." She smiled and lowered her voice so he alone could hear. "If what you're really asking is if I'm well enough to make love, the answer is yes."

He swallowed hard.

"Shall we hurry home, James?"

"By all means."

He paid the tab and they were gone. "You're sure?" he asked as he unlocked the car door and helped her inside.

Sitting in the passenger seat, Summer smiled up at her husband. "Am I sure? James, it's been months since we last made love. I'm so hot for you I could burst into flames."

James literally ran around the front of the car. He sped the entire way home, and Summer considered it fortunate that they weren't stopped by a traffic cop.

"Torture...every night for the last week," James mumbled as he pulled into the driveway. "I couldn't trust myself to even touch you."

"I know."

Her time in Seattle hadn't started out well. The first morning, she'd woken and run straight for the bathroom. James helped her off the floor when she'd finished. He'd cradled her in his arms and told her how much he loved her for having their baby.

Her first few dinners hadn't stayed down, either. But each day after her arrival, the nausea and episodes of vomiting had become less and less frequent. Now, one week later, she was almost herself again.

He left the car and came around to her side. When he opened the door, she stepped out and into his embrace—and kissed him.

James groaned and swung her into his arms.

"What are you doing?" she asked.

"Carrying you over the threshold," he announced. "You've been cheated out of just about everything else when it comes to this marriage."

"I haven't been cheated."

"You should've had the big church wedding and—"

"Are we going to argue about that again? Really, James, I'd rather we just made love."

He had a problem getting the door unlocked while holding her, but he managed. The minute they were inside, he started kissing her, doing wonderful, erotic things that excited her to the point of desperation.

Summer kicked off her shoes.

James kissed her and unsnapped the button to her skirt. The zipper slid down. All the while he was silently urging her toward the stairs.

Her jacket went next, followed by her shirt.

She made it to the staircase and held out her hand. James didn't need any more encouragement than that. They raced to the bedroom together.

Summer fell on the bed, laughing. "Oh, James, promise you'll always love me this much."

"I promise." He tried to remove his shirt without taking off his tie, with hilarious results. Arms clutching her stomach, Summer doubled over, laughing even harder. It was out of pure kindness that she climbed off the bed and loosened the tie enough to slip it over his head. Otherwise, she was afraid her normally calm, patient husband would have strangled himself.

"You think this is funny, do you?"

"I think you're the most wonderful man alive. Will you always want me this much?"

"I can't imagine not wanting you." And he proceeded to prove it....

* * *

James was half-asleep when he heard the doorbell chime. He would have ignored it, but on the off chance it was someone important, he decided to look outside and see if he recognized the car.

Big mistake.

Ralph Southworth was at his door.

James grabbed his pants, threw on his shirt and kissed Summer on the cheek. Then he hurried down the stairs, taking a second to button his shirt before he opened the door. "Hello, Ralph," he said, standing, shoes and socks in hand.

Ralph frowned. "What the hell have you been—never mind, I already know."

"Summer's here."

"So I gather."

"Give her a few minutes, and she'll be down so you can meet her," James told him. He sat in a chair and put on his shoes and socks. "What can I do for you?"

"A number of things, but mainly I'd…" He hesitated as Summer made her way down the stairs. Her hair was mussed, her eyes soft and glowing.

"Ralph, this is my wife, Summer," James said proudly, joining her. He slipped his arm around her shoulders.

"Hello, Summer," Ralph said stiffly.

"Hello, Ralph."

"When did you get here?"

"Last week. Would you two like some coffee? I'll make a pot. James, take your friend into the den, why don't you, and I'll bring everything in there."

James didn't want his wife waiting on him, but something about the way she spoke told him this wasn't the time to argue. That was when he saw her skirt draped on a chair, and her jacket on the floor.

"This way, Ralph," he said, ushering the other man into the den.

He looked over his shoulder and saw Summer delicately scoop up various items of clothing, then hurry into the kitchen.

"Something amuses you?"

James cleared his throat. "Not really."

"First of all, James, I have to question your judgment. When you told me you married a showgirl—"

"Summer's an actress."

Ralph ignored that. "As I was saying, your judgment appears to be questionable."

This was a serious accusation, considering that James was running for a position on the superior court.

Ralph's lips were pinched. "It worries me that you'd marry some woman you barely know on the spur of the moment."

"Love sometimes happens like that."

"Perhaps," Ralph muttered. "Personally I wouldn't know, but James, how much younger is she?"

"Not as much as you think. Nine years."

"She's unsuitable!"

"For whom? You? Listen, Ralph, I asked you to manage my campaign, not run my life. I married Summer, and she's going to have my child."

"The girl's pregnant, as well?"

"Yes, the baby's due September twenty-third."

Ralph's lips went white with disapproval. "Could she have chosen a more inconvenient date?"

"I don't think it really matters."

"That's the primary!"

"I'm well aware of it."

"Good grief, James." Ralph shook his head. "This won't do. It just won't. Once people learn what you've done, they'll assume you were obligated to marry the girl. The last thing we need now is to have your morals questioned."

"Ralph, you're overreacting."

"I can't believe you brought her here, after everything I said."

James gritted his teeth. "She's my wife."

Ralph paced back and forth for a moment or two. "I don't feel I have any choice," he said with finality.

"Choice about what?"

"I'm resigning as your manager."

Summer appeared just then, carrying a tray. "Coffee, anyone?"

CHAPTER TEN

SUMMER SETTLED EASILY into life with James. She adored her husband and treasured each moment that they were together.

Her days quickly began to follow a routine of sorts. She rose early and, because she was feeling better, resumed her regular workout, which included a two-mile run first thing in the morning.

James insisted on running with her, although he made it clear he didn't like traipsing through dark streets at dawn's early light. But he wasn't comfortable with her running alone, so he joined her, protesting every step of the way.

James was naturally athletic, and Summer didn't think anyone was more surprised than he was by how enjoyable he started to find it. After their run, they showered together. Thankfully James's hot-water tank was larger than the meager one back in her Orange County apartment.

This was both good and bad. The negative was when James, a stickler for punctuality, got to court late two mornings in a row.

"You shower first," he told her after their Monday-morning run.

"Not together?" she asked, disappointed.

"I can't be late this morning."

"We'll behave," she promised.

James snickered. "I can't behave with you, Summer. You tempt me too much."

"All right, but you shower first, and I'll get us breakfast."

Ten minutes later, he walked into the kitchen, where Summer was pouring two glasses of orange juice. He wore his dark business suit and carried his briefcase, ready for his workday.

"What are your plans?" he asked, downing the juice as he stood by the table. He sat down to eat his bagel and cream cheese and picked up the paper.

"I'm going to send Julie a long email. Then I thought I'd stop in at the library and volunteer to read during storytime."

"Good idea," he said, scanning the paper.

Summer knew reading the paper was part of his morning ritual, which he didn't have as much time for since her arrival. She drank the last of her juice and kissed his cheek.

"I'm going upstairs for my shower," she told him.

"All right. Have a good day."

"I will. Oh, what time will you be home tonight?" she asked.

"Six or so," he mumbled absently and turned the front page.

Summer hesitated. His schedule had changed. Rarely did he get home before eight the first week after she'd moved in. It seemed that every night there was someone to meet, some campaign supporter to talk to, some plan to outline—all to do with the September primary, even though it was still months away.

In the past week James had come directly home from the courthouse. Not that she was complaining, but she couldn't help wondering.

"What about your campaign?" she asked.

"Everything's under control," was all he said.

Summer wondered.

All at once James looked up, startled, as if he'd just remembered something. "What day's your ultrasound?"

"Thursday of next week. Don't look so worried. You don't need to be there."

"I *want* to be there," he stated emphatically. "Our baby's first picture. I wouldn't miss it for the world. Besides, I'm curious to find out if we're going to have a son or daughter."

"Don't tell me," she said. "I don't want to know."

"I won't," he said, chuckling. He reached out to stroke her abdomen. "I can't believe how much I love this little one, and he isn't even born yet."

"He?" she asked, hands on her hips in mock offense.

"A daughter would suit me just fine. Actually Dad's hoping for a granddaughter. It's been a long time since there's been a little girl in the family."

Summer pressed her hand over her husband's. She'd never been this happy. It frightened her sometimes. Experience had taught her that happiness almost always came with a price.

Walter joined them for dinner Wednesday evening. From the moment she'd met him, Summer had liked her father-in-law.

"Did you know Summer could cook this well when you married her?" Walter asked when they'd finished eating.

She'd found a recipe for a chicken casserole on the Internet and served it with homemade dinner rolls and fresh asparagus, with a fresh fruit salad made of seedless grapes and strawberries. For dessert she picked up a lemon torte at the local bakery.

"Summer's full of surprises," James told his father. His eyes briefly met hers.

"What he's trying to say is no one knew how fertile I was, either."

"That's the best surprise yet," Walter said. He dabbed the corner of his mouth with his napkin in a blatant effort to hide a smile.

"It certainly is," James put in.

Walter studied her. "How are you feeling these days?"

"Wonderful."

"What's the doctor have to say?"

"That I'm in excellent health. The baby's growing by leaps and bounds. I haven't felt him move yet, but—"

"Him?" James and Walter chimed in simultaneously.

"Or her," she retorted, smiling. She stood and started to clear the table.

"Let me do that," James insisted.

"I'm not helpless, you know," Walter added.

Both men leapt from their chairs.

"Go have your coffee," Summer told them. "It'll only take me a few minutes to deal with the dishes."

Walter shrugged, then looked at his son. "There are a few things I need to discuss with James," he said.

"Then off with you." She shooed them out of the kitchen.

James poured two cups of coffee and took them into the living room. He paused in the doorway and looked over his shoulder. "You're sure?"

"James, honestly! Go talk to your father."

Although she didn't know Walter well, she sensed that something was on his mind. Throughout the meal she'd noticed the way he watched his son. James was acting odd, too.

Walter wanted to discuss the campaign, but every time he'd introduced the subject, James expertly changed it. He did it cleverly, but Walter had noticed, and after a while Summer had, too.

She ran tap water to rinse off the dinner plates before putting them in the dishwasher, and when she turned off the faucet she heard the end of James's comment.

"...Summer doesn't know."

She hesitated. Apparently the two men didn't realize how well their voices carried. She didn't mean to eavesdrop, but it did seem only fair to listen, since she was the topic of conversation.

"What do you plan to do about it?" his father asked.

It took James a long time to answer. "I haven't decided."

"Have you tried reasoning with him?"

"No," James answered bitterly. "The man said he has doubts about my judgment. He's insulted me, insulted my wife. I don't need Southworth if he's got an attitude like that."

"But you will need a campaign manager."

"Yes," James admitted reluctantly.

So *that* was what this was about. Summer leaned against the kitchen counter and closed her eyes. Ralph had resigned, and from the evidence she'd seen, James had, too. Resigned himself to losing, even before the election. It didn't sound like him.

"What's the problem?" Walter asked as if reading Summer's mind.

James lowered his voice substantially, and Summer had to strain to hear him. "He disapproves of Summer."

"What?" Walter had no such compunction about keeping quiet. "The man's crazy!"

"I've made a series of mistakes," James said.

"Mistakes?"

"With Summer."

The world collapsed, like a house falling in on itself. Summer struggled toward a chair and literally fell into it.

"I should never have married her the way I did," James elaborated. "I cheated her out of the wedding she deserved. I don't know if her mother's forgiven me yet. The last I heard, her family's planning a reception in November. By then the baby will be here and, well, it seems a little after the fact."

"You can't blame Summer for that."

"I don't," James remarked tartly. "I blame myself. In retrospect I realize I was afraid of losing her. So I insisted on the marriage before she could change her mind."

"I don't understand what any of this has to do with Ralph," Walter muttered.

"Ralph thinks Summer's too young for me."

"Nonsense."

"He also seems to think I've done myself harm by not letting everyone know immediately that I was married. Bringing Summer here to live with me now, pregnant, and saying we've been married all along, is apparently too convenient to believe."

"It's the truth."

"You and I know that, but there's already speculation."

"So? People will always talk. Let them. But you've got to do something about getting this campaign organized. There are worse things you could be accused of than marrying in secret or getting Summer pregnant before your wedding day. As far as I'm concerned, Southworth's looking for excuses."

"I refuse to subject Summer to that kind of speculation," James said stubbornly.

"Have you talked this over with her?"

"Not yet…"

"You haven't?"

"I know, I know." The defeatist attitude was back in James's voice. "I've put it off longer than I should have."

After that, Summer didn't hear much more of the conversation between father and son. Their marriage had hurt her husband; it might have robbed him of his dreams, cheated him out of his goals.

The phone rang long before she had time to gather her thoughts.

"I'll get it," she called out to James, and reached for the extension in the kitchen. Her hand trembled as she lifted the receiver.

"Hello," she said, her voice weak.

"Hello," came the soft feminine reply. "You don't know me. My name's Christy Manning Franklin."

"Christy... Manning?" Summer said, stunned. She hadn't recovered from one shock before she was hit with another. "Just a moment. I'll get James."

"No, please. It's you I want to talk to."

"Me?"

"From your reaction, I'd guess James has mentioned me."

"Yes." Summer slumped down in a chair and closed her eyes. "You and James were engaged at one time."

"That's right. I understand you and James recently got married."

"Three months ago," Summer said, embarrassed by how weak her voice still was. "In Las Vegas," she added a little more loudly.

"I hope you'll forgive me for being so forward. I talked it over with Cody—he's my husband—and he said since I felt so strongly about it I should call you."

"So strongly about what?"

"About you...and James. I'll always regret the way I treated James. He deserved a lot better, but I was younger then. Immature in some ways. At one time I thought I was in love with him. I knew he loved me, and my family thought the world of him. Then I met Cody." She hesitated. "I didn't phone to tell you all this. I'm sure James filled in the details."

"Why did you call?" Summer was sure that under other circumstances she might have liked Christy Franklin.

"I wanted to tell you how happy I am that James found someone to love. I know it's presumptuous of me but I wanted to ask a favor of you."

"A favor?" The woman had a lot of nerve.

"Love him with all your heart, Summer. James is a special, special man and he deserves a woman who'll stand by his side and love him."

"I do," she said softly.

"For quite a while I despaired of James ever getting married. I can't tell you how pleased I was when Mom phoned to tell me

Rich and Jamie had met you. Cody and I want to extend our very best wishes to you both."

"Thank you."

"I know it's a lot to ask, but I do hope you'll keep Cody and me in mind when you count your friends. There's a place in my heart for James. He's been a friend to our family for years. He was a tremendous help to Paul when Diane died, and again later when he married Leah. James helped Rich and Jamie, too, and he's been a good friend to Jason and Charlotte, as well. We're all indebted to him one way or another."

"I do love him so much." She was fighting back tears and not even sure what she was crying about. The fact that Ralph Southworth had resigned as James's campaign manager because of her? Or that James's ex-fiancée still cared for him deeply?

Summer had just replaced the receiver when James stepped into the kitchen. He stood with one hand on the door.

"Who was that on the phone?" he asked.

Summer met his look straight on, waiting to read any emotion. "Christy Franklin."

"Christy?" he repeated. "What did she want?" He looked more surprised than anything.

"She called to give us her and Cody's best wishes. She said it was high time you were married and she can hardly wait to meet me."

"Really?"

"Really."

"And what did you tell her?"

Summer grinned. "I said she's to keep her cotton-pickin' hands off my husband."

James chuckled, obviously delighted by her possessive attitude. "You aren't going to get much of an argument from me."

"Good thing," she said, and slid her arm around his waist. Together they joined his father.

"I don't understand it," Summer muttered. She sucked in her stomach in order to close her skirt. "I can barely zip this up. It fit fine just last week."

"Honey, you're pregnant," James said matter-of-factly.

"Three months. I'm not supposed to show yet."

"You're not?" James's eyes left the mirror, his face covered with shaving cream. He carefully examined her rounded belly.

"Tell me the truth, James. If you were meeting me for the first time, would you guess I was pregnant?"

He frowned. "This isn't one of those trick questions, is it?"

"No."

"All right," he said, then cleared his throat. He seemed to know intuitively that she wasn't going to like the answer. "You do look pregnant to me. But then you *are* pregnant, so I don't understand what the big deal is."

"I'm fat already," she wailed, and felt like breaking into tears.

"*Fat* is not the word I'd use to describe you."

"If I'm showing at three months, can you just imagine what I'll look like at nine?"

His grin revealed pride and love. "I'd say you'll look like the most beautiful woman in the world."

"No wonder I love you so much," she told her husband, turning back to the closet. She sorted through the hangers, dismissing first one outfit and then another.

"Where are you going that you're so worried about how you look?" James asked.

Summer froze. "An appointment." She prayed he wouldn't question her further. She'd arranged a meeting with Ralph Southworth, but she didn't want James to know about it.

"Okay. Don't forget tonight," he reminded her. "We're going to the Mannings' for dinner."

"I won't forget," she promised. "Eric and Elizabeth, right?"

"Right. Knowing Elizabeth, she'll probably spend the whole day cooking. She's called me at least five times in the past week. She's anxious to meet you."

"I'm anxious to meet them, too." But not nearly as anxious as she was about this meeting with Southworth. In setting up the appointment, Summer hoped to achieve several objectives. Mainly she wanted Ralph to agree to manage James's campaign again. And she wanted to prove to James that he didn't need to protect her from gossip and speculation.

James left for court shortly after he'd finished shaving. Summer changed into the outfit she'd finally chosen, a soft gray business suit with a long jacket that—sort of—disguised her pregnancy. She spent the morning doing errands and arrived at Ralph's office at the Seattle Bank ten minutes ahead of their one-o'clock appointment.

She announced her name to the receptionist and was escorted into Southworth's office a few minutes later.

Ralph stood when she entered the room. He didn't seem pleased to see her.

"Hello again," she said brightly, taking the chair across from his desk. She wanted it understood that she wouldn't be easily dissuaded.

"Hello," he responded curtly.

"I hope you don't object to my making an appointment to see you. I'm afraid I may have, uh, misled your secretary into thinking it had to do with a loan."

"I see. Are you in the habit of misleading people?"

"Not at all," she assured him with a cordial smile, "but sometimes a little inventive thinking is worth a dozen frustrating phone calls."

Southworth didn't agree or disagree.

"I'll get to the point of my visit," she said, not wanting to waste time, his or hers.

"Please do."

"I'd like to know why you've resigned as my husband's campaign manager."

Southworth rolled a pencil between his palms, avoiding eye contact. "I believe that's between James and me. It has nothing to do with you."

"That isn't the way I understand it," she said, grateful he'd opened the conversation for her. "I overheard James and his father talking recently, and James said something different."

"So you eavesdrop, as well?"

He was certainly eager to tally her less than sterling characteristics.

"Yes, but in this case, I'm glad I did because I learned that you'd resigned because of me."

Southworth hesitated. "Not exactly. I questioned James's judgment."

"About our marriage?" she pressed.

Once again he seemed inclined to dodge the subject. "I don't really think..."

"I do, Mr. Southworth. This election is extremely important to James. *You're* extremely important to him. When he first mentioned your name to me, he said you were the best man for the job."

"I am the best man for the job." The banker certainly didn't lack confidence in his abilities. "I also know a losing battle when I see it."

"Why's that?"

"Mrs. Wilkens, please."

"Please what, Mr. Southworth? Tell me why you question James's judgment. Until he married me, you were ready to lend him your full support. I can assure you I'll stay right here until I have the answers to these questions." She raised her chin a stubborn half inch and refused to budge.

"If you insist..."

"I do."

"First, you're years younger than James."

"Nine years is hardly that much of a difference. This is a weak excuse and unworthy of you. I do happen to look young for my age, but I can assure you I'm twenty-eight, and James is only thirty-seven."

"There's also the fact that you're a showgirl."

"I'm an actress and singer," she countered. "Since I worked at Disneyland, I hardly think you can fault my morals."

"Morals is another issue entirely."

"Obviously," she said, finding she disliked this man more every time he opened his mouth. It seemed to her that Ralph Southworth was inventing excuses, none of which amounted to anything solid.

"You're pregnant."

"Yes. So?"

"So...it's clear to me, at least, that you and James conveniently decided to marry when you recognized your condition."

Summer laughed. "That's not true, and even if it were, all I need to do is produce our marriage certificate, which I just happen to have with me." Somehow or other she knew it would come down to this. She opened her purse and removed the envelope, then handed it to the man whom her husband had once considered his friend.

Southworth read it over and returned it to her. "I don't understand why the two of you did this. No one meets in Vegas, falls in love and gets married within a few days. Not unless they've got something to hide."

"We're in love." She started to explain that she and James had known each other for a year, but Ralph cut her off.

"Please, Mrs. Wilkens! I've known James for at least a decade. There had to be a reason other than the one you're giving me."

"He loves me. Isn't that good enough for you?"

Southworth seemed bored with the conversation. "Then there's the fact that he kept the marriage a secret."

Summer had no answer to that. "I don't really know why James didn't tell anyone about the wedding," she admitted. "My guess is that it's because he's a private man and considers his personal life his own."

"How far along is the pregnancy?" he asked, ignoring her answer.

"Three months," she told him.

"Three months? I don't claim to know much about women and babies, but I've had quite a few women work for me at the bank over the years. A number of them have had babies. You look easily five or six months."

"That's ridiculous! I know when I got pregnant."

"Do you, now?"

Summer drew in her breath and held it for a moment in an effort to contain her outrage. She loved James and believed in him, but she refused to be insulted.

"I can see we aren't going to accomplish anything here," she said sadly. "You've already formed your opinion about James and me."

"About you, Mrs. Wilkens. It's unfortunate. James would've made an excellent superior court judge. But there's been far too much speculation about him lately. It started with the black eye. People don't want a man on the bench who can't hold on to his own temper. A judge should be above any hint of moral weakness."

"James is one of the most morally upright men I know," she

said heatedly. "I take your comments as a personal insult to my husband."

"I find your loyalty to James touching, but it's too little, too late."

"What do you mean by that?" Summer demanded.

"You want your husband to win the election, don't you?"

"Yes. Of course." The question was ludicrous.

"If I were to tell you that you could make a difference, perhaps even sway the election, would you listen?"

"I'd listen," she said, although anything beyond listening was another matter.

Southworth stood and walked over to the window, which offered a panoramic view of the Seattle skyline. His back was to her and for several minutes he said nothing. He seemed to be weighing his words.

"You've already admitted I'm the best man to run James's campaign."

"Yes," she said reluctantly, not as willing to acknowledge it as she had been when she'd first arrived.

"I can help win him this September's primary and the November election. Don't discount the political sway I have in this community, Mrs. Wilkens."

Summer said nothing.

"When James first told me he'd married you, I suggested he keep you out of the picture until after the election."

"I see."

"I did this for a number of reasons, all of which James disregarded."

"He…he really didn't have much choice," she felt obliged to tell him. "I turned up on his doorstep, suitcase in hand."

Ralph nodded as if he'd suspected this had been the case. "I can turn James's campaign around if you'll agree to one thing."

Her stomach tightened, knowing before the words were out what he was going to say. "Yes?"

"Simply disappear for several months. Stay away from Seattle, and once the November election is over, you can move back into his house. It won't matter then."

She closed her eyes and lowered her head. "I see."

"Will you do it?"

"Summer, I'm sorry I'm late." James kissed her soundly and rushed up the stairs to change clothes.

He was late? She hadn't noticed. Since her meeting with Ralph Southworth, Summer had spent what remained of the afternoon in a stupor. She felt numb and sad. Tears lay just beneath the surface, ready to break free.

This decision should've been far less difficult. She could give her husband the dream he'd always wanted or ruin his life.

Five minutes later James was back. He'd changed out of his suit and tie and wore slacks and a shirt and sweater. "Are you ready?" he asked.

"For what?"

"Dinner tonight with the Mannings. Remember?"

"Of course," she said, forcing a smile. How could she have forgotten that? James was like a schoolboy eager to show off his science project. Only in this case, *she* was the project. She still wore her gray suit, so after quickly brushing her hair and refreshing her makeup, she considered herself ready—in appearance if not in attitude.

He escorted her out the front door and into his car, which he'd parked in front of the house. "You haven't had much campaigning to do lately," she commented.

"I know."

"What does Ralph have to say?" she asked, wanting to see how much James was willing to tell her.

"Not much. Let's not talk about the election tonight, okay?"

"Why not?"

"I don't want to have to think about it. These people are my friends. They're like a second set of parents to me."

"Do they know I'm pregnant?"

"No, but I won't need to tell them, will I?" He gently patted her abdomen.

"James," she whispered. "When we get home this evening, I want to make love."

His gaze briefly left the road and he nodded.

The emptiness inside her could only be filled with his love.

"Are you feeling all right?"

She made herself smile and laid her head against his shoulder. "Of course."

"There's something different about you."

"Is there?" Just that her heart felt as if it had been chopped in half. Just that she'd never felt so cold or alone in her life. South-worth had asked her to turn her back on the man she loved. He'd asked that she leave and do it in such a way that he wouldn't follow. He'd asked that she bear her child alone.

When they got to the Manning home, James parked his car on the street and turned to Summer. He studied her for an intense moment. "I love you."

"I love you," she whispered in return. She felt close to tears.

James helped her out of the car. They walked to the front porch, and he rang the doorbell. When she wasn't looking, he stole a kiss.

A distinguished older gentleman opened the door for them. "James! It's good to see you again."

"Eric, this is my wife, Summer."

"Hello, Summer." Instead of shaking her hand, Eric Manning hugged her.

They stepped inside, and all at once, from behind every conceivable hiding space, people leapt out.

They were greeted with an unanimous chorus of "Surprise!"

CHAPTER ELEVEN

SUMMER DIDN'T UNDERSTAND what was happening. A large number of strange people surrounded her. People with happy faces, people who seemed delighted to be meeting her.

"Elizabeth," James protested. "What have you done?"

The middle-aged woman hugged first James and then Summer. "You know how much I love a party," she told him, grinning broadly. "What better excuse than to meet your wife? I'm the mother of this brood," she told Summer proudly, gesturing around the room. There were men, women and children milling about. "You must be Summer."

"I am. You must be Elizabeth."

"Indeed I am."

Before she could protest, Summer was lured away from James's side. The men appeared eager to talk to James by himself. Summer looked longingly at her husband. He met her eyes, then shrugged and followed his friends into the family room.

Soon Summer found herself in the kitchen, which bustled with activity. "I'm Jamie. We met the other day in the restaurant," Rich's wife reminded her.

"I remember," Summer told her, stepping aside as a youngster raced past her at breakneck speed.

"These two women with the curious looks on their faces are my sisters-in-law. The first one here," Jamie said, looping her arm around the woman who was obviously pregnant, "is Charlotte. She's married to Jason. He's the slob of the family."

"But he's improving," Charlotte told her.

"When's your baby due?"

"July," Charlotte said. "This is our second. Doug's asleep. I also have a daughter from my first marriage, but Carrie's working and couldn't be here. I'm sure you'll get a chance to meet her later."

"Our baby's due in September," Summer said, ending speculation.

The women exchanged glances. "You're just three months pregnant?"

Miserable, Summer nodded. "I think something must be wrong. The first couple of months I was really sick. I'm much better now that I'm in Seattle with James. But I'm ballooning. Hardly any of my clothes fit anymore."

"It happens like that sometimes," Elizabeth said with the voice of experience. "I wonder..." Then she shook her head. "I showed far more with Paul, my first, than I did with Christy, my youngest. Don't ask me why nature plays these silly tricks on us. You'd think we have enough to put up with, dealing with men."

A chorus of agreement broke out.

Elizabeth took the hors d'oeuvre platter out of the refrigerator. "The good news is I was blessed with three sons. The bad news is I was blessed with three sons." She laughed. "My daughters are an entirely different story."

"I don't know what to expect with this baby," Summer told everyone, pressing her hand to her stomach. "We didn't plan to get pregnant so soon."

"I'll bet James is thrilled."

Summer smiled and nodded. "We both are."

"This is Leah," Jamie said, introducing her other sister-in-law, who'd just entered the kitchen. "She's Paul's wife. Paul's the author in the family."

"He's very good," Leah said proudly. "His first book was published last year, and he's sold two more."

"That's great!"

"Let me help," Jamie insisted, removing the platter from Elizabeth's hands. She carried it to the long table, beautifully decorated with paper bells and a lovely ceramic bride-and-groom centerpiece.

"I've been waiting for a long time to use these decorations," Elizabeth said disparagingly. "My children didn't give me the opportunity. It all started with the girls. Neither one of *them* saw fit to have a church wedding. Then Rich married Jamie and Paul married Leah, again without the kind of wedding I always wanted."

"Jason and Charlotte were the only ones to have a big wedding," Leah explained. "I don't think Eric and Elizabeth have ever forgiven the rest of us."

"You're darn right, we haven't," Eric said, joining them.

"They made it up to us with grandchildren, dear," his wife interjected. "Now, don't get started on that. We're very fortunate."

Summer couldn't remember the last time she'd sat down at a dinner table with this many people. A rowdy group of children ate at card tables set up in the kitchen. Twin boys seemed to instigate the chaos, taking delight in teasing their younger cousins. The noise level was considerable, but Summer didn't mind.

More than once, she caught James watching her. She smiled and silently conveyed that she was enjoying herself. Who wouldn't be?

There were gifts to open after the meal and plenty of marital advice. Summer, whose mood had been bleak earlier, found herself laughing so hard her sides ached.

The evening was an unqualified success, and afterward Summer felt as if she'd met a houseful of new friends. Jamie, Leah and Charlotte seemed eager to make her feel welcome. Charlotte was the first to extend an invitation for lunch. Since they were both pregnant, they already had something important in common.

"A week from Friday," Charlotte reminded her as Summer and James prepared to leave. She mentioned the name of the restaurant and wrote her phone number on the back of a business card.

"I'll look forward to it," Summer told her and meant it.

It wasn't until they were home that she remembered her meeting with Southworth. She didn't know if she'd be in Seattle in another week, let alone available for lunch.

Sadness pressed against her heart.

James slipped his arm around her waist. He turned off the downstairs lights, and together they moved toward the stairs. "As I re-call," he whispered in her ear, "you made me a promise earlier."

"I did?"

"You asked me to make love to you, remember?"

"Oh, yes…" Shivers of awareness slid up and down her spine.

"I certainly hope you intend to keep that promise."

She yawned loudly, covering her mouth, fighting back waves of tiredness. "I have no intention of changing my mind."

"Good." They reached the top of the stairs, and he nuzzled her neck. "I wonder if it'll always be like this," he murmured, steering her toward their bedroom.

"Like what?"

"My desire for you. I feel like a kid in a candy store."

Summer laughed, then yawned again. "I enjoyed meeting the Mannings. They're wonderful people."

"Are those yawns telling me something?" he asked.

She nodded. "I'm tired, James." But it was more than being physically weary. She felt a mental and emotional exhaustion that left her depleted.

"Come on, love," James urged gently. He led her into the bed-room and between long, deep kisses, he undressed her and placed her on the bed. He tucked her in and kissed her cheek.

The light dimmed, and Summer snuggled into the warmth. It took her a few minutes to realize James hadn't joined her.

"James?" She forced her eyes open.

"Yes, love?"

"Aren't you coming to bed?"

"Soon," he said. "I'm taking a shower first."

A shower, she mused, wondering at his sudden penchant for cleanliness.

Then she heard him mutter, "A nice, long, *cold* shower."

James had been looking forward to the ultrasound appointment for weeks. He'd met Dr. Wise, Summer's obstetrician, earlier and had immediately liked and trusted the man, who was in his late for-ties. David Wise had been delivering babies for more than twenty years, and his calm reassurance had gone a long way toward re-lieving James's fears.

The ultrasound clinic was in the same medical building as Dr. Wise's office. He'd said he'd join them there, although James wasn't convinced that was his regular policy. Still, he felt grateful.

Summer sat next to him in the waiting room, her face pale and lifeless. She hadn't been herself in the past few days, and James wondered what was bothering her. He didn't want to pry and hoped she'd soon share whatever it was.

They held hands and waited silently until Summer's name was called.

It was all James could do to sit still as the technician, a young woman named Rachel, explained the procedure.

Summer was instructed to lie flat on her back on the examining table. Her T-shirt was raised to expose the bump that was their child. As James smiled down on her Dr. Wise entered the room.

A gel was spread across Summer's abdomen. It must have been cold because she flinched.

"It's about this time that women start to suggest the male of the species should be responsible for childbearing," Dr. Wise told him.

"No, thanks," James said, "I like my role in all this just fine."

Dr. Wise chuckled. Rachel pressed a stethoscope-like instrument across Summer's stomach, and everyone's attention turned toward the monitor.

James squinted but had trouble making out the details on the screen.

"There's the baby's head," Dr. Wise said, pointing to a curved shape.

James squinted again and he noticed Summer doing the same.

"Well, well. Look at this," the physician continued. "I'm not altogether surprised."

"Look at what?" James studied the screen intently.

"We have a second little head."

"My baby has two heads?" Summer cried in alarm.

"Two heads?" James echoed.

"What I'm saying," Dr. Wise returned calmly, "is that there appear to be two babies."

"Twins?"

"It certainly seems that way." As the ultrasound technician moved the instrument across Summer's abdomen, Dr. Wise pointed to the monitor. "Here's the first head," he said, tracing the barely discernible round curve, "and here's the second."

James squinted for all he was worth just to see one. "Twins," he murmured.

"That explains a lot," Dr. Wise said, patting Summer's arm. "Let's run a copy of this for you both," he said, and Rachel pushed a series of buttons.

Within minutes they had the printout to examine for themselves. While Summer dressed, James studied the picture.

"Twins," he said again, just for the pleasure of hearing himself say it. He turned to Summer and smiled broadly. "Twins," he repeated, grinning from ear to ear.

She smiled, and James thought he saw tears in her eyes.

"It won't be so bad," he said, then immediately regretted his lack of sensitivity. He wasn't the one carrying two babies, nor would he be the one delivering them. "I'll do whatever I can to help," he quickly reassured her.

She gave him a watery smile.

"Say something," he pleaded. "Are you happy?"

"I don't know," she admitted. "I'm still in shock. What about you?"

"Other than the day I married you, I've never been happier." He couldn't seem to stop smiling. "I can hardly wait to tell my father. He's going to be absolutely thrilled."

Summer stared at the ultrasound. "Can you tell? Boys? Girls? One of each?" Strangely, perhaps, it hadn't occurred to her to ask Dr. Wise.

James scratched his head. "I had enough trouble finding the two heads. I decided not to try deciphering anything else."

They left the doctor's office and headed for the parking garage across the street.

"This calls for a celebration. I'll take you to lunch," he said.

"I was thinking more along the lines of a nap."

James grinned and looked at his watch. "Is there time?"

"James," she said, laughing softly. "I meant a *real* nap. I'm exhausted."

"Oh." Disappointment shot through him. "You don't want to celebrate with a fancy lunch?"

She shook her head. "Don't be upset with me. I guess I need time to think about everything."

That sounded odd to James. What was there to think about? True, Summer was pregnant with twins, but they had plenty of time to prepare. As for any mental readjustment, well, he'd made that in all of two seconds. The twins were a surprise, yes, but a pleasant one.

"This news has upset you, hasn't it?" he asked.

"No," she was quick to assure him. "It's just that…well, it changes things."

"What things?"

She shook her head again and didn't answer. James frowned, not knowing how to calm her fears or allay her doubts. She didn't seem to expect him to do either and instead appeared to be withdrawing into herself.

"You don't mind if I tell my dad, do you?" he asked. If he didn't share the news with someone soon, he was afraid he'd be reduced to stopping strangers on the street.

She smiled at him, her eyes alight with love. "No, I don't mind if you tell Walter."

He walked her to where she'd parked and kissed her, then walked the short distance back to the King County Courthouse. His thoughts were so full of Summer that he went a block too far before he realized what he'd done.

In his office, the first thing he did was reach for the phone.

His father answered immediately. "You'll never guess what I'm looking at," he told Walter.

"You're right, I'll never guess."

"Today was Summer's ultrasound," James reminded him. Hiding his excitement was almost impossible.

"Ah, yes, and what did you learn?"

James could hear the eagerness in Walter's voice. "I have the picture in front of me."

"And?"

"I'm staring at your grandchildren right this second."

"Boy or girl?"

James couldn't help it. He laughed. "You didn't listen very well."

"I did, too, and I want to know—what do we have? A boy or a girl?"

"Could be one of each," James informed him calmly.

"Twins!" Walter shouted. "You mean Summer's having twins?"

"That's what I'm telling you."

"Well, I'll be! This is good news. No, it's great news. The best!"

James had never heard Walter this excited—practically as excited as he was himself.

It wasn't every day that a man learned he was having not one baby but two!

Summer didn't go directly home. Instead, she drove around for at least an hour, evaluating the situation between her and James. She loved him so much. The thought of leaving him, even when she knew it was the best thing for his career, brought her to the verge of tears.

What she wanted was to talk with her mother, but her parents were vacationing, touring the south in their motor home. They weren't due back for another month. Summer received postcards every few days with the latest updates and many exhortations to look after herself and their unborn grandchild. Wait till she told them it was grand*children,* she thought with a brief smile.

This vacation was good for them, but she really needed her mother now.

Without realizing she knew the way, Summer drove to the Manning family home. She parked, wondering whether she was doing the right thing.

It took her a full five minutes to gather up enough nerve to get out of the car, walk up the steps and ring the bell.

Elizabeth Manning answered the door. Her face lit up with warmth. "Summer! What a lovely surprise."

"I hope I haven't come at an inconvenient time."

"Not at all," Elizabeth said, ushering her in. "I was making meatballs. It's Eric's favorite. Today's his bowling day, so he's out just now. Can I get you a cup of tea?"

"No, thank you."

Elizabeth sat down in the living room.

"Would it be all right if we talked in the kitchen?" Summer asked after an awkward moment.

"Of course."

"I... I'm aware that you barely know me, and it's an imposition for me to drop in like this."

"Not at all. I'm delighted to see you again."

"I...my parents have a motor home," Summer said, wishing now she'd thought this through more carefully before she approached James's friends. "They're traveling across the south."

"Eric and I do quite a bit of traveling in our own motor home. We visit Christy and her sister, Taylor, at least once a year. Montana's become like a second home to us." She dug her hands into the bowl of hamburger and removed a glob of meat. Expertly she formed it into a perfect round shape.

"I really just wanted to thank you for everything you did the other night," Summer said. "The party for James and me..."

She suddenly decided she couldn't burden this woman with her troubles. She would've welcomed advice, but felt uncomfortable discussing her problems with someone who was little more than a stranger to her.

"When you know me better," Elizabeth was saying, "you'll learn that I love throwing parties. James has always been a special friend to our family, and we were so happy to find out about his marriage. Naturally we wanted to celebrate."

Summer nodded. "I didn't think it was possible to love anyone so much," she confessed, and then because tears began to drip from her eyes, she stood abruptly. "Listen, I should go, but thank you. I'll see myself to the door."

"Summer," Elizabeth called after her. "Summer, is everything all right?"

Summer was in her car by the time Elizabeth appeared in the doorway. She hurriedly started the engine and drove off, sure that she'd done more harm than good with her impromptu visit.

Wiping away tears, Summer went home. She walked into the house and up the stairs, then lay down on the bed and closed her eyes.

She had to leave, but she didn't know where to go. If she didn't do it soon, she'd never find the courage. Only minutes earlier, she'd declared to James's family friend how deeply she loved her husband. That was the truth, so doing what was best for him shouldn't be this difficult.

But it was.

Sobbing and miserable, Summer got up from the bed and pulled a big suitcase from the closet. She packed what she thought she'd need and carried it down to the car.

At the last minute she decided she couldn't leave without writing James. She sat at his desk for several minutes, trying to compose a letter that would explain what she was doing and why. But it was all so complicated, and in the end she simply said he was better off without her and signed her name. She read it twice before tucking it in an envelope.

Tears streamed down her cheeks. It wouldn't be so bad, or so she attempted to convince herself. The babies would be less than two months old when the election was over, and then she'd be free to return.

If James wanted her back.

James had seldom been in a better mood. He sat in the courtroom, convinced he must be grinning like a fool.

His assistant didn't know what to think. During a brief recess, he waltzed back to his office to phone Summer, whistling as he went.

His wife might not have wanted to celebrate with lunch, but their news deserved some kind of festivity. Dinner at the Space Needle. A night on the town.

While he was in his office, he ordered flowers for Summer with a card that said she'd made him the happiest man alive. Twice. He wondered what the florist would make of *that*.

The phone rang four times before voice mail kicked in. James hung up rather than leave a message. He'd try again later. Summer was probably resting; he hoped the phone hadn't disturbed her.

"Judge Wilkens?" Mrs. Jamison, his assistant, stopped him as he was leaving his office.

"Yes?"

"Your father phoned earlier. He wanted me to let you know he's been to the toy store and purchased two giant teddy bears.

He also asked me to tell you he'll be dropping them off around six this evening. And he said he made dinner reservations in case you hadn't thought of it."

"Great." James laughed and discovered his assistant staring at him blankly.

"See this," James said, taking the ultrasound picture from inside his suit pocket. "My wife and I just learned we're having twins."

"Your wife? Twins for you and Summer. Why, Your Honor..." Her mouth opened, then shut, but she recovered quickly. "Congratulations!"

"Thank you," James said. Then, checking his watch, he returned to the courtroom.

The afternoon was hectic. James was hearing the sad case of a man who, crazed with drugs and alcohol, had gone on a shooting rampage. He'd killed three people and injured seventeen more. The case was just getting underway but was sure to attract a lot of media attention. James knew the defense was hinging its case on a plea of temporary insanity.

A door opened at the rear of the courtroom. James didn't look up, but out of the corner of his eye, he saw a lone figure slip into the back row. Whoever it was apparently didn't want to be recognized. She wore a scarf and large sunglasses.

Twice more James found his gaze returning to the figure in the back of the courtroom. If he didn't know better, he'd think it was Summer.

Whoever it was stayed for quite a long time. An hour or more. He wasn't sure when the woman left, but James couldn't help being curious.

His best guess was that the woman was a reporter.

When he was finished for the afternoon, James returned to his office and removed his robe. His secretary brought in a stack of phone messages. The one that seemed most peculiar was from Elizabeth Manning. She'd never called him at court.

Leaning back in his chair, he reached for the phone. "Hello, Elizabeth," he said cheerfully. It was on the tip of his tongue to tell her his and Summer's good news, but she cut him off.

"You'd better tell me what's wrong. I've been worried sick all afternoon."

"Worried? About what?"

"You and Summer."

Sometimes she baffled him. "I don't have a clue what you're talking about. I will tell you that Summer and I were at the doctor's this morning and found out she's pregnant with twins."

"Congratulations." But Elizabeth seemed distracted. "That can't be it," she mulled aloud. "She was here, you know."

"Who?"

"Summer."

"When?"

"This afternoon. Listen to me, James, there's something wrong. I knew it the minute I saw that girl. She was upset and close to tears. At first I thought you two might've had an argument."

"No..." James frowned. "What did she say?"

"She talked about her parents traveling in their motor home. I suppose I should've realized she wanted to discuss something with me, but I started chattering, hoping she'd relax enough to speak her mind."

"Tell me everything that happened."

"After the part about her parents' vacation, she said she'd come to thank me for the party, which we both knew was an excuse. Then she apparently changed her mind about talking with me and started to cry. Before I could stop her, she was gone."

"Gone? What do you mean gone?"

"The girl literally ran out of the house. I tried to catch up with her, but with my bad leg, that was impossible."

"She drove off without another word?"

"That's right." Elizabeth sounded flustered. "What could be wrong, James?"

"I don't know. I just don't know. She was fine this morning." Or was she? James had no idea anymore. "I'll give you a call this evening," he assured Elizabeth. "I'm sure everything's okay."

"I hope so. Summer was very upset, James. Oh. That's odd...."

"What is?"

"I remember something else she said, and it was after this that she started to cry."

"What was it?" James asked anxiously.

"She told me how much she loved you."

A few minutes later, when he'd finished speaking to Elizabeth, James was more confused than ever. He tried calling Summer again—but again there was no answer. He left the office abruptly, without a word to his staff.

When he got to the house he burst through the front door. "Summer!" he shouted, his heart racing.

He was greeted with silence.

He raced up the stairs, taking them two at a time. He searched every room but couldn't find her.

What confused him further was that her clothes still hung in her closet, but one suitcase was missing. Surely if she was planning to leave him, she'd have taken more things. The only items that seemed to be missing were her toothbrush, slippers and a book about pregnancy and birth.

Baffled, he wandered back downstairs. He scouted out the kitchen and the other rooms. The last place he looked was in his den. There he found an envelope propped against the base of the lamp.

James tore open the letter. It was brief and it made no sense. All he understood was that she'd left him. He had no idea why, other than that she seemed to think she was doing what was best for him.

He immediately called her cell. No answer.

A sick feeling attacked his stomach. He sat numbly at his desk for what could've been minutes or hours; he'd lost track of time. The next thing he knew, the doorbell chimed. He didn't get up to answer. A moment later the door opened on its own and his father came into the house.

"You might've let me in," he grumbled, setting one huge teddy bear in the chair across from James. "I'll be right back." He returned a couple of minutes later with the second bear.

"How'd you get in?" James asked, his voice devoid of emotion.

"You gave me a key, remember?"

He didn't.

"What's going on around here?" Walter asked. "Where's my daughter-in-law who's giving me twin grandkids?"

"Apparently Summer has decided to leave me. She's gone."

CHAPTER TWELVE

"GONE?" WALTER PROTESTED. "What do you mean, gone?"

"Gone, Dad," James said bitterly, "as in packed-a-suitcase-and-walked-out-the-door gone."

His father quickly sat down. "But...why?"

James couldn't answer that; silently he handed Walter the brief letter Summer had left him.

Walter read it, then raised questioning eyes to James. "What's this supposed to mean?"

"Your guess is as good as mine."

"You must've said something," Walter insisted. "Think, boy, think."

"I've done nothing *but* think, and none of this makes sense. I thought at first that she was upset about the twins. I realize now that whatever it is has been worrying her for some time."

"What could it be?"

"I don't know. I'd hoped she'd tell me."

"You mean to say you didn't ask?"

"No."

Walter glared at him in disbelief. "That's the first thing I learned after I married your mother. She never told me a thing that I didn't have to pry out of her with a crowbar. It's a man's duty, a husband's lot in life. When you didn't ask, Summer must've assumed you didn't care. She probably figures you don't love her."

In spite of his heavy heart, James smiled. "Trust me, Dad, Summer has no fear of speaking her mind, and as for my loving her, she couldn't have doubted that for an instant."

"She loves you." Walter's words were more statement than question.

"Yes," James said. He felt secure in her love. Or he had until now.

"Where would she go?"

This was the same question he'd been debating from the moment he discovered her letter. He shrugged. "No idea."

"Have you tried her cell?"

"Of course," he snapped. "She turned it off."

"Did you contact her parents?"

He would have, but it wouldn't help. James rubbed his face, tired to the very marrow of his bones. "They're traveling across the Southwest in their motor home. Half the time they don't have cell phone coverage."

"What about friends she's made since the move?"

"They're more acquaintances than friends. She's planning to volunteer at the library, but she's only mentioned the children's librarian in passing."

"I see." Walter frowned. "What about the Mannings?"

"She went over to talk to Elizabeth earlier this afternoon. Elizabeth phoned me and said Summer started to cry and then left in a hurry."

Walter's look was thoughtful. "Sounds as if she was trying to reach out for help."

"The only other person I can think of is her former roommate, Julie. I'll call her now."

"Julie, of course," his father said as if he should've thought of her himself.

James looked up the number and spoke to Julie's new roommate for several minutes.

"Julie's contract with Disney was up at the same time as Summer's," he said as he hung up. "Now that I think about it, Summer did say something about Julie being on tour with a musical group."

"So she'd be staying in hotels. Unlikely Summer would go to her."

James closed his eyes. His wife had walked out on him into a cold, friendless world.

"What about her brother?"

After another quick call, James shook his head. "Adam and Denise haven't heard from her. All I did was scare them," he said grimly.

"Did you check the airlines?"

"Where would she go?" James asked, losing his patience.

"I don't know," Walter admitted reluctantly. He began pacing.

His movements soon irritated James. "For heaven's sake, will you kindly sit down?"

"I can't sit here and do nothing."

"Yes, you can and you will," James insisted, making a decision. "I'll take the car and drive around, see if I can find her. You stay here by the phone in case she calls or we hear something."

"Okay. Check in with me every half hour."

James nodded. As he climbed into the car, he felt as if he was setting out on a journey without a map. Essentially he was, he thought as he drove through the narrow neighborhood streets. Try as he might, he couldn't figure out where she'd go. He tried to put himself in her shoes. Alone in a strange city with few friends.

The only thing he could do was ask God to guide him.

The wind blew off Puget Sound and buffeted Summer as she stood at the end of the pier. The waterfront was one of her favorite places in all of Seattle. Not knowing where else to instruct the taxi to take her, she'd had the driver bring her here.

She loved to shop at the Pike Place Market. Every Saturday morning James came down to the waterfront with her, and they bought fresh fruit and vegetables for the week. He'd been wonderfully patient while she browsed in the tourist shops that stretched along the waterfront. Some of their happiest moments in Seattle had been spent on this very pier.

How she hated to leave this city. It was as if everything in her was fighting to keep her in Seattle. Her husband was here, her home, her very life.

The instant she'd walked into James's large house, she'd experienced a powerful sense of homecoming. She'd never said anything to her husband—he might think her reaction was silly—but Summer felt that his house had always been meant for them together.

She'd like to think that somewhere in James's subconscious he'd known he was going to fall in love and marry. The house had been his preparation for her entry into his life.

Tears blinded her eyes. She didn't want to focus on her unhappiness, so she turned her attention to the water. The pull of the tide fascinated her. The dark, murky waters of Elliott Bay glistened in the lights overhead. A green-and-white ferry chugged into the terminal.

Summer closed her eyes, willing herself to walk away. Except that she didn't know where she'd go. One thing was certain; she couldn't spend the night standing at the end of the pier. She'd need to find herself a hotel. In the morning her head would be clearer and she could make some decisions.

She was about to reach for her suitcase when she sensed someone approaching. Not wanting company, even the nonintrusive sort, Summer turned away from the railing. She kept her eyes lowered, but that didn't prevent her from recognizing James.

He sauntered to the railing several feet from where she stood. Wordlessly he stared into the distance.

Summer wasn't sure what she should do. She couldn't very well walk away from him now. It had been difficult enough the first time. She didn't have the strength to do it again.

"How'd...how'd you find me?" she asked.

He continued to stare into the distance. "Lucky guess," he finally said in cool tones.

Summer doubted that James felt lucky being married to her just then. He was furious with her. More furious than she'd ever seen him.

She wanted to explain that she was a detriment to his career, but couldn't force the words through her parched throat.

The tears that had flowed most of the day returned. She brushed them away with her fingertips.

"Was I such a bad husband?" he demanded in the same chilling tone.

"No," she whispered.

"Did I do something so terrible you can't forgive me for?"

Sobbing, she shook her head.

"You've fallen out of love with me," he suggested next.

"Don't be ridiculous," she cried. If she'd loved him any more than she already did, her heart couldn't have stood it.

"Then tell me why you walked out on me."

"My letter..."

"...explained nothing."

"I... I..." She was trembling so much she couldn't speak.

James walked over to her and reached for her suitcase. "We're going back to the house and we're going to talk about this. Then, if you're still set on leaving, I'll drive you to the airport myself. Understand?"

All she could manage was a weak nod.

Thankfully, he'd parked the car close by. Summer felt disoriented. Maybe she shouldn't be this happy that James had found her, but she was. Even if he was angry with her, she was grateful he was taking her home.

James opened the car door for her and set her suitcase in the backseat. He didn't speak so much as a single word on the drive home.

When they pulled into the driveway, Summer saw Walter's car.

"Your father's here?"

James didn't answer her. Nor did he need to. Walter was already out the door.

"Where'd you find her?" he asked, bolting toward them.

"The waterfront."

"Sit down, sit down," her father-in-law murmured, guiding Summer inside and into a chair. She felt she was about to collapse and must have looked it, too.

"Now what the hell is this all about?" James said roughly.

"You can't talk to her like that," Walter chastised. "Can't you see the poor girl's had the worst day of her life?" He turned to Summer, smiling gently. "Now what the hell is this all about?"

Summer looked from one man to the other. "Would it be all right if I spoke to James alone?" she asked her father-in-law. She couldn't deal with both of them at the same time.

It looked for a moment as if Walter wasn't going to leave. "I suppose," he agreed with reluctance. "I'll be in the other room."

"Walter," Summer said, stopping him on his way out the door. "I take it the two teddy bears are your doing."

He nodded sheepishly. "The car's loaded with goodies. I'm afraid I got a little carried away."

"These babies are going to love their grandpa."

Walter grinned, then walked out, closing the door.

James stood by the fireplace, his back to her. Summer suspected he was preparing a list of questions. She wasn't even sure she had all the answers; she wasn't sure she wanted him to ask them. She decided to preempt his interrogation.

"I... I went to see Ralph Southworth," she said in a quavering voice.

James whirled around. "You did *what?*"

"I... I overheard you and your father talking not long ago and I learned that Southworth resigned as your campaign manager."

"So he's what this is all about," James said thoughtfully. His eyes hardened. "What happened between the two of us had nothing to do with you."

"James, please, I know otherwise. I... I knew from the start that Ralph disapproved of me. I'm not sure why, but it doesn't matter."

"No, it doesn't. Because Southworth doesn't matter."

Summer didn't believe that. "Afterward, it seemed like you'd given up on the election. In the last two weeks you haven't made a single public appearance. When I ask, you don't want to talk about it and—"

"There are things you don't know."

"Things you wouldn't tell me."

James sat across from her and leaned forward, elbows on his knees. He didn't say anything for several minutes.

"What was I supposed to think?" she cried when he didn't explain. "Being a judge is the most important thing in the world to you. You were born for this.... I couldn't take it away from you. Don't you understand?"

"You're wrong about something. Being a superior court judge means nothing if you're not with me. I guarantee you, my career's not worth losing my wife and family over."

"I was going to come back," she whispered, her eyes lowered. "After the election..."

"Do you mean to say you were going to deliver our babies on your own? Do you honestly think I wouldn't have turned this city upside down looking for you?"

"I...didn't know what to think. Ralph said—"

"Don't even tell me." A muscle leapt in his jaw. "I can well imagine what he said. The man's a world-class idiot. He saw you as a liability when you're my greatest asset."

"If you truly believe that, then why did you throw in the towel?"

"I haven't," he told her. "I took a few days to think about it and decide who I'll ask to manage the rest of my campaign. It seems there are several people who want the job."

"But Southworth said he could sway the election for you.... He claims to have political clout."

"He seems to think he does," James said tightly.

"We made a deal," she whispered, lowering her gaze.

"What kind of deal?"

"Southworth agreed to manage your campaign if I left Seattle until after the election."

James snickered. "It's unfortunate you didn't check with me first."

"Why?"

"I don't want Southworth anywhere near my campaign."

Summer bristled. "You might've said that earlier."

"True," James admitted slowly. "But I wanted everything squared away before I announced that I'd changed campaign managers."

"So, who did you choose? Who's your new manager?"

"Eric Manning. He's not only an old friend, he was a successful businessman and he's very well connected." He shook his head. "I should've asked him in the first place."

"James, that's wonderful! I like him so much better than Ralph."

James reached for her hands and held them in his own. "What you don't understand is that I wouldn't have taken Southworth back under any circumstances. First of all, I won't allow any man to talk about my wife the way he did. It's true I made some mistakes when we first got married. I blame myself for not publishing our wedding announcement immediately. Frankly, I didn't think of it."

"I didn't, either. And remember, we were talking about an April ceremony back then." Summer wasn't willing to have him accept all the blame.

"You're my wife, and I couldn't be prouder that someone as beautiful and talented as you would choose to marry me. Ralph made it sound as if we should keep you under wraps until after the election, which is utterly ridiculous. I'm angry with myself for not taking a stand sooner."

"What about the election?" She didn't care to hear any more about Southworth.

"I'll get to that in a minute. When Southworth said he questioned my judgment, I realized what a fool I'd been to listen to the man for even a minute."

"But—"

"Let me finish, sweetheart. The best thing I ever did in my life was marry you."

"It was impulsive and—"

"Smart," he said, cutting her off. "I don't need Southworth to win this campaign for me. He had me convinced I did, but I know otherwise now."

"What about his political friends?"

"That's a laugh. A man as narrow-minded and self-righteous as Ralph Southworth can't afford the luxury of friends. He has none, but he doesn't seem to know it. If he hadn't decided to leave my campaign, I would've asked him to resign."

It was a good thing Summer was sitting down. "You mean to say I went through all that grief and left you for *nothing?*"

"Exactly."

"Oh."

James gathered her in his arms. "Summer, whatever I am, whatever I may become, I'm nothing without you."

Summer sobbed into his shoulder.

"Winning the election would be an empty victory if you weren't standing at my side. I want you to share that moment with me. I love you, Summer, and I love our babies, too."

"Oh, James, I've been so unhappy. I didn't know what to do."

"Don't ever leave me again. It was like I'd lost my mind, my heart—everything—until I saw you standing at the end of that pier."

Summer tightened her arms around him.

Walter tapped on the door. "Can I come in yet?"

"No," James growled.

"So have you two settled your differences?"

"We're working on it," Summer called out.

"Then I'll leave you to your reunion."

"Good night, Dad," James said in what was an obvious hint for his father to leave.

"'Night, kids. Kiss and make up, okay?"

"We're going to do a lot more than kiss," James whispered in her ear.

"Promises, promises, promises," she murmured.

"You can bet I'll make good on these."

CHAPTER THIRTEEN

"This is my wife, Summer," James said, his arm around her thick waist. Although she was only six months pregnant, she looked closer to nine.

"I'm so pleased to meet you," the older woman said.

"Who was that again?" she whispered to James.

"Emily Rohrbaugh, president of the League of Women Voters."

"Oh. I don't know how you remember all these names. I'm impressed."

"I'm more impressed that you can remember all your lines in *Beauty and the Beast*," he said. "But here's my little trick for recalling names. I try to tie them in with something else," James told her. "Some kind of object or action."

"Rohrbaugh is something of a challenge, don't you think?" Summer raised her eyebrows.

"Roar and baa," he said under his breath. "Think of a lion and a lamb. A lion roars and a lamb goes *baa*. Rohrbaugh."

Summer's face lit up with a bright smile. "No wonder I married you. You're brilliant."

"I bet you won't have a problem remembering Emily the next time you meet."

"I won't."

"She's a good friend of Elizabeth Manning's," James said, feeding his wife a seedless grape. It was a test of his restraint not to kiss her afterward. One would assume his desire for her would fade after all these months; if anything, quite the opposite had occurred. She was never more beautiful to him than now, heavy with their children.

"Elizabeth Manning?" Summer repeated. "I didn't think she'd be the political type."

"She isn't," James said. They mingled with the crowd gathered on the patio of an influential member of the state senate. "But the two of them have been friends since high school."

"I see."

"Do you need to sit for a while?"

"James," she groaned. "Stop worrying about me."

He glanced down at her abdomen. "How are Mutt and Jeff?"

She circled her belly with both hands. "I swear these two are going to be world-class soccer players."

James chuckled, reaching for an hors d'oeuvre from one of the several platters set around the sunny patio. He gave it to Summer.

"James, I don't believe I've met your wife."

James recognized the voice—William Carr, the president of the Bar Association. He quickly made the introductions. He never worried about Summer saying the wrong thing or inadvertently embarrassing him. She had a natural way about her that instantly put people at ease. She was charming and open and genuine. These political functions weren't her idea of a good time, but she never complained. She seemed eager to do whatever she could to aid his campaign and had proved to be the asset he knew she would be.

"I'm very pleased to meet you," she said warmly as they exchanged handshakes.

The obvious topic of conversation was Summer's pregnancy, which they discussed but only briefly. She managed to deftly turn the conversation away from herself, and soon Carr was talking about himself, laughing over the early days when his wife was pregnant with their oldest child.

After ten minutes or so, Summer excused herself.

"She's an excellent conversationalist," William Carr commented as she walked away.

James did his best to hide a smile. It amused him that Carr

could do most of the talking and then act as if Summer had been the one carrying the discussion.

"It seems strange to think of you as married," the attorney said next.

"When I'm with Summer, I wonder why I ever waited so long."

Carr shifted his weight from one foot to the other. "If I'd given you advice before you were appointed to the court, it would've been to marry."

"Really?" This came as a shock to James.

"You're a fine young man, and I expect great things from you. Just between you, me and the fence post, I think you're doing an excellent job."

"I hope so," James said, but there were some who weren't as confident as William Carr. Generally those under the influence of Ralph Southworth. To James's surprise, Southworth had managed to prejudice several supporters against him.

"You remind me of myself thirty years back," Carr told him.

James considered this high praise. "Thank you."

"But you needed a little softening around the edges. You came off as strong and unbending. Not a bad thing for a judge, mind you, but being a little more human wouldn't have hurt."

"I see." James didn't like hearing this but knew it was for his own good, however uncomfortable it might be.

"It's easy to sit in judgment of others when you live in an ivory tower."

James frowned uncertainly. "I don't understand."

"Until you married Summer, your life was a bit...sterile. Protected. If you don't mind my saying so... A married man knows how to compromise. I imagine you've done things to make your wife happy that you wouldn't normally do."

He nodded.

"In my opinion, marriage matures a man. It helps him sympathize and identify with his fellow humans."

"Are you trying to tell me I was a stodgy stuffed shirt before I married Summer?" James asked outright.

William Carr seemed taken aback by his directness, then grinned. "Couldn't have said it better myself."

"That's what I thought." James reached for a tiny crab puff.

"By the way, I wanted to congratulate you on a job well done. That multiple homicide was your first murder trial, wasn't it?"

"Yes." To be honest, he was happy it was over. The ordeal had proved to be exhausting for everyone involved. The jury had found the young man guilty, and after careful deliberation, James had pronounced the sentence.

His name and face had appeared on television screens every night for weeks. It went without saying that a lot of people were watching and waiting to see how he'd rule. Liberals were looking for leniency, and hard-liners wanted the death penalty. James had agonized over the sentence.

There were more victims than the ones who were shot during those hours of madness. Three families had lost loved ones. Seventeen others would always carry the mark of a madman's gun. Innocent lives had been forever changed.

James had delivered a sentence he felt was fair. He didn't try to satisfy any political factions, although the outcome of the election could well rest on his judgment. He'd sentenced the killer to life without the possibility of parole, with mandatory psychiatric treatment.

It would've been impossible to keep everyone happy, so his decision had been based on what he considered equitable for all concerned. Some were pleased, he knew, and others were outraged.

"Thank you," James said, "I appreciate your vote of confidence."

"The decisions won't get any easier," William Carr told him. The older man grabbed a stuffed green olive and popped it in his mouth.

"The bar will be taking their opinion poll about the time your wife's due to have those babies of yours."

James knew that whether or not the results were published was at the discretion of the bar. The vote could sway the November election.

Summer returned just then, looking tired. Despite her smile, William Carr seemed to realize this. He wished them his best and drifted away.

"Are you ready to leave?" James asked.

"No," she protested. "We've barely arrived."

"We're going." His mistake was in asking her; he should've known to expect an argument.

He made their excuses, thanked the host and hostess and urged Summer toward their parked car. Her progress was slow, and he knew she was uncomfortable, especially in the heat.

"Charlotte's due in two weeks," she said when he helped her inside. She sighed as she eased into the seat. The seat belt barely stretched all the way around her.

James paused. "What's that comment about Charlotte about?"

"I envy her. Look at me, James!"

"I am looking at you," he said, and planted a kiss on her cheek. "You're the most beautiful woman in the world."

"I don't believe you," she muttered.

"You'd better, because it wouldn't take much to convince me to prove it right here and now."

"James, honestly."

"I am being honest."

She smiled, and he couldn't resist kissing her a second time.

After they got home, Summer sat outside in the sunshine. She propped her feet on a stool, and her hands rested on her stomach.

James brought her a glass of iced tea.

She smiled her appreciation. "You spoil me."

"That's because I enjoy it." He sat down next to her. "I don't suppose you've thought about packing up and leaving me lately?"

Summer giggled. "Once or twice, but by the time I finished dragging out my suitcases, I was too tired to go."

"You're teasing."

"Of course I'm teasing."

"Speaking of suitcases, do you have one ready for the hospital?"

"Aren't we being a little premature?"

"Who knows what Mutt and Jeff are thinking." James's hand joined hers. It thrilled him to feel his children move inside her. "And this time you might want to take more than your toothbrush, a book and your bedroom slippers."

"That goes to show you the mental state I was in."

"Never again," James said firmly.

Summer propped her head against his shoulder and sighed. "Never again," she agreed.

* * *

The day of the September primary, Summer woke feeling slug-gish and out of sorts. Getting out of bed was a task of monumen-tal proportions. She felt as if she needed a forklift.

James was already up and shaved. He'd been watching her care-fully all week. To everyone's surprise, including her doctor's, Sum-mer hadn't delivered the twins yet. She'd read that twins were often born early. But not Mutt and Jeff, as they'd been affection-ately named by James.

"Most babies aren't born on their due dates, so stop looking so worried. This is *your* day." She sat on the edge of the bed and pressed her hand to the small of her back.

James offered her his arm to help her upright. "How do you feel?"

"I don't know yet." The pain at the base of her spine had kept her awake most of the night. It didn't seem to go away, no matter how often she changed her position.

"When are we voting?" she asked.

"First thing this morning," James told her.

"Good."

"Why is that good?" he asked anxiously. "Do you think to-day's the day?"

"James, stop! I'm in perfect health."

"For someone nine months pregnant with twins, you mean."

Summer swore that somehow, God willing, she'd make it through this day. James was so tender and endearing, but she didn't want him worrying about her during the primary.

They gathered, together with Walter, at the large Manning home for the election results that evening. Summer was pleased for the opportunity to be with her friends.

Jason and Charlotte, along with their toddler and infant daugh-ter, Ann Marie, were among the first to arrive. Many of the friends who'd worked so hard on James's campaign showed up soon after, shortly before the first election results were announced.

Summer planted herself in a chair in the family room and didn't move for an hour. The ache in her back had intensified.

Feeling the need to move about, she made her way into the

kitchen. She was standing in front of the sink when it happened. Her eyes widened as she felt a sharp, stabbing pain.

"James," she cried in panic, gripping the counter. Water gushed from between her legs and onto the floor. "Oh, my goodness."

"Summer?" James stood in the doorway, along with at least ten others, including Elizabeth Manning.

"I'm sorry," she whispered, looking at James. "But I think it might be time to take me to the hospital."

She saw her husband turn and stare longingly at the election results being flashed across the screen. "Now?"

CHAPTER FOURTEEN

"JAMES... I'M SORRY." The pain that had been concentrated in the small of her back had worked its way around her middle. Summer held her stomach and closed her eyes, surprised by the intensity of it.

"Sorry," James demanded, "for what?" He moved quickly and placed his arm around her shoulders.

"You'd better get her to the hospital," Elizabeth advised.

"I'll phone the doctor for you," Eric added.

James shouted out the number he'd memorized, and five or six Mannings chanted it until Eric found a pad and pen to write it down.

Summer felt as if everyone wanted to play a role in the birth of their twins.

"Toss me the car keys, and I'll get the car as close to the front door as I can," Jason Manning shouted.

James threw him the keys, and Jason hurried out the front door.

"What about the election returns?" Summer asked, gazing at the television.

"I'll get them later," James said as if it meant nothing.

"I'll leave messages on your cell phone," Charlotte volunteered, "and James can call us when he has an update on Summer and the babies."

Summer bit her lip at the approach of another contraction. It hurt, really hurt. "James." She squeezed his hand, needing him.

"I'm here, sweetheart. I won't leave you, not for anything."

Jason reappeared, and the small entourage headed for James's car. It was parked on the grass, close to the front door, the engine running.

"The doctor said you should go directly to the hospital," Walter said breathlessly. "He'll meet you there."

"Don't worry, Summer, this isn't his first set of twins," Elizabeth said in a reassuring voice.

"True, but they're mine," James said.

"James?" Summer looked at her husband and noticed how pale he'd suddenly become. "Are you all right?"

He didn't answer for a moment; instead, he helped her inside the car and strapped her in. Before long he was sitting next to her, hands braced on the steering wheel. Summer saw the pulse in his neck pounding.

"It's going to be fine," she whispered. "Just fine."

"I'll feel a whole lot better once we get you to the hospital."

"Call us," Charlotte shouted, standing on the steps, waving.

Summer waved back, and no fewer than fifteen adults crowded onto the Mannings' front porch, cheering them on.

"James, are you okay to drive?" Summer asked when he took off at breakneck speed. He slowed down and stayed within the speed limit, but there was a leashed fear in him that was almost palpable.

"I'll be okay once we get you to the hospital."

"The birthing process is perfectly natural."

"Maybe it is for a woman, but it isn't as easy for a man."

With her hands propped against her abdomen, Summer smiled. "What's that supposed to mean?"

"I don't know if I can bear to see you in pain," he said, wiping his face as they stopped for a red light.

"It won't be too bad."

"Hey, you saw the films in our birthing class. I don't know if I'm ready for this."

"You!" she said, and giggled.

James's fingers curled around her hand. "This isn't a laughing matter. I've never been more frightened in my life. No, only once," he amended. "The night I came home and found you gone."

"The babies and I are going to be just fine," she said again. "Don't worry, James, please. This is your night to shine. I'm just sorry Mutt and Jeff chose right now to make their debut."

"At the moment, the election is the last thing on my mind. None of it matters."

"You're going to win the primary," she insisted. Summer knew the competition had been steep, and Ralph Southworth had done what damage he could, eager to prove himself right.

"We're almost at the hospital," James said, sounding relieved.

"Relax," she said, and as it turned out, her words were a reminder to herself. The next contraction hit with unexpected severity, and she drew in a deep breath trying to control the pain.

"Summer!"

"I'm fine," she said breathlessly.

James pulled into the emergency entrance at Virginia Mason Hospital and raced around the front of the car. He opened the door, unsnapped the seat belt and lovingly helped her out.

Someone rolled a wheelchair toward her, and while Summer sat and answered the questions in Admitting, James parked the car.

She was on the maternity floor when he rejoined her, looking pale and harried.

"Stop worrying," she scolded him.

James dragged a chair to the side of her bed and slumped into it. "Feel my heart," he said and placed her hand over his chest.

"It feels like a machine gun," Summer said, smiling. She moved her hand to his face and cupped his cheek.

"I need you so much," James whispered.

Summer couldn't speak due to a strong contraction. James clasped her hand and talked to her in soothing tones, urging her to relax. As the pain ebbed, she kept her eyes closed.

When she opened them, she found James standing by the hospital bed, studying her. She smiled weakly and he smiled in return.

Dr. Wise arrived and read her chart, then asked, "How are we doing here?"

"Great," Summer assured him.

"Not so good," James said contradicting her. "I think Summer needs something for the pain, and frankly I'm not feeling so well myself."

"James, I'm fine," Summer told him yet again.

"What your husband's saying is that he needs help to deal with seeing you in pain," the physician explained.

"Do something, Doc."

Dr. Wise slapped James affectionately on the back. "Why don't we let Summer be the one to decide if she needs an epidural? She's a better judge than either one of us."

"All right." But James's agreement came reluctantly.

For Summer the hours passed in a blur. Her labor was difficult, and she was sure she could never have endured it if not for James, who stood faithfully at her side. He encouraged her, lifted her spirits, rubbed her back, reassured her of his love.

News of the primary filtered into the room in messages from Charlotte and various nurses, who caught snippets on the waiting room TV. In the beginning Summer strained to hear each bit of information. But as the evening wore on, she became so consumed by what was happening to her and the babies that she barely heard.

She lost track of time, but it seemed to her that it was well into the wee hours of the morning when she was taken into the delivery room.

James briefly left her side and returned a few minutes later, gowned in surgical green. He resembled a prison escapee, and she took one look at him and laughed.

"What's so funny?"

"You."

James drew in a deep breath and held Summer's hand. "It's almost time."

"I know," she breathed softly. "Ready or not, we're about to become parents. I have the feeling this is going to be the ride of a lifetime."

"It's been that way for me from the night I met you."

"Are you sorry, James?"

"Sorry?" he repeated. "No way!" Leaning over, he kissed her forehead. "My only regret is that I didn't marry you that first New Year's."

"Oh, James, I do love you."

Dr. Wise joined them. "Well, you two, let's see what we've got here, shall we?" He grinned at James. "Congratulations, Your Honor. You won the primary. This is obviously a night for good news."

Two months later Summer woke to the soft, mewling cry of her infant daughter. She climbed silently out of bed and made her way into their daughters' nursery.

There she found James sitting upright in the rocker, sound asleep with Kellie in his arms. Kerrie fussed in her crib.

Lifting the tiny bundle, Summer changed Kerrie's diaper, then sat in the rocker next to her husband and offered the hungry child her breast. Kerrie nursed eagerly and Summer ran her finger down the side of her baby's perfect face.

Her gaze wandered to her husband and she felt a surge of pride and love. The election had been that night, and he'd won the court seat by a wide margin. During the heat of the last two weeks of the campaign, James had let her compose and sing a radio commercial for him. Summer had been proud of her small part in his success, although she didn't miss life on the stage. Her twin daughters kept her far too busy for regrets.

James must have felt her scrutiny because he stirred. He looked up and saw Summer with Kerrie.

"I might as well feed Kellie, too," she said. Experience had taught her that the minute one was fed and asleep, the other would wake and demand to be nursed. Her twin daughters were identical in more than looks. Even their sleep patterns were the same.

James stood and expertly changed Kellie's diaper.

When Kerrie finished nursing, Summer swapped babies with him. James gently placed his daughter on his shoulder and patted her back until they heard the tiny burp.

"Why didn't you wake me?" Summer asked.

"You were sleeping so soundly."

"It was quite a night, Your Honor," she said, looking over at her husband. "I couldn't be more thrilled for you, James. Your position on the bench is secure."

"I couldn't have done it without you," he told her.

"Don't be ridiculous."

"It's true," he said with feeling. "You and Kerrie and Kellie. The voters fell in love with the three of you. Those radio commercials you sang were the talk of the town. I'm the envy of every politician I know."

"Because I can sing?"

"No, because you're my wife." His eyes were dark, intense. "I'm crazy about you, Summer. I still can't believe how much you've given me."

"I love you, too, James." Summer closed her eyes. It had started almost two years ago in Vegas, when it felt as if her heart was breaking. Now her heart was filled to overflowing. Life couldn't get any better than it was right then, she decided.

But Summer was wrong.

Because the best was yet to come.

* * * * *

The Princess's New Year Wedding

Rebecca Winters

Dear Reader,

I was a typical little girl who loved fairy tales. My mother would take me and my four sisters to the library and we would check out as many books as we could. I adored anything to do with princesses, princes, magic spells, castles, crowns and jewels. But I read them too fast and had to wait until she took us to the library a week later to get more. I never had enough reading material and so I would sit on the radiator cover by the window in the living room for hours drawing pictures of a princess in a beautiful gown, or I would use tracing paper to copy some of my favorite pictures out of the books.

One of my favorite stories was *The Twelve Dancing Princesses*. I'd dream about the different kinds of princes who danced with them after midnight. That story stayed with me all my life and was the inspiration for my The Princess Brides series. But instead of twelve, I chose three of the king's daughters and fractured their traditional tale by turning everything around. I won't tell you how, but I hope you like my flight of fancy in this first book, *The Princess's New Year Wedding*.

Enjoy!

Rebecca Winters

Rebecca Winters lives in Salt Lake City, Utah. With canyons and high alpine meadows full of wildflowers, she never runs out of places to explore. They, plus her favorite vacation spots in Europe, often end up as backgrounds for her romance novels—because writing is her passion, along with her family and church. Rebecca loves to hear from readers. If you wish to email her, please visit her website at cleanromances.net.

Books by Rebecca Winters

Harlequin Forever

Holiday with a Billionaire

Captivated by the Brooding Billionaire
Falling for the Venetian Billionaire
Wedding the Greek Billionaire

The Billionaire's Club

Return of Her Italian Duke
Bound to Her Greek Billionaire
Whisked Away by Her Sicilian Boss

The Montanari Marriages

The Billionaire's Baby Swap
The Billionaire Who Saw Her Beauty

The Billionaire's Prize
The Magnate's Holiday Proposal

Visit the Author Profile page
at millsandboon.com.au for more titles.

How lucky was I to be born to my darling, talented mother, who was beautiful inside and out. She filled my life with joy and made me so happy to be alive! I love you, Mom.

Praise for
Rebecca Winters

"Readers will be swept away.... Winters' fine romance unfolds at the perfect pace, so one can digest the relationship and still enjoy the antics of being a billionaire."

—*RT Book Reviews* on
The Billionaire Who Saw Her Beauty

CHAPTER ONE

"*MIO FIGLIO?* I know it's early, but there are things I must talk to you about. *Come to the apartment.*"

Thirty-year-old Stefano sat up in bed. It was a shock to get a phone call from his father at 5:30 a.m., but his father's entreaty shocked him even more.

"You mean now?"

"Please."

"I'll be there as soon as I can."

Stefano realized his father's broken heart wouldn't allow him to sleep, but then Stefano doubted anyone in the palace had known a moment's rest for the past week. Alberto, his adored younger brother—his parents' beloved son and heir to the throne—had just been buried yesterday at the young age of twenty-eight. There was no antidote for sorrow.

Stefano's twenty-seven-year-old sister, Carla, and her husband, Dino, and two children, were just as grief-stricken over the loss of a wonderful brother and uncle. She was now first in line to the throne and would be queen when their father died or could no longer rule. The rules of succession fell to the firstborn, then the second or the third, regardless of gender.

Stefano would never rule.

Since his eighteenth birthday when he'd prevailed on his parents to be exempt from royal duty for the rest of his life, Stefano had been granted that exemption by parliament. From that time forward, he was no longer a royal, but he loved his family and they loved him. They'd all come together for this unexpected tragedy.

With Alberto gone, his mother looked like she'd aged twenty years and had gone to bed after the interment of her second-born son. The funeral had been too much for her.

Stefano had struggled with his pain and was forced to face the fact that he was now the *only* son of King Basilio. Though his father would rely more and more on Carla, he needed Stefano, too, and would lean on him for comfort. Stefano guessed that was why his father had summoned him this early in the morning. Forcing himself to move, Stefano dragged himself out of bed to shower and dress.

Before long he entered his parents' private lounge off their bedroom in the north wing of the palace. His bereaved father turned away from the fireplace to look at him. "Thank you for coming, Stefano. Your mother is still in bed, overcome with grief."

"As *you* are, *Papà*." Stefano gave him a soulful hug. It would be impossible to get over the reality that Alberto had been killed in a car crash a week ago.

Stefano, who'd graduated from the Colorado School of Mines in the US, had been in Canada at the time, inspecting one of the Casale gold mines. Casale being an old family name dating back to the founding of Italy. Nothing had seemed real until he'd returned home to the Kingdom of Umbriano, located in the Alps. His father had met him after the royal jet touched down and they went to identify Alberto's body.

Yesterday's state funeral in the basilica of Umbriano, presided over by the cardinal who had also delivered the eulogy, had been a great tribute to Alberto, a favorite son revered by the people. Dignitaries of many countries had attended, including of course the royal family of the Kingdom of Domodossola bordering France, Switzerland and Italy.

Stefano would never forget the vacant look on the face of Alberto's betrothed, Princess Lanza Rossiano of Domodossola, beneath her black, gauzy veil. He'd met war victims after serving a required year in the military in the Middle East who'd had that same lost, bewildered expression, their whole world wiped out.

The twenty-two-year-old daughter of King Victor Emmanuel of Domodossola had been betrothed to Alberto twelve months ago. Their marriage was supposed to take place a year from now on New Year's Day, and her family had clearly been devastated.

Stefano, who was rarely in the country because of business, hadn't met with King Victor's family since his childhood when both families got together on occasion. Meeting them again at the funeral, he was shocked to see all three of the king's daughters grown up. Not until he witnessed their bereavement did Stefano realize how terrible the news must have been for them. Stefano still couldn't believe Alberto was gone.

"Sit down. We have something vital to discuss."

By vital, his father must mean he wanted Stefano to stay around for a while, but that would be impossible because of Stefano's latest gold mining project in Kenya. He needed to fly there the day after tomorrow to oversee a whole new gold processing invention that could bring in a great deal more money. Hopefully, it would serve as a prototype for all his other gold mines throughout the world. He imagined he'd be gone six weeks at least.

With his hands clasped between his legs, Stefano closed his eyes, knowing his father was in so much pain at the moment that he needed all their support, but he was curious as to what his father wanted to talk about.

"The wedding to Princess Lanza must go on as planned. Since losing Alberto, your mother and I have talked of nothing else. It's imperative that *you* take your brother's place."

Stefano's head jerked up. "Surely, I didn't hear you correctly."

"I know this comes as a shock to you."

Stefano shot to his feet, incredulous. "Shock doesn't describe it, *Papà*."

"Hear me out."

Stefano groaned and walked over to the mullioned windows looking out on the palatial estate with the snow-covered peaks of the Alps in the distance. An icy shiver passed through his taut body.

"Our two countries need to solidify in order to build the resources of both our kingdoms. This necessary merger can only happen by your marrying Princess Lanza."

Stefano wheeled around, gritting his teeth. "Years ago you gave me my freedom by parliamentary decree. I'm no longer a royal."

"That decree can be reversed by an emergency parliamentary edict."

"What?"

His father nodded. "I've already been investigating behind the scenes. Because of the enormity of this tragedy and their eagerness to see a marriage between our two countries happen, my advisors have informed me the parliament will reinstate you immediately."

Stefano couldn't believe it. "Even if it were possible, you're not seriously asking me to marry Princess Lanza, are you? I haven't been around her since she was a young girl. And I'm seven years older than she is."

"That's not a great age difference."

Stefano tried to calm down. "Alberto was the one who was attracted to her. I can't do this, *Papà*. Right now I'm doing everything in my power to develop more lucrative gold mines and invest the revenues to help our country grow richer. We don't need the timber from Domodossola!"

His father shook his head. "What I'm asking goes a great deal deeper than cementing fortunes. Victor and I have had this dream of uniting our two families in marriage since the moment we both became parents of future kings and queens."

"But it's not *my* dream, *Papà*, and never could be," Stefano said, attempting to control his anger. "I'm sorry, but I can't do what you ask."

"Not even to honor your brother?"

He hadn't realized his mother had come into the lounge wearing her dressing gown. The edge in her tone caught him off guard. "What do you mean, *Mamà*?"

"This has to do with keeping faith with a sacred pledge your brother made to Princess Lanza a year ago. She's been groomed to become Alberto's bride. For the past year her life has been put on hold because she wears our family betrothal ring. All this time she's been faithful to their pledge, preparing for their wedding day."

Stefano shook his head. "No one could have imagined this crisis. It changes all the rules."

"Except for one thing your father and I have never told you about because we didn't think we would have to."

Fearing what he'd hear, Stefano's heart jolted in his chest. "What do you mean?"

"On the morning you turned eighteen, your brother came to us in secret. He wanted to give you a gift he knew you wanted more than anything on earth."

His brows furrowed. "What was that?"

"What else? Your freedom."

"I don't understand, *Mamà.*"

"Then let me explain. You never wanted to be a royal. You made it clear from the time you were old enough to express your feelings. Alberto adored and worshipped you. By the time you turned eighteen, he was afraid you'd never be happy. He literally begged us to let you live a life free of royal duty.

"He loved you so much, he promised that he would fulfill all the things we would have asked of you as a royal prince who would rule one day so *you* could have the freedom to live life without the royal trappings. That was the bargain he made with us."

"A bargain? *That's* why you suddenly gave in to me?"

His father nodded solemnly. "The only reason, *figlio mio.* You two were so close, he put you before his own wants or desires. He convinced us you had to be able to go out in the world free to be your own person. Otherwise you'd die like an animal kept in a cage."

Alberto had actually told them that?

"All he asked was that we agree. Then he would do everything and more than we expected of him as a crown prince, *and*...he consented to become betrothed to Princess Lanza on whatever date we chose. He knew how much we loved her growing up. She was always a delight. In truth, he wanted his elder brother's happiness above all else, and made that request of us out of pure love."

Stefano stood there rigid as a piece of petrified wood. His parents had never lied to him. He had to believe them now. Because of his brother's love and intervention—and *not* because of his parents' understanding—Stefano had been able to escape the world he'd been born into all this time.

His mother walked over to him and put her hands on his shoulders. It pained him to see the lines of grief carved in her features.

"His only desire was that you never know how he pled for you. He worried that if you ever found out the truth, you would always feel beholden to him. That request was his unselfish gift to you."

Unselfish didn't begin to describe what Alberto had done to ensure his happiness.

In Stefano's mind and heart, it was an unheard-of gift. He'd always loved his younger brother, his buddy in childhood. Alberto's noble character made him beloved and elevated him above the ranks of ordinary people. Many times he'd heard people say that the good ones died young. His brother was the best of the best, and death had snatched him away prematurely.

Overcome with emotions assailing him, Stefano wrapped his arms around his mother until he could get a grip on them, then he let her go. He was amazed his parents had so much love for their sons that they'd gone along with both his and Alberto's wishes at the time. It was humbling and gave him new perspective.

Her eyes clung to his. "Would you be willing to do what Alberto can't do now? Take on the royal duty you were born to and marry Princess Lanza?"

He inhaled sharply. "Do you think she would consent when she'd planned to marry Alberto?"

"King Victor says his daughter will agree. You and Lanza knew each other in your youth and you have a whole year to get reacquainted."

"But that will be close to impossible, *Papà*. My schedule has been laid out with back-to-back visits of all the mines through the next eighteen months. There's no time when so many managers are depending on me, especially with the new mining process I've developed."

His father cocked his head. "After we inform her and her parents of your official proposal of marriage, surely you could find a way to visit her once and stay in touch with her the rest of the time? Both King Victor and I have already talked to the cardinal, who has given this marriage his blessing."

Stefano could see the die had been cast.

His mother eyed him through drenched eyes. "Our two countries have been looking forward to this day since you were all children. The citizens know that your business interests throughout the world have contributed to our country's economy. Umbriano will cheer your reinstatement and honor your name for stepping into your brother's shoes, believe me."

Stefano found all this difficult to fathom. There wasn't time for him to get reacquainted with Princess Lanza. Even if parliament voted to reinstate him as a royal, he had crucial business issues around the globe.

His father walked over to them. "I've never asked anything of you before, Stefano. I've allowed you to be your own person, free of all royal responsibilities, but fate stepped in and took Alberto away too early. Now is the time when your parents and Lanza's are asking this for the good of both our countries."

"Alberto told us he hoped to have a family." His mother stared at him with longing. "I'm sure Princess Lanza was planning on children, too. That dream is gone, but you could make a whole new dream begin. I've had that dream for you, too, Stefano.

"On all your travels for business and pleasure, you've never brought a woman home for us to meet, let alone marry. We were prepared that you'd eventually want marriage and have a family, but it has never come to pass. If there's a special woman, you haven't said anything."

Stefano sucked in his breath. This whole conversation was unreal, including a discussion of a woman in his life he couldn't do without. He'd met several and had enjoyed some intimate relationships, but the thought of settling down with one of them hadn't entered his mind. As Alberto had said, he liked his freedom too much.

"Have you even considered Princess Lanza's feelings?" he asked them in a grating voice, struggling to make sense of this situation.

His father nodded. "King Victor and I talked about it before the funeral. He's as anxious as I for this to happen and has probably discussed this with her already. Victor assures me it's in her nature to do what is good for both countries."

No normal woman worth her salt would agree to such a loveless marriage, but a royal princess was a different matter if she believed it was her duty. Over the phone a few months ago, Alberto had told him in private that Princess Lanza had a sweet, biddable disposition.

Maybe she did. But the many royal princesses he'd met in his early teens were very spoiled, full of themselves, impossible to please, moody and felt entitled to the point of absurdity.

His vague memory of Lanza was that she was nice, but that was years ago and she'd been so young. His brother was a kind, decent human being. Alberto always tried to find the best in everyone and had probably made up his mind to like her.

After hearing what his parents had just told him about the sacrifice he'd made for Stefano, it was possible Alberto hadn't liked Princess Lanza at all. But he would have pretended otherwise to fulfill his obligations after making the incredible bargain with their parents. It was Alberto's way.

Stefano shook his head. He wasn't born with that kind of greatness in his soul. Humbled by what he'd learned, tortured by the decision his parents were asking him to make, he started for the door. "I need to be alone to think and will be back later."

Once outside in the chilling air, he drove his Lancia into the city to talk to his best friend, Enzo Perino, who managed his own father's banking interests. Stefano found him in his office on the phone.

The second Enzo saw him in the doorway, he waved him inside. After he hung up, he lunged from the chair to hug him. "I'm so sorry about Alberto."

"So am I, Enzo."

"Chiara and I couldn't get near you at the funeral. There were too many people." Stefano nodded. "Come to our house tonight for dinner so we can really talk."

He stared at his best friend who'd recently married. They'd been friends throughout childhood and had done everything together, including military service. Stefano had been the best man at their wedding three months ago.

"I need help."

Enzo chuckled. "Since when have you ever needed a loan?"

Stefano sat down in one of the leather chairs. "I wish money were the problem, but it isn't."

As Stefano's father had emphasized, this suggested marriage had a lot more riding on it than financial considerations.

"You sound serious."

"More serious than you'll ever know."

"Go ahead. I'm listening."

"My father woke me up at the crack of dawn to have a talk." In the next few minutes he told Enzo the thrust of the conversation with his parents, including the necessary part about being reinstated by parliament.

"Our marriage will make me heir apparent to the throne of Domodossola since King Victor has no sons. He doesn't have any married daughters yet. According to their rules of succession, a woman can't become queen in their country. He'll have to rely on a son-in-law."

His friend whistled and sank down in the chair behind his desk. "I know this used to happen in the Middle Ages, but not today." He looked gutted. "Who will take over Umbriano when *your* father can no longer rule?"

"My sister, but I imagine that's many years away. Our country doesn't run by the same laws. You know that. Since I was granted my freedom, she's been raised to be second in line should anything happen to Alberto. Which it did," he said in a mournful tone.

"But if you're reinstated—"

"No—" He interrupted him. "My destiny lies with the throne of Domodossola, the only reason for reinstating me."

Enzo slapped his hands on the desk. "There goes the end of our friendship."

"Don't you ever say that!"

He smiled sadly. "How can I not? With you living in Domodossola, you'll be a prisoner running the affairs of government, hardly ever free to leave the country or have time for me. What will you do with all your mining companies?"

"I still plan to run them, of course."

"Then you'll be carrying a double load. I thought it was too good to be true when your father released you from your princely duties on your eighteenth birthday. We should have known it would all come to an early end."

Stefano closed his eyes for a minute, never imagining he'd lose his brother so young. "I haven't told my parents what I'm going to do. Not yet."

While he'd driven into town, he'd considered the huge decision his parents had made to give Stefano his freedom. In searching his soul, one thing became clear. He could solve his parents' dilemma about the marriage situation by unselfishly taking Alberto's place. How could he not when his brother had willingly done his double royal duty to make up for Stefano's absence?

"It'll happen," Enzo muttered. "I know how much you loved Alberto. You'll never let your parents down now that you know of your brother's sacrifice. As for Princess Lanza, she'll agree to marry you. After all, you are Alberto's brother and she knew you when your families got together as children."

"That's true, but I was hoping for some much-needed advice from you."

They stared at each other for a long time. "All right—there's only one way I can see this working. You need your freedom, so do her the biggest favor of her life and yours. You've got a year before the wedding. Let her know *before* you're married that you plan to be your own person and continue doing the mining work you love while you help her father govern. It'll mean you'll be apart from her for long periods. Give her time to adjust to that fact, know what I mean?"

Pain wasn't the right word to describe Lanza's feelings since returning from the funeral in Umbriano four days ago. Shock would be more precise. Prince Alberto had always been kind to her when they had met. She'd never felt uncomfortable with him.

The second-born son of her father's best friend, King Basilio of Umbriano, had been mild-mannered. Over the years and occasional family get-togethers, both families felt their two children were the perfect fit. Since they'd wanted the marriage to happen, they went ahead with the betrothal on her twenty-first birthday.

According to what her parents had told her, they'd believed that out of her two sisters, Lanza had the right temperament and disposition to be the wife for Prince Alberto, who'd shown an interest in her.

From that time on Lanza had spent several weekends a month

with Alberto, both in Domodossola and Umbriano. They'd developed a friendship that helped her to get ready for her marriage. She'd enjoyed being kissed by him, but they hadn't been lovers.

The fact that he was nice-looking had made it easier to imagine intimacy in their marriage. She'd liked him well enough and believed they could be happy. But now that he was gone, one truth stood out from everything else.

She hadn't lost the love of her life.

Furthermore, his death had made her aware of her own singlehood in a way she would never have anticipated. Since the betrothal she'd known what her future would be. For the past year she'd been planning on the intimacy of marriage and family, the kind her parents enjoyed. Yet in an instant, that future had died with him.

His life had been snuffed out in seconds because of a car crash on an icy, narrow mountain road when he'd swerved to avoid a truck. The accident had robbed her of the destiny planned out for her. But as sorry as she was for Alberto and his family, a part of her realized that she was now free to make different plans.

There was no law of succession in Domodossola since a female couldn't rule. Now her parents would have to look elsewhere for a prince who would marry one of her older sisters, either Fausta or Donetta.

The sad, legitimate release of her betrothal vows gave Lanza a sense of liberation she'd never known before. Heaven help her but the thought was exciting. So exciting, in fact, she was assailed with uncomfortable guilt considering this was a time of mourning, and she *did* mourn Alberto's death.

In an attempt to help her deal with the fact that Prince Alberto had been taken prematurely, the palace priest, Father Mario, had been summoned. He counseled her that she should be grateful Alberto hadn't been forced to live through years of suffering. If his life had been spared, he might have lost limbs or been paralyzed.

Of course she was thankful for that and appreciated the priest's coming to see her, but no one understood what was going on inside her. No longer would she be marking time, waiting for her future with Alberto to start. There was no future except the one she would make from here on out. In truth, Lanza found the thought rich with possibilities.

Since returning from the funeral, it hit her with stunning force that she was alone and dependent on herself to make her own decisions, just like her sisters had been allowed to do. This strange new experience wasn't unlike watching a balloon that had escaped a string and was left to float with no direction in mind. But she knew what she wanted to do first.

With this new sense of freedom, she planned to visit her favorite aunt, Zia Ottavia, who lived in Rome with her husband, Count Verrini. They could talk about anything and Lanza loved her.

A knock on the door of her apartment brought her back from her thoughts.

"Lanza?" Her mother's voice. "May your father and I come in?"

She assumed they wanted to comfort her and she loved them for it. Lanza hurried across the room and opened the door, giving them both a long hug. "Come in and sit in front of the fire."

They took their places on the couch. She sat in her favorite easy chair across from them where she often planted herself to read. She'd been a bookworm from an early age.

"We asked Father Mario to visit you. Did he come?"

"Yes, and he gave me encouragement."

"Oh, good," her dark-blonde mother murmured, but Lanza could tell her parents were more anxious than ever and looked positively ill from the shock they'd all lived through. "We don't think it's good for you to stay in your apartment any longer. I've asked the cook to prepare your favorite meal, and your sisters are going to join us in the dining room for an early dinner."

Her distinguished-looking father nodded. "You need to be around family. It isn't healthy for you to be alone."

"Actually, I've needed this time to myself in order to think. Please don't be offended if I tell you I'm not hungry and couldn't eat a big meal."

"But if you keep this up, you'll waste away," her mother protested.

"No, *Mamà*. I promise that won't happen. Right now I have important things on my mind."

"We do, too," her father broke in. "It's time we talked seriously."

She sat back. "What is it, *Papà*?"

He got to his feet and stoked the fire. "I've been on the phone with Basilio almost constantly for days."

"That doesn't surprise me. I'm sure Alberto's death has brought you two even closer. He and Queen Diania must be in desperate need of comfort."

Her father blinked. "You're really not all right, are you, my dear girl?"

She frowned. "What do you mean?"

"You…don't seem quite yourself," her mother blurted.

If Lanza's parents had expected her to fall apart and take to her bed, then they truly didn't understand.

"I've shed my tears, but all it has done is give me a headache. I have to pull myself together and deal with the here and now. Honestly, I'll be fine. In fact, I'm thinking of taking a trip to Rome to visit Zia Ottavia.

"She phoned me last night and asked me to stay with her for a few months. She's planning to take a long trip to the US and wants me to go with her while Zio Salvatore has to stay in Rome on business. I love being with her and told her I'd come after I talked to you."

He shook his head. "I'm afraid you can't go."

What? She sat forward. "I don't understand."

He cleared his throat. "Alberto's brother, Stefano, has asked for your hand in marriage and wishes to marry you on New Year's Day in a year as planned."

CHAPTER TWO

A STRANGE LAUGH broke from Lanza, who got to her feet. Maybe she was having a bad dream.

"*Stefano?* What kind of a joke is this? For one thing, that's impossible! He was relieved of his royal duties years ago by their parliament."

Lanza had taken a personal affront to the news at the time, even though she knew it didn't have anything to do with her. How could it? She'd only been eleven years old.

But she still remembered how shocked she'd been when she'd heard Stefano had walked away from royal life. She'd always found him more attractive and headstrong than Alberto, but she'd never told anyone her true feelings.

Her father shook his head. "His royal title has just been restored to him through an emergency act of that same parliament. Now he has officially proposed marriage to you."

Lanza let out a cry, incredulous that Stefano wanted to marry her when he'd hardly noticed her growing up. "Is it so important that our two countries combine our money and resources to the point that Stefano has been sent in to salvage the situation? He's the brother who wanted nothing to do with royal life!"

She knew she'd shocked her parents with an outburst that was totally unlike her. Never in her life had she dared speak her mind to them like this. But she felt frustrated and angry.

Her mother stood up and walked over to her. "We can understand your anger, darling, but please just listen. These have been dark days for all of us, but it's true that Stefano wants to take his brother's place and honor his commitment to you. It's what both our families want."

"But it's not what *I* want and I'm over twenty-one!" Lanza stared at her parents in sheer disbelief. What they were asking went beyond rational thought. "You *do* know Stefano gave up the royal life years ago because he hated it."

"That's in the past," her father murmured.

"*Papà*—he's a gold-mining engineer and, according to Alberto, has had various love affairs with women where he's lived around the world. You're asking me to marry *him*? Are you serious?" she cried out.

Her mother's eyes implored her. "We're asking you to think about it and what it will mean for our two countries, for the future of both royal lines."

"I'm getting older every day," her father murmured. "Worse, I'm plagued by a fatigue that is growing more serious. I need a son-in-law to lean on who is fit to be king. Prince Stefano was raised like his brother, Alberto, and will make a splendid husband for you."

"But he's been a playboy!"

"No," her father argued. "What he has done in his nonroyal past is what most men do before they find the right woman. There's been no scandal about him in the media. He's brought no shame of any kind. Quite the opposite. His brilliant business acumen is known around the world and has helped enrich his country. He's Basilio's son, after all."

"But Father—"

"Hear me out, Lanza. His private life before now has no bearing on the future. That part is over."

"How do you know he doesn't have children somewhere? I'm not trying to be cruel by saying that, only practical."

His expression hardened. "I'm going to forget you said that. He's prepared to be a husband to you."

Lanza was too stunned to talk. She studied her father, worried if it was true that he was ill. This was news no one had told her about. "Why haven't I heard about your health before now, *Papà*?"

She'd noticed he moved a little slower these days, but she attributed it to his growing older.

Her mother put a hand on her arm. "Because we didn't want to burden you while you were preparing for your wedding day. We were assuming you wouldn't have to worry about it, but with Alberto dying, everything has changed. Under the circumstances we'll leave to give you time to think about everything." She turned to Lanza's father. "Come on, Victor."

As Lanza watched them go, her two older sisters came in and shut the door. She sucked in her breath. "I take it you could hear us talking."

They nodded.

"Is it true? Is *Papà* ill?"

"I only know what *Mamà* said." Donetta spoke first. "*Papà*'s physician is concerned about his health and says he needs to slow down."

Fausta nodded. "I have a feeling it's his heart, but they won't tell us."

Lanza shivered and walked over to the fireplace. "Why didn't you two tell me?"

Donetta drew closer. "We were ordered not to."

"In other words, I'm the baby who can't handle bad news."

"No. They've been living for your wedding and didn't want anything to mar it."

She closed her eyes tightly. "What they've asked me now is impossible, but I shouldn't have gotten so upset with them."

"Yes, you should have!" Fausta blurted. "I'm proud of you. You haven't seen Prince Stefano in years. Naturally, we're all worried that something is wrong with *Papà*, but even so, you shouldn't let this news make you do what you don't want to do."

Donetta nodded. "I hate to tell you this, Lanza, but you've always been a lot like Cinderella from your favorite fairy tale. She, too, was sweet and believed everything would turn out in the end. But you don't have a fairy godmother to save you. Otherwise, Alberto wouldn't have died. You need to wake up before it's too late."

"She's right!" Fausta chimed once more, adding to Lanza's turmoil. "Cinderella was a fool. She should have gone out into the world to find a man of the people, not some puppet prince, and enjoy a life away from a royal world. That's what I'm planning to do."

Lanza understood her sisters well. Twenty-five-year-old Donetta had no intention of getting married and her parents knew it. But the day would come when they would demand that she marry some prince they approved of.

She'd grown up wanting to be queen, with no man telling her what to do, but it would be impossible because of the succession law of their country that excluded women from ruling.

As for Fausta, their twenty-four-year-old sister, she'd dreamed of marrying a commoner and having a life like her close friends in the city. Fausta thought she was safe, but in the end their parents wouldn't allow it and she'd end up marrying a prince they'd picked out for her.

That left Lanza as her parents' hope for finding the perfect royal son-in-law. But Alberto's death had rendered that null and void. Or so she'd thought!

"We know how upset you are. Would you rather be alone?"

Lanza turned to Fausta. "If you don't mind, I've got a lot to think about."

"We'll eat dinner and then come back up to talk. We're here if you need us." Donetta gave her a peck on the cheek before they left the apartment.

Lanza turned toward the fire once more. What in the name of heaven was she going to do? She loved her father. The last thing she'd ever want would be to disappoint him or her mother, or do something that could make his condition worse.

But to be asked to marry Stefano, who'd turned his back on everything in order to be free...

She remembered one weekend in August when Alberto had come to see her and she'd asked him why he sometimes seemed sad. Lanza wanted to know the truth so she could understand him better.

Alberto told her he missed his elder brother terribly since he no longer lived at the palace. They'd been incredibly close. A few days later Alberto sent her a letter with a picture of Stefano enclosed, looking gorgeous in a safari shirt. He'd been twenty-two in the photo, taken when he'd been working in Kenya.

"I love that smile of his, Lanza. He's my idol and always has been. There are times when I miss him like crazy. After you and I are married, I hope he'll come around more often. I'd give anything to see more of him."

Lanza stoked the fire, recalling those words that had come straight from Alberto's heart. He'd gotten his wish far too late. Stefano was back, and had proposed marriage to *her*.

Stefano was an important, sophisticated man of the world and had been intimately involved with various women over the years, according to the media, so there were no surprises. If Alberto had been with other women this past year, Lanza knew nothing about it, but assumed he'd had a few girlfriends in the past.

Marrying Stefano would mean having a normal intimate relationship that would produce a family in time. Her attraction for him had never changed, even though they hadn't seen one another for a long time, but for some reason the thought of having relations with him made her nervous. She was an inexperienced and naive virgin. A shudder passed through her body.

Would she be a disappointment as his wife?

Could she bring herself to accept another royal proposal of marriage?

If she did, it might increase her father's longevity and give him the help he needed to rule. She loved her father. Perish the thought if he died early because she'd refused to go through with this marriage. How would she be able to bear the burden of that knowledge?

Lanza was a mess.

Her sisters were right. Her favorite fairy tale *had* been about Cinderella, who'd met her heart's desire at the ball and had lived happily-ever-after with her prince. But that was never going to happen to her now.

When Lanza finally turned away from the fire, she accepted the fact that she'd been a fool her whole life...

I'll never know love or be in love.

On that note she left the apartment to find her parents and tell them she'd made her decision to accept Stefano's proposal, but was stopped on her way out the door by her personal maid.

"This came for you personally by courier from the royal palace in Umbriano, Your Highness."

"Thank you, Serena."

Lanza went back into the apartment to open it. Letters of condolences had poured into the palace for days through the post, but this had been hand delivered. There was no writing on the outside of the envelope. Who would be sending her a letter?

Curious, she opened it and found a brief missive.

Dear Lanza,

What you and I are about to do is unprecedented. I've already had to leave the country for Kenya, where I'll probably be working for at least six weeks. After that I must fly directly to Australia, and from there Bulgaria.

I'll try to get to Domodossola at some point to see you. If I can't, I'll email you so we can talk regularly and get prepared for the wedding. Phone calls are difficult because the mines where I work rarely have cell phone service.

I'm afraid our life will have to begin after we meet at the altar.

Don't worry about our wedding night. We'll spend it away from everyone while we sort out the rules of engagement.
Stefano

She gasped in surprise. Before she'd even given her parents or him her answer, Stefano had already sent this message assuming she would have fallen in line with their parents' wishes.

What on earth did he mean about the rules of engagement, unless he was implying he had a solution they could live with?

Lanza sank down on the side of the bed, confused and unsettled as she reread it. Stefano's work truly did take him around the world. When would he have time to help her father? Maybe she shouldn't marry him, after all.

"Lanza?"

"Just a minute." Hearing her sisters' voices, she quickly buried the letter beneath a cushion on her bed and hurried over to the door to open it. "Come on in."

"We thought you might want company."

She didn't know what she wanted.

"Have you decided what you're going to do?"

"Not yet. *Papà* said this marriage has the blessing of the cardinal. He says the citizens of both countries will accept it. But I think it seems like a sham and I feel guilty about it. Do you think it sounds honorable for Stefano to take Alberto's place?"

Fausta eyed her with concern. "It's a year away, and they were close. I do remember that."

"But I don't love him."

"Did you love Alberto?"

She lowered her head. "No, but I liked him well enough. If I say yes and agree to marry Stefano, it will be because *Papà* needs a son-in-law to rely on."

"No." Donetta came back with a friendly smile. "That won't be the reason. You can't fool Fausta and me."

"What do you mean?"

"We both know you always had a crush on Stefano. Who could blame you? As the tabloids say, he's the dishiest bachelor on the planet."

CHAPTER THREE

One year later...

A WINTRY NEW YEAR'S DAY brought thousands of people to line the streets of the capital of Domodossola for the royal wedding. A national holiday had been declared and the sound of bells rang out.

The kingdom had been preparing for this event since her betrothal to Alberto two years ago. Now that day was finally here with a different prince walking her down the aisle. Every shop was open to welcome visitors from all over Europe and beyond.

Lanza sat across from her father in the gold leaf closed carriage that took them toward the cathedral in the distance. With every step of the matched white horses in trappings of red and gold bells that jingled, huge cheers from the masses rang out to celebrate this day unlike any other. Excitement filled the air to see the king accompanying his daughter to the long-anticipated wedding ceremony.

Over the year she'd received dozens of long emails with pictures from Stefano while they'd discussed the plans for the wedding in the cathedral and the festivities afterward at the palace.

She'd asked him questions about his locations and work. He'd explained a lot of technical things about mining she'd enjoyed. His descriptions of the people and mountains painted pictures that lived with her. Lanza hadn't counted on him being such a satisfying letter writer, and she'd found herself eagerly looking forward to reading them when they came.

But they hadn't touched on their personal, intimate relationship yet. She was still anxious to talk to him about the *rules of engagement*. Those words had been dancing around in her head since his letter had arrived close to a year ago.

What had Stefano really meant? If only he'd explained, it might have helped her get through this ordeal without so much angst. Those words had sounded cold and unfeeling coming from a worldly man who'd managed to avoid a royal life until now. Now that they were about to exchange vows, her fraught nerves had made her too jumpy to concentrate on anything.

What she'd give to get out of the carriage and run for her life. Then she glanced at her father with his salt-and-pepper hair, who looked splendid despite the fact that he did move slower these days. The love in his eyes when he smiled at her helped her remember one of the reasons why she was going through with this farce of a marriage.

Her father had been living for this day for years and might be granted a longer life because she'd agreed to marry his best friend's only son now that Alberto was gone.

"You look so beautiful in all that silk and lace, my angel daughter."

"Thank you, *Papà*, but I'm not your angel." He'd always called her that, but since the day she'd learned her parents expected her to marry Stefano, she hadn't felt very angelic.

Through her mother, who talked constantly with Stefano's mother, Lanza had learned Stefano planned to whisk her away for a two-week honeymoon to a secret spot in the Caribbean. She now had a wardrobe of beachwear.

Two weeks alone in paradise.

"I'm going to miss you around the palace while you're on your honeymoon, my sweet girl."

She wasn't as sweet as her father thought. "I'll miss you, too. Today you look magnificent, like the king you are. I love you and I'm sorry abou—"

"Let's not talk about that day," he interrupted. "We were all beside ourselves. You've brought me joy your whole life and it's all in the past. Promise me you'll forget it."

Her eyes smarted. "If you can, then I will, too."

But she would never forget. By agreeing to marry Stefano, all hope for personal happiness had died. Her mind kept going back to the note he'd had couriered to her.

They were definitely doing something unprecedented.

Soon the closed carriage drew up in front of the steps of the fourteenth-century cathedral. One of the footmen opened the door. She held her bouquet of white roses and stephanotis as he helped her step out, giving the press an opportunity to see her in all her wedding finery and take pictures.

Her chestnut-colored hair had been swept back and cascaded beyond her shoulders. The lace veil draped over the pearl tiara worn by her great-great-grandmother fell to her chin in front and flowed down her back to meet the hem of her gown with its long train.

Her father got out behind her and accompanied her up the steps to the roar and cheers of the thousands of people filling the streets. Lanza's mother and sisters, along with her aunts, uncles and cousins, had already gone inside with the other dignitaries and waited in the pews. By now Prince Stefano's entire family from Umbriano, including their future queen and her young children, would have already entered and been seated.

Once inside the doors, Lanza heard the glorious organ music and choir, catching her off guard. She took a deep breath, realizing the moment had come when she had to pledge her life to a man who'd lost a brother, hated royal life and was as unhappy as Lanza.

The wedding march sounded, alerting her this was it. Her father turned to look at her. "Are you ready?"

No...

Like an automaton, she put her free hand on his left arm, and they walked into the Romanesque nave that was packed wall to wall with the invited guests turned out in elegant dress. The fascinators worn by the women made the scene resemble a garden even though it was winter.

With each step that took her closer to the altar where the cardinal stood resplendent in red and gold robes, her legs felt less substantial. Then she saw Stefano waiting in a magnificent royal suit of navy and gold braid. Across his chest from shoulder to waist he wore the bright blue sash of his office as Prince of the Realm of Umbriano.

At the funeral she'd hardly noticed him with everyone around. They'd all been in mourning. Lanza had been in such deep shock, she hadn't realized that over the years he'd grown taller than Alberto. Looking at him now, he probably stood six foot two and was built of rock-hard muscle.

A little closer and she gasped quietly. His burnished complexion reflected his work and travel in hot climates. Mesmerized, her gaze roved over his chiseled features set beneath dark brows and wavy black-brown hair. The boy had become a breathtaking man.

As the tabloids had claimed leading up to the marriage, he was a dashing male specimen. She suspected he had to shave twice a day and was more gorgeous than her idea of any prince in an old fairy tale.

Her heart tripped over itself. Stefano was going to be *her* husband. The man she would go to bed with and whose children she'd bear. She gripped her father's arm harder and continued walking until they reached the cardinal, who put out his arms.

"Come stand in front of me."

Stefano moved to Lanza's side. She let go of her father's arm and handed Donetta the flowers, then turned back to meet his dark, penetrating eyes. A thunderbolt passing through her body couldn't have been more electrifying. Shaken by emotions new to her and an instant awareness of him, she transferred her gaze to the cardinal, who opened with some prayers, before proceeding to the marriage ceremony.

"Stefano Amadeo Piero Casale, wilt thou have this woman to thy wedded wife, to live together according to God's law in the holy estate of matrimony? Wilt thou love her, comfort her, honor and keep her, in sickness and in health; and, forsaking all others, keep thee only unto her, so long as ye both shall live?"

"I will," he said in a deep voice Lanza felt resonate to her toes.

"Lanza Vittoria Immaculata Rossiano, wilt thou have this man to thy wedded husband, to live together according to God's law in the holy estate of matrimony? Wilt thou love him, comfort him, honor him, keep him, in sickness and in health; and, forsaking all others, keep thee only unto him, so long as ye both shall live?"

"I will."

"You will now exchange rings."

Stefano, not missing a heartbeat, reached for her left hand and slid a ring with the royal Umbriano crest on her finger. She in turn put the gold band with the Rossiano crest on his ring finger. She felt tense and wondered if he could tell. "In as much as Stefano and Lanza have consented together in holy wedlock, and have witnessed the same before God and this company, and thereto have given and pledged their troth either to other, and have declared the same by giving and receiving of a ring, and by joining of hands, I pronounce that they be man and wife together, in the name of the Father, and of the Son and of the Holy Ghost. Amen.

"You may kiss the bride, Your Highness."

A year ago Lanza had worn the black veil of mourning. Since then Stefano had been imagining this moment. When she'd approached him at the altar—a vision in white silk—her white lace veil had given him enticing glimpses of her lovely features and deep blue eyes. As he lifted it, what he hadn't counted on was her true classic beauty or the voluptuous shape of her mouth.

His heart pounded hard as he lowered his head to kiss her. Much as he wanted to taste her fully, he held back and only brushed his mouth against hers. The soft sweetness of her lips sent a sensation not unlike electricity through his body. The princess he'd met when she was just a young girl had grown into a breathtaking woman who was now his wife. *His wife!*

"We'll talk in the carriage," he whispered against the fragrant silky skin of her cheek before he lifted his head.

Organ music filled the cathedral while he took her hand in a firm grip. Donetta came forward to give her the flowers and they started down the aisle. He was now a married man who'd made promises to his new bride, who walked at his side. They made their way outside to the ringing of the cathedral bells, followed by bells ringing out all over the city.

He felt like they were part of a dream as he helped her into the same carriage he knew she'd ridden in with her father. Stefano climbed in and sat opposite her, hoping she'd meet his eyes. "This is where we have to wave at the crowd. They're eager to see the beautiful princess and take pictures."

"If the temperature keeps falling, maybe everyone will go home."

He studied her features. "You know they won't. This wedding has been anticipated for two years."

She nodded. "We're part of the fairy tale meant to be exciting for them, but by midnight it'll all be over and the real test of living will begin."

Stefano sat back. "I am guessing from that comment you received the message I sent you when we got engaged. But in all our emails, you never mentioned it."

She continued waving. "I'm sorry that I didn't. If you want to know the truth, it was like a breath of fresh air."

One dark brow lifted. "Why do you say that?"

"You indicated that there are ways to negotiate our situation. It gave me hope that you have something brilliant in mind. Alberto said you were born with the real brains in the family."

So saying, she turned to the windows on the other side of the carriage. For the next little while she fulfilled her part in acknowledging the crowds cheering and taking pictures.

They weren't really going to have a chance to talk properly today; that would have to wait till they left to go on their honeymoon. That time couldn't come soon enough for Stefano. He didn't want their marriage to start off with this kind of tension.

"Uh-oh!" she exclaimed. "Don't stop waving, *Signor* Casale. Alberto told me that's the name you go by at your many gold mines throughout the world. Time's not up yet. We only have to endure this display for the masses for a few more minutes."

The woman who'd sent him enchanting emails he'd thoroughly enjoyed was not in evidence right now. Soon the carriage arrived back at the fifteenth-century palace. She faced him with a smile. "All we must do now is endure this endless day a little longer."

The footman opened the door of the carriage, but Stefano got out first to help her. No matter her true feelings, whatever they were, he was determined to behave in every way like an adoring bridegroom, even arranging her veil and train. With her flowers in one hand, he grasped her other hand and they ascended the steps past the palace staff who'd assembled to welcome them.

He walked her through the rotunda where their families awaited them. After many hugs, she turned to him. "I'm going down the hall to freshen up, but I'll be back."

"Would you like me to go with you?"

"Thank you, but I won't be long."

"Then I'll wait right here for you."

"You don't have to."

His eyes searched hers. "Don't you know I want to?"

CHAPTER FOUR

STEFANO HAD SOUNDED like he'd meant it. Lanza went to the waiting room more confused over her feelings about him than ever before returning to the rotunda. He saw her coming and walked toward her.

"Are you all right?"

"Of course. Why do you ask?"

"You look a little pale."

"I'll be fine when I eat."

He cupped her elbow, and they joined the guests in the enormous ballroom decorated for their wedding feast. According to her mother, no expense had been spared to make this the most lavish affair since her father had been crowned king.

They sat at the head table with their royal parents on either side of them. Stefano couldn't have been more accommodating, seeing to her every need as they ate. His behavior and noble bearing were impeccable.

The way he waited on her and was so attentive, she had the impression he'd convinced everyone this was a match made in heaven. She was bewildered because deep inside her she knew he hadn't wanted this marriage.

Her father gave the first toast. "To my new son-in-law, Stefano, who has made me and my wife the happiest people in Domodossola, except for our daughter. Her radiant countenance speaks for itself. To the bride and groom and a lifetime of joy!"

Everyone drank from their champagne glasses. Stefano touched his flute to hers with a smile. "I'm relieved to see more color in your cheeks."

"I didn't realize how hungry I was."

"Is there anything else I can get you?"

"No, thank you."

This should be the most exciting, thrilling night of her life, but Stefano didn't love her and she wasn't foolish enough to pretend otherwise.

At that point Stefano's father stood on his feet. "Victor took the words right out of my mouth. My wife and I are overjoyed. Over the years we've been delighted to anticipate the day when Princess Lanza would become our daughter-in-law. Now it is here. To Stefano and Lanza. We couldn't ask for a greater blessing."

Again, Stefano touched her glass with his and they sipped their champagne. Then to her surprise, he stood up. Looking down at her he said, "Lanza? Will you stand up with me?"

After she got to her feet, he slid his arm beneath her veil to get it around her waist and pulled her next to him. "I'm the luckiest of men today. There's no bride to compare to her. Wouldn't you all agree?" His comment produced cheers and clapping.

Warmth filled her cheeks. When she looked at her sisters sitting next to her mother and father, she knew what to say in response. "With three daughters, my parents have waited a long time for a son. Who better than the son of my father's best friend, a man he reveres?"

Then everyone got to their feet for one more toast. King Basilio sent her a special smile that seemed to come from his heart. Then everyone sat down.

She watched her father get up again. "The fireworks are starting. We'd like to invite everyone to go through the side doors of the ballroom to the balcony. Stefano? If you and Lanza will lead the way. The crowds are waiting for you."

He helped her up, and they walked together. On their way out in the chilly night air he pulled her close again. "You made my father very happy just now."

"They're all happy," she murmured back. Without waiting for a response, she moved ahead of him to the balcony railing.

The sight of their winter wonderland kingdom waving and cheering at them from the lighted palatial estate came as another emotional moment, like the one when she'd stepped inside the cathedral and heard the magnificent music of the organ and choir. How sad their marriage was such a travesty of a proper wedding.

Stefano joined her and found her hand, holding it with enough strength that she couldn't shake it off. Of course she wouldn't have.

Before everyone got too cold, they went inside and cut the eight-tiered wedding cake. Her awareness of him was growing so strong, she could hardly eat any of it. Lanza despised her own weakness for being vulnerable to anything to do with him.

His dark gaze found hers. "Our bags have already been taken out to the limo. We need to leave soon to make our flight. I'll meet you in the rotunda in a half hour."

"Maybe that's possible for you. But it's obvious you've never had to get yourself out of a wedding dress with thirty tiny buttons holding it up. My sisters will do their best."

She nodded to Donetta and Fausta, who left their parents to accompany her out of the ballroom to her suite on the second floor of the palace. On the bed, Serena had laid out the designer eggshell-colored two-piece suit with lace on the hems of the sleeves.

After they helped Lanza remove the veil and tiara, they turned her around. "How do you feel now?" Fausta wanted to know as she worked on the bottom half of buttons. Donetta stood on her other side to undo the top ones.

"I'm so exhausted, I have no idea how I feel. Tomorrow when I'm lying on a beach, I'll be better able to tell you."

"Good grief, he's handsome!"

"You can say that again," Donetta commented. "The women must be crazy about him."

Fausta nodded. "But he's out of circulation now."

"One can hope."

"Oh, Donetta, what a thing to say."

Lanza didn't like hearing any of it and stepped out of her gown. She didn't want to believe Donetta's teasing comment. He was her husband now. "Thanks for helping me."

Wanting to avoid talk, she gathered up her new underwear and hurried into the bathroom for a quick shower. Afterward, she swept her hair back on her head and secured it with a pearl comb. It matched her pearl earrings and the single pearl on a gold chain Stefano had sent her ahead of time as a wedding gift.

She fastened it around her neck, touched up her lipstick, then came back out to dress in the suit. Once she'd put on her high heels, she slipped on the new beige cashmere coat that fell above the knee and tied with a sash at the waist.

Her gaze flew to the clock by her bed. She'd already been gone an hour. Lanza reached for the cream-colored leather handbag and kissed her sisters.

"You look beautiful," they both said at the same time.

"Thank you. See you in two weeks."

They caught up to her at the door. Donetta eyed her with concern. Fausta looked just as worried. "Are you all right?"

She stared at them, deciding to be honest. "No, and I'm not sure I ever will be again, but you two already know that. I won't be throwing the bouquet, and you both know why." Donetta didn't want to get married. One day Fausta would find her man of the people, but unfortunately their parents could intervene and turn their wishes around.

Lanza blew them another kiss and hurried through the palace and down the stairs. The girls, uncharacteristically quiet, followed her.

Stefano stood out from everyone at the bottom of the elegant staircase beneath the rotunda. Her striking new husband had changed into an elegant dark gray suit, shirt and tie, reminding her of a highly successful, sophisticated CEO. He wore an overcoat close to the color of hers and was surrounded by their families, who were waiting to wave them off.

"Here she comes," her mother said as both her parents rushed toward her and gave her a hug. "You look perfectly lovely, darling."

"Thanks, *Mamà*."

"You'll never know how happy we are for you," her father murmured.

He was wrong. She knew exactly how they felt, but her dad looked weary tonight. It had been such a long day. Lanza had to pray that if nothing else came of it, this marriage would add a few years to his life.

She hugged him extra hard. "Relax and enjoy this time now that the wedding is over, *Papà*. We'll be back before you know it."

"Lanza?"

She let go of her father and walked over to him. "Yes, *Signor* Casale?" she said in a quiet aside. When she saw his slight grimace, it brought a smile to her face.

He put his arm through hers and they left the palace in the biting cold for the limo waiting below. After they got inside and the chauffeur drove them around the drive to the road in the distance, Stefano turned to her.

"I'm curious to know the real reason why you insist on calling me *Signor* Casale." He sat next to her rather than opposite her like they'd done in the carriage.

"I'm sorry and won't do it again. One of my favorite novels is *Pride and Prejudice*. In the story, the mother of the four Bennett daughters always speaks to her husband as Mr. Bennett. She never uses his first name, never calls him honey or darling or sweetheart or dearest. She's absolutely hilarious and I laugh every time."

"You read it often?" He wasn't able to hide his surprise.

"I've read it a lot in my life. Are you a reader?"

"When I have time."

"What's one of your favorite novels?"

"I'll have to think about that."

She let the comment go and crossed her legs at the ankles. "While we're alone, let me thank you for the lovely necklace you sent me. I'm wearing it now."

"I noticed. It's made from the gold of one of our mines in Umbriano."

"That was very thoughtful. I'll treasure it. What about the pearl?"

"I purchased it in Japan a long time ago." It looked like a pregnant pear.

"I can always replace it with something you would like better, perhaps a diamond?"

"Don't you dare." She touched it with her fingers. "I'm sure there's not another pearl like this one in existence." Actually, she loved its unique shape.

She had a gift for him, but it was packed in her luggage.

Before long they reached the airport and were driven to the area where the private planes landed. In a minute they arrived outside the royal jet with the King of Umbriano's insignia.

The steward came down the steps of the jet and loaded their luggage. Stefano got out of the limo to help Lanza. Cupping her elbow, he walked up the steps with her into the luxurious interior and introduced her.

"My name is Corso. I'm honored to meet you, Your Highness. It's a privilege."

"I'm very happy to meet you."

Stefano led her to the club compartment and helped her off with her coat.

She felt those dark, probing eyes rove over her as she sat down and fastened her seat belt.

"You look stunning in that suit."

Lanza wondered how many women he'd said that to in the past, but she needed to stop thinking about what had gone on before. The last thing she wanted to act like was a jealous wife.

"Your gift gave it the touch it needed."

The engines fired and she saw the fasten seat belt sign flash. He sat across from her and buckled up. She knew he was anxious to get going. That was fine with her, but Lanza couldn't imagine anything more nerve-racking than going to a beach with him. She barely knew him, and part of her wished this was a bad dream and she'd wake up to find herself alone.

"If you'd like something to eat or drink, I'll tell Corso."

"Nothing for me, but thank you."

Exhausted after such a long day, she closed her eyes, anxious to fall asleep and avoid the inevitable small talk neither of them had any desire to engage in. By the time she awakened, they would have landed somewhere in the Caribbean.

But it seemed like she'd barely dropped off when she heard the ding of the fasten seat belt sign and opened her eyes. They couldn't possibly have been in the air very long. She could feel increasing turbulence. Lanza darted him a glance. "Do you know why we had to land?"

He eyed her intently. "Unbeknownst to our families, I changed our honeymoon destination and instructed the pilot to fly us to Umbriano."

The jet was starting to descend against strong winds. This part of the Alps was known for its fierce weather. "Apparently right into the heart of winter," she drawled. "This must be why you told me to hurry."

"I heard a storm front was moving in fast."

"I presume you had no taste for a beach honeymoon, either, but our families will continue to fantasize. This is *their* wedding day, after all, the one they've dreamed of since we were children."

She undid her seat belt, but before she could get up, Corso came in carrying a pair of women's leather lace-up boots he handed to Stefano.

Her husband had already gotten to his feet and put on his over-coat. "You'll need to remove your high heels so they won't get ruined in the snow."

"Thank you. You've managed to think of everything." As soon as she'd taken them off, he put them inside his coat pockets. The man was full of surprises.

While she tied the boots, Corso took their luggage out of the plane. Stefano helped her into her coat and together they walked to the entrance and down the steps. Snow had been falling, spattered by the wind.

An attractive man with blue eyes and dark blond hair she'd met at the wedding reception stood outside an all-terrain vehicle. Right now he was wearing a ski hat and parka. The steward loaded their bags at the back.

Stefano turned to her. "Lanza? You remember my very best friend, Enzo Perino."

"Of course." They shook hands.

His eyes played over her features in male admiration. "I couldn't be more honored, Your Highness. You were a vision today when you walked down the aisle in the cathedral with your father. Stefano is the luckiest of men."

Hardly... But for some reason she liked his friend on sight.

"Thank you, Enzo. Please call me Lanza."

He flashed Stefano a smile before opening the rear door for them. "You're going to freeze to death if you don't get in where it's warm."

How funny. Other than her coat, she hadn't brought a stitch of winter clothing with her.

Stefano followed her inside and shut the door. It felt good to get out of the freezing wind. He helped her find the seat belt so she could fasten it. Every time he brushed against her, she smelled the scent of the soap he'd used in the shower and she was increasingly aware of his potent male aura. Her attraction to him was blinding her to the pragmatic reason why they'd married.

Enzo got behind the wheel. Before starting out, he said, "I'm very aware of my precious cargo and will drive as safely as I can."

That was a very thoughtful thing for him to say considering Alberto had been killed on a winter road.

They headed out of the airport. Obviously, their flight had landed just in time. Snow had started falling and pelted the windshield. They'd barely made it here ahead of the storm.

She assumed they were headed for a hotel, but she couldn't have been more wrong when she saw the turnoff he'd taken for the mountains.

"Where are we going?" she asked in a quiet aside.

"Home to my chalet. We'll be there within forty-five minutes."

"So you had a home here when you returned to Umbriano after your various trips?"

"For the last ten years, yes."

"That's one secret not leaked to the public. It means you were given your own hideaway at eighteen along with your freedom." Every young prince dying to be released from the royal trappings should be so blessed.

"Actually, I purchased it with my own earnings."

Lanza swallowed hard at her unintentional gaffe. "Did Alberto envy you?"

She had to wait for his answer. "Alberto loved it as much as I did. My wedding present to him was that he bring you to the chalet for your honeymoon after you were married. It was going to be a secret from everyone else."

His response was so unexpected and touching, she could hardly breathe. Alberto had been planning to bring her to Stefano's hideaway in the mountains?

Lanza wished she hadn't brought up his brother's name while he was still grieving.

Unsettled, she leaned forward. "Enzo? Did you spend time at the chalet with Stefano when you two were young?"

"All the time. We skied, mountain climbed, hunted, fished, camped out and had parties."

"I'll bet. Sounds like heaven."

"But as we got older we haven't had as much time to do that as we've been busy pursuing our careers."

"What kind of work do you do?"

"I went to university and got my degree in finance. Since then I've worked in my father's bank. Lately I've taken over more and more of his duties because his health is failing."

"How wonderful for him to have a son like you."

Stefano would be doing the same thing for her father. *But not Stefano's own father...* Though she knew his sister would be queen one day, she wondered how King Basilio really felt about losing his firstborn son this way. Was Stefano conflicted, as well?

"It's very generous of you to drive us to the chalet this late, Enzo."

"After all the things Stefano has done for me in my life, I'll never be able to repay him." She heard real affection in his tone. Stefano remained quiet.

The snow continued relentlessly as they climbed in altitude to the higher peaks. Enzo was being very careful. Few cars were on the treacherous mountain road, the kind where Alberto had lost his life.

She sat back, growing more anxious because they'd be alone soon in his private home away from civilization.

Before long Enzo turned off the main road and drove along what seemed like a path lined with snow-swept pines winding for several miles. Eventually, he pulled up to a massive gate that swung open electronically. He drove on through and around to an alpine chalet whose roof was covered by at least two feet of snow, but she could barely see the outline.

Stefano got out to help her. She was glad he'd thought ahead and had brought her new boots to put on. The snow was deep. Under the fresh layer coming down lay more snow from other storms. Enzo took the bags from his car, and they entered Stefano's secret domain.

A light went on. The lower level housed everything; shovels, hunting gear, skis, snowshoes, camping gear, snowboards, a snow-shoveling machine, a generator, a freezer and a washer and dryer. Stefano could live here self-contained.

"Shall we go upstairs?"

Lanza followed him and Enzo to the next floor where several lamps went on. She was struck immediately by the light wood floors and rafters. On one wall she saw an enormous fireplace set behind glass, lending the vaulted room a chic yet rustic elegance. Stefano turned it on so the flames lit up the interior. Instant heat.

Attractive twin couches in a claret color faced each other in front of a low, large square coffee table with a colorful ceramic pot. It was probably from Mexico where she'd heard one of his gold mines was located.

On one wall stood a massive breakfront with books on two shelves. There were many small pictures of Stefano's family on a third shelf. The bottom one contained magazines and board games.

She turned around to view the floor-to-ceiling windows that would give a spectacular mountain outlook during the day. There was a refectory-style table and chairs off the kitchen with its wood cabinets and slate floors.

Enzo had disappeared down a hallway with their luggage. When he reappeared, he paused at the stairway. "I wish the two of you every happiness and a wonderful honeymoon. Now I've got to get back to my own wife."

"Thank you for everything, Enzo."

"My pleasure."

"Be careful going down the canyon. That's a heavy snow out there."

He smiled. "We're used to it, aren't we, Stefano?"

Her husband nodded. "I'll walk you out." Before he left the room, he turned to Lanza. "I'm sure you must be exhausted. Your bedroom is down the hall to the left. Just so you know, earlier this month I asked Carla to buy you some winter clothes. When I returned to Umbriano a few days ago, I put them in your closet."

"That was very thoughtful. Thank you."

He nodded. "If you're hungry or thirsty, make yourself at home in the kitchen. I have things to do so I'll see you in the morning and we'll talk then." The two men disappeared down the stairs.

In the letter Stefano had couriered to her a year ago, he'd warned Lanza there'd be no wedding night. She'd taken him at his word and there'd been no mention of it during their exchange of emails.

While they were gone, Lanza explored the rest of the chalet. There were two bedrooms with light wood floors, rugs and ensuite bathrooms. Her bags had been put in what was obviously a guest bedroom with a queen-size bed and dresser. A TV sat on top of it. She removed her coat and boots, putting them in the closet where she saw the winter clothes.

After finding a pair of flats in one of her cases, she put them on and decided to do the rest of her own unpacking in a little while.

Curious to see everything, she went across the hall. Stefano's bedroom showed signs of being permanently occupied with a cubby full of various winter wear. He had his own TV and radio. A mural that showed the Casale gold mines around the world took up one wall. She intended to study it, but not when he was around.

The desk on the other wall contained a state-of-the-art computer and printer, ledgers, mining books, everything he needed for his work. His bags had been placed at the end of the king-size bed.

Afraid to be caught trespassing in his thoroughly masculine domicile, she hurried back to the living room and wandered into the kitchen. The fridge appeared stocked with food and drinks. Over the past few days Stefano must have been busy getting all this ready.

She reached for a cola and walked back to the main room to examine some of the books. *The Thirty-Nine Steps* by John Buchan caught her attention. She wondered if Stefano had read it recently, or even read it at all. She took it to the bedroom with her and shut the door.

How bizarre to be alone with a strange man who'd only been her husband for about nine hours.

Needing to unwind, she opened her cases and unpacked the

rest of her clothes. In one of the pockets she'd packed her wrapped gift for Stefano. She pulled it out and put it on the dresser to give him in the morning.

When everything was done, she took a shower, then brushed out her hair. Eventually, she was ready for bed. Though she'd brought reading material in her luggage, she decided to read the book she'd taken from the living room.

Once she'd climbed under the covers, she turned on the bedside lamp and started to read. Soon she found it hard to concentrate because she kept listening for sounds that Stefano had gone to bed, too. Inside the chalet it was quiet as a tomb. Beyond these walls the wind moaned and snow pelted the bedroom windows.

She turned off the lamp and snuggled deeper under the covers. In one way Lanza had never felt so isolated and alone, but in truth she loved it. Her life had always been planned out. Her parents had done her thinking for her. The wedding that had been organized for a year was over and now she was a married woman.

To the wrong prince.

But her parents were happy. So were his. Perhaps it meant her father's life had been preserved for a few years longer. Her thoughts wandered. Alberto would have brought her here for their honeymoon. Stefano was attempting to fulfill all his younger brother's wishes.

Before she fell asleep she wondered what her new husband would have wanted and done if he were in love with her.

When morning came Lanza walked over to the window. Snow was still falling, revealing a white world. She checked her watch: 9:40 a.m. What a surprise! She rarely slept late.

Slipping into a new pair of black wool pants and a red sweater, both of which fit her to perfection, all she had to do was fix her hair. It fell from a side part she gathered at the nape with an elastic band. After applying lipstick, she reached for Stefano's small gift and left the bedroom.

On the way down the hall she smelled coffee. She had no idea how long he'd been up because there'd been no sound. Last night she hadn't been hungry. This morning she was starving and headed for the kitchen.

Lanza found him cooking what she considered a full American

breakfast. Eggs, bacon, toast. Why not? He'd received his education in Colorado. After exchanging emails for the past year, she'd learned Stefano had spent a lot of time in the States at his gold mine in South Dakota.

This morning he'd dressed in a navy hoodie and jeans that molded his powerful thighs. His five-o'clock shadow and disheveled hair added to his disturbing male presence. Her unwanted attraction to him was growing. Perhaps he'd been outside already and had worked up an appetite.

"Good morning, Stefano."

CHAPTER FIVE

STEFANO HAD BEEN wondering when his wife would awaken and make an appearance. He couldn't prevent his gaze from traveling over her beautiful face and curvaceous body, not missing one inch of her. Her long chestnut hair against the red sweater took his breath.

"Buon giorno, sposa mia."

She smiled. "You look like you slept well. What can I do to help?"

"Our food is ready. Come in the dining room and we'll eat. I've already fixed our coffee." He carried their plates and put them on the table. She followed him and placed her gift next to his food before sitting opposite him.

He eyed it with curiosity. "Am I to open this now?"

"Whenever you'd like, but I'm afraid it's not like the gift you gave me because it has no monetary value."

"Now you've intrigued me. I think I'll wait until later."

She spooned sugar into her coffee after pouring some from the carafe. Without waiting for him, she dug in and helped herself to two more helpings of bacon, which pleased him.

"This breakfast is delicious. I could get used to it. You're welcome to do all the cooking for as long as we're here."

He stopped munching on his toast. "We'll be leaving tomorrow."

"Why?"

"Because it occurred to me you might not like it up here. Alberto wasn't entirely sure, either. In that case, I've planned to drive us around some of the Mediterranean countries you mentioned you hadn't visited in your emails."

"That's very considerate of you." She finished eating everything and eventually sat back to eye him through her dark lashes. "You're an awesome bridegroom. Feed your bride an excellent meal before doing anything else. But before we discuss how to spend our honeymoon, I'd like to hear you lay out the rules of engagement."

Her response let him know she'd not forgotten that message he'd sent her a year ago. But he was in an entirely different place now.

"That wasn't my best choice of words at the time. I wish I'd put it a different way. Let's agree this situation wasn't what either of us had anticipated. For want of a better word, I see our marriage as one of convenience for a way to begin."

Her eyes pulsed a deep blue. "Didn't that quaint expression get thrown out decades ago?"

"Possibly," he murmured, wishing he hadn't used that word, either.

"Please go on and explain the details. I like the sound of it if it means we can do whatever we want and open the door of our cage to unknown possibilities."

He took a long time to finish drinking his coffee. "Not all the time. When there are public duties, we'll have to do them together."

"Naturally, but you're the one my father is going to lean on, not me," she emphasized. "He doesn't believe a woman should rule. I'm afraid you've gotten the brunt."

Stefano rubbed the back of his neck in frustration. "There'll be times when I'll have to be gone for long periods."

"You mean that you'll leave to do your engineering work and come back each time to rule when you've finished your business. In that case, when you're away I'll be able to indulge myself without anyone telling me I can't. This could work."

He frowned. "You do understand what I'm saying. For the time being we'll be living in separate bedrooms."

"Of course. I took that for granted the moment I read your missive a year ago about not having a wedding night. In fact, I assumed as much before I told my parents I would accept your proposal. How long do you see our separate bedrooms lasting?"

If she only knew he didn't want separate bedrooms. He already desired her. "Shall we say until we've become comfortable with each other?"

"That sounds reasonable. I'll admit that marrying you has already given me the freedom I didn't think I'd ever have."

"What are you insinuating?"

"Alberto and I were trapped and understood our duty." Stefano was stunned. Had she honestly felt that way when she'd been engaged to his brother? "But marriage to you under the rules you've set out means we'll both be able to do whatever we desire to a greater degree, right?"

He didn't like what she was saying. Not at all. "At some juncture we'll have to talk about having children."

She sat back. "That's true. As you said, we need time to become comfortable with each other."

"Alberto's death changed many things for me. I find I'm looking forward to having children with you."

"Even though you gave up the royal life at eighteen?"

Stefano cocked his head. "But I took it back again to marry you. Sometimes people and circumstances change."

She eyed him over her coffee cup. "If we do this thing right, it will let us off the hook in more ways than one, *if* you know what I mean."

"I'm not sure I do," he said.

"While you're off doing gold-mining business around the world, I can be busy carrying out my charity works, which are considerable."

"Alone?"

She stared at him. "What are you implying?"

"You know what I'm asking. Has there been another important man in your life? It would be understandable, of course. I just want to be clear about where we stand."

"Only Alberto." Hearing that admission didn't help Stefano's understanding. "I'm afraid I'm one of a dying breed. Your parents and mine made sure I'm pure as the proverbial snow burying us alive as we speak.

"Alberto was my betrothed for a year. And, according to him, you were never bound to one woman. In case you only suspected it, Stefano, he adored you. The only time he truly showed passion was when he talked about you."

Her mention of Alberto had again reached a private region of his soul. Before he could say another word, she got up from the table. After taking her dishes to the counter in the kitchen, she returned to the dining room.

"I need to be excused for a few minutes, but I'll be back. Maybe now would be a good time for you to open your wedding present. When you see what's inside, you'll understand why it really should belong to you. During the twelve months we were engaged, it's the only thing Alberto ever sent to me."

Surprised that Alberto had anything to do with Lanza's wedding present to him, Stefano was more bewildered than ever. Worse, he hated that his eyes lingered on her womanly figure as she disappeared to the other part of the chalet.

He'd never spent a more uncomfortable hour with a woman in his life, and she was his wife! The fact that she had an allure that appealed to him only compounded his frustration.

Unable to concentrate on anything, he got up from the table and cleared the rest of the dishes. After he'd cleaned up the kitchen, he walked back to the dining room.

Her gift lay on the table unopened. He couldn't imagine what she might have given him relating to his brother. The youngest daughter of King Victor could be unpredictable, so it seemed.

When he realized he was making too much of it, he undid the gold paper around the flat, three-by-four-inch box. As he lifted the lid, he saw his own face looking up at him. The black-and-white photo took him back in time. He remembered sending it to Alberto, who was always after him to send him pictures.

A friend had taken it while he was in Kenya at the mine. He drew it from the box. There was a note folded beneath it. He smoothed it out.

Dear Lanza,
After I returned home from my last visit to Domodossola,
I decided to send you this photo of Stefano at twenty-two

because you said you wanted to get to know me better and asked me what I treasured most.

As I told you, I've always missed him and wished he were here. No one ever had a better brother.

I'll never stop loving him and hope this helps you to understand the sadness you sometimes glimpse in me. I've always considered him my other half. Life has never been quite the same without him.

Alberto

Stefano closed his eyes tightly, squeezing the paper in his hand. Gripped by emotions churning inside him, he remained there for countless minutes. When he could function, he dashed down the stairs for his ski outfit and gloves. The need to be alone propelled him outside into the storm, which hadn't abated. He was surprised it had gone on this long.

The deep snow made it difficult to walk, but he was so churned up, nothing mattered. He kept going for several hours, working off the adrenaline surging through him.

He would never have credited Lanza with enough sensitivity to give him a priceless treasure like the one in the box. Though he'd believed his parents, the note and photo to Lanza was further verification that everything they'd told him about his younger brother's desire for Stefano to be free was true.

He found himself suffering all over again for Alberto's willingness to rule while Stefano was allowed to wander the globe doing exactly what he wanted. Stefano had missed his brother, too, so much at times he'd wondered if his freedom had been worth it.

Where Lanza was concerned, he felt remorse for insinuating that she might have been unfaithful to Alberto. What in the hell had prompted him to use words that made her feel like he was treating her as an enemy with that couriered message? She'd been as much of a victim as he had.

Guilt plagued him over his behavior. He'd made her feel that she was trapped in a loveless, sexless marriage and could never have his heart because he hadn't wanted to be a royal.

During their conversation he'd meant it when he'd told her he was looking forward to having children with her. If she hadn't acted excited at the prospect, it was because she'd been guarding herself with good reason. He realized he'd done a lot of damage with his words. Those emails were a paltry excuse for the time alone they'd needed. She had every right to think of him as a beast.

While he'd been out walking in the snow, he'd been contemplating a plan to make her happy. If she wanted freedom, they would work out an arrangement.

Who was she, really?

The woman who'd exchanged vows with him yesterday had the face of an angel and eyes the color of a deep blue fjord. But after the conversation they'd exchanged at breakfast this morning—which had turned him inside out—he couldn't get her off his mind.

Had Lanza been grief-stricken at his brother's funeral, or had it been an act? Stefano would give anything to know if the wife he'd only been married to for twenty-four hours was the same woman Alberto had talked to over the year they'd been betrothed.

Enzo's words to him at the bank a year ago hadn't left his thoughts. *Let her know before you're married that you plan to be your own person and continue doing the mining work you love while you help her father govern. It'll mean you'll be apart from her for long periods. Give her time to adjust to that fact, know what I mean?*

Stefano's best friend had turned out to give him the wrong advice. That wasn't Enzo's fault. Stefano had been wrong to follow it and was the only one to blame for making Lanza feel insecure about a marriage forced on her.

To his shock it was already late afternoon by the time he made it back to the chalet. He'd been gone much longer than he'd realized and imagined he looked like the abominable snowman. But he didn't have to worry about Lanza, who hadn't been concerned how long he'd been gone, nor had she rushed downstairs even if she'd heard him come in.

When he removed his gear and eventually went upstairs, he saw her engrossed in a book on one of the couches facing the fireplace. She looked so enticing he wanted to lie down and take her in his arms.

To his chagrin there was no sign of a hysterical wife who was out of her mind with worry because she'd been left alone too long in a strange place and felt unprotected. Stefano had the deep impression she didn't know what time it was and didn't care. Again, it was all his fault. He needed to change things—and quickly.

He walked down the hall to his bedroom to freshen up. Before he joined her, he went to the closet for his overcoat. The pockets still held her high heels. He picked them up and placed them inside her bedroom door.

An odd sensation passed through him when he thought of her standing on them throughout their entire wedding day. She stood five feet four, but they'd made her taller. Taking a deep breath, he had to admit he'd found her exquisite with that lace veil covering her features in an almost seductive way.

No doubt Alberto had been attracted to her from the beginning. That would explain why it hadn't been hard to go along with the betrothal. Stefano couldn't help but wonder if Lanza had been physically drawn to his brother. Alberto, who resembled their mother, had enjoyed girlfriends behind the scenes before becoming engaged to Lanza.

Irritated because he was dwelling too much on the two of them, he headed for the living room. His wife had curled up on one end of the couch with a throw blanket covering her.

"Is that a book you brought with you?"

She turned her head to look at him with a passive gaze. "No. One of yours. It's a good spy novel."

"I'm glad you're enjoying it. In truth, I didn't mean to be gone so long."

A small smile lit her lips. "This is your world. For the last month all you've done is get ready for our wedding. But it's over at last. You can relax for a little while and do what you want from here on out. I know I'm loving the freedom."

There was that word *freedom* again. It had driven him away from his family. Now it was driving him and his new bride apart if he didn't take steps to make their marriage work.

"Are you hungry?"

She shook her head. "I ate earlier, but I imagine you are and know exactly what you're going to fix. As I told you earlier, you're a great cook."

His hands curled into fists, not because of her remarks, but because of his earlier behavior toward her. "Before any more time passes, let me thank you for the gift. The note Alberto wrote to you is priceless to me. I'll always treasure it."

"You and your brother clearly had an exceptional relationship. For you to take his place and marry me is beyond extraordinary. What you've done is almost unbelievable."

Lanza was wrong. Alberto had laid down his life for his brother, who'd been spoiled and hadn't thought about anyone but himself. But what was almost unbelievable was Lanza's willingness to marry Stefano.

"What's extraordinary to me is that you accepted my proposal. For what it's worth, you've made me very happy, Lanza."

Her eyes finally looked away, but not before he saw them light up. Hopefully, she'd believed him.

"Tomorrow morning Enzo will be here to take us down to the city. From there we'll leave and start our trip. After ten days we'll return to Domodossola."

She sat up. "I have an even better idea. Why don't you plan to go where you want while I visit Zia Ottavia in Rome? She invited me to come at the wedding. I promise I won't tell a soul." So saying, she went back to her novel.

He'd never been dismissed before. That was what it felt like. But in truth, he'd been the one to set the rules. Damn if she hadn't taken him at his word on everything, but this was going to change. He planned to change the rules until she welcomed him in her arms and her bed.

After making some sandwiches and coffee, he disappeared down the hall to his bedroom for the night. A ton of work had piled up while he'd been getting ready for his marriage. He dug in and arranged for his next travel plans to include the Casale mine in South America.

But to his chagrin, he had a devil of a time staying focused on his work. He kept replaying her unexpected remarks in his head. It wasn't as much what she said as the tone of her delivery. In his gut he knew that somewhere deep inside her lovely facade lived the real Lanza. He was convinced that neither he nor Alberto had ever met her.

* * *

Lanza woke up the next morning to discover sunshine had filled the bedroom. Loving the light, she scrambled out of bed and padded over to the window. A blue sky had chased away the blizzard.

Glorious, dazzling snow resembling trillions of diamonds covered Stefano's playground. That was what it was, and secretly she loved this hideaway of his. Wouldn't every man or woman kill to live in such splendid isolation? This was her childhood dream come true. She had always fantasized about having freedom from her royal life. And here there was no one dogging her footsteps or telling her what she could and couldn't do.

More than anything she wanted to go out and play in the scrumptious white stuff no human had touched. She'd give anything to stay longer. If only Enzo weren't coming. Nothing sounded worse than having to leave on a driving trip to fill time when they had paradise right here.

If she only could stay, Lanza would borrow some of Stefano's winter clothes and fix them so they'd fit. Luckily, he'd bought her boots. In her dreams she'd go outside for hours and have a blast. Too bad that wasn't going to happen.

Knowing that Enzo could be here at any moment, she showered and put on another sweater and pair of wool pants. Once she'd done her hair and makeup, she made her bed and packed her bags. It had surprised her that she'd found her high heels inside the door when she'd gone to bed last night. She smiled when she remembered Stefano putting them in his elegant coat pockets.

With everything done, she reached for her coat and carried her cases down the hall to the living room. There was no sign of Stefano, but she noticed that his cases had been placed near the stairs. She put her things there, too. Maybe he was outside waiting for Enzo.

Lanza walked into the kitchen that looked spotless. She reached for a small apple in the bowl on the counter. While she ate it, she wandered over to the living room windows. Once again her breath caught at the beauty of the Alps in winter. Then a noise from below caused her to turn around. She saw her husband walk into the room with a concerned expression.

"*Buon giorno*, Stefano."

His gaze traveled over her in that way that told her he missed nothing. It made her feel fluttery inside.

"*Buon giorno*, Lanza."

"I'm all packed and ready to go. Has Enzo arrived?"

He shook his dark head. "He's late and there's no cell phone service. The storm must have knocked it out along with the electricity. There's no email, either."

So *that was* what was wrong. But the news couldn't have made her happier. "How long have you been outside waiting?"

"About an hour. I walked to the gate in case he couldn't get in and shoveled, but I didn't see him. There were no cars going in either direction."

"I'm sure he'll be here as soon as he can. Have you eaten yet?"

"No. I'd planned to take you to brunch after we got back to the city."

He had no idea how delighted she was to have to stay here longer. "Since we don't know how long we'll have to wait for him, I'll fix us some frittata." Lanza loved an omelet eaten with the kind of crusty Italian bread he had on hand. "You have a generator, right?"

He blinked. "You noticed—"

"I can even cook when I have to."

The first real smile she'd seen broke out on his handsome face. So...food played an important part in his life, *if* he didn't have to make it. Or maybe he did like to cook, having been on his own all these years.

"I'll go downstairs and turn it on." Soon she heard the sound of the generator. They had power.

She removed her coat and walked through to the kitchen to put her apple core in the wastebasket. Next, she made coffee. After finding a bowl and pan, she reached for eggs and other ingredients out of the fridge to start their meal. Before long she'd made large, fluffy ham and cheese omelets cooked in butter.

Because he'd stocked the fridge with items for salad, she added mushrooms, red peppers and chives. Once everything was ready, she prepared two plates that overflowed with chunks of the bread and put them on the table.

Stefano appeared in time to carry the coffee and silverware to the dining room. He eyed the food. "These look fabulous."

"The palace kitchen staff taught me and my sisters how to cook from the time we were little."

They both started to eat. His food disappeared in a hurry. "They taught you well. This is the best omelet I've ever tasted."

"Thank you. You want me to make you another one?"

"Would you?"

They were good if she said so herself. "I want another one, too. I'm starving."

Quickly, she went to the kitchen and whipped up another batch. He brought their plates to the stove, and she slid the cooked food onto them. "Uh-oh," she cried. He chuckled because one of the omelets almost slid away from her.

Lanza happened to look up at him and caught the intense way he was staring at her out of those beautiful black eyes. She quivered in reaction, wishing he would kiss her. She wanted to feel his mouth on hers. What was happening to her?

Back at the table they dug in once more. But she could only eat half of hers and shoved her plate toward him so he'd finish it, which he did, as well as the rest of the bread.

When she saw him pull out his cell phone to make a call, Lanza got up to clear the table and do the dishes. He followed her into the kitchen. "There's still no service."

"Do you often have blackouts here in winter?"

"No. This is very unusual." He put the leftover ingredients back in the fridge while she loaded the dishwasher. "I'll check to see if Enzo has emailed me."

"That's a good idea."

He returned to the kitchen a minute later. "No message yet. Something tells me Enzo won't be coming today."

CHAPTER SIX

YES! LANZA DIDN'T want to leave.

She was loving this time with Stefano and didn't want anything to change. "It's so beautiful out. Do you have some winter clothes for outside I could borrow?"

Her question seemed to take him by surprise. "There's a closet downstairs with my sister, Carla's, ski outfit and skis. She's a little taller than you, but I'm sure they'll fit. You're welcome to use them."

"Thank you."

"Come with me and I'll show you."

She trailed him to the lower level where he opened a closet with half a dozen outfits. He pulled out a woman's stylish white parka and black ski pants. He found her everything—gloves, a white ski hat, ski socks and boots.

Elated, she stepped into the pants and put on the socks and boots. Then she zipped up the parka and tugged the wool hat over her head. Everything fit just fine.

"You look perfect, Lanza." In the next instant he kissed her briefly on the mouth the way she'd wanted when they were in the kitchen. Her heart almost palpitated out of her parka.

While she pulled on her gloves, she looked over and noticed him getting on his ski clothes. "Where are you going?"

His eyes roved over her, setting her on fire. "Outside with you."

Her heart turned over. It hadn't occurred to her that he might come with her, though she wanted him to be with her with every atom of her body. "Have you ever been snowshoeing?"

"Never."

"This is the perfect kind of snow for it." He reached for the snowshoes. "Come outside with me and I'll help you put them on."

Lanza walked out into the brilliant sunlight, thrilled to be entering this glistening white world with Stefano, who'd just kissed her because he'd wanted to. Maybe some dreams could come true.

With her pulse racing, she leaned against his broad shoulder while he knelt down to center her boot in the binding. She never expected to be doing something this exciting with her handsome husband, who was taking amazing care of her.

He wrapped the heel strap around the back and through the buckle to tighten it. "Does that feel snug?"

"Yes."

"Now we'll do your other foot." Within a minute she was ready. "Keep your legs apart as you start to take steps. It requires more energy than you'll be used to, but it won't take long for you to work into a rhythm."

While she experimented, he went inside for his snowshoes and came back, shutting the door. In seconds he'd fastened his straps with a finesse that revealed years of experience. She gave him a covert glance because she couldn't stop herself from looking at him.

Her husband really was a gorgeous male no matter what he wore. Lanza found herself wildly attracted to him. She'd never expected this to happen and it shocked her that she wanted him so badly in every way.

Lanza took off across the front property of the chalet toward the white shrouded pines in the distance. Stefano caught up to her within seconds.

"Where's the fire?"

The last thing she wanted him to know was that his kiss had set off an explosion inside her. She wanted more. So much more. "I'm just excited to be out here making fresh tracks. It's a surreal feeling, as if we're on top of the world."

"I love it, too."

She could tell he did. In time, they came to the trees. Lanza kept going, marveling over the sculptures created by the wind and snow.

As they penetrated deeper, she thought she heard a yapping sound. She stopped walking and turned to Stefano. "Did you hear that?"

"I did." He reached out to grasp her arm with his gloved hand in a protective movement. "Don't go any farther."

"If I didn't know better, I would think it was a dog."

He shook his head. "Not a dog."

"Whatever it is, it sounds wounded."

"Wait here while I go look." Again, she was touched that he wanted to keep her safe. But the second he let go of her and went on ahead, she hurried to catch up. The yapping continued. Two hundred feet farther along, she saw him approach a small animal with red fur and a snout half buried in the snow beneath the boughs of a fat pine tree.

"Oh, Stefano, it's a little fox." She couldn't imagine it weighing more than seven or eight pounds.

"Stay back, Lanza."

"They're not dangerous and it can't hurt anybody. Listen. It's in pain." She pulled off her gloves so she could remove her parka. "Wrap it inside my coat to keep it warm and we'll take it back to the chalet."

"*Lanza—*" he muttered in exasperation.

"Don't worry about me. I'll be fine in this sweater. Please— we've got to help it before it's too late. It's so sweet."

To her relief he swaddled it like a baby and stood up. The fox kept yapping. She put her gloves back on and together they returned to the chalet as fast as they could go. "It must have gotten injured during the storm and couldn't go any farther."

When they reached the entrance, it was her turn to help Stefano. "I'll undo your snowshoes so you can take it inside to the fireplace." She got down and unfastened his straps so he was free to go in. It was a pleasure doing something for him when he was doing everything for her including taking care of the fox.

Another minute and she stepped out of her snowshoes. Then she carried all four of them inside and shut the door before going upstairs. Stefano had found a blanket where he laid the yapping fox and kept the parka over it to retain warmth. She turned on the switch that lit the fire, then knelt down beside him.

"The poor thing is frightened and needs food. I'll warm some milk. I could dip a cloth in it and then let it drip into his mouth. What do you think?"

"I think you're the most amazing woman I've ever known."

His compliment filled her with warmth. "Why do you say that?"

"Your kindness and lack of fear. Your concern for a wild animal. All of it."

"I could say exactly the same thing about you." Quickly, she hurried to the kitchen and warmed a pan of milk. After finding a clean washcloth, she carried the items over to the blanket.

"If you'll force its mouth open, I'll squeeze the liquid into it."

For the next hour they worked together feeding the fox, who eventually stopped yapping.

Stefano's eyes smiled into hers at last.

"He's still alive thanks to your quick thinking, Lanza. I believe you got a cup of milk down him."

"Him?"

A chuckle escaped his lips.

"It may not be enough. Don't tell your sister what we did with her parka, Stefano."

"When I brag about what you did, she'll never mind. If you'll stay right here, I'll find a box and make a bed for him. He'll feel safer and more comfortable if he's enclosed."

"Do you think he's been injured?"

"That's hard to tell, but I don't think so."

"Maybe he developed hypothermia."

"That's possible." After he disappeared down the stairs, she checked beneath the parka. The fox was warming up and stirred at the touch of her hand. In a minute, Stefano returned with a two-by-three-foot carton. He gathered the blanket holding the fox and placed it inside.

She tucked the parka around it before glancing at Stefano. "His home has to be somewhere near the chalet. If we can get him strong enough, he can be released."

Stefano studied her features. "I didn't know you went to vet school," he drawled.

Lanza smiled. "Nothing so admirable. When we were young my sisters and I often found injured creatures and birds around the estate and nursed them, but it had to remain a secret. Fausta was a natural tending them, but *Mamà* didn't want us touching wild things that had diseases. Our parents were too protective of us."

"Don't they know you're fearless?"

"You should see Donetta in action. She's a real warrior. The way she rides a horse, you would think she was born on one and has won every international *concorso* she's ever been in. Her trophies need their own room to be displayed. My sister would make a great king."

"King?"

"Yes. The word *queen* loses too much in the translation for her."

Deep, rich laughter burst out of Stefano, the kind she loved.

"From my earliest memories of her, she has always wanted to rule. But not with a husband! That's probably the real reason she didn't get picked to be Alberto's intended in the first place. As for Fausta, she has always refused the idea of marrying a prince. She intends to find a man of the people in the city. That left *moi*."

Stefano started to say something, then seemed to think the better of it.

"If my father would have that absurd ancient rule changed proclaiming only a man can rule, Donetta would make the perfect head of Domodossola. She's brilliant and innovative. That would be really lucky for you since you'd be free to spend even more time away doing your thing."

Lanza had only told him she would like to go to her aunt's while he did what he wanted, because she was afraid to spend any more time with him. Now she was growing increasingly drawn to her husband, which was dangerous. She'd be a fool to enjoy any more of his company when she feared he could never fall madly in love with her. That was what she wanted.

CHAPTER SEVEN

MY THING?

Here Stefano had been feeling comfortable with Lanza for the first time since their wedding and she suddenly interjected a discordant note. Did she mean his mining business or something else? If it was the latter, then she had every right to question his future associations with women. He'd insinuated the same thing about her relationships with other men during her betrothal to Alberto.

"It's a good thing you stocked milk. Are you a big milk drinker, Stefano?"

"Yes. I like it with my muesli. Sometimes it's all I eat when I'm busy. Since I didn't know if you wanted some, I made sure we had it on hand."

"That was lucky for Fausto."

He angled his head at her. "Fausto?"

"Yes. I've named him that because it means lucky. Our little fox was lucky Enzo didn't come for us and we were able to find him." Lanza stood up. "I'm going to heat more milk." She left his side and walked into the kitchen with the empty pan and rag.

Stefano stared into the flames. Something unprecedented was happening to him since his wedding day. He realized he was becoming enamored of his wife and wanted her in all the ways a man wanted a woman.

When he'd committed to marrying her, he'd promised himself

to make it work, but his desire for her had already happened. She had a charm that took him by complete surprise.

Thank heaven something had prevented Enzo from making it up here. It gave him and Lanza more time together in his favorite place on earth. He could tell she loved it here, too, and he wanted their honeymoon to begin in earnest. Since it would be another day before Enzo arrived, Stefano was excited at the thought of spending more time alone with Lanza.

She returned and they again started the process of squeezing milk into the mouth he eased open. "Look—Fausto's tongue is curling around the drops. He *likes* it!" she cried in real pleasure. The fox was coming back to life. "At this rate I think he'll want some solid food before long."

Her caring and tenderness reached a place in his soul he didn't know was there.

She lifted jewel-blue eyes to him. "It's almost time for dinner. I'll fix some ham sandwiches and feed him part of mine. Do you think he should have ham?"

He grinned. "If not, we'll find out."

Again, she carried the pan and cloth to the kitchen. While she was gone, the fox stirred enough that Stefano removed the parka so it could have more breathing room. It lay on its side, but he could see it trying to right itself. More food would make a difference.

Before long she returned to kneel by him. "Your sandwiches are on the counter."

"Thank you, but first I want to help you by opening its mouth so you can put some ham on its tongue."

She teased the fox by dangling a small piece of meat in front of its nose. That brought out its tongue. Lanza pushed the ham inside and they kept up the process until all the ham in her sandwich was gone.

Stefano chuckled. "It's working. He likes it."

"Now *I'm* the one starving to death."

"I'll get up and make you another sandwich. Then we'll eat here together to keep him company."

Before long he was back with their food and a small, shallow bowl of water. Stefano put it in a corner of the box near its head. He sprinkled some on its snout and it produced a reaction. The fox moved its head and pretty soon they watched it start to lick the water.

"Oh—you're thirsty, aren't you?" She looked at Stefano. "Do you think he would like some of your muesli?"

"Probably. I'll put a little in another bowl and we'll see what happens."

Within an hour the fox had turned over on its own and was eating and drinking.

"By morning we might be able to put him outside the chalet with more food and water and see what he does. If he seems fit, I'll carry him back to that tree where we found him so he can find his way home."

"I'll help you because I know it's the right thing to do, but I'd love to keep him for a pet." Her eyes focused on the fox. "He's so sweet. I hope Enzo doesn't come for a long time. That way I can keep an eye on Fausto and know he's going to be all right until we have to go."

It was getting late. Instinct told him Enzo wouldn't be coming tonight. "If you want to go to bed, I'll stay up with the fox for a while."

She turned her head toward him. "I was going to say the same thing. I know you always have mining business to take care of and we've got internet now because of the generator. I'll stay right here by the fire a few more minutes so he knows he's not alone."

Stefano had a feeling she knew how attracted he was to her and wanted to kiss her, but he decided not to press it yet. "Then I'll say good-night and see you in the morning." He leaned over to kiss her cheek. *"Buona notte,* Lanza."

He got up from the floor and headed for his bedroom. The first thing he did was shower and get ready for bed in his navy sweats. Anything to take his mind off his delectable wife sitting in the firelight.

Next, he went over to his desk and discovered that Enzo had just sent him an email.

Stefano, a major blizzard has hit the area and thousands are without power. Including me until I could start up our generator. Worse, there was an avalanche that has covered the road two miles south of you. It could be close to a week before it's passable again because there are too many other areas in much more need of help. I'll come as soon as I can. If you need help before then, I can notify your father to send a helicopter for you. Please advise.

He took a deep breath before responding. In his gut he knew Lanza didn't want to be rescued and not just because of the fox.

Enzo. Thank you, but there's no reason for urgency. Don't tell anyone where we are. Let me know your schedule when you know more. S.

While he waited to hear back, he left his bedroom to tell Lanza the news.

The sight before his eyes caused him to stop in his tracks. Her lovely body lay on its side by the box sound asleep. She had an angelic look in profile. The lambent flames from the fire brought out the strands of reddish gold in her luxurious chestnut hair. Stefano had the desire to run his hands through it.

Much as he'd like to lie down next to her, he didn't dare for too many reasons to consider. He could try to wake her up, but she probably wouldn't appreciate being disturbed. The news from Enzo could wait till morning. On impulse, he left to get a blanket for her and turn down the fire.

The fox had been curled up, but immediately lifted its head when Stefano drew near to cover her. Who was guarding whom? A smile broke the corner of his mouth before he stole back to his room for the rest of the night.

In case she needed him, he left his door open and went to bed. But he didn't sleep well because he kept listening for any sounds from her or the fox. When morning came he got dressed and shaved, eager to find out what was going on in the living room.

He found Lanza on her knees once more, hand-feeding some bits of apple to their patient with all the joy of a child at the zoo. She saw Stefano out of the corner of her eye.

"I thought you'd sleep longer."

"I couldn't until I knew how you got on. We have news, Lanza.

Enzo sent me an email late last night. The storm knocked out the electricity and triggered an avalanche farther down the mountain. There are so many other regions needing emergency assistance, he's heard it might be a week before the road is cleared. He'll come to get us as soon as he can, but we might have a long wait."

Her smile widened, telling him everything he wanted to know. "Thank you for the blanket you threw over me. Because of it I had a wonderful sleep."

"That's good. I'll get Fausto some more food and water." He reached for the empty bowls and went to the kitchen. After replenishing the dishes, he brought them back to the box.

"Look how hungry he is!" she cried.

He nodded. "The ham didn't bother him. Now it's time I fixed our own breakfast."

Stefano went back to the kitchen to make scrambled eggs and bacon. She came in to fix the coffee and toast. In a few minutes they sat down to eat at the dining room table.

"I'll admit I'm glad we've been given more time to stay here."

"Me, too," he murmured. She had no idea. "We have a lot to talk about. I've wanted to explain the reason I didn't come to visit you this past year."

She lifted searching eyes to him. "Why didn't you?"

"I knew you were trying to get over Alberto's death. So was I. Though we agreed to get married and please our parents, I felt like you and I needed the past year apart to sort out our feelings before meeting again. I was half-afraid that seeing me before the wedding would have made you run the other way."

"By now you know that's not true," she laughed gently.

"But I was wrong to stay away."

"No," she countered. "Not wrong. It's true I was in limbo, but the emails really helped me get a sense of your life."

"The same for me, Lanza."

"I'm glad things worked out this way."

He covered her hand and squeezed it. "You really mean that?" "Yes."

"Then let's go downstairs and get ready to enjoy this day."

She followed him below. He opened the closet door for her. A few minutes later she appeared in his sister's ski outfit. Her womanly figure drew his attention. No matter what she wore, he found himself unable to keep his eyes off his new wife.

He carried the box outside with some food. "If you want, we'll put on our snowshoes and trek across the property to that pine tree. Maybe he'll follow us. I'll tuck a bag of food inside my parka in case he trails us."

Together they strapped themselves into their snowshoes and started across the expanse, retracing their own former tracks that stood out in the snow. Every so often they looked back, but the fox had stayed in the box. Eventually, they reached the pine tree where they'd found Fausto.

Lanza shot him a guilty glance. "Maybe I did the wrong thing to feed him. Now he's spoiled and doesn't want to leave our protection."

He put his hands on his hips. "You did the right thing. Not everyone would have done that."

She bit her lip. "But it might have been a mistake." In the next breath she turned and started walking farther into the trees. She handled the snowshoes like a pro.

"Stefano!"

Her cry drew his attention and he started after her. It was an older stand of forest. He noticed a lot of debris and some trees had been downed during the ferocity of the storm. "What is it?"

"I need your help."

Alarmed, he hurried toward the sound of her voice. When he came upon her, she was standing at the end of a toppled tree that was dead in spots. "What's wrong?"

"This top would make the perfect Christmas tree. If we could break it off, we could drag it back to the chalet and pretend it's Christmas Eve. All the pine cones make perfect ornaments. Thanks to the wedding, I feel like Christmas passed me by this year."

He stared at her in disbelief. "You didn't celebrate Christmas?"

"We had a tree at the palace, but getting ready for the wedding took precedence over everything. I feel like I missed it altogether. From childhood I dreamed of finding my own little tree in the woods near the palace and putting it in my room. But that was never allowed." She averted her eyes. "Please forget I said anything. It was a silly idea."

With a flushed face, she worked her way past him to reach the clearing.

Stefano walked over to the tree and took a good look to see if separating it was possible. After bracing his boot against the dead part near the top, he grasped the trunk and pulled hard. To his surprise it gave. He kept tugging until he pulled it free.

The little tree couldn't be more than five feet in length, light and easy enough to pull behind him. Over the years he'd often spent the holidays at the chalet, but he'd never put up a tree, let alone one from his own property. The novel idea seemed to be important to his wife and he wanted to please her. When he got it back to the chalet, he could fix a stand for it and set it up in the living room.

All these years he'd put off the idea of getting married because he loved being free. When he thought about it, he realized that the relationships he'd sought over the years had always fallen short of anything lasting.

Though his mother had hit a nerve, she hadn't been off the mark when she'd reminded him he hadn't brought a special woman home for them to meet. That was her argument to convince him he had no reason not to marry Lanza and fulfill his duty.

But now he was beginning to think that wasn't the real reason that had stopped him from settling down. Maybe it was possible that the only reason he'd remained single this long was because he'd never met the right woman until Lanza...

CHAPTER EIGHT

LANZA KEPT WALKING toward the chalet, feeling like a fool. It had been the height of idiocy to talk to him about a Christmas tree. He must think she was stupid. But she knew she'd fallen in love with her husband and was living out her private fantasy of sharing Christmas with the man she wanted to spend the rest of her life with.

As she trudged on, there was no sign of Fausto. Maybe he'd run away while they'd been gone. That would be a good thing. He belonged in the wild.

Maybe her eyes were deceiving her, but when she reached the chalet she saw the fox creep out of the box, almost as if he was greeting her.

"Fausto—I thought you were gone." He moved around, keeping his distance, but he didn't run off. "You're not ready to go home yet and I suspect you're hungry. Don't worry. We'll feed you in a minute."

She removed her snowshoes and took them inside. When she went back out, she was met with another surprise. In the distance she saw Stefano's tall, striking physique coming closer. He dragged the little tree behind him that he'd broken off for her.

The trouble he'd gone to in order to make her happy caught at her heart. This husband of hers was turning out to be a very different person from the man she'd envisioned.

being together while they were snowed in. Once they returned to Domodossola and he was free to make plans, they might not have this closeness again.

"Stefano, can we talk frankly this evening?" She needed some answers.

He cast her a level glance. "Isn't that what we've been doing?"

"Before you heard that Alberto had been killed, what was your situation at the time? I'm not talking about your business affairs. I imagine you might have been involved with a woman you possibly loved. If that was the case, the shock of having to leave her and fly home to your family to deal with your pain had to have devastated you."

Lines carved his features. "Tell me something first. I know gossip abounds, but what makes you think there's been a particular one?"

"It's a natural assumption." Before he could say anything else, she asked him another question. "Before the wedding, did you have time to see her one more time? If there was a woman, there would have been so much to discuss about the huge change in your life that meant taking on your royal duty by marrying me."

"I don't like that word," he bit out.

Heat filled her cheeks. "Neither do I, but that's what it was," she fired back. "We both knew what was ahead of us, and now it's done. But the real test of living has only begun. I'm asking about your love life because I'm concerned. Four days after the funeral my father told me you'd asked for my hand in marriage.

"If there was a woman you were close to, then you weren't able to see her in person before our fathers set the seal on our marriage. Were you able to fly over and spend time with her during the year?

"If so, I can't imagine how she would have handled it. Is it possible she'll try to hurt you in some way and cause damage to our marriage that will be all over the media? If you and I hope to endure a lifetime together, then I would like to be aware of what we could be up against."

"You're afraid of public scandal?"

"I don't want to be."

He poured both of them more wine and swallowed part of his. "I'm prepared to give you all the honesty in me. I've known my share of beautiful, exciting women, but never lived with one. To answer your question, *if* I'd found the woman you're talking about—the one I couldn't live without—I'd be married by now. Believe me, there's no one out there who's going to make trouble."

"Thank you for that reassurance." She swallowed the rest of her wine. "My case is different because there was no other man from the moment I was betrothed."

"Not even a special man before?"

"No."

"Then can we talk about my brother for a minute? How did you feel about losing Alberto?"

Lanza had wondered how much he'd thought about it. His probing question, demanding an honest answer, had taken them to the heart of the matter.

"The shock of his death was one thing. But not having been in love, I didn't grieve over him. Of course I liked and admired him. The only way I can explain is that I felt guilt because I hadn't experienced acute grief. My parents were very upset I didn't fall to pieces over the news."

Stefano shook his head. "No one on the outside would expect you to feel grief since you and my brother didn't have a relationship like a man and wife."

"I'm glad you understand that, but we're talking about you. Your case is totally different because you've enjoyed a nonroyal life and have probably been intimate with a woman, which would only be natural."

"Now that I know the truth about you, will you humor me with a little more honesty and tell me how you felt about Alberto having to marry me?"

He took another drink of wine. "I didn't consider it until I fell for a local girl before going into the military. That was the first time I'd given his betrothal any serious thought and it gutted me to the point that I never stopped feeling sorry for him."

His frankness made her smile. "Did you tell him as much?"

"Yes. Every chance I got. But when I could see that my needling didn't make a dent in his good nature, I eventually stopped and tried not to think about it anymore."

"Alberto wasn't the flappable type."

"He was my total opposite. Now it's my turn. How did your sisters feel about your having to be the sacrificial lamb?"

She chuckled to hide her pain. "Donetta was overjoyed not to be in my shoes. Fausta pitied me because I was the baby. She teased me for always minding our parents."

"Why did you?"

Her delicate brows lifted. "Mind them, you mean?"

He nodded.

Stefano didn't know her father was ill. If she told him that was why she'd agreed to this marriage, it could change things. He'd hoped to have a lot of freedom to travel for his work. She wanted that same freedom, too, which was why she had no intention of telling him the truth.

"Donetta said it was because I didn't have a backbone."

His eyes narrowed on her mouth. "Donetta doesn't have a clue who you are."

Neither did Lanza, but being married to Stefano had thrust her into a whole new realm of existence. She was praying for this marriage to work. At the moment she appreciated him for being forthright. She could live with that when he was around, which wouldn't be that often.

While she was deep in thought she heard a little yip. For a while she'd forgotten about the fox. "Sounds like he wants attention." She got up from the table to give Fausto a few bits of her steak. "Uh-oh. You're out of food again."

Stefano pushed himself away the table and stood up. "I'll fix him some more muesli and apple bits. Tomorrow I'm taking him to the tree and leaving him. He's too dependent on us already."

"I hope he has family close. What will he do if he finds himself alone?"

"Survive like all of his species."

"I want to believe you."

The tremor in Lanza's voice found its way to Stefano's heart. So did the concerns she'd voiced for fear of scandal from his past that could hurt them. More than ever he needed to do everything he could to reassure her he meant them to enjoy a loving, wonderful marriage.

After he'd prepared more food for Fausto, he did the dishes with her. When it came to the dumplings pan, he finished what was left before putting it in the dishwasher and saved one for later. "They're better than dessert," he quipped when he caught her smiling at him. Soon their work was done. She blew out the candles.

Now that darkness had crept over the mountains, Lanza went back into the living room. She spread a blanket on the floor by the box and sat next to it so she could see inside.

He walked over to the breakfront and reached for a deck of cards. "How about a game?" he asked and found a spot next to her.

She took a look at them. "Judging by how well-worn they are, I don't know that I dare play with you."

"Just a few hands of Scopa."

Lanza flashed him a mischievous smile. "Do your best."

He dealt three cards and the game began. The idea was to sweep the board and take tricks until you accrued eleven points. Right away she started to outplay him and he knew he was confronting an expert. For the next hour they were fully engaged and he'd never had so much fun in his life.

"You play like an old salt. Who taught you?"

"The head gardener's father, Duccio. He was in the merchant marines and was an invalid with a bad leg. After his wife died, I used to go to their cottage on the estate with a treat for him and he'd teach me to play all sorts of card games.

"Being with Duccio made me realize the plight of the disabled navy men who ought to have more health care and financial help after serving their country."

Stefano flicked her a glance. "I don't know who was more brilliant, the teacher or the pupil. You'll have to introduce me."

"I can't." A somber expression broke out on her face. "Duccio died last year."

"I'm sorry."

"So am I. He was a good friend who could tell the most amazing tales and kept me mesmerized."

No doubt she'd brought sunshine into his life. "Is his son a cardsharp, too?"

"No. Antonio says they're a waste of time when there's a world of growing things to cultivate and provide beauty."

Her imitation of his words and the way he said them made Stefano laugh. The sound brought Fausto's head up.

"Oh, he's so adorable," she crooned.

Fausto wasn't the only adorable creature in the living room. "You've made a friend, Lanza."

"I know. It's got me worried."

"Tomorrow we'll try to wean him so he'll survive on his own. For now I'm going to take him downstairs. He'll be warm enough down there." Stefano wanted Lanza's complete attention and the fox needed to be on his own. "I'll be right back."

In a few minutes he'd returned. "I want a rematch of Scopa to repair the dent to my ego."

This time she made a sound of protest. "You don't fool me. I bet you let me win."

"I swear I didn't! Don't you trust me?"

Her eyes fused with his. "Of course I do."

His heart thundered in his chest. "I'm glad. Your turn first."

They played a long match. "You won, Stefano."

"It was a hard-fought battle. Now I want to claim my prize." She'd been lying on her stomach to play. Before giving her any time to think, he lay down next to her and rolled her into him. "I've been waiting to do this all night."

So saying, he lowered his mouth to kiss her the way he'd been dreaming about since that chaste kiss at the altar. She had a mouth to die for and he couldn't get enough of her. He was feverish with longing, loving the feel of her body and her response that was giving him a heart attack.

"Lanza—" He was breathless with desire. "You have no idea how delightful you are." In the next breath he tangled his legs with hers and pulled her on top of him. It was heaven to plunge his fingers into her fabulous long hair and kiss the daylights out of her.

"Stefano…" she murmured.

"I'm going too fast, aren't I, *bellissima*?" The hardest thing he'd ever had to do was stop making love to her. But she wasn't quite ready, so he moved her off him gently, allowing her to get to her feet before he did. His wife swayed a little and looked thoroughly kissed.

With her eyes glazed over she said, *"Dormi bene*, Stefano."

In a flash, she disappeared from the room, leaving him bereft. Being alone with Lanza had set off a fire that brought him alive in a whole new way. He hadn't been ready to call it a night. Far from it. They'd actually been communicating on a level he hadn't expected to happen this soon.

He gathered the scattered cards and put them away, but his body was trembling. Once he'd folded the blanket and put it on a chair, he turned down the fire.

Letting out a tormented sound, he headed for his bedroom, knowing he wouldn't be able to sleep for a long time. Thank goodness he could get on his computer, but she had nothing. It made him feel guilty.

He paused outside her door. Of course there was no sound. On a whim, he knocked on it.

"Lanza? Would you like my radio to listen to? I have plenty of batteries."

After ten seconds he heard, "You're sure you don't want it?"

She needed help going to sleep, too. "I'm positive. Give me a minute and I'll put it by your door."

"Thank you. *Sogni d'oro*, Stefano."

"Sweet dreams to you, too, *sposa mia*."

He hurried into his room and brought the transistor radio to her door. He knocked once more. "It's here. Enjoy." After putting it down, he went back to his room and shut the door.

After getting ready for bed in a fresh pair of sweats, he sat down to a new batch of emails. Enzo had sent another update a few minutes ago, but nothing had changed in terms of the mountain road being cleared. Among the messages was one that came from the Casale Mining Company near Zacatecas, Mexico.

He hadn't been there for four months and wouldn't be going again for another four or five. The message was sent from Alicia Montoya, the only woman he'd been intimate with for a short time in the past three years. She worked in the main office, but he hadn't given her a thought in all this time.

Stefano let out a small groan. From the moment he'd learned she had a husband and hadn't told him, he'd stopped seeing her because he had no desire to get involved with a married woman.

He found out she and her husband lived apart, but they couldn't divorce because of religious reasons. Stefano understood her pain, but the revelation had changed the situation for him. Unfortunately, she had access to the files in the office.

Stefano, I have to see you. We must talk. I've been confiding in my priest. He thinks a divorce might be possible because I've lived apart from Julio for over a year with no hope of reconciliation. Answer me back and tell me you still want to be with me. I can't bear this separation from you any longer. Alicia.

He rubbed the back of his neck while he gathered his thoughts. There'd been a time when he'd enjoyed Alicia's company. But even if he hadn't gotten married and Alicia was now divorced, Stefano knew it had never been an affair of the heart and wouldn't endure.

The fact that she hadn't told him she was still married caused his feelings to undergo a complete change. It wasn't difficult for him to compose his answer.

Alicia, if it's a divorce you want, I hope it's granted for your sake, so you can be happy. But my circumstances have changed. I'm now a happily married man and won't be seeing you again. Believe me when I wish you the very best in the future. Stefano.

He'd promised Lanza no scandal would ever touch their marriage and he'd meant it.

Once he'd pressed Send, he read through the messages from the managers of his other mines and answered where he needed to. The next meeting in Mexico wouldn't come until after his visit to Bulgaria.

When he finally climbed into bed, his mind was on Lanza. He couldn't wait to spend tomorrow with her. It didn't matter what they did because on top of the qualities he'd been discovering about her, her mind intrigued him. That distinction made her stand out from all the other women he'd known.

His last thought before he fell asleep had to do with her and Alberto. If he hadn't died in that crash, he'd be here on his honeymoon with Lanza right now. When Stefano tried to imagine his brother being married to her now, he no longer felt sorry for him. If anything, it was just the opposite…

He must have fallen off because the next thing he knew, Lanza was knocking on his door. "Stefano? Are you awake?" She sounded panicked.

In one bound he was out of bed and pulled on his robe before running over to the door to open it. She stood there wrapped in a stunning peach-colored robe.

"What's wrong?"

"Fausto's gone! I can't find him. When I went downstairs this morning to see if he needed more water—he'd tipped over the box."

"He has to be around here someplace."

"I've looked everywhere."

"Come on. We'll find him. He couldn't leave the chalet."

Her glorious chestnut hair flounced around her shoulders as they hurried below. The second he flipped on the light at the bottom of the staircase and called out, he heard yapping.

"Fausto?" She'd heard it, too.

Stefano headed for the door to the wood bin where he'd taken out some pieces for the tree stand. He opened it and Fausto sprang out. Laughter burst from him as their little pet darted up the stairs.

At this point she'd started laughing. "Curiosity killed the cat, but not our fox. What do you suppose he came down here for?"

"Since our doors were closed and he was hungry, he probably went on the hunt for food. He must have been shocked when the door closed on him."

"I'll fill his bowls." She started up the stairs.

He followed after her, wanting to put his arms around her and pull her back against him the way he'd done last night. This urge to feel her next to him wasn't going to go away. For the moment the only thing to do was channel his energy with something physical.

While they fixed breakfast and fed the fox, he had an idea. "Have you ever skied?"

"Once in a while."

There were many things Stefano still had to find out about her, but her answer pleased him no end. "As long as the good weather is holding, how would you like to go cross-country skiing with me today?"

"That's something I've never tried. I'd love it!"

She'd answered without thinking about it. That was easy and excited him. "We'll take Fausto to the tree with some food and leave him there while we go exploring."

"I saw that you have a backpack downstairs. I'll make some sandwiches for us so we can be gone as long as we want."

She seemed indefatigable, another trait he welcomed. But more important, she wanted to be with him. That meant everything. "We'll take drinks and a pack of biscotti, too."

"Sounds perfect."

"I'll find an old blanket."

Within a half hour they were ready to go. Her figure did wonders for Carla's ski outfit. She'd fastened her hair at the nape with a band and pulled on the white wool hat that looked sensational on her.

He wrapped the fox in the blanket. When they were ready to take off, he put Fausto under his arm and they headed across the snow toward the forest of trees. Today they saw signs of animal tracks that delighted Lanza.

"Maybe Fausto's family is out here looking for him."

"Why not?" he murmured, willing to humor her.

When they reached the big pine tree, he spread the well-worn blanket on the ground against the trunk and put Fausto down with a pile of food he poured out. "That ought to last him for quite a while."

She lifted concerned blue eyes to Stefano. "I'm almost afraid to leave him, but I know we have to do this for his sake."

"He'll be fine. But if he's unwilling to leave us, we'll take him to a wildlife shelter after we get to the city so he'll survive."

"That will be the right thing to do."

"For the time being, let's stop worrying about him and blaze a new trail. You never know what we might find on our trek today."

CHAPTER NINE

FOR LANZA IT was enough to be out in nature and bask in a white, sunlit world with Stefano. Her love for him was brimming to the surface. It was the kind of love you never got over.

There was no one like him. Since the moment she'd taken vows with him in the cathedral, she'd felt a stirring that had grown into white-hot heat. Being at his fabulous chalet, perched on a mountain as beautiful as this, was her idea of heaven. She couldn't help staring at him. Stefano was a gorgeous man. When he smiled, Lanza was left breathless.

At this high altitude she felt light-headed just looking into those dark eyes that seemed to swallow her alive. Last night he'd kissed her into a new realm of existence. Incredible to think she was so happy today when on the morning of her marriage, it had felt like the end of the world.

Being married to him opened her up to a world of intimacy. Every day with Stefano was turning into an adventure. Lanza hadn't had brothers and had never lived around a man. It made her realize what a sheltered life she'd led as a betrothed royal princess with two sisters and a doting mother. The duties of her father running the country didn't allow a lot of quality time with him.

Today she was so excited to be alive, she wanted to shout it to the world. But it might set off another avalanche. Being up here

Stefano was modest, too. He removed the pack from his shoulders and opened the flap so she could pull out what she wanted. Lanza noticed he was hungry, too. She relished this moment with him as they ate their fill and finished off their meal with some biscotti.

"Mmm, that tasted good."

Stefano looked around. "We've come a long way and the afternoon wind has started to pick up. It might be smart to head back."

She squinted at him. "You wouldn't be worried about Fausto?" she teased.

"Would you be surprised if I admitted I was?"

Lanza put her empty water bottle back in the pack. "Like I told you a little while ago, I don't regret marrying you and this is one of the reasons why."

"I'll take that as a compliment."

"You should. Not everyone would care that a larger predator could come along and snatch him for prey." There was a goodness and tenderness in Stefano that made her love him all the more.

"We'll have to hope the last dumpling I fed him last night has made him strong enough to ward off his enemies."

She laughed. "You gave him one?" When he told her things like that, she was touched by his words, but tried to hide it.

"You never saw anything disappear so fast. He has good taste."

Stop, Stefano. Every word and gesture enamored her. Already it was killing her that he planned to live part of his life away from her when he left for his various mines. "When you're starving, any morsel will do. By the way, what kind of meat do you have in the freezer?"

"As I recall, there are several salmon steaks and a couple of lamb roasts."

"What sounds best to you and I'll fix it for dinner."

"Whatever is easiest."

She smiled. "The steaks will thaw faster. That settles it. Now I'm ready to take off and have to admit I'd like to find out what Fausto has been up to all day."

"First, I want this." He wrapped her in his arms and gave her a long, hungry kiss that robbed her of breath. Finally, he let her go. "You taste so good I never want to stop."

His words caused her to blush before they started across the snow, avoiding their old tracks. It took less energy to make new ones. They spotted some chamois and watched a golden eagle make its way to a peak. Eventually, they reached their destination and skied in through the trees to the one where they'd first found the dying fox.

The sight of the blanket with no food and no Fausto caused her spirits to plummet. "It looks like our plan worked," she murmured, trying to keep the disappointment out of her voice.

"That blanket should have been thrown out long ago. We'll leave it here."

Lanza felt tears sting her eyelids. "He won't be back, which is the way it should be." She shoved on, not wanting to dwell on where he was or what might have happened to him. There'd been no sign of a struggle or blood. That was a good thing.

They kept going without looking back. She hated that this day was almost over. The joy of skiing with Stefano, of watching and loving him in this private world, was almost too much for her. Though the sun was close to falling behind the mountains, she wasn't ready to call it a day. She'd never forget today, but her legs would pay the price in the morning for trying to keep up with him.

Once they reached the chalet, she undid her skis and carried them inside with the poles. Next, she got out of her ski clothes and removed her hat, putting them in the closet. Not waiting for Stefano, she hurried up the stairs to her bedroom. Though she was worried about the fox, her mind and heart were centered on Stefano and how he made her feel.

A hot shower was exactly what she needed; after which she dressed in black wool pants and a tan pullover. Later tonight she'd wash and dry her hair, but right now she needed to thaw the fish in the microwave and get the pasta started for their dinner. He would be hungry and she was eager to fix food he liked. She'd seen boxes of fettuccine noodles on the shelf.

On her way to the kitchen, she stopped in her tracks to glimpse Stefano hunkered down by the box in front of the fireplace he'd turned on...*feeding Fausto!*

"What on earth...?" She rushed over and knelt down next to him.

"Our little fox followed us home. I was just walking inside the chalet with my gear when I heard yipping and saw him coming running toward me."

"All the way across in the deep snow? I don't believe it!"

"I let him inside and brought up the box."

This time the tears overflowed her lashes. "Oh, Stefano—"

Before she could take another breath, he slid an arm around her shoulders and looked into her eyes with an expression she hadn't seen before, suffusing her with heat. "Somehow he knows he's loved."

Before she realized what was happening, Stefano's dark head descended and he covered her mouth with his own the way she'd been aching for all day. This kiss was transforming her.

Suddenly, he was coaxing her mouth open to take their kiss deeper and longer. The divine sensation stopped her from thinking. She went where he led, never wanting him to stop.

Alberto had kissed her each time he'd been with her, but it was nothing like this. With all the reading she'd done, all the films she'd seen and accounts she'd heard from friends, nothing in this world had prepared her for the experience of being kissed by her exciting husband.

Little did he know he was changing her whole world as he pulled her so close she could hardly breathe. Helpless against such pleasure, she slid her hands up his chest and around his neck.

His hands roaming over her back and hips lit a fire inside her. It was real and not a part of her imagination. Anything she'd felt with Alberto bore no resemblance to the rapture Stefano was creating with the slightest touch of his hands and mouth. His enticing scent and the slight rasp of his dark beard against her skin drove her growing desire for him to a wild pitch.

The sensual part of her nature had come alive in his arms and she didn't want to bring it to an end. Lanza was embarrassed for being such a vulnerable mark. It bothered her that the virginal princess was easier prey than Fausto would ever have been *if* he hadn't followed them back to the chalet before dark because he sensed danger.

The way Stefano kissed and held her, she was reeling out of control. Her wholehearted response to his lovemaking meant that he could be in no doubt what he was doing to her. She cried out his name as her body throbbed with desire for him.

But at that moment he unexpectedly relinquished her mouth and put her away from him in a gentle gesture. It produced a protesting moan from her.

"I'm sorry for crossing a line with you, Lanza," he murmured and got to his feet.

"But you didn't." She rose to her feet. "I could have stopped it and you know it."

He shook his head. "The thing is, I made a promise to help you get comfortable with me first."

"Can't you tell that's what's happening?"

"I don't want you to think I'm taking advantage of you. I don't want to make any more mistakes with you like I did in the beginning."

How ironic that she was learning how to do what he did and live in the moment. In fact, that was what she intended to do until they left the chalet. For now she would pretend Stefano could really love her as she loved him. Once they were back in the real world, she feared all would be different.

Lanza stood up and went into the kitchen to start dinner. Stefano took the fox downstairs. When he came back up, he undid a package marked salmon he put in the microwave to thaw. "I'll freshen up and be back."

While he was gone, she set the table with wine and candles, and made some bruschetta for an appetizer. When she noticed he'd come back to the living room freshly shaven, she turned on the grill and cooked the salmon. The steaks only took a few minutes. Finally, everything was ready including the coffee.

"La cena è pronta, Stefano," she called to him.

"Meraviglioso." He came into the kitchen and took their laden plates to the table without glancing at her.

She followed with the tray of coffee and cups, drinking in how incredibly appealing he was, wearing navy trousers and a white pullover. No man in Domodossola or Umbriano could measure up to him, not in looks or charisma.

Tonight was like déjà vu, but instead of dumplings, he wolfed down the bruschetta so fast she had to bring more to the table.

He lifted his head. "You could open a restaurant, Lanza. Do you know that?"

"That's been a dream of mine for a while."

He'd already made inroads into the fettuccine and salmon. "How so?"

"Recently, I've urged father to have a soup kitchen constructed in the western part of the city next to the new housing for the homeless and immigrants. He thinks it's a good idea, but there are other needs that have more priority. It's a case of raising more money."

She smiled at him. "Perhaps because you're his new son-in-law, you could talk him into allocating some funds as an experiment. Maybe match them with donations from some of our wealthier citizens. I'd love to at least get it started and run it until I can find volunteers who'll be happy to work there full-time. Many people everywhere would help if given the opportunity."

He stared at her in surprise. "You'd really like to take on that kind of responsibility?"

"A soup kitchen is only one of my interests."

Stefano put down his fork. "What else?"

She was flattered by his interest and plunged away. "I told you about Duccio, who taught me how to play cards. He, like so many of the disabled naval veterans still do, needed housing and better health care. They've fought for our country and we have a moral obligation to pay them back."

"Alberto never told me you were a philanthropist at heart."

She sipped her coffee. "Don't assume I'm a Mother Teresa–type with a list of a dozen causes that are underfunded and don't have the right people with organizational skills. But you can't live in this world without seeing problems. I would hope that's true, even if I'm a royal."

"So what *did* you and my brother talk about if it wasn't about the needs of the people?"

"Between elaborate breakfasts, lunches and dinners, we rowed on the lake out in back of the palace and went horseback riding. Our conversation centered mostly on his duties for your father and my schooling.

"We both agreed we got annoyed with our tutors. Instead of learning Latin and studying the Punic Wars, we would have much preferred to get into the latest inroads in technology and become computer savvy. He once told me that if he'd been granted one wish, he would have become a space scientist."

That brought a sad expression to Stefano's face. "I remember when he was given a telescope that was set up in his room. He'd look through it all the time and should have been allowed to pursue his studies in science."

She swallowed hard to hear his pain. "Now he's in heaven, where he's learning amazing things."

"I'd like to believe that."

Lanza eyed him directly. "Don't you believe in an afterlife?"

"Do you?" He turned the question on her.

She wondered if her answer was important to him, wishing it didn't matter. "Definitely. This beautiful world wouldn't have been created only for everything to end once we'd lived out our lives here. After what we learn, it wouldn't make sense not to take that knowledge to the next world."

As he'd been thinking ever since he'd married Lanza, Stefano thought she was the most intriguing female he'd ever met in his life. There were so many parts that made up the whole of her; he knew he hadn't even skimmed the surface.

After holding her in his arms and kissing her earlier, he also discovered she was the most desirable woman he'd ever been with, and he'd been with a lot of them over the years. His heart still hadn't recovered from the shock since her mouth had opened to the pressure of his. Her response had shaken him to the foundation.

The two of them had experienced an overwhelming surge of passion earlier that had been real. But he shouldn't have acted on his desire this soon when he'd told her they'd give their marriage time until she was ready for intimacy. The chemistry between them had made it almost impossible for him to let her go.

Following that thought came a sensation of guilt when he realized that his own brother would have been the one to make love to her if he hadn't died. He closed his eyes tightly. What he needed to do was shut off those thoughts.

With a sharp intake of breath he said, "After that fabulous meal,

I'm going to do the dishes while you relax. When I've finished, are you up for another game of cards before we go to bed?"

"Yes."

He eyed her in amusement. "I was thinking of playing Briscola. Let's play for higher stakes."

"You're on." Her eyes glowed like gems.

Stefano's mind went back to the planning stage of this supposedly quick trip to the mountains. After two days his intention had been to take her on a sterile drive to the Mediterranean while they made desultory talk trying to get to know each other.

Not in his wildest dreams would he have imagined being snowed in with Lanza enjoying a domestic scene like this with a wife who thrilled him. Eager to join her, he finished up in record time, but when he went to get the cards, he saw that she'd already taken them from the breakfront and was looking at the back side of one.

"What's caught your eye?" He sat down next to her.

"The drawings of clubs and swords. And of course *denari* for gambling. But I guess that's not unusual considering it was the warriors who passed time playing cards until their next war."

Everything she said was unexpected and kept him fascinated. "What would you have drawn?"

"I have no talent, but my sister Fausta does. She would probably have designed the heads of dogs and birds. She's a wonderful artist and could sell her work." Lanza looked up at him. "If you're ready, I'll deal." The glint in her eye told him she was prepared to do battle and would give him no quarter.

At the end of three rounds, he'd won the first two, but she won the last one. "Bravo, Lanza. Let's go another round."

"I'm in, but I swear you're better at this than I am. Do you play cards a lot during your downtime at the mining camps?"

"Hardly ever. Mostly I eat and sleep after putting in twenty hours work a day."

"Do the wives join their husbands at the camps? I'm talking about your managers."

"No. There'd be nothing for the women to do."

"Does that mean you would never take me with you?"

He stared hard at her. "I can promise you wouldn't be happy. It's not a place to be if you don't have a job there."

"Could you give me one? I enjoyed learning about the things you told me in your emails. Your work is so important I'd like to be a part of it if I could. At night we could be together whether it's in a tent or sleeping in the out of doors. The six weeks you have to be gone on your various trips wouldn't matter if we were together."

Stefano couldn't believe what he was hearing. "What if you became pregnant?"

"Then I'd travel with you until I couldn't."

"Your family wouldn't approve."

"But you're my husband. I vowed to honor *you*."

Perhaps it could work since his wife wanted her freedom. All along she'd maintained that was what she craved. With Stefano's influence, his new father-in-law might not be averse to Lanza traveling with him once in a while.

To have his wife at the mines and go to bed with her every night would be heaven for him. But he'd have to figure out a job she could do. It was something to think about.

They played another round, and she won. "Now that I'm the winner, will you promise to figure out a job for me to do when you have to leave for your next mine visit?"

"That will be in Argentina."

"Hmm. I've never been there, but I've studied Spanish with my language tutor."

"I promise to see what I can do."

She got up from the floor. "It's been a wonderful day. I'm going to say good-night and hope you get a good sleep."

Stefano didn't want her to go to bed yet, but after he'd brought a halt to their lovemaking, what did he expect? He sat there in shock while she left the living room.

The thought of her traveling with him and having his baby was exciting to him. If any woman was meant to have children it was Lanza. He knew she wanted him. He had proof of that in the way she'd clung to him. Otherwise, she would have pushed him away and run to her bedroom the second he'd put his arm around her.

In hindsight Stefano recognized that a part of him had put off marrying anyone and having children because he hadn't met Lanza yet. But there was more to it. Deep inside he'd known he couldn't escape the fact that he'd been born royal. Bringing a child into the world wouldn't exempt it from being titled, no matter how he much he wished it otherwise. But he didn't feel that way any longer.

Their marriage had already made a big change in him. The more he thought about it, the more he admitted what a coward he'd been. For the first time in his life he felt shame at what he'd done by running away. He'd left it to Alberto and his sister to carry on. To his chagrin, his actions had resulted in unintended consequences.

Lanza honestly hadn't believed he'd wanted children. How could she when he'd made it clear they would be living separate lives when he wasn't helping her father? By promising her fidelity to him, she'd set herself up to exist in a childless marriage. How selfish was that!

He'd hurt her in ways he'd hadn't dreamed of and now he had a huge problem to repair. As he got ready for bed, Stefano realized this was going to take time to fix, including figuring out a job she could do if she went with him on his trips. So far he'd practically kissed her into oblivion and was already aching to get her in his arms again.

After a restless night, he got up early, took Fausto outside where he could eat and play, then made a big breakfast. Not wanting to knock on her door when she didn't come to the dining room, he phoned her.

"Are you up? I've made breakfast."

"I just washed my hair and am drying it." All that glorious hair… "I can't come for a half hour."

"Fine. I'll keep it warm for us."

"Thank you."

While he waited, he walked back to his bedroom and got on the computer. He spotted Enzo's email first.

Hi, Stefano. Electricity will be restored by the end of the day. No news yet on the road opening. Hope you two are all right.

Stefano smiled to himself. They were more than all right.

He knew what his friend was really asking. The last time the two of them had gotten into a serious talk, Enzo knew Stefano was dying inside over having to marry his brother's fiancée.

In fact, he'd been dreading it and couldn't face a vacation in the sand and sun with a woman he could never love. He and Lanza had been on the same wavelength about a beach vacation being the place if you were in love.

He'd brought her to the chalet because it had been his wedding present to Alberto, but he hadn't believed she would like it here. With the diversion of a driving tour, they'd somehow be able to get through the two weeks of *ennui*.

It was incredible how wrong he'd been about everything. Nothing was as he'd assumed or imagined.

You're a great friend. It's all good news, amico. Thanks for keeping me posted. S.

No doubt Enzo would be in shock when he received this email. One day soon Stefano would confide in him about the true state of his feelings over his marriage.

He pressed Send and moved on to the next message. Farther down he saw a return message from Alicia Montoya.

Tell me it isn't true that you're married, Stefano. I asked the head boss. He said it was, but nothing else. I don't understand.

Stefano had kept his royal identity a secret all these years except from his head mining engineers. Unfortunately, Alicia couldn't let this go.

Alicia, I am married to a woman I met very recently. It was sudden and I'm happy. I hope in time you will be, too.

He wouldn't respond to her again.

Once that was sent, he checked his other messages before going back to the living room. Lanza had gone to the kitchen to take their plates out of the oven. She was wearing a pair of tan pants and a print blouse.

Stefano couldn't take his eyes off her figure or her hair. She'd put it in a becoming braid that made her look younger than her twenty-three years. Whether on top of her head, flowing over her shoulders or fixed like this, she was a vision.

He took one of the plates from her. "How did you sleep?"

Her eyes swerved to his. "Too well." They walked to the dining room table and sat down. "I awakened with aches and pains from our workout yesterday and the day before. Today I'm going to lie near the fire and read."

"Sounds good. After we eat, I need to make some repairs around the chalet. The wind loosened some of the shutters and there's a basement window that needs fixing." They tucked into the scrambled eggs and sausage he'd cooked. He was glad to see her appetite hadn't suffered.

"Where's Fausto?"

"Outside somewhere."

"Was he still in his box this morning?"

Stefano nodded. "I think he learned his lesson about staying put so he wouldn't get trapped again."

"He's a little rascal."

"I agree. By the way, Enzo wrote. We're supposed to get electricity by this evening."

"Yes. I heard as much on the radio a little while ago, but they still haven't cleared the road covered by that avalanche."

"Lanza, if you're anxious to leave, Enzo will have a helicopter sent for us."

"Oh, no!" she cried immediately. "I mean… That is…unless you've grown restless."

That little outburst was worth its weight in gold to Stefano. There was the proof that she loved it here as much as he did. It revealed another truth to him. This intimate time with his enticing wife had grown on him to the point that he didn't want to budge from his favorite spot.

CHAPTER TEN

LANZA NEVER WANTED to leave the mountains and was embarrassed to have reacted so strongly. The longer they stayed away from everyone, the happier she would be. Once they were back at the palace, the world would descend on them. While they were here, she had Stefano to herself.

She feared he could never love her the way she loved him. But she cherished the fact that this would probably be the only time in her life when they would have this kind of privacy. It was incredible that no one knew where they were except Enzo. If they were trapped here for a month, she'd love it.

After clearing the table, she went back to the bedroom for her spy novel and came out to the living room once more to lie on the couch and finish the book. Her only problem was her inability to concentrate. Snatches of earlier conversations sent her down one road after another, each tidbit of information giving her insight into his character.

Out of the corner of her eye she saw their Christmas tree, the one he'd brought home for her when he didn't have to. Fausto's blanket still sat in front of the fireplace. Stefano had made the box into a home for the fox with bowls of food and water. It was right there that he'd kissed her close to senseless. Her body still throbbed from the sensations that had sent her spiraling to a different universe.

Love's first kiss, the famous line delivered in angry mockery from the lips of the evil queen in a certain childhood fairy tale, had taken on new meaning for her. She'd never get over what his hands and mouth had done to her. The feel of his hard body was a revelation. Lanza had been transformed into a different person. That was Stefano's doing.

By midafternoon Lanza grew restless and got up from the couch. She would have to finish the story another time. The Vacherin and Gruyère cheeses in the fridge had been calling to her. She could make up a pot of *fondue au fromage*. They could eat it with one of the loaves of French bread from the freezer.

Stefano had been outside a long time and no doubt was hungry. His supply of wines included Kirsch cherry wine, a perfect one to add flavor. She got busy grating cheese and hurried downstairs to the freezer so the bread could thaw in time for dinner.

Lanza had always enjoyed cooking, but had never cooked on a regular basis in her life until now. Of course, even if she couldn't boil water, that wouldn't have bothered Stefano. He knew how to cook and had been fending for himself for years. But it made her happy she could do her part while they were cut off from the world for a little while. She adored him and couldn't do enough for him.

Before long he came in for a drink of water, bringing a draft of cold air with him. "Um, that fondue looks good enough to eat."

She laughed. "Let's hope. It's ready when you are. Did you get all the chores done?"

"Yup. I'll freshen up and be right back."

While he was gone she set the table with the fondue forks and put on a bottle of white wine to go with their meal. By the time he returned, she'd brought the pot of bubbly yellow fondue to the table.

"Food for a king!" Stefano exclaimed, his dark eyes shining with excitement as he sat down.

"That's what you will be one of these days, or have you forgotten?"

"I'm trying," he said under his breath, but she heard him and couldn't believe she'd said it when she knew how hard he'd fought to be a nonroyal.

"I'm sorry, Stefano. I wasn't thinking when I said that."

"I shouldn't have said what I did, either." His apology meant a lot. "How did you know this is my favorite dish after being outside in the snow all day?"

"It's mine, too. Who stocked all your shelves and freezer for you?"

"I have a housekeeper, Angelina, who lives in the city. When I asked her to do some shopping for me because I was bringing my bride to the chalet for our honeymoon, she told me to leave it to her."

"You found yourself a real treasure."

"She's been with me for five years."

"I hope you give her a big bonus for supplying us with so much food. She couldn't have known about the avalanche."

"She goes overboard when she finds out I'm coming with my friends. This time she wanted to make it special for you."

"We've been blessed."

His eyes held hers for a moment. "I'll tell her what you said. It will mean the world to her." That brought a lump to her throat.

He started inhaling his dinner. "This fondue is divine."

"At the rate you're going, I'll have to make another pot."

She waited for him to say, "Would you?" But to her surprise he said, "I'll make the next batch. It won't be as good as yours."

Unbelievably, he did get up after he'd finished off the food and started making another meal.

"While you do that, I'll go downstairs and see if Fausto is ready to come in."

"He was gone all day, but I'm sure he's back now. It's dark out and the temperature dropped this afternoon. There might be another storm, but not like the last one."

With the cozy atmosphere inside the chalet, Lanza hoped it was a big blizzard. She went down and turned on the light. To test if the electricity had come on, she turned off the generator. Sure enough there was a flicker, but the lights stayed on. Stefano would be pleased.

Next, she went over to the door and opened it. "Fausto?" He must have been waiting because he bounded inside and crawled inside his box. What a change from the day they'd found him barely alive.

"Wherever he's been, he was ready to come home," she announced at the top of the stairs. "And guess what? The electricity did come on, so I turned off the generator."

"That's good news. Enzo and his wife will be pleased, because they've had to use their generator, too. But if I know my friend, he's made the best of it and they're enjoying it."

Lanza imagined they did since they'd only been married a few months. Her stomach clenched. Because Stefano had been forced to marry her, it meant he wouldn't be able to see Enzo or his other friends nearly as often as before. Besides the royal duties that would infringe on his business interests, he would now be living in Domodossola and forced to give up an enormous part of his former life.

Life hadn't been fair to either of them.

Lanza had been forced to marry another man. After Alberto had died, she'd assumed she'd be free to make a new life for herself, but her parents had insisted that the New Year Wedding would take place. She knew her father's health wasn't good, but they could have insisted that one of her sisters get married to one of the available princes on their short list. It didn't have to be Stefano.

No one except her aunt had ever considered how she'd really felt about her betrothal to Alberto, or how close she'd come to running away and never returning. Only Ottavia's promise that one day she'd find a man she could love had helped her to survive this long.

Ironically, her words had been prophetic and Lanza found herself deeply in love with the man she'd married. Her eyes watered. If he could never return her love…

Lanza started doing the dishes, but she was all stirred up inside. So much for living out her fantasy with Stefano while they were alone. If she went on playing that delusional game, it would be to her detriment.

"Stefano?" Lanza walked into the dining room. "I'm going to say good-night so I can finish my book. See you in the morning."

His head shot up. "You can't go yet. I've got Scrabble all set up for us."

Her spirits lifted immediately. He wanted to be with her. "Then watch out. I'm a good speller."

They played until late. He walked around the table and squeezed her shoulders. "I love being with you no matter what we do." She got up from the chair and turned into his arms. His kiss didn't last long enough. He'd said he wanted to go slowly, but that was ridiculous when she was on fire for him. Somehow she needed to find a way to speed things up.

Taking the initiative, she cupped his face. "Get a good sleep, Stefano." She said it with a smile before heading to her bedroom. From here on out she would do what she could to entice him until he realized she was so comfortable, she wanted to climb into his bed and stay there.

For the next three days they kept Fausto fed and cooked breakfast together. She'd done a wash of her clothes and the fox's blanket. Lanza adored going cross-country skiing and got quite good at it. She relished every minute with him.

They did three different exciting trails where they saw all kinds of wildlife, including a moose. Their strenuous ski adventures wore her out. Sometimes they raced each other, but he always won and they ended up kissing each other beneath a glorious sun. His sensuous smile melted her bones, leaving her limp with longing.

Every time they returned to the chalet, they'd make a sandwich, then lie on the floor in front of the fire and listen to music from his radio. He'd start to kiss her and she'd kiss him back, but he never tried to do anything more. She ended up taking long, hot showers, then getting into bed with the novels she'd brought.

After a week had gone by, they had news. When she appeared in the kitchen to fix breakfast dressed in wool pants and a cherry-red sweater, Stefano was waiting for her in trousers and a tan sport shirt. The sight of him always made her breath catch, but there was a different aura about him this morning.

"We have phone service."

No.

"Enzo called me a minute ago and the snow has been cleared from the mountain road enough for him to make it up here. He'll be bringing my car." Stefano sounded so happy, her heart plunged to her feet.

She reached for an apple. Their supply had grown low. "How soon are you expecting him so I can start packing?"

He rubbed the front of his chest in an absent gesture. "I was waiting to talk it over with you. Do you want to take the driving tour I'd planned for us?"

Lanza had to suppress a moan. "I'll do whatever you'd like." Did he want to leave? She couldn't bear it.

His dark eyes narrowed on her features. "We'll take Fausto with us when we drop Enzo back at his office. Then I'll drive you to one of my favorite restaurants for a big lunch and we'll talk about plans."

"Does this mean you'll be assigning security for us?" She dreaded the idea of it. Here they'd been free of everything and everyone. "I guess you'll have to because people will recognize us. Our secret will be out."

"Not if we disguise ourselves in our ski outfits and sunglasses. We'll look like typical tourists. On our way out of the city we'll leave our little fox at the wildlife shelter. I'll make a donation so they'll look after him."

That last comment told her he'd gotten attached to Fausto, but she still felt ill. This was the end of her idyll, the happiest time she'd ever had in her life, all because of Stefano. With the opening of the road, this whole glorious time had come to an end.

"Go ahead and call Enzo back. I'll get started packing."

With a heart so heavy she wanted to die, Lanza hurried to the bedroom and began putting things in her suitcase. It didn't take long since she hadn't worn the clothes meant for the tropics. Once she'd packed her cosmetics, she was ready.

An hour later, after making the bed, she put her hair in a braid. No one would recognize her wearing her hair like that. She slipped on Carla's ski outfit and carried her cases to the stairs. Lanza found Stefano in the kitchen making coffee. He handed her a mug to drink.

"I'll take the box downstairs to load in the car."

Lanza followed with her cases. He must have already taken his down. She couldn't look at the Christmas tree in the corner of the living room. It hurt too terribly. She was in excruciating pain when she remembered the thrilling moments in here they'd shared, especially the rapture she'd experienced in his arms. Sobs welled in her throat. Somehow she had to find a way to stifle them.

Enzo's voice carried as she reached the door entrance. The two men sounded thrilled to see each other. She opened it into the sunlight and walked out to the car, glad for her sunglasses.

"Buon giorno, Enzo," she called to him. Today he appeared without a ski hat and was dressed in a suit and tie. Stefano had told her they'd be driving him to the bank."

"Lanza—" He hurried around the car toward her. "I hope you don't mind my calling you that."

"I want you to."

He smiled. "It's good to see you again, but I have to admit I wouldn't have recognized you in that outfit."

"Or my braid?" she teased.

"Exactly." His blue eyes played over her with even more masculine interest than before. "I'm sorry you had to wait so long to be rescued."

"Since you've stayed at this chalet many, many times, then you know how comfortable we've been. We appreciate your coming."

"It's my pleasure, believe me." Stefano had already put the box on the back seat of the car. No man on the planet could look as jaw-droppingly handsome as her husband in his ski clothes and sunglasses. She opened the car door and got in next to it.

Her husband walked over to her. "I'd like you to ride in front with me."

He didn't need to keep up the pretense in front of his friend. She fastened her seat belt. "If you don't mind, I'd like to be by Fausto until we have to say goodbye to him. Will that be all right?"

Lanza heard him take in a quick breath. "Of course." He shut the door and put their luggage in the back end of the vehicle. Then he slid behind the wheel.

Enzo got in the front passenger seat, and they made their way out to the mountain road, using the remote to open the gate for them. It was astounding how much snow had fallen the night of the blizzard.

She couldn't break down sobbing, but she wanted to. Instead, she looked inside the box at Fausto, who had no idea what was going on. He had to be anxious. "We're taking you to a place where you'll be safe and cared for, but I'm going to miss you."

Enzo wanted to know all about him and directed his questions to her while Stefano maneuvered their car through so much snow she didn't know how they would make it.

She gasped when they reached the avalanche area. It had been a massive slide. A dozen men and vehicles were working to clear the road completely. Once they got past everything, the snow wasn't quite as deep and it only took them a half hour to drive on snow-packed roads to the main city of Umbriano, the same name as the country.

Stefano drove him to the city center and drew up in front of the bank where Enzo worked. He leaned over to press her hand. "My wife and I hope to see you soon." Then he turned to Stefano and the two men hugged before he got out of the car. "Talk to you later." He flashed them both a big smile and hurried inside the building.

Before Stefano pulled out into traffic, he looked over his shoulder at her. "I think we'll drop off Fausto first. Then we can take all the time we want to eat."

"Bene" was all she could get out at the moment.

Five minutes later he drove into the parking lot in front of a building attached to a spacious preserve on the edge of the woods. The sign said *Rifugio Faunistico di Umbriano*.

She felt a pain in the pit of her stomach as Stefano got out and opened the back door to get the box. His face was taut with emotion, mirroring her anxiety that the fox was going to face a whole new life. But her thoughts had gone far beyond Fausto. She was already in mourning that this precious time with Stefano was coming to an end. If only he knew how much she loved him...

Lanza slid out her side and held the door open for him so he could carry the box inside. The reception room had a long counter with a man in glasses and a lab coat working behind it. Stefano put the box down and explained why they'd come.

"Cute little fellow. Where did you find him?" So far the man hadn't recognized them or he would have addressed Stefano as *Your Highness*. That was a good sign.

"On Monte Viso, above the area of the avalanche, right after the storm."

"He was close to death," Lanza asserted. "After we fed him and he recovered, we took him back to the exact place where we'd found him, but he refused to run away."

"He got a taste of your food. That's natural."

"Can you introduce him back into the wild?"

The older man nodded. "That's our job. We'll do everything possible."

Stefano slipped him some euros. "My wife and I will be interested to know how he does and make inquiries."

"Of course."

"His name is Fausto," Lanza blurted. Just saying the name caused the fox to lift its head.

The worker laughed. "He has a name already?"

"My wife is very attached to him."

"I can see that, but he wouldn't make the most satisfactory pet. Not like a dog or a cat."

"I know."

"You brought him to the right place. We'll do all we can."

"Bless you," she murmured before running outside to the car. In a few minutes Stefano followed in time to shut her door. By the time he'd gone around to the driver's side, she'd broken down in tears. While her face was buried in her hands, she felt Stefano's arm go around her and pull her against him.

He kissed the side of her face and hair. "I know exactly how you feel. As I told the man, we'll call in a few days and find out how he's getting on."

"Thank you." Shaken by his tenderness, she wiped the tears with the backs of her hands and moved out of his arms though she'd wanted to stay in his arms forever.

He started the car, but instead of taking them to a restaurant, he drove them to a farm. "Why are we coming here?"

"I thought you might enjoy a sleigh ride before we eat."

"You're kidding! How exciting!"

An older man came out of the barn and told them to get in the sleigh pulled by two horses. He'd supplied blankets for their comfort and they took a half hour's journey along the path through the nearby woods.

"What made you think about this?"

"I knew we'd both be upset to have to leave Fausto and thought we might enjoy something different to get our minds off him."

Her heart pounded in her chest. "This is a wonderful surprise. I love it. Thank you, Stefano." Every minute with him brought new thrills and bonded her to him.

When it came to an end and they'd thanked the farmer, he drove them to Ristorante Alasso, an elegant restaurant that served the best burrata antipasto she'd ever eaten. The shell of mozzarella contained a semisoft white Italian cheese made with cream and was to-die-for. Delicious ravioli followed with a dessert of cappuccino and cannoli.

Stefano smiled at her after she took her last bite. "Feel better?"

"What a question. This was a superb meal."

"But it hasn't taken the sadness from your eyes."

"Nor yours, but I have an idea. If you'll take me to the airport now, I'll fly to Rome to visit my aunt. That will leave you free to be gone for a week. I'll fly to Domodossola Airport when you return and we'll take a limo to the palace together."

Stefano leaned forward and eyed her intently. "I'm going to be honest with you. There's no place on earth I'd rather be than the chalet. If it hadn't been for Fausto, who needs attention, I would have told Enzo not to come for us until we had to leave at the end of our two weeks.

"Are you serious?" she cried, so overjoyed she couldn't find words.

"We haven't even gone skiing yet and the Monte Viso resort is a mere twenty minutes away. This kind of snow calls to you, but maybe you've had enough of it."

He was begging to go back!

She felt it in every atom of her body. In fact, she was almost sick with excitement at the prospect of being isolated with him for another week. Anything could happen now.

"I'd much rather ski than travel around the Mediterranean," she stated. "On our way back to the chalet, why don't we pick up fresh salad and some pastries to last us for another week."

"Don't forget chocolate," he added. There was no mistaking the light shining in those dark eyes before he sat back. "Now I can breathe again."

He didn't know the half of it.

She watched him put money on the table before they left to find a store. Another new experience awaited her when she went into a grocery store to shop. Lanza had always wondered what it would be like to do anything as ordinary as walk around a store with the husband you loved.

Being with Stefano was an adventure she loved with every fiber of her being. They laughed while they planned their meals for the week and ended up buying more food than they would need, but he insisted more was much better than less.

To her amazement he bought half a dozen bottles of Almond 22 Pink India Pale Ale. He admitted to developing a taste for it over the years and dared her to try it. In her euphoric mood, there was no way to deny him. "I'll have some tonight."

"While we play some more Scrabble, right? You won't go to bed on me too soon?"

Surely, he was joking. She had no plans to disappear on him. His plea connected to her in a way he wouldn't have believed. "I promise."

"I'm going to hold you to it," he said in his deep voice that wound its way to her insides, turning them to jelly.

After loading the car, they headed for the turnoff on the outskirts of the city. "Before we go any farther, do you want to check on Fausto?"

"There's nothing I'd love more." Lanza adored him for suggesting it. "But if we did that, we might as well have not taken him to the refuge in the first place."

"Thus speaks my rational other half."

Even to her own ears, her remark had sounded like a nitpicking wife. She never wanted to be that kind of wearisome woman a man couldn't wait to get away from.

Lanza lowered her head. "I'm afraid that didn't come out right. I was thinking of his welfare without realizing you're missing him, too."

He reached over to clasp her hand, instilling her with warmth. "We'll have to stay busy so we don't worry about him. Oh—while I think about it, take a look at the photo on my phone." He pulled out his cell phone. "I took a picture of him for us to remember before I ran after you."

She did his bidding and found an adorable headshot of Fausto. He was looking up from the box.

Stefano... I love you, I love you.

CHAPTER ELEVEN

THAT EVENING STEFANO set their table on a blanket by the fireplace with all kinds of treats. They'd bought pizza they could warm up. He opened two bottles of beer for them before settling down to play Scrabble while they ate.

After an afternoon of skiing, they were comfortably tired. Tonight there was a special glow about Lanza in the firelight. This evening she wore her hair long. He wished she always wore it this way, loose and flowing. The flush on her cheek was new. He hoped her heightened color before she'd started drinking the beer meant she loved being with him, too.

For his part, he was happy in a way hard to articulate. He couldn't think of another place he'd rather be. As for being with a woman, he had all the woman he wanted right here. Day after day his desire for her had been escalating. Though he'd been sexually attracted to other women, he hadn't felt like this. Being with Lanza was different. She excited him on too many other levels and he worried what her true feelings were for him.

He couldn't tell if she was ready to be loved into oblivion. But before the week was out, he intended to show and tell her how much he wanted her. Forget being comfortable together. They were beyond that.

But if, heaven forbid, he learned that she only tolerated him and the sex that was expected—which he couldn't believe—then things would have to change. They would have a long talk about the best way to make her happy. Lanza didn't deserve to live in a cage if that was how she still felt about their marriage.

"How do you like the beer?" She'd just taken her first sip.

Her enticing mouth smiled at him. "I didn't think it would be this delicious."

"You're a good sport."

"I'm telling you the truth. I really liked it. What a surprise."

He studied her out of half-veiled eyes. *She* was the surprise. Watching her ski today and witness how fast she improved with just a few tips was another exciting revelation to him. Stefano realized his wife could do anything and made the most wonderful companion he could ever have dreamed of.

"Are you tired, Lanza?"

"Pleasantly so. I should have told you before now that you out-skied everyone on the piste today. Are you sure you weren't on the Umbriano ski team in another life?"

He chuckled. "Would it surprise you to know Alberto had that distinction for a season?"

She got to her feet. "I had no idea, but I believe you could out-ski anyone."

"You think?" He loved bantering with her.

"I know."

She started cleaning up, but he didn't want this night to end. "The dishes will wait."

"I can tell you're tired, too. It's better to do them now before all that beer gets the best of us."

"Slave driver."

"I heard that." Her grin got to him.

He followed her into the kitchen with the items that needed to go in the fridge. While she stood at the sink to load the dishwasher, he wanted her so much he couldn't resist sliding his arms around her waist. In an instant his plan to go slowly and woo her for a few more days had just gone up in smoke.

Stefano pulled her against him. "Do you have any idea how good you feel? How marvelous you smell?" he murmured against her nape, bringing her closer. "I've been wanting to do this all day."

He turned her around and saw the startled look in those heavenly blue eyes. "I need to kiss you again before I go mad."

Stefano didn't give her a chance to breathe as he closed his mouth over hers. He was so hungry for her, he was close to devouring her. His lips roved over every beautiful feature before kissing her again and again. When she clung to him like she'd done before, he knew she wanted this. Desire wasn't something you could hide when it was the real thing.

Unable to stop what was happening, he picked her up in his arms and carried her to one of the couches where he lay back and pulled her down. She trembled as he locked her to him, loving the feel of her hands and mouth that were driving him crazy.

The more they kissed and found ways to bring each other pleasure, the more he discovered he couldn't assuage his longing.

"Stefano." She suddenly said his name. To his chagrin, she eased herself away from him before getting to her feet. She was breathing hard.

He sat up. "Have I done something to offend you?"

"It's not that."

"Yes, it is. I'm going too fast."

"No." She shook her head. "I've been enjoying this time with you a great deal more than I thought I would. That's something I hadn't anticipated. But I guess I still need a little more time."

"That's what I was afraid of."

"It isn't that I don't want to make love, Stefano, but this is all happening so fast."

"That's true, but things have changed, or so I thought."

"You know they have." She folded her arms. "Perhaps because you're a man, you can follow through with your natural inclinations when it appeals to you. Obviously, I've had no problem in that regard, either. But we're not in a hurry, are we?"

"Of course not."

She'd just hung him with his own words by reminding him of that terrible message he'd sent to her about no wedding night. But within a very short amount of time, that man had disappeared. He wanted to take it all back and start over. A lance piercing his body couldn't have done more damage and it was his own fault.

On a groan, Stefano got up from the couch. "We have a lifetime to work everything out. There's one thing I know about you already. I'll always be able to count on your honesty."

Though it was going to take time, Stefano was determined to win her heart. She was a prize beyond all others. Time was all he had now that he was her husband. Hopefully, their marriage would last for the rest of their lives.

"I depend on yours, too," she murmured. "If you'll excuse me, I'm going to bed." She picked up the radio to take with her.

"I'm sure you're tired and bed sounds good to you."

"It does." She started for the hallway.

"We have another exciting day of skiing tomorrow," he reminded her.

"I can't wait," she called over her shoulder.

He believed she meant that. So far they'd enjoyed doing everything together whether cooking, tending Fausto, playing cards or talking. Among other things his wife was a natural at sports, and a moment ago she'd been on fire for him, displaying a hunger for him that was thrilling.

There was no way she could turn off those feelings at will any more than he could. But she didn't have that much experience dealing with desire. He had to ease her into making love with him.

Tomorrow they'd eat dinner at the lodge in disguise once they'd had their fill of skiing. He couldn't wait. Afterward, he'd take her into the bar for dancing where he would have a legitimate reason to put his arms around her and feel the mold of her beautiful body close to him.

He put the game away and turned down the fire before heading for his bedroom. Once he'd looked at his emails, he'd take a quick shower and crawl into bed. Alone. But he didn't intend for this state of affairs to last much longer.

Lanza threw herself across the bed and broke down sobbing into her pillow.

Lying in Stefano's arms tonight, relishing the taste and feel of him, had brought her ecstasy. But she was afraid he didn't love her. The thought that his heart might not be involved had sent a chill through her body and she'd been the one to break it off.

The thought of his making love to her if he wasn't in love the same way she was hurt her so much she couldn't lie there any longer. It would be better to keep her distance from him and not succumb to her own longings. He'd never take her with him to one of his mines, and she'd spend part of her life in pain every time he went away.

Things would get easier once they'd returned to the palace. The difficulty lay in getting through the rest of this week while they were alone. Yet, there was nothing she wanted more in this world than to stay here with him indefinitely.

Lanza decided she had to be out of her mind. Donetta would tell her she was crazy not to live it up the way a man would do, especially with a husband who looked like Stefano. She could hear her sister now. *Forget being in love. There is no such thing. Enjoy!*

Fausta would have a different take on it. She would tell her there was no reason why she couldn't have her own secret lover. It wasn't natural to be forced to stay in a marriage with no joy. Her sister was right, but Lanza couldn't see herself being unfaithful, or even getting interested in another man. What would be the use? Stefano was in a class of his own.

At four in the morning Lanza awakened, shocked to realize she'd never gotten ready for bed. The wind had picked up during the night and moaned around the bedroom windows.

She hurried into the bathroom to change into her nightgown and brush her teeth. When she got into bed, she turned on the radio to a music station to blot out the howling of the wind. There hadn't been a sign of it during the day, but the weather changed fast up here in the mountains.

Lanza finally fell asleep again and didn't get up until ten in the morning. The wind was even stronger than before and the sky had grown dark. That meant another storm was on the way. They wouldn't be able to ski today. She doubted any lifts could run with these gusts.

She scrambled out of bed to get dressed and brush her hair, which she tied back at the nape. Once she'd done her makeup, she headed for the kitchen, hungry for a pastry and some juice. When she opened the fridge, she saw that the leftover pizza was gone, providing Stefano with breakfast. He'd probably gone outside after eating.

Lanza took her food into the living room where he'd turned up the fire and switched on a lamp. Though Stefano had watered their Christmas tree, it didn't look well. She wandered over to the window while she munched. The spectacular view of the mountains never ceased to exhilarate her, especially with the clouds moving in.

Maybe if Stefano didn't have any other plans for today, she could ask him to show her his huge map of the mines and learn what he did. The wealth he brought into his country staggered her.

As she turned to go back to the kitchen, he walked into the living room, dressed in jeans and a pullover with a look of concern on his face. "I'm glad you're up," he said in his deep voice that told her something was wrong. "I was about to waken you."

Her heart pounded. "What is it?"

Lines bracketed his mouth. "I was doing some work on the computer this morning when I received an emergency alert message from my mining manager in Zacatecas, Mexico. There was a cave-in at the Casale mine that has trapped some miners. I have to go and have arranged for the jet."

No. Her heart lurched. "Of course you do. I'm so sorry this has happened. Those poor men and families. What can I do to help?"

"I contacted Enzo. He'll be here at two to help close things up and get you to the airport so you can fly home to Domodossola."

"Please don't worry about me. I'll be fine."

He shook his head. "This wasn't the way I planned for the rest of this week to go."

"Accidents happen, Stefano. You think I don't understand?"

"That's the thing. I know you do, thank God. Where's your phone? Besides Enzo's, I'm putting in the number at the main office at the mine in case you can't reach me and there's an emergency here at home." When that was done, he gave it back to her and grabbed his suitcase.

She walked him downstairs. Wind almost knocked her over when he opened the door before they hurried to the car. "I wish you didn't have to fly out in this."

"Don't worry. This is nothing." He tossed his bag into the back seat, then turned to her. "I'll call you after I've arrived and give you an update."

"Please be safe."

"You took the words right out of my mouth, *Signora* Casale."
He gave her a long, hungry kiss, then got in and shut the door.
She watched through tear-filled eyes until she couldn't see him
anymore.

That kiss had reduced her to the lovesick wife she was fighting
hard not to be. Little did he know he was taking her heart with him
before she went inside the chalet where she'd known the greatest
happiness of her life.

Her thoughts were reeling. The last thing she wanted was to go
home to the palace. A part of her had hoped he would ask her to
fly to Mexico with him. How ridiculous was that?

When she got upstairs she called her Zia Ottavia. Everyone believed she and Stefano would be on their honeymoon in the Caribbean until the end of the week. No one would be the wiser if
she spent time with her aunt. Hopefully, by then, Stefano would
be able to fly home and they would arrive at the palace together.

Her mother's older sister was the best friend she'd ever had. She
answered on the second ring. *"Pronto?"*

"Zia Ottavia? It's Lanza."

"Lanza! Are you calling from the tropics?"

"No, no. It's a long story, but you can't tell a soul. Are you up
for a visitor?"

"How soon?"

"Today."

"Ehi? I don't understand."

"I'll explain later, but only if your invitation is still open."

"I want you to come anytime. You know that!"

Lanza was on the verge of tears. "Thank you for being so wonderful. I probably won't be at your house before evening. I'll take
a taxi. *Fino a tardi*, Zia."

She hurried to the bedroom and phoned the airport. There was
a flight to Rome at four-thirty. If Enzo got here on time, she'd be
able to make it.

Once she'd made the reservation, she phoned him and he assured her he would be there by two at the latest. After she hung
up, she started packing and made her bed. Then she fixed breakfast and cleaned up the kitchen.

At quarter to two she turned off the fireplace switch and went downstairs with her bag and coat. Enzo had just pulled up to the door. He did a quick final inspection of the chalet before they left for the city.

"Stefano is so lucky to have a friend like you. I really appreciate your helping me."

"I'm delighted to do something important for him. He was very worried about leaving you alone."

"I'm the one who's worried. A mine cave-in is so awful. If anyone dies, I know he'll take it on."

"He will, but he can handle anything. I've found that out over the years."

When they reached the airport, he walked her inside with her bags. She turned to him. "You've done enough. Please don't think you have to stay with me."

"I want to and I promised Stefano I'd wait till you boarded your flight. I told him I'd arrange for someone from the palace to meet your plane."

"No, no, Enzo. That won't be necessary, but thank you. I'm flying to Rome to stay with my aunt. She invited me to stay with her at the wedding. Now I'm taking her up on it."

His eyes widened.

"I'm hoping Stefano will be back in time for the two of us to arrive at the palace together."

"I see."

They walked to the gate for the flights going to Italy. "Please don't tell him. When he calls me, I'll let him know I'm in Rome."

His eyes danced. "Your wish is my command, Your Highness."

She laughed. "Don't you dare *Your Highness* me! Since our marriage I've forgotten all about being titled. If I'd had the courage to tell my father I didn't want to live a royal life, I would have been long gone like Stefano."

Enzo's demeanor underwent a drastic change with that comment. He looked nonplussed over what she'd said. Lanza decided she could confide in him a little more.

"Stefano and I had to give up our dreams when we were forced to marry, but we've worked out a solution that gives us as much freedom as possible to do our own thing without question.

"Under circumstances that could have spelled the end of happiness for both of us, we've found the perfect way to have freedom and I couldn't be happier," she asserted, keeping a smile pasted on her face while she was in agony. "I believe he's happy, too. Of course I could be wrong. You've been his friend forever and would be the best judge of that."

He went quiet just as her flight was announced for boarding. She jumped up from the seat and gave him a peck on the cheek. "Thank you for being such a good friend to him. Stefano loves you like a brother and I'll never forget your kindness."

It was after 8:00 p.m. when the driver from the Casale mine picked up Stefano at the Ruiz airport outside Zacatecas. He drove him to the mining office, which was on a high plateau that rose to eight thousand feet. The temperature was in the thirties. He felt right at home in the cold air as he walked inside to meet with his other mining officials.

Dozens of workers and family members milled around while Jose Ortega, the chief engineer, apprised him of everything that was happening. Teams of workers would be working through the night taking turns trying to reach the three trapped victims using the latest equipment. Safety inspectors were still trying to piece together why there'd been a collapse in the structure in the first place.

Stefano was determined to find out why all their precautions to avoid such an accident had failed. So far this had never happened before at any of his mines. He'd been proud of the safety records and would be devastated if there was a loss of life.

He stayed in the office where he could sleep on a cot in the back room. To his relief Alicia hadn't shown up tonight. He planned to avoid her if it was at all possible and got to work at his desk.

First, he needed to look over the plans of the mine where the cave-in had happened. Many factors had to have been in play, including the strength and weight of the soil combined with the porosity and amount of moisture.

When he checked with the environmental factors like weather conditions, he discovered there'd been some ground uplifting and tilting two months ago along the Acapulco Trench that included the

Tehuantepec Ridge. His mine couldn't be found in fault, but right now he was more concerned that the miners would be rescued.

As the men came in and out giving him updates, he made a call to Enzo, wanting to know how everything went before he phoned Lanza. It was 11:00 p.m. here.

"Sorry, Enzo. I know it's the middle of the night for you. I haven't called Lanza yet because I wanted to talk to you first."

"She's fine. What I want to know is, how are you? Have the trapped miners been rescued?"

"We're just getting started, but I want to know about my wife."

"I only have one thing to say. She's not the person I thought she was."

Stefano sucked in his breath. "Is that good or bad?"

"What in the hell do *you* think? I steered you wrong when you asked me for advice in my office that day. Before I put her on the plane, I called her *Your Highness*. She forbid me from ever saying that to her again." Stefano chuckled. "She's nothing like what I'd conjured in my imagination."

He closed his eyes tightly. Amen to that. "I owe you, *amico*."

"Good luck and come home safe. *Ciao*."

"*Ciao*."

Relieved with that report, he phoned Lanza while no one needed to talk to him.

To his satisfaction she answered after the first ring in an anxious voice. "Stefano? Are you all right? What about the trapped miners?"

"Yes and yes. As for the miners, I'll find out soon. There are three of them, but it's going to be difficult reaching them and could take longer than I'd hoped."

She moaned. "Now that you're there to investigate, how do you think it happened?"

"I know exactly what caused it. The graphs showed there was a noticeable ground settling of the earth after tremors along the Acapulco trench a couple of months ago. The collapse couldn't have been prevented."

"Thank heaven you can't be blamed."

"But I will be anyway, and won't be happy until the miners are found and able to be home with their families. I bet your parents were surprised to see you arrive early without me. When I know more, I'll email your father to explain."

"Please don't," she begged.

He frowned. "Why not?"

"I didn't go home, Stefano. I flew to Rome and am staying in my Zia Ottavia's villa. I adore her and she's being wonderful to me. I plan to stay here until you're able to return. If you don't mind, I'd rather meet you at the Domodossola Airport when you fly in from Mexico. We'll arrive back at the palace together."

That explained his conversation with Enzo. She'd mentioned going to her aunt's before. Enzo couldn't have talked her out of it and she'd sworn him to secrecy.

Stefano grinned. His wife was her own person in every way and heavenly shape. "I'm glad you're safe and happy. I'll try to get back as soon as I can."

"Thank you for calling and letting me know you got there without incident. I'll pray those men get out alive."

He swallowed hard. "That means a lot, Lanza. I'm hoping to see you soon. *Buona notte, sposa mia.*"

After hanging up, he left the office to join the other rescue workers. The next few desperate days and nights would keep him from reliving those moments on the couch before Lanza had pulled out of his arms. She'd been life to him, but he had to correct that remark and admit, she *was* life to him.

CHAPTER TWELVE

THOUGH LANZA LOVED spending time with her aunt, her mind wasn't off Stefano for a second. Other than two text messages that said they were still searching for the men, she'd had no other news.

By the fifth day she couldn't stand it. She had to talk to him! But first she called Enzo, who told her he hadn't heard from Stefano, either.

Lanza was fretting that Stefano might feel he had to go down the mine. She had no doubt his life could be in danger if he did and there was another tremor that caused more cave-in. The thought of losing him was too horrendous to contemplate. If she could just hear his voice...

After dinner she went to her room and phoned him on his cell, something she'd promised herself not to do. It was night there. All she got was his voice mail. Lanza hung up, but she couldn't stand not knowing anything.

On impulse she called the mining office number he'd programmed. Someone would be able to tell her what was going on if they were there. She pressed the digit and waited for the call to go through. After a moment, *"Bueno?"* said a female voice.

"Buenas noches, señora. Is there someone in your office who speaks English? I need information."

"Sí."

Frustrated, she said, "I need to speak to Señor Casale, please."

"No disponible," she rapped out.

Thanks to the Spanish she'd learned from one of her tutors, Lanza realized that meant Stefano wasn't there and squeezed her phone tighter. "This is Señora Casale. Will you ask him to call me when he can?"

She could have sworn a half minute passed before she heard the woman say, *"Sí."*

After that one word there was a click that cut them off.

It had to be the shortest phone call in history. Beside herself because she still had no information, Lanza clicked off. The woman hadn't been of any help and probably didn't know English or Italian, but maybe the situation there was as desperate as Lanza had feared.

She hardly slept that night. If she didn't hear from him tomorrow, she would see if her father could get answers she couldn't.

Lanza's prayers had eventually produced results.

Six days after the cave-in, all three men had been rescued to cheers and tears. They would soon be released from the hospital.

Stefano got the cleanup underway and wound up his affairs. At last, he was able to fly straight to Rome to pick up his wife. Six days away from her was too long. He'd gotten used to being with her. Nothing or no one would ever take her place.

En route to the jet he phoned her. "Lanza?"

"Stefano!" she cried. "I've been out of my mind with worry. Thank goodness that woman in the office got my message to you."

"What do you mean? What woman?"

"I phoned last night and a woman answered, but she said you were unavailable. I asked her to tell you to call your wife."

Alicia...

He knew she'd been around, but he'd avoided her. She'd paid him back by not giving him the message from Lanza.

"I would have been difficult to find, but none of it matters. I have the best news! The men are all out and safe. I'm on my way to Rome."

He heard a break in her voice. Hopefully, she was glad he was coming for her. After a minute she said, "How soon do you expect to land?"

"At six-fifteen p.m. your time. Can you meet my plane at the airport?"

"Of course."

"Our families will never know we weren't in the tropics all this time."

"I'm afraid I don't have a tan like yours," she murmured.

"Your ski tan is enough for everyone to be fooled."

She was being too quiet. He imagined she was nervous about them returning to the palace to begin their life together. The best thing that could have happened had been for them to be alone at the chalet. He wished they had another two weeks of freedom ahead of them.

"How's your aunt?"

"Amazing. We've always been close."

"One day you'll have to invite her to the palace to spend some time with us."

"I'd love that."

This chitchat was driving him crazy. "Do you have any news to share?"

"Yes!" All of a sudden she came alive. "I called the refuge. The man who helped us said Fausto adapted well and yesterday they took him out in the woods. This morning he didn't come back."

"That means he's found a way to survive."

"I know. I'm really glad. We know he'll be happy now."

Stefano gripped his phone tighter. "How do you feel about that?"

"Fausto is back home. What more could we ask?"

"We couldn't."

He heard her sigh. "You've got a long flight ahead of you."

"Not too bad. I'll sleep most of the way. We'll have dinner on the plane for the short flight to Domodossola. Now I have to go. We're getting ready to take off. See you tonight."

"Be safe."

"You, too."

He hung up and climbed the steps, anxious to get back to Lanza. After chatting with his pilot and steward, he walked to his bedroom. Once they'd attained cruising speed and the seat belt light had gone off, he prepared to pass out until it was time for the descent.

The whole nightmare of the cave-in was over and his wife would be meeting him at the airport in Rome. Maybe now he could actually get some sleep.

Stefano couldn't believe it when the steward knocked on his door and told him it was almost time to fasten his seat belt. He really had needed the sleep. They were about to make their approach.

He shaved and freshened up, then slipped on the same gray suit he'd worn the night they'd left on their honeymoon. His pulse picked up speed as he moved to the club car to check on the dinner menu and get ready for the landing.

The jet taxied along the tarmac. The second it came to a stop, he leaped from his chair. His steward opened the door so he could rush down the stairs.

Like magic, Lanza stepped out of the taxi parked nearby. She, too, had chosen to wear the same suit with the lace hem. She'd even done her hair up with the same pearl clip and the necklace he'd given her. Princess Lanza Rossiano was in evidence once more.

He drew closer to her, noticing a nerve throbbing at the base of her throat where the pearl lay. She was even more beautiful than he remembered when they'd said goodbye at the chalet. Those blue eyes met his for a breathless moment.

Stefano wanted to crush her in his arms, but this wasn't the place in front of his staff or the taxi driver. Instead, he pressed a kiss to her cheek and cupped her elbow. "Come on. Our dinner is waiting for us."

He helped her up the steps and inside to the club compartment of the jet. The steward brought her coat and luggage. After she sat down and fastened her seat belt, he did the same and before long they were in the air. The moment they could unbuckle, the steward served them a pasta dinner with shrimp.

"I told him to serve us soon because this flight won't take us long."

She started to eat. "You asked me earlier if I had any news. I decided to wait and tell you what my aunt told me. She said that while we were gone, my parents had the second floor of the east wing of the palace restored to a home for us.

"It has three bedrooms, a kitchen, sitting room, den, an office with the latest computer software for you, a terrace, two bathrooms, a living room, everything we could want. It's their wedding gift to us."

"That's very generous of them. I'll thank them as soon as possible. Now I'd like some advice from you."

"What is it?"

"I have to fly to Argentina the day after tomorrow. The timing is terrible since I've just returned from Mexico."

She didn't react to the news, but he knew it came as a surprise that he was leaving again so soon. "This meeting with my engineers in Puerto San Julian in the northwestern part of the country was planned before Alberto died and can't be changed."

"Father wouldn't expect you to."

But what about you, Lanza?

"We've been putting in a new process, which increases the purity of gold by electrolysis. I won't bore you with all the details, but by use of an electric current the gold can be restored to a highly pure metallic state, leaving the impurities separate."

"It sounds complicated."

"More than that, it takes time to make sure it's all working satisfactorily and has involved some engineers from Chile, Bolivia and the States. I have to be there to oversee everything. Yet, I know your father is expecting to meet with me in the morning to discuss what responsibilities he expects me to start handling. I'm concerned he'll be offended when I tell him I have a prior commitment before I can give him quality time."

She finished her coffee. "He'll understand. How long will you be gone? Four, five weeks?"

"It could be that long."

"Then tell him the truth and say you'll probably need five weeks before you're back. That way he won't have expectations you can't meet."

Stefano nodded. "That's sound advice I'll take to heart. I'm sorry I'm going to have to leave you the moment we're back."

She stared at him in a way he couldn't tell what she was thinking. "We knew this would be our life."

Yes, he knew, but he hadn't counted on being crazy about his wife. "What will you do while I'm gone?"

A small laugh escaped her lips. "What I've been doing for several years. I organize benefits to raise money. At present my efforts are for our various homeless shelters. As I told you earlier, there's a new low-income housing project going up on the other side of the city. I'm anxious to get enough money donated to start a soup kitchen.

"And after that, I'm planning to find a billionaire who might be willing to donate land for the building of new housing for our naval vets. Again, it all takes money and sometimes I reach out to our allies who are willing to invest a little."

He heard what she was saying, but she wasn't the same woman he'd been with at the chalet. It was as if she'd lowered a shield between them he couldn't get past.

In several prior conversations with her, she'd told him her sister Donetta, who wanted to be king, would make a great one. To Stefano's mind Lanza was the sister who would make the best ruler.

The steward came in to remove their trays. After he left them alone Stefano said, "I phoned your father's chief assistant, Marcello, earlier and told him we'd be arriving shortly."

One delicate brow lifted. "I would love to have shown up unannounced, but you did the right thing and will be in his good graces. My father dislikes surprises."

"So does mine. Any other advice to help me?"

"You don't need it. Do you know what he said when he told me you'd asked for my hand? 'Lanza? Prince Stefano was raised like his brother, Alberto, and will make a splendid husband for you. His brilliant business acumen is known around the world. He's Basilio's son, after all.' There could be no greater praise."

But Stefano knew Lanza hadn't believed what her father had told her about him at the time. That was because he'd hurt her too deeply.

Our life will begin after we meet at the altar. Don't worry about our wedding night. We'll spend it away from everyone while we sort out the rules of engagement.

Looking back on what he'd said to her crushed him now.

The fasten seat belts sign flashed on.

She smiled at him. "We're almost home. Happy New Year, Stefano."

The waiter poured Lanza more coffee after a working dinner with Matteo Fontana at a restaurant in the western part of Domodossola City. Earlier in the day she'd walked through the new low-income, three-story housing facility with him. She enjoyed working with the young, good-looking, wealthy businessman in charge of overseeing this big project, one of her pet projects.

"It's fabulous. How soon can it be opened?"

His warm brown eyes played over her. "One week, Your Highness."

"You've accomplished everything in such a short time. I'm awestruck."

"I'm glad you're delighted. Our office is pleased, too."

"Did you have a chance to look over my ideas for a series of soup kitchens? I'm still working on getting the funds, but what do you think?"

"I went over them with my architect, Marco. They're brilliant and desperately needed. If you give me the go-ahead, they can all be built within six months."

"Wonderful. It will make a big difference to the problems in this area of the city. I'm running another couple of fund-raisers in the next two weeks. Hopefully, we'll go over the top with donations and I can phone you with the good news."

To her surprise he suddenly got to his feet, staring beyond her. "Your Highness!"

Who on earth was Matteo addressing? She turned in the chair and almost fainted to see Stefano standing behind her. With his dark hair and eyes, he was so incredibly striking, and looked so handsome in a navy business suit, she could hardly believe that it was her husband standing there.

Stefano had only been gone ten days and wasn't expected back from Argentina for at least three more weeks! She got to her feet. "Stefano—"

Her husband's dark, penetrating gaze took in Matteo before

focusing on her. "I got through early with my project and hurried home. Marcello told me I could find you here."

She was in shock. Not only had he come home ahead of time, he'd also gone out of his way to find her. If she wasn't clutching the edge of the table, her legs wouldn't support her.

"L-let me introduce you to Matteo Fontana," she stammered. "He's the dynamic businessman in charge of the fabulous housing project I told you about. We've been talking about the date for the opening."

"It's an honor to meet you, Your Highness." She could tell Matteo was flat-out intimidated because Stefano wasn't only the crown prince, he also had a sophisticated aura that made him stand out from other men.

"My wife has talked a lot about this project. I'm pleased to meet the man responsible."

"The privilege has been mine to work with her. She's one of the most enlightened people I've ever met."

He was very kind. "Thanks, Matteo."

"I couldn't agree more," Stefano murmured before he flicked his gaze to hers. "Have you finished your business dinner, or shall I come back for you later?"

"We're through, Your Highness," Matteo rushed to assure him. Then he smiled at Lanza. "Let me know about those fund-raisers and I'll give Marco the okay to start drawing up the blueprints."

"You're talking about the soup kitchens?" her husband wanted to know.

Matteo nodded.

Stefano eyed her intently. "You've accomplished a great deal in the time I've been gone."

"Your wife is a dynamo and so easy to work with." Matteo looked at her one more time. "Thank you for meeting me for dinner."

"It was my pleasure. *Buona notte*, Matteo."

He nodded to Stefano. "Your Highness. If you'll excuse me."

As he left the restaurant, Stefano put a hand on the back of her chair. "Are you through eating?"

"Yes."

"Then let's go back to the palace. I have the limo waiting."

She walked through the restaurant with him. When he helped her into the back, she could smell the scent of the soap he used in the shower. Her desire for him was off the charts. He sat next to her. With a sideward glance she could see he'd either shaved on the jet, or he'd gone to the palace first to freshen up before coming to get her.

The sun had set as they drove through the city, a magical time with the lights turned on. They hadn't had snow for at least a week, which made it easier to walk around the building site with Matteo.

"How did the process go in Argentina?"

"Good. I felt confident to leave earlier than planned. Tell me how long you've known *Signor* Fontana."

She blinked. "We met about a year ago at a state dinner at the palace when the plans for the project were only in the embryo stage."

"Do you meet with him often?"

"I've seen him dozens of times in the past year and almost every day for the past week."

"Are you aware he's crazy about you? I didn't see a wedding ring."

Was it possible Stefano had developed husbandly feelings for her, and that was why he'd come home early? Lanza's heart almost jumped out of her chest.

"He's not married."

"It seemed to me he forgot you were married, too, until he noticed me walk over to the table."

"Why do you say that?"

"He was eating you alive with his eyes. I'm not sure it's a good idea for you to meet alone with him."

She felt a fluttering in her chest, but chose not to respond to that comment because deep down she knew Matteo did have a tiny crush on her. But more important, she'd never seen this domineering side of Stefano before.

Lanza had thought often about her short conversation with the woman at the mine. Stefano had played dumb about it, never letting on who it was. Perhaps she'd been one of the women he'd once had an affair with.

That relationship might be in the past, but he'd come home to

Lanza, who was still unfinished business. Was that it? Could that be the problem challenging him? Was she his only failure when it came to seducing a woman? Her thoughts darted hither and yon.

Before long they reached the palace and the driver took them around to the east entrance. Stefano helped her out of the limo. A staff member opened the large palace doors so they could walk up the steps. Once on the second floor, they entered their apartment, the size of the average person's house.

Ten nights ago he'd gone to one of the bedrooms to get some sleep early because he'd had to leave for the airport at five o'clock the next morning. Lanza had stayed up to talk to her sisters about her trip and hadn't gone to bed until one in the morning in another of the bedrooms.

Tonight was different.

Stefano was in a strange mood she didn't understand unless she was right and he hadn't liked seeing her with another man. Had it brought out his egotistical side, and now he was feeling possessive? If so, it wasn't enough for her.

He removed his suit jacket and undid the top buttons of his shirt where she saw a dusting of black hair on his chest.

After he pushed his sleeves up to the elbows, he hunkered in front of the fireplace to put more logs on the fire. While it crackled and the flames lit up the semidark room, she couldn't take her eyes off his well-honed physique. Right now she was having to fight overpowering feelings of desire for him.

She stood near the long, rounded green velvet couch facing the fireplace. Its color was reflected in the background of the huge tapestries hanging on the walls depicting medieval forest scenes with animals.

"Why didn't you phone that you were coming tonight, Stefano? I would have planned to have dinner waiting for you."

He stood up and turned to her, putting his hands on his hips in a totally male stance. "I wanted to surprise you and take you out for a meal."

"That would have been very nice. I couldn't believe it when Matteo called out and said, 'Your Highness.'"

"I know for a fact he wasn't happy to see me."

"You're wrong, you know. It's just that you're bigger than life to everyone and it intimidates them, even Enzo, who worships you."

"You're mistaken."

"No, Stefano. I witnessed it with my own eyes."

Maybe that was true, but Lanza had been deeply engrossed in conversation with Matteo when he'd walked into the restaurant. Even from a distance, Stefano could tell the man was totally entranced with her.

At that moment Stefano had experienced a flare of jealousy, which was so foreign to him, he'd felt violent inside. What made it worse was that Lanza seemed to enjoy Matteo's attention. Seeing them together like that had disturbed him so much he couldn't seem to calm down.

She was always gracious and charming with a style all her own, but Stefano had felt deflated that she hadn't shown more excitement at seeing him tonight. Ten days away from her had felt like death.

"My father will be thrilled to know you're home."

"He already knows. We talked for a moment and I've been asked to have breakfast with him and your mother."

Lanza smiled. "She's anxious to give you a tour of the stables and the kennel. She is an animal lover like me and my sisters."

"I'm sure that will be enjoyable, but aren't you going to come with us?"

"I can't. While you've been gone, I've had a full schedule of duties. Tomorrow I have to leave early enough to visit a school of students at risk by eight in the morning. I'm making an assessment of their needs in order to gather donations of books and other supplies they lack."

He admired her work ethic more than she would ever know, but he missed the intimacy of the chalet. It seemed that nothing was the same here at the palace.

"I understand, but now that I'm back, I'd like to spend more time with you. We need to coordinate our activities."

To his disappointment, Lanza simply smiled and said, "I agree, but could we leave it for now? I'm dead tired after a full day and need to get to bed."

"Don't go yet— We have to talk."

"Can't we do that tomorrow after I return?"

She seemed so distant. He longed for the closeness they'd had in the chalet.

"No. This can't wait."

Her brows furrowed. "What's wrong?"

He rubbed the back of his neck absently. "I don't like what's happening to us."

"Because I wasn't here when you flew home from Argentina?"

"That and other things."

"Oh." Lanza looked perplexed. "If you don't mind me asking, why do you care? We both agreed to do our own thing, no questions asked. I can't help it that you came home from your trip early. Now you're breaking your own rules. Which is it, Stefano? You can't have it both ways."

Frustrated beyond reason, he reached for her, pulling her against him. "I cut my trip short by three weeks because I missed you and couldn't get home fast enough. I want us to have a real marriage."

Lanza pulled away and looked at him, confused.

"No, you don't," she argued back. "You made it clear to me from the start that this was going to be a business arrangement."

"I know," said Stefano, sighing. "But I do now, and I think you want it, too. When you kissed me back at the chalet, I knew you wanted me even though you wouldn't admit it. It's not something you can hide."

Lanza moved out of his arms, cutting him to the quick. Her eyes stared at him as if she didn't know him.

"What's happened to you? I can't believe you could change this fast without a reason. Does this have anything to do with my father? Don't tell me he demanded that we produce an heir before the year is out? Is that what this is all about?"

"Lanza—"

How could she think that? But then again, he had never spelled out to her that his feelings for her had changed. No wonder she wouldn't listen to him. She carried on in full flow.

"Is that why you came home early? Did you feel guilty? Or did my father insist you hurry home to get me pregnant ASAP?"

As it happened it was Stefano's father who had brought it up during a phone conversation he'd had with him while he'd been in Argentina. He'd been upset that Stefano had barely come home from Mexico before flying off to South America so soon. "How can you and Lanza have a family under these circumstances?" he'd complained, and Stefano had had to admit he was right.

Her cheeks were flushed, and he could see she was agitated and upset. "When I agreed to marry you, I was planning on normalcy until you warned me of your rules of engagement and told me ours would be a marriage of convenience. It killed something inside me."

He groaned. Why had he sent her that note? "I know that now. I was so wrong and I'm sorry I've hurt you. I would love to start again. Please, can you forgive my foolish mistake?"

"It's not a case of forgiveness, Stefano. I guess I'm not like other women. My sisters tease me for being naive and gullible. They reminded me that this is a business arrangement, even if I let myself believe for a time in the chalet it could be more than that. But you managed to take off my blinders. If you want to try for a baby tonight, let's do it!" Stefano looked at her in shock. Had he really made her feel like this? He felt ashamed that he had hurt her so badly.

"You deceived me with this marriage and were my second choice. Not that I actually had one."

Stefano tried to protest, but she had started for her bedroom. When she reached the door, she turned around. "Well? Are you coming to fulfill your next duty to produce an heir? Let's get it over with."

Minutes passed before Lanza realized Stefano wasn't going to follow her. She went into the bedroom, but before the door closed, she saw that the color in his face had turned ashen. She felt so sick and heartbroken, she wanted to die.

Heaven help her. What had she done? While he'd stood there begging her forgiveness, she'd cut him off.

In reality he *had* come home from Argentina much earlier than planned. Stefano had told her he'd missed her. He'd displayed a jealousy she couldn't have imagined when he'd found her with Matteo. But she'd dismissed all that. She'd been angry with him and lashed out, but now she felt terrible for the way she must have hurt him. She'd seen the stricken look on his face as she'd left the room.

Lanza stood with her back against the door, burying her face in her hands while the tears gushed. How could she have let her pain turn her into someone she despised? What she needed to do was beg *his* forgiveness.

Without hesitation, she left the bedroom and hurried across the apartment to his bedroom, praying he hadn't left the palace already. He would have had every right.

"Stefano?" When he didn't answer, she knocked. There was no response so she opened the door. In the semidarkness she saw him sitting on the edge of the bed with his head bent and his arms clasped between his powerful legs.

She was so thankful he hadn't gone, she hurried toward him. Standing in front of him she said, "Stefano? Can you ever forgive me for what I said to you? I didn't mean any of it." Her voice throbbed.

He lifted his dark head and looked up at her. "There isn't a cruel bone in your beautiful body. You spoke the truth when you said *I'm* the one who deceived you. What frightens me is that you'll never believe I've fallen in love with you. I love you, Lanza. So terribly in fact that I don't know myself anymore."

She knew those words had come straight from his heart and she launched herself at him.

"Darling—" She threw her arms around his shoulders. "Can you ever forget the awful things I said to you? I can't believe I said them. I love you so much I can hardly breathe. By the time we took the carriage ride on our wedding day, I knew I loved you because I'd already had help from Alberto."

"What do you mean?" he whispered against her throat.

"Your brother idolized you. When you asked what he and I talked about when we were together, most of the conversation was about you. He told me story after story and wished he could be half the man you were."

"He said those things?" Stefano sounded incredulous.

"Yes, and much more. He made me fall for you long before I met you at the altar. But I fought my feelings with all my might because I never dreamed his brilliant, dashing elder brother could ever fall in love with me."

"*Lanza—*"

Stefano didn't give her a chance to say another word. He followed her down on the bed and began to devour her, kissing away her tears. She lost all sense of time and surroundings as they attempted to assuage their longing for each other. Being loved by her husband was absolute heaven.

Lanza had been convinced she'd never find love, or never know how it felt to be adored and ravished by a man like Stefano, who was worshipping her with his body.

The rapture he brought her was beyond anything she could have comprehended. They gave each other continual pleasure throughout the night and morning. In their euphoria, they forgot the world and only sought to bring each other joy.

"Have you really forgiven me, *bellissima*?" It was midmorning and he'd tangled his hands in her hair. "I was out of my mind to say and do what I did to you."

She kissed his mouth hungrily, never able to get enough of him. "To be honest, I was shocked you would actually marry me after you'd given up the royal life for so many years. I still can't believe you went through with the wedding. I'm the luckiest woman on earth."

He cupped her face in his hands. "There's something you need to know that will explain why I agreed to our marriage." In the next breath he told her about Alberto's sacrifice. As the story unfolded, tears welled in her eyes once more.

"Oh, Stefano—that explains the picture he sent me of you."

His gorgeous dark eyes filmed over. "You were right, *amore mio.* There was no man more honorable and I was a coward for running away as long as I did. When I found out he never intended for me to know what he'd done for me, I knew I had to follow through in his place. But what I don't understand is why you were willing to marry me."

"I have a secret, too. One I hope won't upset you too terribly."

"Now that I know you love me, I'm too happy to be upset about anything."

She covered his face with kisses, loving him to distraction.

"When my parents told me you'd asked for my hand and that they wanted me to marry you, I rebelled until they told me my father had a health problem. They still haven't explained exactly, but I'm pretty sure it's his heart. *Papà* told me he needed a son-in-law to lean on."

Stefano kissed her long and hard. "I already knew."

"But you couldn't! They didn't tell anyone."

"My father figured it out during a visit two months before our wedding and told me Victor was slowly fading. When I heard that admission, I thought that if the woman I was about to marry could love her father enough to make a sacrifice that earthshaking, then I had to have faith that we could eventually make a good marriage. But like you, I fought it hard in the beginning. The day my parents told me I had to marry you, I went to see Enzo and get his advice."

An impish smile broke out on her succulent mouth. "What did he say?"

"You want the exact translation?"

"You know I do."

"He said, 'All right—there's only one way I can see this working. You need your freedom, so do her the biggest favor of her life and yours. You've got a year before the wedding. Let her know *before* you're married that you plan to be your own person and continue doing the mining work you love while you help her father govern. It'll mean you'll be apart from her for long periods. Give her time to adjust to that fact, know what I mean?'"

Lanza burst into laughter first. "I love Enzo. When he drove me to the airport, he was surprised that I was flying to Rome. I told him you and I had to give up our dreams when we were forced to marry, but we worked out a solution that gives both of us as much freedom as possible to do our own thing without question. To think that little monkey was the architect of your rules of engagement."

"In a manner of speaking." Stefano grinned before kissing the hollow in her throat.

She kissed him back. "I also told him our circumstances could have spelled the end of happiness for both of us, but we found the perfect solution through freedom and I couldn't be happier. Enzo must be laughing his head off about now."

Stefano pulled her on top of him and looked into her eyes. "I talked to him the other day. He told me he thinks I'm the lucki-est man on the planet and I better be good to you. What he didn't know was that I already wanted you beyond reason."

So saying, he covered her mouth with his own and gave her another long, passionate kiss that went on and on. When he fi-nally lifted his head he whispered, "You have no idea how much I missed you. Every night when I went to bed, I dreamed of you. The next time I have to leave, I'm taking you with me."

"Darling—"

"Just promise me one thing."

"What is it?"

"That you'll forget that letter I sent you and the things I said to you on our first morning at the chalet. I'm in love with you and plan to be so good to you, you'll love me forever."

Her eyes shone like hot blue stars. "Is that your way of saying you believe in forever?"

"You've convinced me there's something to it because I can't imagine life without you. When you went to the other bedroom last night, it felt like death. I never want to experience that feel-ing again."

"I know because I felt it, too. That's why I came flying back into you. Thank you for forgiving me."

She burrowed her face in his neck. "I love you, love you."

"Enough to have my baby?"

"Oh, Stefano—I can't wait to get pregnant."

"We'll have beautiful royal babies because you'll be their mother." He bit her earlobe gently. "Do you think they'll hate us for bringing them into the world?"

"They'll get over it."

"How do you know?"

She gave him an illuminating smile. "*We* did."

* * * * *

A New Year's Eve Proposal

Kim Findlay

Kim Findlay is a Canadian who fled the cold to live on a sailboat in the Caribbean and write romance novels. She shares the boat with her husband and the world's cutest spaniel. Bucket list accomplished! Her first Harlequin Heartwarming novel, *Crossing the Goal Line*, came about from the Heartwarming Blitz, and she's never looked back. Keep up with Kim, including her sailing adventures, at kimfindlay.ca.

Books by Kim Findlay

A Hockey Romance

Crossing the Goal Line
Her Family's Defender

Cupid's Crossing

A Valentine's Proposal
A Fourth of July Proposal

Visit the Author Profile page
at millsandboon.com.au for more titles.

Dear Reader,

Thanks for coming on this journey with me as Carter's Crossing transforms into Cupid's Crossing. This third book in the series was an additional challenge, as it starts before *A Valentine's Proposal* and continues past the events of *A Fourth of July Proposal*. The transformation of the mill that happens in this book was the major event to make the town the romance center it aspired to be, so this was an important part of the series.

The story idea began as I imagined an architect who'd had problems with a crooked contractor on his last job coming to Carter's Crossing and meeting a female contractor who'd had it up to here with mansplaining and people questioning her fitness for a traditionally male job. From there, I just needed to get them to see that they needed each other. No problem!

Over the course of construction, they learn to trust each other, but of course, it's not an easy journey. I hope you enjoy Trevor and Andie's story. Maybe something has happened to you that damaged your confidence in others and yourself. Or maybe you have had to adjust your dreams or found your dreams have changed over time. But always, we want to find our special someone.

Thank you for taking this journey with me.

Kim

To Lara, Ritchard and Grant,

who all helped with technical things I know nothing about,

with my apologies for my mistakes in the Cupid books.

CHAPTER ONE

SHE'D BEEN STARING at the glass of soda and ignoring the people in the pub around her for fifteen minutes. At least. Arms crossed and leaning on the bar countertop, she watched the glass like it held the secrets of the universe.

He knew it had been that long because he'd arrived fifteen minutes ago, and she'd already been deep in her staredown with the fizzy liquid. The stool beside her had been the only empty seat in the place when he came in, so he'd sat down and ordered a beer for himself. He tried not to watch her, but it was hard, because she was right *there*. Staring at her soda.

He hadn't planned on this stop at the Goat and Barley, but he'd needed to clean up after helping a senior citizen change her tire. Changing the tire hadn't made a mess, but her Great Dane had managed to lick his face and hands, and he preferred to not wear a layer of dog saliva. It seemed only right to order a drink in return for use of their restroom.

Now he thought he might stay for a bit. It was better than spending the afternoon on his own, and it *was* New Year's Eve.

Something about his barstool neighbor pricked his attention. She looked sad. That was obviously not his problem, but it seemed wrong to ignore her distress.

Something jammed into his ribs, and he turned as cold liquid dripped onto his pant leg. He looked up and met the shocked gaze of an older man.

"My apologies. I lost my balance and..."

From the smell, it was Scotch now dripping over his thigh. The man reached forward to rescue the glass from the bar top, and Trevor got a blast of more Scotch.

He wiped at his leg, but it was no use. The whiskey had soaked into his pants.

"I'm sorry. Let me buy you another, um, whatever..."

Trevor's beer was only half gone. He didn't want to drink another, since he still had to drive. He shook his head and forced a smile.

"No problem. Accidents happen."

The man blinked at him for a moment, then his phone buzzed, and he moved a shaky hand to his pocket.

"Rachel? What? I can't hear—"

The man wandered away, weaving through the crowd, people moving out of his way as he blundered into them.

"Are you okay?"

Trevor turned his attention to the bartender wiping the bar top. He'd taken the spilled glass and was watching for Trevor's reaction.

"I'm fine." Trevor glanced over his shoulder. "Is he alright?"

The bartender glanced toward the door, with a frown. "I called someone for him. He'll be good for now."

Trevor reminded himself he didn't know these people, and they could undoubtedly take care of themselves.

The bartender moved away, and Trevor turned to the woman on the stool next to him. She hadn't moved. She'd ignored the whole incident.

He should just leave her alone, but he was in a strange place on this day of celebration, and he was tired of fixating on his own problems. Some variety would be a distraction, if nothing else.

The only thing that had changed with the woman since he'd arrived was her soda was less fizzy. It would soon be flat.

He was rusty at this, no longer at ease in social interactions. But tonight was about ending the old and starting anew. He could start a conversation. If he could think of something to say.

"Are you breaking up?"

Had he actually said that? He wouldn't normally do anything like this, but that unwavering stare at the flattening pop was… eerie.

She blinked and looked at him for the first time since he'd sat down next to her.

While she'd been leaning over, a curtain of brown hair had hidden most of her face, and he hadn't gotten a good look at her. Now frowning hazel-green eyes met his. She had a straight nose, strong jaw and pink lips without makeup.

She raised her eyebrows, and he felt his cheeks warm. He should have kept silent.

"What?"

She'd had to lean toward him to respond, and a whiff of some clean scent, soap perhaps, tickled his nostrils and gave him courage to continue.

He nodded at the drink.

"Are you two breaking up?"

She looked back at the drink, as if it might have changed in the last thirty seconds.

"Am I breaking up?"

This was awkward. He was out of practice and was making a fool of himself. No one could say he didn't follow through, though.

"With your drink. You've been frowning at it since I sat down here."

A reluctant grin pulled up the corner of her mouth. It added a sparkle to her eyes, and he realized with a jolt that she was pretty. And that maybe he hadn't completely embarrassed himself.

She turned her gaze back to the glass.

"No, it's not a breakup. It's more of…an anniversary."

It obviously wasn't a happy anniversary, but he didn't know her and didn't want her story. He wasn't sure why he'd felt the need to break into her reverie, but he wasn't going to pry.

"What about you two?" she asked, looking at the half-empty glass of draft beer in front of him.

She was interested in talking, in spite of what was going on with her and her beverage. He was surprised he wanted to talk to her, as well.

He cocked his head, considering his response, thinking of something light, easy.

"This is what I'd call a blind date."

Her smile grew, and he felt good. Like he'd accomplished a challenging task.

She lowered her voice to a whisper.

"How's it going?"

He leaned in, playing the game with her. "Nice, but I don't think this is the one."

She nodded, solemnly. "Well, you have to drink a lot of toads before you find your princess."

A laugh snorted out of him. He hadn't made a sound like that in…forever.

"You did not just say that. That is the grossest—" he said, shaking his head.

Her lips were pulled between her teeth to prevent her own laugh, but the eyes dancing above them gave her away. "I have three brothers. *Gross* is their forte."

Brothers. The smile slipped away from his face.

He didn't want to talk about family, not now. He felt her gaze on him, but he kept his face turned to his beer.

"You're not from around here."

She changed the subject, and he appreciated it. He made sure he had a polite expression on his face when he turned back to her.

"What gave me away?"

He thought he looked like most of the other customers. Sweater and jeans, warm jacket hanging on the back of his seat. Utility boots, whether for working or simply for keeping warm. Once he'd left the outskirts of New York City, the temperature had dropped and kept dropping as he'd driven for hours to get here.

Here being a small town named Carter's Crossing. He'd signed on for a yearlong project in the hopes of keeping his firm alive so he wouldn't have to go back to working for someone else.

"I grew up here. Lived in Carter's Crossing all my life. I know all the locals."

That must be what it was like in a small town. No anonymity. Presumably, most of the people in this bar were locals, but none of them had come over to see if she was okay. Interesting.

"I'm from New York. The city. I'm not familiar with this part of the state." He considered his next question. He could call this research. "What's this place like?"

She seemed to think for a while and then come to some decision. There was a trace of a smile on her face, so he thought the decision was in his favor, and that warmed him. Maybe he hadn't lost all his social skills over the past two years.

"Do you know anything about small towns?"

He shook his head. He'd been born and raised in New York City. He was accustomed to crowds and lights and the sounds of people all the time. A feeling of hustle even when sitting still.

Her lip quirked on one side, and he found his gaze hooked there. He noticed her lips, their shape and color, and he wondered what it would be like to kiss them.

Whoa. He gave himself a mental slap, met her gaze again and listened to the words coming from that mouth.

"It's small, which means there are no strangers. It's great when you want people or when you need help, because everyone gathers around, but it's more difficult when you want to be alone. And it's hard to keep secrets."

Trevor was suddenly aware this woman was on her own by choice, and that the people in this bar, who would all know her, had left her alone because that's what she wanted. He was intruding. He *was* still missing some of those social skills.

He leaned back slowly, reluctantly. He felt himself flushing as he realized he was one of those guys convinced a woman on her own needed his company.

"I'm sorry. I didn't mean to intrude."

She made an abrupt movement with her hand, as if she was reaching out to touch him, to keep him there beside her. But she stopped it, and her face reddened.

"No, it's okay. As you might have guessed, this isn't a happy day. I'm bracing myself to get through it. I appreciate the distraction of talking to someone who doesn't know and isn't anxiously asking me how I'm doing."

He could relate to that. She had no idea how tired he was of the same. Enough that he'd driven out to Carter's Crossing on New

Year's Eve to take one more look at the place he'd agreed to work, just to be out of the city and away from those sympathetic eyes.

He held her gaze, letting her know he understood. Empathized. Was avoiding his own stuff.

"I'll promise not to ask you about your business if you promise the same."

She gave a slight nod and then continued the conversation as if there hadn't been that break. "Carter's. It's a pretty town, for the most part."

He'd noticed as he'd driven through.

"It was a lumber town until just a couple of years ago. The better-off people lived around the park in their nice Victorian homes. When you cross the train tracks, heading to the mill, you have the places where the workers lived. As the mill had to lay people off, those homes got a little more run-down."

The buildings in a town said a lot about a place, and he'd been reading Carter's story on his visits.

"There's a literal wrong side of the tracks?" He meant it as a joke, but all sign of humor left her face.

"If you judge by money, then yes. And maybe people were a little more likely to break the rules on the poorer side, but it's only because not having money is one of the things that can limit your choices. I know good people on both sides."

For some reason, he was upset that he'd been put into the group of people that judged by money. The kind who would consider the worker side of the railroad to be the wrong side. He was mortified he'd leaped to those conclusions and that she'd seen that.

"I'm sorry." He shrugged. "I've been fortunate enough that even though I've never exactly been rich, I've had choices."

Until his choices had been taken away. He would guard against that in future. He suspected she might not have had many choices, and that maybe limits had been imposed on her by others.

He didn't think poverty was her problem. Even though she'd ordered a soft drink and then simply sat looking at it, her clothes were clean, almost new, and good quality. Her skin was clear, and her eyes weren't shadowed from lack of sleep. There were lines at the corners of her eyes, but her mouth was still positioned for smiling, not pulled down at the corners by endless struggle.

It was something else, and he'd guess it was connected to the anniversary drink in front of her, but he'd promised not to ask. He hadn't thought he'd want to.

She closed her eyes for a moment. "I didn't mean to be judgmental. Most of my people live in that part of town, so I may be a little protective of them."

She had people? "Which side do you live on?"

It was a little pushy. They had an unspoken agreement not to probe too closely, didn't they?

"Neither, really. My family's place is just outside of town, so you could say we have a foot on both sides."

We? Family *we* or partner *we*? He hadn't thought she was with someone. No ring on the fourth finger, no mention of someone before this. It had been a while since he'd been curious about someone else, but talking to this woman kept him from feeling sorry for himself or second-guessing his decision to come to Carter's Crossing. Knowing about the town and its people would help.

"You've never wanted to leave?"

She narrowed her eyes, and he realized he'd touched on something.

"I did once. Maybe I will again someday, but for now, this is where I am."

He glanced over at the glass of soda and wondered if that was connected to her reason for staying, but again, they weren't allowed to dig deep.

She talked about leaving, without someone with her. That pleased him. He wanted to keep talking with her.

"Tell me more about Carter's Crossing. I promise I'll withhold judgment."

Her lips twisted as she considered his request.

"Okay, if you'll tell me about living in the city."

He held out his hand. "Deal."

She lifted her hand to shake his, and he noticed hers was rough and calloused, the nails short. This was a woman who worked with her hands. He was so curious, but he ignored the impulse to ask her any questions, as well as the jolt of awareness that skin-on-skin contact provided. Instead, he took his hand back and had another sip of his beer.

He'd promised not to pry.

She sat back in her seat, a smile playing on the corners of her lips. "This reminds me of the city mouse and the country mouse. You know, that kids story? Only, I can't remember the ending. Did the city mouse move to the country or the country mouse to the city?"

He might come to a town like this to work, but his home was in the city, and that wasn't going to change.

He shrugged. "The country mouse probably stayed in the country and the city mouse in the city."

She shook her head. "In real life, the country mice tend to end up in the city. Only a few of us stay in the country."

Andie wasn't sure what it was about this guy, but talking to him was fun. She wasn't Andie, business owner, responsible for her family and her employees. She wasn't poor Andie, reliving the worst day of her life. She was just a woman in a bar, talking to an interesting man.

He was interesting and not just because he was from somewhere else. Not just because she liked his rangy build and the way a lock of dark hair fell over those deep brown eyes framed by tortoise-shell glasses. She felt a connection with him.

He had secrets, wounds he didn't want to share. She could tell by the way he respected hers. He knew the burden of sympathy, and how it refused to let you forget.

He listened as she told him about Carter's Crossing, the mill town now trying to reinvent itself as a romance destination. He talked about his experiences in New York. Nothing personal, nothing too revealing, but even those bits did expose glimpses of who he was.

He had respect for people. He had a sense of humor. He didn't mention friends, and she wondered if he was lonely.

He didn't mention his family, either. He'd flinched when she'd mentioned her brothers, so she suspected he had family issues. On the other hand, who had a family without some kind of issue? When he described New York City, he often described the buildings as if they were residents, part of the population that made up the city, and she found that fascinating.

Her phone pinged with a text message, and that was the first she became aware of how much time had passed. The pale winter sunlight was gone, leaving the windows dark. It was almost dinnertime, and her mother would be worried about where she was. Of course she would be, on today of all days.

Andie picked up the phone and quickly responded, assuring her mother she was at the Goat and Barley, wasn't drinking and would leave now. She knew her mother wouldn't relax until she pulled into the driveway.

She sighed.

She was dreading tonight. She looked up at the man beside her, who was watching her with raised brows. Had he thought of asking her to eat with him? To stay for the evening and see in the New Year?

Andie didn't do that. New Year's wasn't a time to party or celebrate. It hadn't been for a long time. And she had to leave, now.

"I'm sorry. I have to go."

That was disappointment she saw in his eyes, wasn't it? She told herself it was. That would be her comfort for the rest of the night.

"Thanks for the chat. This is a bad day, and you helped me get through some of it. I hope this new year is good to you."

He stood as she pulled her coat on and grabbed her bag.

"Thank you. I've enjoyed talking to you, too."

She wondered if he was going to ask her name? Her number? Was there any point, when he was traveling through and she was stuck here?

Her phone rang, this time a call from her brother. She answered it, already edgy as she anticipated his reason for calling. His excuses soon filled her ears.

"Joey, that was your responsibility," she said, interrupting him. "Can you not do anything I ask you to? I'm supposed to be your boss, not just your sister. Mom is already freaking that I'm late."

More excuses, more dragging her back to her regular life. The man with the soothing voice had sat down and tactfully turned away to give her privacy.

It was probably for the best anyhow. She had no time for interesting men, even if they were staying in the area. She had responsibilities and decisions and ties, and until she was free of those, she couldn't be distracted. Maybe one day she'd be able to leave.

She smiled at the stranger who was almost a friend, and he nodded at her before she headed for the exit, winding her way through the people who knew her, cared for her, and who watched her with sympathy and pity.

It had been nice to talk to someone who didn't know what today was about, but her family needed her now. This night, above all others in the year.

Her brother was supposed to check out all the sites they were working on before he went home, but he'd already had a few to drink and couldn't drive. Andie was going to need to check out those sites while her mother sat at home worrying about losing another family member.

If only she had someone to help her deal with Joey, some way to get him to grow up and be responsible. She wished there was someone to reassure her mother, to take charge of the company and worry about finances if these romance initiatives didn't keep Carter's Crossing alive.

She wished she could be the kind of woman who could meet a strange man in a bar and exchange names and go for dinner and visit New York City.

For now, she just wanted this night over. Maybe some of her wishes would come true this year.

CHAPTER TWO

HE'D ALMOST ASKED her what her name was after that text when it became apparent she was going to leave. He'd even thought of asking for her number, but then her phone rang again and broke whatever there was happening between them.

It was a reprieve. He didn't need to know her name or talk to her again. She walked out the door, and it was not disappointment he felt. Impossible.

He wasn't here to make friends or find dates. He wasn't going to stay in this town after his year was done. He planned to restore his reputation and get his life back on track. In New York.

He was here in Carter's Crossing on New Year's Eve because he'd decided to take one more look at the place and try to get a feel for it. When his new client, Abigail Carter, owner of the mill wasn't around to curate his impressions. A year was a long commitment, and if this went badly… Stomach acid roiled in his belly.

He'd chosen New Year's Eve to accomplish several goals simultaneously. He didn't want to spend the holiday with his family or his former friends. They couldn't hide their pity, and he'd had to deal with too much of that this past couple of years to handle that, as well. Not today.

He found his hand rubbing over his leg reflexively. The one with the prosthetic.

He'd thought New Year's Eve would provide him an opportunity to drive in, check out the building again and head out without attracting any attention or arousing any suspicion.

He'd been successful at the mill. He'd taken pictures, imagining the final building once he'd finished. Abigail Carter had asked him to keep the project quiet until everything was ready to go, so he'd been aware every minute that he might be discovered by someone wanting to know his business.

Once he left the mill undetected, he'd decided against driving back to the city. There was no reason to rush back. He'd find someplace nearby to take a break, grab a beer and maybe spend the night.

He'd driven by a woman standing outside her car, frowning at a flat tire. She'd looked about eighty and slight enough for the wind to blow her over. He hadn't seen the dog until he'd already stopped, and it was too late to escape. He wasn't sure how he'd missed the Great Dane.

After putting on her spare and refusing offers of food, money or recognition, he'd needed a place to wash off the dog spit. He'd pulled into the Goat and Barley on a whim. That whim had led him to the woman contemplating her glass of soda.

She was gone now, and the pub was filling up, the stool beside him already taken. Newcomers were looking for a seat, and it was time to leave. He paid for his beer, leaving a good tip, and made his way cautiously through the crowd to the cold air outside.

According to his phone and the internet, there was a slightly larger town about a forty-minute drive away. It had a couple of chain motels, something Carter's Crossing was lacking. He made a reservation through an app, not needing to interact with an actual person, and got into his car.

The hotel room was bland and surprisingly quiet. He'd intended on spending his New Year's Eve reviewing his designs and ideas for the mill, but he was restless and edgy.

Meeting that woman in the bar had brought up feelings and memories that he'd ignored for a long time. Something about her had drawn him in. Then she'd made that comment about having problems with her employee. It reminded him of the disaster of his last job and how that had led to his prosthetic, the end of his engagement to Violet and almost the end of his career.

The woman in the bar was lucky she wasn't in his shoes. He couldn't afford another mistake. He needed to talk to someone tonight. It was three hours later in California. Howard had probably not gone out yet.

Howard was someone who'd been in his corner after the whole debacle of his last job. He was in graphic design and had moved to the West Coast, so they weren't able to see each other often, but they kept in touch, and Trevor counted him as one of his friends.

He threw himself down on the bed and called the familiar number.

After three rings, he thought Howard must be out or be with someone. He was about to hang up when he heard, "Hello, Trev!"

No one else called him Trev.

"I hope I didn't disturb you."

"Nah. It's fine. Just getting ready to head out later. Are you back from Cowlick Cove yet?"

Trevor shook his head. "Carter's Crossing. And no, I stopped at the next town and got a room. I didn't want to drive back tonight."

There was a pause. Trevor closed his eyes, waiting for Howard to chastise him.

"You can't keep hiding. You gotta move on. Unless you got an invite in Redneck Woods for a party tonight?"

Trevor opened his eyes, a smile crossing his face. He knew Howard worried about him. Trevor worried about himself, too.

"No, I'm not going out. But I did talk to someone."

"A female someone?"

"Definitely."

"That sounds promising. Pretty? Young? Single?"

"I think so. I mean, she was pretty, near our age, and she wasn't wearing a ring." He frowned. She hadn't acted like she was with anyone.

"Who is she?"

"I don't know. She got called away before I could ask her name." He didn't know how to explain their unspoken agreement to keep it light.

"Maybe you'll see her again while you're stuck in Boonieville."

"Maybe you should insult this place less since you're the reason I'm here, Howard."

Howard laughed. "I know. This year will be great, though. You'll get back on track, and life will return to what you want."

"Will it?" Trevor hated that he felt the need to ask. It wasn't as if Howard had a crystal ball. But Howard had heard about this job through his channels—he'd kept up with everyone even after he'd left New York for LA—and he'd asked Trevor if he would consider working in a small town on an intriguing project to get his career kick-started again. Something to keep his business going.

Trevor had appreciated the lead, and Howard's support.

"Trevor, you're great at what you do. Don't let one setback ruin architecture for you. You love it, you're great at it, and you deserve to have your career back. Just be careful."

Yes, that was the problem.

"I will be."

He'd learned the hard way that not everyone was trustworthy. That people might smile and joke with you, spend time with you as if they were your friends, and still stick a knife in your back. It had been an expensive lesson in many ways, but he had definitely learned.

"This time, I'm going to make sure everything on this job is done right."

"Good," Howard encouraged.

"This time, I'll check on everything. I can't trust people to do their jobs and risk another accident. It's a local contractor, and I don't know if they've done anything this big before."

"That's a reasonable concern. Don't go overboard, though, Trev. Not every contractor is crooked."

"Well, Compton's was supposed to be good."

"And it was, until his son took over. There's no way you could've known that the kid was going to cut corners."

No, but he was prepared for it now. Just in case.

"I hope nepotism isn't a thing out here. People should be hired based on their abilities, not who their parents are."

Howard grunted.

Neither of them was familiar with how things worked in a small town, but Trevor suspected nepotism would be possible here, as well. He thought of the woman at the bar, with a brother working for her who didn't listen. She'd also talked about her mom. Maybe she had a family business like Compton's, where family didn't do what they were supposed to.

Real damage could be done if someone wasn't in control and let things slip. He hoped the woman in the bar managed something simple, like a gift shop. He hoped the local contractor he'd be working with was good—knowledgeable and skilled and organized. He'd micromanage as necessary if they weren't.

Once this job was done, and done correctly and safely, he could return to New York City and restart his firm. He'd get his do-over.

He could supervise the contractor, but he wondered about the owner of the mill.

"Mrs. Carter has a good reputation, correct?"

"I'd never have given her your name if she didn't. She's apparently tight with Gerald Van Dalton, so if she's happy with you, you might get some work from his companies back in the city. I promise, Trev, I checked this out for you. Besides, you met with her. She was good, right?"

"Yes, she was. Sorry, I'm just nervous. It will be fine. I can keep an eye on the contractor, and if they can't do the job, I'll make sure Mrs. Carter knows about it. And if she won't do the right thing, I'll have to walk away."

"It's not going to come to that, Trev. This is going to work. Hey, maybe you'll meet the pretty woman and have some fun while you're in Sticksville Station."

Trevor thought of the woman from the bar. It would be nice to see her again.

But this job was important. Too important. He couldn't afford distractions. He remembered those hazel eyes, and the laughter in them as she looked at him.

She could definitely be a distraction, especially if she was having trouble with managing her own business. He didn't have bandwidth for that.

"No, no fun till this project is done. This time next year, maybe."

"I'm gonna hold you to that. If you can't find a New Year's party on the East Coast, you'll have to come out here. Are you sure you don't want to move west? I could hook you up with some people."

It was a generous offer, one Howard had made before. But

Trevor wasn't running away. He was going to work his way back to where he'd been.

All that stood between him and a triumphal return to New York City was this project, and he was going to make sure it was done right.

He wished Howard a happy New Year and finished his call. Then he pulled out his laptop, opened up the 3D BIM model, and checked and rechecked his work to make sure he was confident about every aspect of the project. That was all he was going to focus on while he was here, but somehow, his mind kept drifting to the woman in the bar.

It was late when Andie turned into the drive beside the Kozak Construction sign. She saw her mother pull the curtains aside. She must've been listening for the truck. That meant there was no time for Andie to bring her irritation under control.

She shoved open the truck door and faced the evening chill. She drew in a lungful of cold, sharp air, reminding herself that her brother, Joey, was the baby. Her mother spoiled him, and when Andie came down on him, he sulked.

Her mother asked her to be more patient with him, and Andie did try to bite her tongue. But when their world blew up, Andie didn't get more patience. She hadn't in the years since, either.

Andie let the cold air, now warmed by her lungs, cloud into the dark sky. Her mother opened the door, as if needing to see her daughter in person, whole, before she could relax.

Another irritation. Andie forced a smile.

She was more than thirty years old. She didn't want her mother checking on her all the time, like someone fifteen years younger. Part of the dream of leaving Carter's Crossing was just to win her own independence.

When she'd first taken over the company after her dad's death, she'd hated how people had wanted to check and double-check her work. But she'd been new, young and untested then. Some people still did it, new people she worked with who assumed she didn't know what she was doing because she was female and had taken over her father's company. Those people were in the minority now, and she didn't allow them to get away with it.

She didn't micromanage her crew—except maybe for Joey, but she had good reason for that—and she didn't want anyone micromanaging her, either. Not at work or at home.

Andie had established herself with the people of Carter's Crossing as the head of Kozak Construction, one of the biggest employers in the county. She was competent, trustworthy, someone they came to when they had questions or wanted advice, but she still lived like a high school kid in her mother's home.

She'd contemplated moving out. Several times. When she'd had her first serious boyfriend, she'd considered it every day.

Part of the problem was the expense. With four siblings in school incurring tuition and boarding costs and the need to ensure there was a financial buffer for the business downturns that happened, spending money on a place here in Carter's seemed pointless. Decadent. Definitely not practical.

Moving out into her own place in Carter's Crossing also signaled that she'd given up on her dream of leaving. That she was settling in, ready to stay for the rest of her life. No more school. No more dreams.

She refused to do that.

Another reason not to move out was that her mother worried. All. The. Time.

Somehow, her mom wasn't as worried about the three kids who'd moved away. All the fear that resulted from her dad's accident was focused on Andie, because Andie was the one who'd been with him that afternoon before the accident.

Andie waved to her mom, breathing the cold air in and out again, hoping her irritation would dissipate with it. It would be cruel to contribute to her mother's anxiety. Especially today.

Andie couldn't do it. She walked into the house, closed the door behind her and hung up her coat in the same closet, just as she had her whole life. She pulled off her boots and set them on the boot tray at the side of the door, where it had always been. She tossed her hat and gloves into the basket that had held jumbles of mittens and scarves for as long as she could remember.

"Smells good, Mom." She kept the irritation out of her voice. Her mom was a good cook. She tended to prepare meals for the family that used to live here, not the three of them still here now in the house. Andie took leftovers to work for lunch almost every day.

She didn't get to eat out like her siblings did, because that would be wasteful. She shoved the thought away, not sure why she was more on edge today. She could only blame some of it on the anniversary.

Her brother came down the hallway when her mother called them for dinner.

"Joey, you were supposed to check the sites today."

She did her best to keep her voice level. She couldn't let him slide on every responsibility.

"My friends are all going out to parties tonight. I just wanted to see them before they left," he said as he slid into his usual chair and reached for the salad. Andie sat down, as well.

People came back to Carter's Crossing to visit family for the holidays and then returned to their real lives. Andie's siblings had left over the last few days—back to their work commitments, families, etcetera. They didn't want to be here, in this house, tonight. And she couldn't blame them.

Still, since she had to be here, it would be nice if they'd have helped share the burden.

"You could have gone to see them after you did your job." Andie bit her tongue so she didn't say more.

"Oh, Andie, he deserves some time off." Her mother was always defending him, always treating him like a child, not a twenty-two-year-old man.

"So do I."

The silence was louder than any words. Andie didn't usually say things like that, but tonight, she wasn't able to keep the peace.

Joey didn't read the room. "You're the one afraid something is gonna happen. Nothing does. Ever. So if you're worried, you check it out."

Andie opened her mouth to tell him that the reason nothing ever happened was because she always checked things out, but her mother was watching her, expression pleading.

Not tonight.

Andie bit back the words and asked her mom to pass the rolls.

The meal was mostly silent and awkward. Her mother asked Joey about his friends, and he answered sulkily.

He didn't like being stuck in Carter's Crossing, but he had no idea what else he wanted to do. He didn't want to leave without money, and Andie refused to give him her college savings or her mother's retirement fund to go and explore his interests, which changed frequently.

Their siblings had found their passions on their own initiative, and with their own money. Joey wanted a shortcut.

After the mostly silent meal, Andie offered to clean up the kitchen. Joey didn't feel any need to help, and she was happy to have him keep her mom company anyway.

Fourteen years ago tonight, their dad died. He'd had a heart attack while driving home after checking the work sites. For years after, her mother had made New Year's Eve a memorial for him, but as her siblings began to find reasons not to be around, it had changed to a family night. They'd watch a movie, watch the ball drop and her mother would cry.

It was draining, but she couldn't leave her mother alone. Not on New Year's Eve.

It was Andie's least favorite night of the year.

It was a relief when her phone rang, and she saw the familiar name.

"It's Denise."

Her mother nodded, eyes welling with tears.

Andie escaped to her room. "I'm so happy to hear your voice," she said.

"How's it going, Andie?"

Andie didn't need to keep up the fake cheer with Denise. Her best friend had been here that night. She'd been here every New Year's since, until her husband was transferred to Florida.

Andie flopped down on her bed. "It's… Well, it's what it is, but Joey is doing his best to make it worse."

"What did he do?"

"He was supposed to check the sites before he called it a day. He didn't, so I had to do it after I was at the Goat."

Denise knew Andie went to the pub every New Year's Eve.

"Did you tell him off?"

"I tried. Mom got upset, and I can't do that to her, not today."

Denise gusted a sigh. "You've got to do something, Andie. He's gotta grow up."

"I know. He's good at some of the job. He just doesn't like to be the boss. And I don't know how to push him without riding him all the time. I can't do that."

Not only would it make home life impossible, it wasn't how she operated. She had faith in the people she hired, and she trusted them to do their jobs.

It helped that in a small town, no one was a stranger, so she knew who she could count on.

"He's gotta step up, Andie. If you're leaving this fall—"

"I'm not."

Silence.

"What? Andie—"

"I know, I know. I'm just putting it off one more year. We've got this new project with the mill. Abigail Carter has big plans for the town, and if we get the mill done, there's going to be a lot of work. I'll use this job to push Joey, to get him ready to take over, and then I can go."

More silence. Andie knew Denise wouldn't like this plan.

"Andie, it wasn't your fault."

Andie closed her eyes. "But—"

"No, Andie. We've been through this. What happened to your dad?"

"A heart attack."

"Exactly. It was nothing to do with the fact that you and he stopped at the Goat and that you went to a party. That didn't make him have a heart attack."

Andie swallowed.

"But if I'd been with him—"

"Andie! What would've happened if you'd skipped the party and driven with him?"

Andie couldn't form the words, even though they'd talked this over so many times.

"Andie, he'd still have hit the tree. The roads were slick. You couldn't have stopped it. And you might have been hurt, and then what would've happened to your family?"

Denise waited, letting her work it through again. She knew Denise was right, but on New Year's Eve, with her mother still weighed down by grief, she couldn't help playing the what-if game. What if she'd done this differently, or that?

No matter how many times she played, though, she couldn't what-if away the heart attack that had caused her dad's death.

"Thanks, Denise. I'm sorry I'm such a pain."

"You're not a pain. You're a good person who's had a lot of crap to deal with. I just wish I could be there."

"I know. But you're not. So tell me what you two are doing tonight."

By the time Denise hung up to get ready for her own evening, Andie was back in control of herself and ready to spend the rest of the evening with her mother and Joey.

She was ready to say goodbye to another year. She didn't know if New Year's Eve would ever be something to enjoy again.

CHAPTER THREE

TREVOR LOOKED AROUND the house he would be living in here in Carter's Crossing for the next year.

It was nice. It had the conveniences he required. What claimed his attention, though, was the knowledge that tomorrow he would meet with the contractor and Abigail Carter, and after that the mill project would begin.

He had concerns about the contractor, but he reminded himself he'd had the same concerns the first time he met Abigail, at the restaurant in New York City.

It had been his most promising lead since the accident. Trevor had recovered physically but found returning to his place in the building industry to be a challenge. He could go to another firm and work for someone else, but his dream had always been to have his own business. So instead of approaching others, he'd looked for new work.

The offers he'd been presented with were from clients looking for someone crooked or stupid. Trevor was neither. What he was, was cynical.

Trevor had agreed to meet with Abigail Carter, but his expectations were low. It wasn't a surprise that Abigail had exceeded them, but he'd still been surprised that she'd asked him to come to the prospective site to check out the project.

That had been in September, on-site in Carter's Crossing. Trevor had driven up, a mixture of excitement, hope and suspicion churning inside him the whole way. He'd met Abigail in the parking lot of the building.

"Thank you for taking the time to come, Mr. Emerson."

"I can't start planning a project until I know what it is."

Abigail turned to the building, and Trevor took a look at what was a functional, seemingly well-built, ugly mill.

"As I mentioned, I admire your work, and I think you can do a good job here, but I'm sure you want to examine the place. Would you like to look inside first?"

He nodded, inspecting her as well as the building. He'd done his own research into Abigail Carter. She'd been widowed young and took over running the family business while raising her children. Generations back, her family had been among the first to settle in Carter's Crossing, and they'd built the first mill structure. The current mill had closed recently, but there was no indication that the Carter family didn't have money.

Abigail herself was tall with silver hair. She was dressed in expensive clothing and was composed. Whether they could work together was still up in the air, but she would not be a pushover. This was someone who would want to understand what was happening. Would she give him room to work?

He was going to need space to check things out in detail. He planned on being more involved than many expected an architect to be. Abigail pulled out keys and opened the door. He followed her into the building. He stopped, surprised at what he saw.

He'd expected a dusty, crowded space. She'd told him the mill had been closed for two years. She hadn't mentioned that it had been emptied of all equipment and was being maintained, based on the lack of dust or dirt.

He examined the ceiling and let his gaze run down the walls to the floor.

"You've done some work here. The old equipment is gone, and the place has been kept up. That wasn't done just for this meeting, was it?"

He fought to keep any notes of suspicion out of his voice.

She shook her head. "The equipment was sold for salvage value so we could maintain the retirement fund. I've been hoping to make use of this space again, to find a way to keep the town alive. It was only sensible to keep it up.

"I've got a wedding planner coming to Carter's Crossing to show us what we need to make this a wedding destination. The mill will be at the heart of that. And that's where you come in."

Trevor nodded. *If* he came in.

"You mentioned you want a commercial kitchen for catering and space for large events. Anything else?"

She considered him for a moment. "Why don't you look around and get your own impressions? Then we can discuss options."

He nodded again. He had to be cautious, but he was also curious. He had come up with a few ideas after their initial meeting, but now he could see what he had to work with and make actual plans.

The space where they'd first entered was large, at least two stories high. It was empty. He examined the walls, looked over the beams and crossed to the far wall. There were a couple of windows, but this was the side that faced the river. He wanted to see what was there. Adding windows here would open up the view and offer a lot of possibilities.

The newer parts of the building were set back from the water, leaving a space between the building and the riverbank. There was enough room to create a patio. The view across the water showed trees and a gentle hillside. There was no sign of the town from here. They needed to take advantage of that. This side of the building should be opened up.

He turned from the windows and the possibilities he saw out there and headed to the back of the building. In this rear section, the height of the building had been split into two stories. There was a metal stairway leading upstairs. He bypassed that to see what was on the main floor behind the doors and the partition that separated it from the main space.

A hallway led to storage, washrooms and what must have been a small kitchen and lunchroom at one point. At the far end was an exterior door. The windows in the back of the lunchroom showed a parking lot.

He did a quick check of the plumbing and the electrical, then he returned to the main room and climbed the stairs to the second floor. Abigail Carter was where he'd left her, reading something on her phone, giving him space and time to check the place over.

He appreciated that. He was going to need to change the way he usually interacted with a contractor to monitor the job more carefully, and that would be unsettling enough. He didn't want to have to change how he dealt with his client, as well.

Upstairs were the former offices. The largest one in the back corner overlooked the river and had good-sized windows to bring in the view. There were additional washrooms, and while the construction wasn't innovative, it was functional and well-built.

He returned to the open space and Abigail. "I'll look around outside, if you don't mind. You don't need to come with me."

She nodded.

The mill was outside the town, and no other homes or businesses were visible. Across the river was a sloping hillside where leaves were starting to change on deciduous trees. There were hints of the vibrant reds and oranges that would light up the view shortly. This was what he wanted to bring into the mill.

The parking lot needed to be redone. The outside of the mill was…functional. That was the best word to describe it. The setting was incredible, and a facelift to the exterior, just enough so that it didn't compete with the beautiful setting, should be sufficient.

He took photos as he walked around, barely feeling his prosthetic leg, noticing the lack of noise and crowd. He wasn't used to that, but it was soothing. He heard a few birdcalls and the gurgle of the water. A car went by, but that was the only sound of civilization.

If they did this right, people would love to get married here. Violet had been looking for something like this. He forced those memories out of his head. They were no longer engaged, and there were no wedding plans. He hadn't seen her in months.

He opened the door to return to Abigail, blinking as his eyes adjusted to the dimmer light inside the mill. She put away her phone and gave him her full attention.

"The place has definite possibilities, but I need to know what your budget is and how much you want to do here."

Trevor had lost his ability to charm and schmooze. He wanted to get to the point and know what he was dealing with before he got excited about the project.

Which he might not even get.

"I have neither the time, budget nor inclination to tear this building down and create a new one."

"I assumed as much, or you wouldn't have asked me to tour through the building."

There was a half smile on her lips. "You're not going to try to talk me into that?"

He shook his head. He didn't know if she was testing him or if other architects she'd talked to had tried to sell her on a new building, but it was her project and her bank account. He didn't think it was his place to try to change her plans.

If the building had been decrepit or impossible to bring up to code, that would have been a different discussion.

"However, I also don't want to simply move a couple of walls and paint the building to try to make this work."

He'd barely knew Abigail Carter, but he already understood she wouldn't want something cheap and superficial. That was good. Cheap often meant shortcuts.

"As for the rest, I can be somewhat flexible on budget if I'm convinced it has long-term benefit. I'm not a fool."

No kidding.

"I don't know exactly what all has to be done or how much it will cost, but I have an upper limit. I will spend up to that amount, if necessary, to make this space what it needs to be," she added.

He wondered if people had tried to take advantage of her in the past, if they'd assumed because of her gender and her looks that she could be fooled.

He was quite confident that she'd taken care of those people, and that they hadn't had a second chance. She could probably teach him a lot.

He pointed at the wall facing the river.

"If you want this space to be beautiful, we need to open that up. This is where I think you should spend most of the money."

"I agree." She nodded.

"Also, the outside of the building needs a change. You can't make this a place people come to get married with the way it looks now. It needs to fit with its surroundings, but the changes we can make depends on your budget and timeline."

"The building has never been known for its appearance. Obviously, we need to deal with that. What else?"

"Inside, we can put your commercial kitchen on the main floor, where the kitchen and workrooms are now. Upstairs can be offices, if you want them, or storage." He decided to test her limits. "I'd also want to install an elevator."

Abigail's brows lifted. "I hadn't considered that, but we should. The building should be fully accessible."

"There aren't any stairs from the parking lot to the main doors, so that will make entrance from the exterior easily accessible. I'd also like to put in a patio outside by the water, and maybe around back, as well."

Abigail looked around the space, evaluating what he'd said, or maybe remembering what the place had been.

She turned back to Trevor. "I appreciate you driving all the way to Carter's Crossing. I went through the recommendations I was given carefully, and I only asked two people to come out here to see the space. I saw examples of your work and liked your vision."

Trevor felt something moving inside him in gentle ripples. It might be hope. Was he one of only two candidates? Were his odds that good? Could he get his career and his business back on track? His life?

"Your vision is the closest to mine, which means you're the front-runner."

The ripples inside him were getting bigger and starting to interfere with his breathing.

"I'd like you to take the initial steps. Survey the building and do some drawings for me. I will of course pay you, but if they come out as well as I expect, I'll offer you the job of renovating the mill. Also, as I mentioned, this town needs some more pedestrian work from an architect. We don't have anyone local. There are a lot of beautiful homes here that we're hoping to open as bed-and-breakfasts, and they'll need to be adapted. If this project takes off the way I hope it will, this town will be rejuvenated, and there will be jobs and opportunities for everyone who wants them."

Redesigning an older home to add some bathrooms was far from glamorous work. But Trevor could show his vision and his talent here at the mill. The home renos would feed his bank account, even if they didn't feed his soul.

"I guess the project will take approximately a year. I'd like you to consider relocating for that amount of time."

A year. Leaving New York City for a year. He hadn't anticipated that.

"You wouldn't need me on-site every day."

"You would know that better than me. But I'm anxious for this to be done as soon as possible. I don't want delays because the roads are in bad condition or you have other commitments and can't get to Carter's Crossing from New York."

"A year?"

"I think so. Does that seem reasonable?"

Trevor ran through potential problems in his head. "I can't promise the project will be finished in that timeline. There are things out of my control. I don't do the inspections and approvals."

Abigail nodded. "I have enough clout to make sure that we don't lose our place in line when it comes to those things."

She must have read the concern on his face.

"I'm not talking about taking shortcuts or paying bribes. Just that if someone in my town overbooks, they won't cancel on me. I've earned that, and I will take advantage of it.

"The mill bears my family's name, and I don't want my reputation damaged. If I thought you were at fault for the accident last year, I wouldn't be speaking to you."

It sounded good, but Trevor had learned to be cautious.

"I'd like time to think it over. And I need to know everything will be done by the book."

Abigail took a moment to study him. She must know why he'd stipulated that.

"Some things will be different here since we're dealing with a small town. There's only one contracting firm who can handle this kind of work, but we will do everything as it should be done. You have my word."

"I'll want to monitor things closely."

"That's fair. But I don't want to wait too long. If I don't hear from you within the week, I'll speak to the other candidate."

She knew he wanted this. She was intelligent and observant,

and he'd probably showed his excitement on his face. But *she* also wanted *him*. She needed someone who could do this. Getting this project and finishing it, doing the job well and without problems would give him a chance to get back on his feet and back on track.

He could make this big, hulking building into a beautiful place for people to celebrate.

Sure, life in a small town might be a little dull for a year, but he could survive that.

He'd agreed to her terms. And now he was committed, living in Carter's Crossing, ready to start. And ready to meet the local contractor, Kozak Construction.

Andie parked her truck in the mill parking lot.

It was still cold here near the end of February, but soon March would bring warmer temperatures, and her life would get busier.

There were no other vehicles around, so she was the first one here for the meeting. That was how she'd planned it. She'd come half an hour early, just so she could have time on her own to check the place over.

Abigail Carter had given her a set of keys, and Andie walked around the building, her footprints leaving marks in the fresh snow.

She'd grown up in Carter's Crossing, but she'd never been inside the mill. While it was open, the mill had had its own employees to take care of its maintenance, and she couldn't remember Kozak Construction ever coming in to work on the building during her lifetime.

It wasn't an attractive building. She'd forgotten just how functional it looked, but it had been constructed well. She liked to think one or more of her ancestors had been involved in the original construction, but it was long done before her grandfather opened their company, and she didn't know if there were records to show who'd built the original structure or the later additions.

Abigail had said she maintained the building, and Andie saw no signs of worrisome neglect. Still, no one would want to get married here, not with the way the building looked now.

She'd circled the exterior and was now back at the main door. She pulled out the keys she'd been given and slid one into the lock. It turned with a soft click. She pushed the door open and stared.

It was a huge space. Clean and empty, ready for whatever work was needed. Andie moved over, eager to check out this space where some demolition would undoubtedly be needed first. She walked toward the back of the building, noting the rooms and condition of the various sections. She made notes on her phone, taking photos to match, until she heard voices from the entry and made her way there.

"Andie? Is that you?"

Andie pushed open the door to bring her back into the main part of the mill. She saw Abigail looking as polished and at home in this empty space as she did at town events, and her mouth curved up in a smile.

There was someone with Abigail, the architect, presumably. Abigail had asked Andie here to meet him so that they could start to plan the renovations. Andie had been impressed by the drawings Abigail had shared and was looking forward to this project.

She was excited about tackling something new and challenging, and it was a chance to work closely with an architect from New York, someone with a vision she admired. On small jobs, she'd see the architect only at the beginning and end.

This would be Kozak's biggest project yet. That should mean more meetings, more time with the person who'd draw up the plans. She hoped they could talk and maybe she could get some advice for her own aspirations after this job.

At first, she saw only his back. He was a little taller than she was, and dark hair touched his collar. He was wearing a warm jacket and sturdy boots and had a large computer bag slung over his shoulder. She saw the frame of a pair of glasses resting on his ear. Then he turned.

She did a double take. The man standing with Abigail stared back at her in equal shock. It was the man from the bar.

She recognized the dark brows, the straight nose, the lines fanning out from his eyes. She'd stared at those while they'd talked at the Goat.

She'd hoped to see him again, but she'd no idea it would ever happen. Her smile widened.

She'd regretted the calls from her mother and Joey that had interrupted them at the bar. She'd thought he'd been about to ask what her name was. She'd wanted to thank him for making that horrible day a little better, at least for a while.

One major drawback of a small town was that you knew everyone in your potential dating pool, and most of the men in hers had either left town or found someone. Andie was out of pool buddies, and she'd liked the man at the bar.

She crossed to where Abigail was standing ready to introduce them. She'd finally know his name.

"Andie, this is Trevor Emerson, our architect. Trevor, this is Andie Kozak, of Kozak Construction, the firm that will be undertaking the work here."

Andie was close now, almost close enough to shake hands. Close enough to see the expression on the man's face. Trevor's face. She knew his name now.

He knew hers, as well. And he looked stunned.

Andie's smile faded. She had no idea why, but he didn't look happy to see her. In fact, he looked upset.

What was his problem?

CHAPTER FOUR

ANDIE SHOVED HER hands in her pockets while she tried to make sense of this. He'd been friendly, fun, attentive in the bar. What had changed?

She glanced at his hands, but his left was hidden in his pocket. There hadn't been anything on his ring finger on New Year's Eve, but she'd bet there was now.

Her face stiffened. Great. She worked with mostly men, mostly married, but they didn't try anything with her, not after the first time. She shut that down immediately.

Guess Mr. Emerson was worried what she might say. She nodded at the man, irritated that he didn't start to look as distasteful as he acted.

"Mr. Emerson."

His lips were pressed tightly together, and he nodded back. "Ms. Kozak."

Abigail's glance flickered between them. "Have you two met before?"

Andie wasn't about to lie to Abigail Carter. Kozak Construction did a lot of work on projects Abigail was connected with.

"I ran into Mr. Emerson at the Goat and Barley on New Year's Eve, but we didn't exchange names."

She heard Trevor suck in a breath. Too bad for him. She wasn't jeopardizing her working relationship with Abigail for a cheating scumbag.

She'd fantasized about this job at the mill, about meeting with an established architect from New York and getting advice, mentoring, perhaps a future reference.

She'd also had fantasies about running into the man from the bar again and spending more time with him.

Apparently, those fantasies were closer to nightmares now that they'd coalesced into one. She just needed to concentrate on her job.

Abigail's expression softened for a moment. She knew what New Year's meant for the Kozak family.

Abigail's glance shot back to Trevor, who still looked shocked. Trevor didn't say anything, and Andie wasn't explaining.

"I've had the heat on so we can work and for the Valentine's Day planning. I brought in a table and chairs to my old office. Shall we talk there?"

Abigail headed to the metal stairs, and Andie followed, Trevor somewhere behind her. Abigail's heels clicked on the metal treads, while Andie's boots thudded. She didn't hear Trevor over her own treads. Her boots were heavy and steel toed. Work boots.

Maybe that was part of his problem. Maybe he didn't like women in traditionally male roles. Too bad. She'd dealt with that before, a lot more than she should've.

Men.

Between Joey and Trevor Emerson, she was ready to be done with them.

Abigail had arranged to have a folding table and some chairs set up. She sat down at one end, and Andie sat beside her. Trevor sat across from them, and Andie kept her attention on Abigail.

Abigail took the lead. Andie imagined she'd chaired many meetings in this room.

"I've looked at your drawings, Trevor, and your budget. I'd like to focus initially on the interior, and if we run behind, the patio and driveway can be done after the snow clears in about fifteen months. I've shown Andie the drawings so we can go over them together."

Andie saw the frown cross Trevor's face from the corner of her eye.

Trevor reached into his bag and pulled out a laptop as well as some papers. Andie restrained herself from reaching for them. She had copies she could access as needed. Instead, she pulled out her tablet and stylus, ready to take notes. She set it on the table, raised her gaze and caught Trevor staring at her, still frowning.

His hands were on the table now, not hidden in his pocket. Andie noticed the ring finger was still bare. She took the few extra seconds to look for a white circle at the base, where a ring would normally be. Nothing.

So maybe he was the kind of married man who didn't wear a ring. No matter, she was still keeping her distance. She wasn't interested in a cheater.

Abigail looked at Trevor, waiting for him to begin.

He cleared his throat. "I'm used to dealing with the contractor himself. I'm sure Ms. Kozak takes excellent notes, but…"

Andie felt the familiar bile rising. Chauvinist. She'd dealt with many of them, had finally established herself in this community. It had taken years. She was so tired of it.

She didn't appreciate that she would need to convince this man that she was capable of doing her job.

She stared at him, waiting till he met her gaze. Abigail Carter let the silence hang, trusting Andie to deal with this.

Abigail was her idol.

"Mr. Emerson. Kozak Construction is *my* company." At least, it would be until Joey was ready to take over and she could finally leave for school.

"I *am* the contractor. I sign the checks. I choose the jobs. I oversee every subcontractor and employee who works on a Kozak Construction site. I have the license, and the buck stops with me. While you might be more comfortable dealing with someone with a Y chromosome, my brother is ten years younger than me and has minimal experience, so it would probably be best if we don't wait until he's up to speed."

Andie waited for his response. Her arms were crossed, her chin raised. Would there ever come a time when she wouldn't have to deal with this crap?

Trevor glanced at Abigail, as if for help. Was he that bad at reading the room? Did he not realize Abigail had dealt with this same attitude while managing the mill?

The older woman's expression was no longer pleasant. "Kozak Construction is the best firm in ten counties, and we're fortunate that they are local and available for this project. Do you have a problem working with them?"

Andie relaxed, a little, knowing that Abigail was backing her up. Andie had been looking forward to this project, and now part of her wanted to throw up her hands and say they could find someone else. But she couldn't dwell on hurt feelings. She was a businesswoman, and this was her job.

She shot a glance at Trevor. His cheeks were red, and he was looking down at his papers.

"I apologize. I didn't mean any disrespect. Most of the contractors I've dealt with have been older, and I made a poor assumption. I've worked with women before, and that has not been an issue. I have no problem working with Kozak Construction if they have no problem working with me." He glanced over at Andie before settling his gaze on Abigail.

Andie didn't buy his apology. She wasn't any happier with someone negging her for her age than she was for them doing it for her being female. Too often, the one was an excuse for the other.

She held her tongue.

There'd be more meetings with the man than on a usual job, since this was a big project. He might want to be around for inspections. But she would do her best to make any interactions short and infrequent. Her idea of spending additional time with the architect on this project was obviously not happening, and she was sure he wouldn't want to spend any more time with her than necessary. If she was lucky, she shouldn't need to see him more than once a week. This project would raise the profile of Kozak Construction, and she'd leave a successful and sound company in her brother's hands to provide a safety net for her mother and siblings.

Then she could finally pursue her own dream. Surely there were architects out there who didn't specialize in being chauvinistic jerks.

Abigail considered the two of them for a moment. "I like your drawings, Mr. Emerson, and I know Kozak's work, which is impeccable. Together, we can make this mill what it needs to be to keep the town alive. Let's start now."

Andie waited till Trevor looked back at her and then gave him a big smile. Totally fake, and she didn't try to hide that.

"I do take excellent notes, by the way."

She thought she heard what sounded like a well-covered snort from Abigail's direction.

Trevor held her gaze and nodded. "I'll keep that in mind."

Andie would like to think she'd come out on top in the encounter, but she had her doubts. She'd show him, though. She'd done nothing but immerse herself in this business for the last fourteen years, and before they were done, he'd have to acknowledge he'd been wrong about her.

She looked up and caught those brown eyes staring at her. A shiver ran down her spine.

Trevor opened his computer and started to talk about the job. Andie kept her mind on his words, taking notes of the things she needed to know. She did her best to focus on the equipment and outside contractors she'd need to arrange, anything new she'd have to do some research on, the kind of timeline they'd be following.

She'd show him what a woman could do.

Trevor slammed the door of his rented house behind him. He kicked off his boots, venting his irritation on them. He dropped his bag on the dining table and pulled off his scarf and coat.

Then he took a deep breath and swore.

This was supposed to be an easy job. It was too important for him to mess up, and he'd almost done that at the first meeting with Abigail Carter and her.

The woman from the pub.

He'd spent too much time since New Year's Eve remembering his conversation with her. That night he'd laughed like he hadn't since the accident, and he liked to think he'd brightened the sadness from her expression.

But then there had been the problems with her employee, a relative, making this another job with a contractor with family issues.

When Abigail Carter told him he had the job, he'd been excited.

It was his chance to get his career back on track. To show everyone that he really was good at his profession. To get his confidence back. His business back.

Part of that excitement had been the memory of the woman in the bar, and that maybe he'd have the chance to get to know her while he was in town. She'd said she was a local, and it was a small place. He'd hoped he'd see her again. He just hadn't expected it would be as the contractor on his job.

His plan had been to get the mill project set up and established and then maybe try to find her again, but only once he was comfortable with how the mill was going. No distractions until then.

Now he was second-guessing that encounter in the bar. What if Abigail had told Andie about her plans and about the architect she'd hired? What if she'd known who he was?

If the town was so small that people recognized every stranger, Andie might have deliberately tried to soften him up, get on his good side in the hopes of keeping him from checking up on her.

Wasn't that almost the playbook Geoff Compton had used on Trevor's last job? Had Andie known who he was? Was that meetup a setup?

He sat in a chair, huffing a frustrated breath. Was he paranoid? Probably. Didn't mean he was wrong.

He couldn't have something like that happen again. It would destroy his reputation. Permanently. He'd been approached by people he knew were shady, after the Compton job. If anything like that happened again, it was either his fault or his judgment was far off.

He scrubbed his face with his hands.

He'd liked Andie and was horrified when he found she was someone he had to work with, someone he couldn't be involved with. He'd hoped she just worked for the company, then they might have been able to see each other.

But no. She was the contractor. How experienced was she? He needed to know, since she was the person essential to getting this job done, to getting his life and career back on track.

How in the world could he trust that she was a capable contractor? She was young. He'd heard her on the phone and knew she was having problems.

This was such a big job. Could she handle it? And would she try to use anything from their first meeting to take advantage?

Abigail Carter had hired the two of them, but she knew and trusted Kozak Construction. Unless he had a better reason than anything he had come up with so far, she was going to trust Andie if it came down to a choice between them.

Abigail Carter said that the company was good. Maybe it was, for this tiny town and whatever jobs they had around here. That didn't mean Andie and her company were capable of doing what he'd envisioned for the mill.

The mill was why he was here. He was going to take that functional, ugly building and make it a place people came for their dream weddings. He was going to make it a thing of beauty. It was going to take a lot of work. Work that Kozak Construction had to carry out. Carry out to his specifications. No shortcuts. No mistakes. No crew making their own decisions without his approval.

He had to make sure of that.

He was good at his job. He'd been doing well until that last project, the first he'd done solo. And though he'd done everything right, he'd been blamed when it had gone wrong. Since he'd been in the hospital, he hadn't been able to defend himself.

He'd been exonerated later, but no one remembered that. They remembered the immediate aftermath, when his contractor and the owner had placed all the blame on him. That couldn't happen again. He wasn't going to be blamed for something he didn't do. And no one was going to take any shortcuts on his project.

That meant he was going to have to be involved, to be really hands-on, checking and double-checking everything.

Abigail Carter had mentioned there would be other work here in Carter's Crossing. Buildings being renovated, new businesses, things that would keep him busy and pay the bills.

During the day, he was going to be at the mill. Every time someone was working on the structure, he'd be there. He'd make sure this job went perfectly.

It would mean spending a lot of time with Andie. Maybe he could show her how to keep control of her crew. It would mean they'd have to keep a professional relationship. No laughing over stupid jokes at the pub. No noticing hazel eyes or the way she bit her lip. No discovering whatever had her staring at a drink on the bar on New Year's Eve.

Not now.

He stood up, restless, his leg bothering him as he moved to the kitchen. He'd brought food with him and stocked up the empty cupboards. Tonight, he planned to go over his drawings and specifications with a careful eye, checking what his contractor would be starting on.

Waiting for his food to heat up, his brain conjured up a pleasant daydream. One where Andie wasn't someone he'd be in conflict with. Where she did some other innocuous job here in Carter's Crossing. Like being the town dentist. He'd run into her once the mill project was well under way and no longer requiring constant supervision. Maybe they'd bump into each other on the sidewalk somewhere, and her face would light up to see him. Like it had in the mill, before she'd lost that sparkle. After he'd probably looked as shocked as he felt.

He needed to stop thinking about the woman from the pub, to put those thoughts well behind him. Now she wasn't the woman from the bar. She was Andie Kozak, the contractor who could ruin his job and his future with just a small amount of incompetence.

He urged his brain to get on board. He opened his laptop, plugged it in, and with a plate of food in front of him, went through his work one more time, carefully focusing on what was on the screen and not remembering the hazel eyes that had stared at him with dislike.

"How can anyone in this day and age possibly think I can't do my job because of my age or gender? Really? I mean, he's supposed to be from New York City, not redneck central."

Denise laughed over the phone. "You don't think there are misogynists in New York?"

Andie huffed a breath. "I know, but to try something like that in front of Abigail Carter? I thought she might fire him on the spot. I hoped she would."

Andie could still hear the laughter in Denise's voice. "That does take nerve. Why do you think she didn't?"

Andie squirmed against the pillows on her bed, getting herself comfortable.

She missed Denise. They'd been friends since high school, and Andie didn't have a lot of time to make new friends. She wished there was an app for that, but in Carter's Crossing, it wasn't likely that she'd find anyone with or without an app. It was as difficult as finding someone to date here.

"I hate to admit this, but his work is good. Really good. That mill is the least appealing building I can imagine, the way it looks now, but in his drawings, it's…totally romantic."

"Can buildings be romantic?"

Andie thought they could. Buildings weren't just wood and concrete. Andie had always found the variety in them appealing, intriguing. It was why she'd always wanted to be an architect.

Working on building sites with her dad, growing up, she'd had a close-up look at structures and the variety of things that could be done with them. There were the basic bones of something, like the mill. The things needed for functionality. If you left it at that, you had…well, the mill. It stuck out against its setting, against the beauty of nature that surrounded it. It was nothing but functionality.

With some imagination and a plan like Trevor had designed, you could bring in beauty and warmth. You could make people feel better. They could *be* better in a home or workplace that did more than just provide the necessities.

"When we get done with the mill, you'll see how romantic a building can be. I'm going to make it beautiful."

"I know you will."

Andie relaxed against her headboard. That was Denise. Always supportive, always on her side.

"But enough about me. How are things in Florida?"

"Oh, no. I can tell you about Florida after we're done with this."

"What do you mean, done with this? We're done. I vented, and you agreed Mr. Emerson is a jerk, and now we're moving on."

"Uh-uh. Not till you tell me about him."

"I did."

"No, what does he look like? How old is he?"

Andie paused.

She hadn't told Denise about the New Year's Eve encounter at the Goat and Barley. She wasn't sure exactly why she hadn't.

It hadn't really been anything, of course. Two people talking. It was just that New Year's Eve was a bad day for her, so being distracted had been a good thing. It had obviously colored her impression of Mr. Emerson.

Denise was too good at seeing through her. She hoped she could describe Trevor without giving anything away.

"Well, he's a little older than us."

"Thirty-five? Forty? Fifty?"

"Stop it! You think fifty is just a little older than us? How old are you? I'm only thirty-two, thank you."

"Okay, so he's more like thirty-five." Andie brought up his face. "Yeah, probably something like that. If he's got his own firm now, he has to be at least that old."

"And ugly, right?" The amusement was back in Denise's voice.

If only. If he had been, she'd still have enjoyed their conversation on New Year's Eve but probably not thought about it again. Somehow, she'd started imagining meeting up again, talking more. Maybe more than talking...

"Andie? You there?"

Andie brought herself back to her phone call. "Yes, I'm here. Where else would I be?"

"Tell me how good-looking this guy is."

"Who said he was good-looking?"

Andie could imagine her friend's eyes rolling.

"I said he was ugly, and you disappeared, at least mentally. That tells me he's the opposite of ugly."

Yeah, that's what happened when someone knew you so well.

"No, he's not ugly. His hair is brown, a little long. His eyes are brown, too."

They were brown with flecks of gold near the pupils. And there were streaks of gray at his temples when he brushed that slightly too long hair back behind his ears.

"Well, that sounds...boring? Tall, short, fit, beard..."

"Tallish."

When he'd stood up, he'd been taller than her, and she was tall for a woman.

"And?"

"Lean." He'd looked like a runner, or a swimmer. Not a guy who lifted weights in a gym or beers in a bar. "No beard."

Or moustache. But there'd been a bit of stubble...

"Andie!"

She'd drifted off again. "Sorry, Denise. I'm here."

There was a pause.

"He's good-looking, isn't he?"

Andie sighed. "Yes, he is."

"Why do the good-looking ones have to be jerks?"

There was a grumble in the background.

"You're the exception to the rule, darling." Andie could hear Denise talking to her husband despite the hand she must have placed over her phone.

Denise and her husband were stupidly in love. Andie would agree Don wasn't ugly, but he wasn't her idea of a great-looking guy. Which was good, since he was married to her best friend.

"Hey, Denise, tell him needy isn't a good look on a guy."

Denise gurgled a laugh. "I know. But there are a limited number of non-jerks, so I take what I can get."

Andie smiled, her grin broadening as she heard the muffled "I'm joking!"

"Sorry, dealing with Mr. Needy. So you have to work with the good-looking jerk for a while. Will it be worth it? Maybe, I don't know. Is Joey ready to step up a bit?"

Andie shuddered. "No, he's not ready yet. But I can handle Mr. Jerky. I doubt he'll be around much. If he does his job and leaves me to mine, we'll be fine. Fine-ish."

"Andie, you did an incredible job taking over that company after your dad died, and you are great at it," Denise said, her tone growing serious. "You've earned the respect of the guys who work for you, and this guy will learn to respect you, as well. I believe in you."

Andie swallowed a lump. She'd needed this call. She'd needed Denise.

"Can't you talk Mr. Needy into moving back up here? I miss you."

"I miss you, too. But we're doing really well down here."

"Don't mind me. I know you're doing well. Tell me about it."

Andie would be fine. Denise was just a phone call away. Andie was normally much stronger on her own, but something about this thing with Trevor had unsettled her.

She *would* be fine, though. She was good at what she did. She just had to do a good job on this project. Like she always did.

CHAPTER FIVE

TREVOR RUBBED A HAND over his face. Things were not going well. He needed to fix this relationship with his contractor. Andie.

They'd had a few emails back and forth, and he'd sent through an article on dealing with employees. It wasn't just the cold New York winter giving him frostbite.

He should reach out, try to build a bridge. He'd injured her pride, and that wasn't the man he normally was.

At least, it wasn't who he'd been before. The individual he was now was still a work in progress. There'd been a lot of changes to adapt to, and he had yet to feel settled in his own skin. He didn't want this new person to be a jerk.

He pulled up his laptop and opened his email.

Ms. Kozak
I think we should meet in person and talk. I apologize that our first meeting did not go well and would like to clear things up.
Trevor Emerson

He considered it for a moment and, with a shrug, hit Send. Then he realized that, actually, their first meeting had been great. It was the second meeting that had blown everything up.

It seemed he was doomed to keep messing up with her. He considered sending a second email to clarify but figured it wouldn't help. He'd just have to wait and see how she responded.

Andie did respond, and that was how Trevor found himself in the town diner on a cold Monday evening. He was early. Driving on his own on a regular basis was an adjustment, and so was being able to get anywhere in town in a matter of minutes. In New York, he took cabs and allowed an ample time buffer for traffic.

He supposed a nonexistent commute time was an advantage to a small town. He didn't think it really offset the limited offerings of places to meet. He couldn't suggest the Goat and Barley again, and the only other sit-down restaurant in town was a place called Moonstone's, which appeared to aspire to fine dining. He didn't want to imply this meetup was a date, so he'd picked the diner.

The place was warm, and there was a buzz of chatter. After a pause near the door, he realized there was no one to seat him, so he made his way to an empty booth. He wanted this to be a private conversation, and the booth offered the most in the way of privacy. A waitress came over with a coffee carafe. She stood for a moment at the end of the table, waiting, so he turned over his coffee cup, and she poured.

"Creamer? Sugar?"

He forced a smile. "No, thank you."

She turned and left him dubiously assessing the coffee.

"Andie! How are you doing?"

Trevor looked up and saw Andie in the doorway being greeted by the waitress with a lot more warmth than she'd shown him. More people called out to his contractor, and he managed to rotate the handle on his cup around three times before she got to the table.

Not that he was nervous.

Andie took off her parka and hung it by the hood on a hook at the end of the booth seat before sliding in across from him. He didn't have time to greet her before the waitress was back, flipping over Andie's cup and filling it. She dropped a creamer beside the cup and asked if they were going to order food.

Andie looked at him for the first time.

"I haven't eaten, so I hope you don't mind if I do. I wasn't sure what you intended, and I was out late on a site."

Trevor stiffened. This was supposed to be a business meeting. He hoped Andie realized that and didn't consider this a potential date. He'd been clear in his email, hadn't he? Their first meeting had been…unprofessional, but he had no plans to revisit that easy camaraderie they'd enjoyed. He was not going to let any personal entanglements interfere with business. He was here to work and had already eaten. If only he had an office or there was a coffee shop in town.

She was watching him, her face a polite mask. She'd lost the warmth she'd had in her friendly greetings to the other diner customers.

That's good, he reminded himself. They needed to be professional. He couldn't allow any attraction to her to affect his performance on his job or the way he planned to scrutinize everything.

He didn't want to think about why it felt like he was missing out on something. It wasn't the first time he'd felt it, but he had to swallow before answering.

"I've eaten, but please, go ahead."

She narrowed her eyes, but with a flash of something on her face, she turned to the waitress.

"Guess it's just me, Jean. Burger and fries, the usual."

The waitress looked at him and sniffed before leaving.

Andie added the creamer and sugar to her cup and took a sip. She set it back down and met his gaze, head slightly tilted.

Right. He'd asked her to come here to talk. "Since we're working together on the mill, I wanted to discuss your processes."

She let the silence sit for a minute. "My processes."

He nodded. "I've worked exclusively in the city so far, so I'm not sure how your tendering process worked, and I wanted to see the bids."

She was still looking at him. He couldn't read her expression. He slid his glasses up his nose with one finger, pointlessly, since they were still sitting exactly where they should.

Then she sighed. "Mr. Emerson, I'm going to guess you've never worked in a small town."

He stiffened. "I grew up in New York City. Went to school there, and that's where I've worked."

Her lips twisted. "Yeah, I remember you saying that, and even if you hadn't, I would have guessed. I don't think you understand what life is like here."

He didn't need to understand anything. He had no interest in moving to a small town. His singular goal was to do a good job here and get back to the city where he could do the work he really wanted to do. With a blemish-free project on his resume to prove he was back to being the same architect he'd been before the accident.

Andie waved a hand around at the diner. "We have this diner. We have Moonstone's, which is as close to fine dining as we get."

Trevor nodded. He'd done the research. He knew this was all there was.

"So when you wanted to meet, you had two choices. That's all."

He wasn't sure where she was going with this. If they weren't going to meet in whatever places they each called home, those were the only two options. He had definitely noticed the limits of the town.

"So how many tenders do you think we can get for a job here?"

A chill ran up his spine.

He didn't care if this was a small town that had limited options. If this woman intended to use that as an excuse for not following specifications or for using inferior materials or not keeping to a timeline...

He sat up, crossing his arms. "This project isn't someone's basement renovation. This is a big job that needs to be done properly."

He recognized the expression on her face now. She was angry. Her cheeks were flushed, and she was sitting equally at attention.

"You do realize you're questioning both my ethics and skills? With absolutely no reason? We may not have a lot of options here—"

Their waitress arriving with Andie's burger and French fries stopped her rebuke. She placed the plate before Andie, along with a wooden rack containing condiments.

"Cook added some extra cheese for you."

Andie's expression was a lot happier as she turned to their server. "Thanks, Jean. I appreciate it."

"Need more coffee?"

The three of them looked at the level of creamy brown in Andie's cup. "I'm good, thanks. Maybe some water when you have a chance."

"Sure thing, Andie."

Jean flicked Trevor another glance but didn't offer him more to drink. His cup was almost empty. The coffee was better than he'd expected.

He hoped Jean not offering him more coffee was an oversight and not intentional, because he felt that more coffee might be needed to finish up this conversation. However, he suspected it had been deliberate.

Andie took a bite of her burger, moaned and wiped a napkin on her lips. The food smelled really good. She swallowed and set the burger down. Then she speared a fry.

"The burgers here are excellent. And the fries. You should try one."

Trevor opened his mouth to refuse. He was here to discuss the work on the mill, and he'd eaten already. They'd been arguing, so he didn't know why she wanted to be nice to him. He had been…rude.

The food did smell good, and it wouldn't hurt to bend a little. They weren't on the clock now. It would be beneficial to know what the quality of the food in the diner was like. He might want to eat out at some point, and this place was convenient.

"Thank you." He reached over and grabbed one of the golden sticks. It was still on the verge of being hot, but it didn't burn his fingers.

He took a bite and almost moaned himself. He didn't often allow himself fried food, but this… This was temptation in a deep-fried bit of potato.

If the rest of the food here was of the same quality, he could occasionally indulge himself. He would check the menu to see if there was anything healthier for more regular visits.

Andie had taken another bite of her hamburger, and he suddenly wished he hadn't eaten before arriving here.

She set the burger down again. Her expression was more relaxed, and the tension in her jaw gone. If the burger was as tasty as the fries, he could understand why.

"Good, isn't it?"

"Very good." He might be a little regimented when it came to his diet, but he was also honest.

She smiled at him. Apparently, the burger had really improved her mood.

"The diner here is convenient. Locals come here because it's not worth driving too far for a cup of coffee. But they couldn't survive selling only coffee. If the food wasn't good, people would go to the Goat and Barley for meals."

Trevor held his expression still when Andie mentioned the pub where they'd met.

"Just because this is a small town with limited choices, doesn't mean those choices are rubbish. We might not have sophisticated palates, but we're not without standards."

Trevor understood where she was going now.

"My company might be the only one in this area, but if all we did was shoddy work on basement renovations, we'd have gone bankrupt or closed our doors a while ago.

"Over and above those considerations, I'm a craftsperson. I take pride in my work. I may work in a small town, but I need to know I've done my best. If someone is unhappy with the results, it bothers me. I wouldn't be able to face people around town if I did a bad job on their homes."

Andie leaned forward, holding his gaze with the passion behind her words.

"We did the renovation for Benny Gifford's place. He's in a wheelchair. I went to school with Benny, and I would never cut corners when it could result in another injury.

"We don't always have a lot of options, or alternate suppliers and workers. But I know my customers, and I protect them. I know my workers, and if they don't do their jobs properly, they don't work for me again."

He leaned forward now. "But you don't have to limit yourself to locals. You could ask for bids from firms elsewhere in the state."

Andie pointed a fry at him before she took a bite of it. "And where would they stay? We're about to start demolition, and it's still winter. We don't have hotels in Carter's Crossing. We won't have functioning B and Bs until some of these old homes have work done on them.

"The mill might be the biggest job we've had here for a while, but it's still not big enough for someone to pay for hotels and crews to commute from Oak Hill or farther."

Trevor leaned back, away from the tempting fries. Andie was making a convincing argument. He could believe that *she* believed her words. She wanted to do a good job for the people she knew. He just wasn't sure of her competence. By her own admission, this was going to be her biggest job. It might be beyond her skill set. And her crew's.

She had sat up again and was eating her burger. She shot a glance at him, waiting for his response to a very pointed argument.

He wasn't unreasonable. He appreciated her points about the inherent problems in bringing in crews from farther away, even if they were more competent. He understood budgets and had every intention of bringing this job in on time and on budget.

She'd made her case. Unless Abigail Carter wanted to increase her spending to include vendors and workers from farther away, he was working with Kozak Construction and the local people they had relationships with.

That meant *he* was going to have to make sure the project was a success. He'd have to be on-site every day. He'd check over who was working, what they were working on and how well they did their work.

He had a lot riding on this. If this job was messed up, he'd never get more clients. He'd have to beg for a position with another firm and would be stuck working on someone else's projects.

Besides his reputation and future being at stake, he also had to be vigilant so that no one would be hurt again...

"You won't mind if I check the work, will you?"

The burger was gone, and Andie pulled the plate of fries closer to her edge of the table.

"I've worked with architects before. I'm accustomed to the process. Unless you mean something more by that?"

"You said this is going to be the biggest job you've done."

"You do realize we've done a lot more than basement renovations, right?"

He shrugged.

"Does 'check the work' mean oversee? Do my job? Micromanage the project?"

There was fury in the tone of her voice and in the snap in her eyes.

He shrugged. "Unless you have something to hide?"

"Check what you want. I don't 'hide' anything."

Jean returned with a glass of water and the coffeepot. As Trevor glanced around the diner, he realized people were watching their… argument? Discussion? Andie had a lot more fans around here than he did.

He stood, keeping his distance from the pot of hot coffee. From the look on Jean's face, she was tempted to pour it on him.

He reached into his pocket to grab his wallet. He took out a five-dollar bill, more than enough to cover his coffee, and tossed it on the table and grabbed his jacket.

"I'll see you tomorrow morning at the mill."

Andie's arms were crossed, and the glare she had focused on him made him uncomfortable. She gave him a short nod, and he walked out of the diner as quickly as dignity allowed.

Outside, he took a deep breath, and the cold air burned his lungs.

He'd hoped to reach a rapprochement with his contractor. That hadn't happened. It wasn't a problem, though, not really. He was here to do a job, not make friends. This wasn't his town, and he had no desire to stay here.

He just wished the woman at the bar, the one he'd liked talking to so much, wasn't the one he was going to be checking on for the duration of this project.

It might have been nice to have one friend here.

CHAPTER SIX

ANDIE WAITED AT the door. It was still dark out, but it was time to go. She tapped her foot while she watched her brother fill a coffee travel cup.

Joey was hard to get moving in the morning. Andie, on the other hand, made it a personal mission to be the first one on-site each day. Normally, they took two vehicles, but Joey's was in the shop for repairs, so they were traveling together in Andie's truck.

It was the first day working on the mill, and she needed to be there before Trevor. Andie was determined that Mr. Emerson would have nothing to complain about. *Nothing.*

She was used to misogyny and guys who thought women couldn't do this job. After her dad died, it had been a struggle to keep the company afloat. There were nights she'd cried herself to sleep, but she'd done it when no one could hear her.

Now her crew respected her, or at least they kept their opinions to themselves if they didn't. It hadn't been easy.

She knew these guys and did her best to be fair. She wouldn't tolerate shortcuts or shoddy work, but if someone worked hard for her, she worked hard for them. Construction slowed during the winter, but she did her best to keep her crew employed as much as possible.

Even though it was still winter, they could start demolition and renovations inside the mill, in the section that wasn't having drastic external changes. Now that the Valentine's Day events the town had arranged to kick-start the romance initiative were wrapped up, the mill was available to them. One event that had included most of the town had been held there, an appropriate beginning to what everyone hoped would be a successful and prosperous transformation.

Andie had enjoyed Dave and Jaycee's engagement party. There'd been skating on the river next to the mill, music and lights, and everyone had warmed up with hot chocolate. It had been beautiful and fun, and it had given everyone a sense of optimism.

If Abigail Carter could make this town a tourist destination for people wanting romance, engagements and weddings, it would breathe in new life. And would keep Kozak Construction busy for a long time.

Andie tried to hang on to that feeling of optimism as her brother slowly pulled on his boots and hat. It was as if he was moving through molasses.

"Come on, Joey. This is a big day, It's the start of our biggest project to date. Let's get on it."

"Jeez, Andie, it's still dark out."

Andie counted in her head. Ten wasn't enough. Neither was twenty. She let out a careful breath. "It's the first day. I have to be there to get things started. It's expected when you're the boss."

"When I'm the boss, we'll start an hour later."

Andie shook her head. "I wish that was possible."

Andie was tired, too. She'd spent too much time last night thinking of what could go wrong in front of Mr. Emerson before she'd finally fallen asleep.

She hustled Joey out the door and jogged over to the truck, breath frosting in the air. The seats were stiff and cold under her as she turned the truck engine on and started blasting air through the vents.

Joey turned down the fan. "Wait till it's warmed up."

Andie resisted the temptation to dial the fan back up. It was her truck, after all, but Joey had been struggling this year. It wouldn't hurt her to concede on the little things.

The truck moved stiffly as they left the yard, towing a trailer full of tools. Andie checked the road for traffic out of habit, but things were dark and still at this hour.

In spite of her gloomy brother and the grouchy architect, there were bubbles of excitement working through her veins. The first day on a new site was like the first day of school. There would be challenges, but right now, it was all possibilities.

She was going to turn the empty space into something beautiful and functional. She might not be the architect in charge of creating the vision, but she would implement it, make it real. And that was enough for now.

The excitement bubbles took a hit when she finally got to the mill. There was a car already there.

She knew that car. The day they went through the mill, there'd been Abigail's Lincoln, her truck and this car.

Trevor Emerson's car.

She'd really wanted to be here before him. She checked the time. Five minutes later than she'd planned. She might have beat him if Joey hadn't been dragging his feet.

Andie backed her truck in carefully, leaving the doors of the trailer accessible, then she headed in to see Trevor. Mr. Emerson. Trouble.

He was standing near the side of the building with the kitchen and bathrooms. This would be where they would focus most of their efforts until the weather warmed up.

The people staging last week's skating party had left the space heaters behind, as arranged. The right side of the main space also had some tables, chairs and boxes waiting to be picked up, but they were in the far corner and wouldn't be in the way. Joey had followed Andie inside, and she nodded at a space heater. They'd need them blowing warm air toward the back where the crew would be working.

Andie picked up one, as well, and started carrying it toward the spot where Trevor was standing. He turned, and a frown creased his forehead.

If she hadn't met him at the Goat, she'd never believe he knew how to smile.

"Should you be carrying that?"

Andie heard Joey snort behind her.

"Are you asking whether I'm incapable or stupid?"

She slid the heater to the ground with a bit more force than normal.

Trevor's gaze moved to Joey, following behind her.

"Is that your equipment? I thought they were from the party."

Andie crossed her arms, and Joey went back for another heater.

"Did you think we just commandeered them? They belong to Kozak. We loaned them out for the skating party. They were left behind because they're ours."

Trevor swallowed and seemed to regain control. "I see. Are you planning to set up an office in one of these rooms?"

Joey was back with another heater. He answered for her. "I ordered the trailer for the office to be delivered first thing, sis. Want me to check on it?"

Andie gave her brother a smile, both for the support and for getting his task done.

"Sure, Joey. Once it's here, Sid will get it hooked up. Want to check on those gennies that are coming, as well?"

Joey nodded and headed toward the door.

Trevor put his hands in his pockets, but they didn't fit well with his thick gloves. He took them back out and crossed his arms.

"So we'll have a trailer to work in."

Andie kept a level gaze on him. "Yes, since we're planning to do a lot of demo in here, we'll keep the paperwork and electronics in a trailer to keep them safe."

"Good, good."

Andie had had enough. She wasn't an idiot, and she knew how to do her job, but this man seemed determined to think her deficient in some way.

"I hear my crew arriving." She turned and headed to the door, happy to be with people who respected her and valued her.

As she opened the door, she looked back at Trevor. He was staring at the floor, looking...sad.

She felt a twinge but reminded herself that she wasn't the one double-checking to see if he was able to perform his job. He'd apparently come into town determined to think the worst of them and the work they'd do.

That was all on him.

* * *

The crew fell into a familiar first-day rhythm. They got the office set up and the gennies and other rented gear in place. Andie gathered the crew, mostly men but with two other women—who were also working on breaking the concrete ceiling in the industry—and ran over the expected schedule and the order in which the work would be completed.

The team had questions, and she answered them. She introduced Trevor, though everyone already knew who he was.

This was a small town.

There was a rumble of welcomes for the newcomer and a lot of curiosity on their faces. They asked if he was finding everything he needed, and he nodded.

Then Sid blurted out the million-dollar question. "Will we be seeing much of you?"

Most of their jobs were smaller, and they didn't see the architect that often. Sometimes, Andie was the only one who interacted with them. She'd get the plans and discuss the work they'd do, and then they'd look at the completed job.

Trevor nodded. "Yes, I hope to be here every day."

Silence.

Andie turned to him. "Every day?"

What would he possibly do here every day? She might not have worked on a lot of major construction projects, but she knew the architect wasn't normally on-site every day unless it was a very big project. Something bigger than would ever be built in Carter's Crossing.

His arms were crossed again, his feet spread. "Yes, I think it's going to be very interesting."

The crew were watching her, waiting to see her response. She'd like to tell him she didn't need a babysitter. She'd like to tell him what he could do with his 'every day' and his 'interesting'. She'd like to tell him a lot of things, but she wasn't going to do that, because she was a professional.

She also wasn't going to tell him that it was fine or that she was looking forward to it. She wasn't going to lie. Instead, she turned back to her people.

"Let's get started on the kitchen. We're gutting it. We've got a bin arriving here in ten minutes. I want to have it filled by lunchtime. Bathrooms are next.

"Are the porta potties here yet, Joey?"

Joey cocked his head. "I think I hear them now."

Andie walked with her brother back to the big door. She wondered how Mr. Emerson was going to enjoy using porta potties *every day.*

The trailer was too small.

It was a standard trailer for a job like this. There was room for a desk for him and one for Andie and a table. It would soon be covered with a confusing litter of odds and ends as the work went on. There was a water cooler and a small fridge with a coffee maker on top. Somehow, it felt too small on this project.

As Trevor sat with his laptop on the desk in front of him, he swore he could feel Andie breathing. The first day was winding down. So far, things were going well. The site was organized, and the work had started and was progressing as expected. Andie was going over paperwork on her end, and he could hear the muted sounds of the work site through the walls.

There was a knock on the door, and Joey appeared, reminding him yet again that this was a family firm.

"We're wrapping for today, sis. I can get a lift home with Badger, so take whatever time you need."

Andie looked at the watch on her wrist and nodded. "Everything's cleaned up for the night?"

"Yes, boss."

Trevor tried to decipher Joey's tone. Was he upset? Did he mind working for his sister?

"Tell Mom I'll call when I'm on my way."

Joey closed the door, and Trevor heard truck and car doors slamming, voices crossing over each other, and the sounds of vehicles pulling away. Andie's head was back down, her fingers clicking on the keyboard as she worked away.

How late did she work? Was she always the last to go? Was it a first-day thing? Or was she doing this to assure him she was capable? To impress him, make him trust her?

She rubbed a finger up and down the middle of her forehead

and then moved it back to the keyboard. Her hair was pulled back in a tie but ruffled from being in a hard hat while she'd been on site. She'd taken off her parka and a flannel shirt was peeking out over the neckline of her sweater.

No makeup, no jewelry. Her feet were still in work boots, crossed under the desk. Her gaze moved upward and caught his. He felt his cheeks heating and concentrated on his screen again.

"Is there anything you want to say?"

He looked back up. She was staring at him, mouth in a tight line. He couldn't tell her he'd been wondering if she was staying in the trailer to impress him or if she wanted to spend more time with him. That would be epically bad.

She wouldn't like him to ask how much nepotism played in her company's operations, either.

"Not really."

She nodded. "If you have any questions, any problems on-site, I'd appreciate it if you speak to me in private first."

He frowned, considering her words. She huffed a breath.

"If I don't deal with the issue, then you can take it further, but I can usually handle it. That's my job."

"You don't want me talking to your crew?"

Her lips thinned. They'd soon disappear.

"You can talk to anyone you like. But if you see a problem, please talk to me first. If someone isn't doing their job, that's my responsibility. If anything goes wrong, the buck stops here."

Her fingertip tapped on the tabletop in front of her. "I'd like a chance to explain to you if the problem isn't what you think it is. I don't want my crew thinking you're here to critique them. Tell *me* first."

Her phone rang, and she answered it, leaving him dismissed.

"Okay, Mom, I'll head out now. Give me fifteen minutes to pack up here and check the site."

She shoved her phone in her pocket and closed her laptop. "I can trust you to lock up the trailer?"

"Yes."

She shoved her laptop in a bag and straightened some papers. Pulling on her coat, she tossed him a key.

"I'm gone after I do this walk-through. You have my number if you need me."

Her coat was zipped, and a hat was pulled over her ears. She left the trailer without any further words. He stared at the door for a long time before he shook his head and focused on his computer. He finished up his notes for the day and looked over at Andie's desk. She'd taken her laptop but left a pile of papers weighed down with a rock on top of the desk. He was curious about those papers.

He remembered Geoff Compton shoving papers in his briefcase, laughing that details like this were the bane of his life, and that Trevor was lucky not to have to deal with them.

That paperwork had later showed Geoff had been making substitutions. Ones that had led to the accident.

He shouldn't look at Andie's paperwork. It really wasn't part of his job.

He opened up an email from Abigail Carter. She wanted to meet with him and some of the locals about renovations to their homes to set up B and Bs. He agreed to meet her tomorrow afternoon, and then his gaze wandered to Andie's desk again.

It wasn't like she was even at the stage where any substitutions could be made. And she probably wasn't making any mistakes. She was on the level and capable enough to do this job.

It was just the memories were returning, over and over again, making him anxious and tense. The story on TV and in the papers, where his picture was captioned with words like *suspected* and *at fault*. The interviews with the owner and contractor looking so earnest and concerned, blaming him for the accident.

His hand rubbed his leg.

He hadn't been able to tell his side, not at first. He'd been in hospital. Some had called it karmic justice that he'd been hurt.

It hadn't been karma. It had been his contractor in collaboration with the building owner, cutting corners, ignoring safety issues to save money, bribing inspectors. When that had led to the accident that brought the south wall down, a good portion of it on his leg, they'd been quick to blame him.

Maybe they'd hoped he wouldn't recover. But he had. And he'd fought back. He'd been exonerated, but not in the court of public opinion. That court had closed up session long before he'd been able to participate.

It had been his first major project since going out on his own, and it had almost crushed his dreams along with his leg.

This project here in Carter's Crossing was his chance to show what he could do on his own, without someone else's company to back him up. He couldn't risk a contractor cutting corners. Not again.

He stood, went to the trailer door and opened it. He looked and listened, but the winter sun was long gone and the place quiet and dark. He closed and locked the door.

He went over to Andie's desk, picked up her paperweight rock and set it aside. Then he scanned the pages. Invoices for the trailer and generators. Deal memos with the crew. Nothing looked out of the ordinary.

He set the papers down and carefully replaced the rock. Then, since he'd already crossed the line, he looked through the file cabinet under her desk, finding nothing but empty folders. Was that suspicious? Or was there just nothing to file because it was the first day?

There was a notepad at the side of the desk. She'd written down a name, a supplier of hardware. He took note of that. He'd check what other companies competed with them, make sure there wasn't too cozy a connection between them and his contractor.

He felt…dirty. Dishonest.

He didn't really know Andie. He'd done some research, and Kozak Construction had no red flags online that he could find. He wished he could believe that was enough proof, but his previous contractor had had a good reputation, as well.

He rubbed his leg again. The cold was making it ache. As his hands ran across the hard plastic of his prosthetic device, his resolve hardened.

He'd lost too much to a shady contractor and conspiring owner. It didn't matter what Andie thought of him or if he was snooping. It might not be nice, but next time, it might be worse than someone losing a limb. Someone could lose their life.

CHAPTER SEVEN

ANDIE CHECKED THE time and made her way through the debris of the former kitchen to find her brother.

"I need to head out now. Sure you don't want to come?"

Joey shook his head. "Nah, I'd rather be here working than sitting in Abigail Carter's parlor while she talks with the old ladies about bathrooms."

Andie shook her head.

"We'll talk about *bedrooms*, too. And you're going to have to learn to do the customer side, as well."

Joey shrugged. "You're staying for a while yet, right? So no rush."

Andie checked her brother's expression. "Would you rather I'd planned to go to school this fall?"

He rolled his eyes at her.

She was the oldest of the family, and Joey was the youngest, so they had the biggest gap in age, and in relationship, as well. Andie felt she understood him least, even though they were the only two still living at home.

Andie had been the de facto boss of the family company after her father died. That responsibility, added to her status as the oldest child, meant that she and Joey didn't have a normal sibling relationship.

Each of her siblings in turn had left to go to school and found the careers they wanted somewhere other than Carter's Crossing. Andie had been sad to see them go but had encouraged them to follow their dreams.

Abigail Carter was hoping to rejuvenate the town so that people could pursue their ambitions here in Carter's Crossing. It was too late for her siblings, but Andie supported the initiative and hoped there would be more opportunities for other kids growing up in town to stay if they wanted.

There were worse places to live.

Joey had gone away to school, but he hadn't found what he wanted. Like all the Kozak kids, he'd worked for the company on weekends and during the summer. He seemed happy to continue working here, waiting to take over. Was he tired of waiting?

Andie had been trying to get him more involved with the company and to take more of a leadership role. When she was off-site, he was the guy in charge. If they split between two sites, he managed the second one. But she didn't think he was ready to take over, not yet. So far, he'd shown no interest in meeting with clients or handling the paperwork that seemed to grow with every job.

Was it her fault? Had she prevented him from being more of a leader because she didn't know how to step back?

"Hey, Joey. Sure you don't want to take this meeting? I could stay here."

Joey gave her a puzzled look. "Why would I do that? I don't know the right things to ask anyway. Go. I can take over here."

He turned back to his work, and Andie, untypically uncertain, turned and headed to the office to get her bag.

Trevor was there putting his laptop in his computer bag. He'd been quiet this morning. He'd walked through the site first thing and then again before lunch. No one had complained, but none of them were used to being watched like this.

She knew he was going to the same meeting as she was, and despite their conflicts, they did need to work together. So far, she'd smiled and let the crew think she was fine with what Trevor was doing. She wasn't. She hated feeling like she needed to prove her competency, but if it would help them get along, she'd do it. Maybe if they spent time not talking about work, he'd feel like he could trust her?

"Want to share a ride to Abigail's?"

Trevor looked up, startled.

"Abigail's? You're going, too?"

The dismay in his voice irritated her. What was with this guy?

"Yes, I am. Since Kozak Construction will be doing a lot of the work, it only makes sense that I'm there to help with scheduling."

Trevor frowned.

Andie didn't have to ask what his problem was with her being there. Her very existence was a problem for him. She just didn't know why. This had never happened before or, at least, not since the early days when she'd taken over after her father died. She hadn't liked it then, and she liked it less now.

"You know, I might prefer to have more choice in architects around here, as well, but here we are. It's supposed to snow soon, so I'm offering to give you a ride since you don't have snow tires on your vehicle. That's all. I'm fine on my own. See you there."

She shoved her computer in her own bag, grabbed her jacket, and prepared to head out while doing her best to pretend Trevor was invisible.

"I would appreciate a ride, thank you."

Andie's head snapped up. Trevor stood in front of her, wearing clothes that looked a heck of a lot nicer than her work wear, ready to go and without a frown. He'd flipped in the few moments she was getting her coat on. Talk about Jekyll and Hyde.

Andie wanted to ask if he really trusted her to drive, but if he could pretend to be polite, so could she.

"Okay. Joey has a key to the trailer if anyone needs something, so we can lock up."

Trevor raised his brows, but he merely waited while she turned the key in the door, and followed her to her truck.

Bertha was big and functional and not pretty. She could drive through almost anything, and she could carry a lot while she did so. Trevor's car was fancier, but Andie could be sure of arriving almost anywhere, in almost any conditions. She wasn't apologizing for Bertha. She hated that she'd been tempted to do so.

She beeped open the locks, climbed in and turned the ignition on to get some heat going. There was a bag of assorted hardware on the passenger seat. Trevor had opened the door but paused. Andie glanced over and picked up the bag.

"Sorry, leftovers from our last job. I need to return it or get Joey to."

"Mind?" he asked, gloved hand hovering over the button to warm his seat.

"Go for it."

He hit the button for her seat, as well. Andie stayed quiet, putting the truck in Drive and heading out from the parking lot to the road. The first few flakes started to fall as they turned onto the asphalt.

It took only a few minutes to make their way to Abigail's home. She assumed it was Trevor's first chance to see the place, and she watched for his reaction. She saw appreciation in his stare and felt vicariously proud. There were several cars parked in front of the house and lining the drive. Andie didn't bother trying to squeeze Bertha in. She stopped at the end of the driveway.

"If you get out here, I'll pull up just ahead."

There wouldn't be any room for Trevor to get out of the vehicle without falling into the ditch once she'd done that.

He paused for a moment before thanking her and opening the door.

He puzzled her. The man she'd met in the bar had been warm and had exhibited a strong sense of humor. The architect she was trying to work with was prickly and suspicious. And he had these exasperating pauses, as if he considered everything before he spoke or acted.

She was curious about what those pauses meant. She wished she wasn't. And while she was at it, she wished she was working with the man from the bar instead of the architect she saw on-site.

It had been a long time since she'd felt just like Andie, a woman someone found interesting, instead of Andie, head of Kozak Construction. But she was Andie the contractor now, as far as Trevor was concerned. And he didn't like his contractor.

Shaking her head, she parked the truck as close to the side of the road as she could and climbed down.

Trevor had waited on the drive for her instead of rushing ahead to get in first. She wasn't sure if it was manners or some kind of power play, but she walked beside him and went first up the steps. With some guys, she might suspect he was checking her out, but not with this one.

Mavis Grisham opened the door. She acted as Abigail's second in command. Andie was glad to see she hadn't brought her dog, Tiny, with her. The Great Dane wasn't good at remembering his manners, and she had no desire to shove his nose out of her crotch in front of Trevor.

"Andie! So nice to see you. How's your mother?"

Andie returned the embrace, careful of Mavis's tiny form.

"We're all good, thanks. How are you? Have you met Mr. Emerson?"

Mavis held a hand to her chest. "You're the lovely young man who helped me with my flat tire on New Year's Eve! That was very sweet of you. I don't think I properly thanked you before you rushed away. But I'll be sure to bake you a cake to show my gratitude, now that I've tracked you down."

Really? Andie wouldn't have guessed that about him. But Mavis kept on.

"I wondered if you were the architect. Abigail told us a bit about you. I'm Mavis Grisham, but you can call me Mavis. I'm so looking forward to you working for me. So handsome."

Andie shot him a glance out of the corner of her eye. Trevor looked startled, but he responded appropriately, falling somewhere on a scale between the man she'd first met and the guy she knew now.

Andie pulled off her coat and added it to the pile already on the chair in the entry.

"You all got here early?" Andie jerked her chin at the coats.

They were dry, so their owners had arrived before the snow started.

Mavis nodded. "Oh, yes. We've been having a committee meeting. We'll just roll that over into talking to you two. Mariah's in charge of the romance iniative, and she's been going on about us setting up websites and getting the B and Bs going. It's really happening!"

Mavis had a huge smile on her face. She was right. It was happening. With every wall coming down at the mill, with the orders

Andie was making for new materials, Carter's Crossing was becoming something new. That bubble of excitement was returning, despite Mr. Emerson beside her.

This was all going to be worth it in the end.

Trevor had made a lot of notes by the time the meeting was done.

It had been difficult to keep things straight. The women in the meeting tended to start telling him about their homes and the work they needed done to adapt them, and then they'd divert into stories about people he'd never heard of, many who appeared to no longer be part of the town. Then someone else would start, and after two more stories, the original speaker would add something else to her list.

Andie was making notes, as well, but it was easier for her. She had the advantage of knowing these people she was talking to and also the ones in the stories. She wouldn't start noting something that George had done to a home, only to discover George had left town or died more than twenty years ago and then his house had burned down or had been sold to Harold.

It was enough to give him a headache. Except, it didn't. The stories were rambling, but he itched to see these homes. He expected some of the work that had been done in the past would probably not meet current codes, and some had undoubtedly marred the beauty of the original structures. But he loved buildings and the stories they told. The homes in this town, especially the ones in the more prosperous downtown area, had decades and sometimes more than a century of stories to their brick and mortar and wood. He wanted to read the stories.

The ladies finally began to trickle away, leaving Trevor and Andie and Abigail to evaluate their notes and plans.

Abigail looked at him with a smile at the corners of her lips.

"I hope you were able to keep up, Trevor. Sometimes we older people can ramble a bit."

"A bit" was an understatement. But Abigail wasn't one to ramble.

"I'll need to see the homes, but today gave me an introduction."

"That's a nice way to express it. Honestly, I've been in Eloise's house at least once a month for as long as I can remember, and I couldn't keep what she was talking about straight."

Trevor allowed a smile in response to her comment. He thought Eloise was the one with the white Victorian with green shutters, but George might have painted them blue.

Abigail closed her own notebook. "I'd suggest Andie set up a schedule for going over the homes."

Trevor stilled. Was he going to be able to do anything without involving Andie?

"It will take an hour to get Eloise to settle on a start time. At least Andie will know what she means when she talks about the day before the bazaar meeting. Also, these women know her and will be more comfortable settling things with her. In a small town, you're a stranger for a long time."

Trevor nodded. He'd figured out that several of the women were widows. He could certainly allow them the comfort of not having a strange man set loose in their homes. Though, they'd need to be a little more accustomed to it if they were going to rent out rooms. That, however, was not his problem.

"Also, Harriet will tell you that her son can do most of the work, but he won't. Andie will make sure she allows time for that in her schedule, for when he sprains his spleen or some such thing."

Huh.

Trevor hadn't worked on small jobs like renovating a few bedrooms and a bath for years. And he'd never been the architect in charge of projects like that. He was used to working with professionals.

Personal vagaries were going to be a factor on these jobs. Andie's local knowledge would be an asset. Perhaps he shouldn't be upset that they were apparently going to meet with the homeowners as a pair. It would give him more opportunity to watch how she worked and evaluate how trustworthy she was.

Andie stood. "Thanks for arranging this, Abigail. Do you have a date when you hope things will be completed?"

"Most of the timeline will depend on when the mill is ready. I don't want to add pressure on the two of you, because I know there will be factors outside of your control that can delay the work. I'll do what I can to smooth your path, but I won't make any major plans until we are closer to that being done."

Andie's forehead creased, her brows almost meeting over her straight nose. Trevor reminded himself that her nose was none of his business.

"Things went so well on Valentine's Day. There's nothing else going on?"

Abigail smiled. "As if Mariah would be content to let things ride. We aren't making any plans that include the mill or require the B and Bs to be functioning, but we have at least one major event planned for this summer, and there will be some smaller things, as well."

"That's good," Andie said. "People need that to look forward to, to give them hope."

Abigail's smile disappeared. "Exactly. I don't want to delay any more than I have to. Not to pressure you, but…"

Trevor knew Abigail had a lot of clout here, and this project of hers was going to keep the town and Kozak Construction busy. Was this maybe a nudge to take shortcuts to speed up the process?

He didn't want to think so. He admired Abigail Carter, but he'd been burned before, and he couldn't let it just ride.

"Do you mind, Andie, if I talk to Trevor for a bit?"

Trevor went very still. This was the first time someone appeared to want to separate the two of them for a discussion. He wondered what Abigail wanted to talk about and how Andie would respond.

"Not at all, but we rode over together."

Abigail shrugged. "This isn't a secret, so I'm not trying to keep anything from you. It just involves a potential project that could use Trevor's expertise after the mill is done, but it might not happen. If it does, you'll probably be gone from Carter's Crossing by the time a contractor is needed, so I don't want to keep you from your work. I know you're busy."

Wait. Andie was leaving town? When? Why?

Andie didn't appear to have a problem with being left out.

"It's fine, Abigail. I can stay here and answer emails. Or would you like me to go to the kitchen? I won't offer to wait in the truck, not today."

Trevor hadn't been watching the weather, but a glance out the window showed him that the wind had picked up and snow was blowing in the gathering dusk.

"As long as you can keep this quiet, Andie. If things go well with Cupid's Crossing, I'm considering converting this place into an inn."

Trevor was mildly surprised, but Andie's eyebrows were now climbing to her hairline.

"An inn? But you—your family…"

Trevor didn't know Abigail's family, and he wasn't sure he could handle more names today.

Abigail looked out the window. "My grandson Nelson's the only family I have in town, and he won't be moving in here. I expect he'll do something about that house on his farm. This place is too big for just me, and I don't know that any of the others are coming back."

Andie was nodding, so Nelson and the others were familiar to her.

"But where would you live?"

Suddenly, Abigail didn't look sad. There was a look of mischief on that elegant face.

"I might not stay in Carter's—or rather, Cupid's—Crossing. I suspect Mariah will remain, and she can take care of things."

Andie was blinking, her mouth slightly open. Apparently, the idea of Abigail leaving town was a surprise. Trevor suspected finding out about Santa had been less of a shock.

It didn't surprise him. Abigail was beautiful, intelligent and incredibly competent, and he was more surprised to know that she'd lived in this small town her entire life. She had connections outside this place. She hadn't invited him to come and work here randomly. Someone in the city had given her Howard's name.

"Do you want me to look around and maybe come up with preliminary drawings?"

Abigail shook her head. "Not quite yet. But I'd like to show you around and get an idea of whether a conversion would be a big job, or a huge job."

Trevor smiled, pleased at the prospect of taking a closer look at the house. It was beautiful, both outside and from what he'd seen inside. He was pretty sure George hadn't done the work on this one.

"I'd love to see more of your home. It's beautiful. And I could probably give you a quick-and-dirty estimate of time and money."

Abigail turned to Andie. "Do you want to join us?"

Andie shook her head. "No, I should answer some of these messages. I'll just sit here and come to terms with the idea of Carter's Crossing without Abigail Carter."

Abigail's mouth twisted. "We're changing the name to Cupid's Crossing. And nothing is determined yet."

That might be true, Trevor thought, but Abigail looked like she'd set her mind on something, and he suspected she was not a person who failed often. If he lived here, he'd be changing his address to Cupid's Crossing.

CHAPTER EIGHT

ANDIE HAD HER phone in her hands but hadn't opened her email yet.

Abigail leaving?

That would be news. And a big change for the town. She couldn't imagine Carter's Crossing without Abigail Carter. Nelson Carter was here, true, but he was the town vet and showed no interest in taking up a leadership role.

Andie could see his fiancée, Mariah, stepping up. Those two had gotten engaged on Valentine's Day. Andie wondered if Abigail had had a hand in that. She shook her head. Nothing was set yet, and she had a couple of messages from her brother to deal with.

Trevor and Abigail took a while. She heard their voices echoing down the stairs as they examined the upper floors, and when they passed though the room she was in, she heard Abigail recounting the history of the building. Meantime, she agreed with her brother about sending the crew home since the wind and snow were now threatening the roads.

When they finally came back, Andie stood up, eager to get going. Her mother would be anxious, and she hated to make her worry. Most of the time, her mom's concerns were excessive, but when the weather was like this, she had good reason to be worried.

"I hope you don't mind, Abigail, but we should head out now. The roads are getting bad."

"You've got your truck?" Abigail asked.

Andie nodded.

"That's good. Would you like me to call your mother and tell her you're on your way? Maybe keep her talking for a while?"

Andie took a long breath. "That would be wonderful, Abigail. She'll fuss with the roads like this, and I need to return Trevor to his car back at the mill."

Abigail crossed to the window and pulled back a curtain.

"Maybe you should just drop him off at his place and take him to the mill tomorrow. The temperature has dropped."

Andie stood beside Abigail and looked out at the snow. Abigail was right. This snowfall had taken a twist toward snowstorm. She turned to Trevor. She didn't think he'd be very keen on that idea, but after taking a look out the window himself, he nodded his agreement.

"As I've been told, I don't have snow tires, so it might be wiser."

Andie shot him a glance. She would bet that if Abigail weren't here, he'd have argued rather than accept assistance.

"You're on Second Street, aren't you, Trevor? That's not far out of Andie's way."

Those eyes turned to her. "Do you mind, Andie?"

It was the first time he'd said her name. Why did she know that?

"No, I don't mind. We don't want to lose our architect."

She wasn't being sarcastic, not really, but she saw the slight narrowing of his eyes and the pinching of his mouth before he quickly wiped away the expression.

They bundled up in their outerwear. Abigail watched them as they headed out to the driveway and promised to call Andie's mom as soon as the truck was moving. Andie climbed in, turned on the heat and reversed so that Trevor could access the passenger door.

He slipped on his way up and gripped the door tightly. "Abigail was right. It's getting very slippery."

Andie was grateful for Bertha's snow tires and firm grip on the road.

Trevor didn't double-check her driving, which was a relief. She concentrated on the road, turning onto Second Street and inching down the slick pavement until she arrived at the house he indicated. She was familiar with it. Kozak Construction had worked on it back when her father was alive.

She pulled to a careful halt in front of the house. She'd wondered where he was staying but had avoided taking any steps to find out. She didn't ask herself why.

"Flick the lights on once you're inside, and I'll head home."

His mouth opened, and she knew he was going to tell her not to bother, but then, he closed his mouth and swallowed.

"Thank you for the lift. Send me a text when you head out in the morning, and I'll be waiting on the sidewalk for you."

Andie nodded. She liked the idea that he wasn't going to arrive before her.

Trevor gathered his things and was careful exiting the truck, mindful of the slipperiness of ice under the coating of fresh snow.

He was very careful walking to his front door. The ice appeared to bother him. Maybe he didn't go out a lot in New York City when things were icy. Perhaps they didn't have a lot of ice like this in the city. If she stayed home when things got slippery, she'd stay home a lot.

Trevor made it to the door and used his key to open it. She put Bertha in Drive and kept her foot on the brakes, waiting for him to flick on the light that would release her.

She waited. It was dark enough now that she'd see a light, even in a back room. She frowned. It was very dark. She bent to peer through the windshield.

The streetlight beside her wasn't on. She could see one lit up farther down. The wind-driven snow whipped through its glow, but the one in front of Trevor's house was dark. So were the houses beside his.

He reappeared in the doorway. Andie put the truck in Park and hopped down, her boots and grip on the door keeping her upright. She headed up the sidewalk, remembering how he'd been cautious and wanting to save him another trip on the ice.

"What's wrong?"

He was frowning, phone in hand.

"The lights aren't working, and the heat is off. I'm calling the landlord."

Andie looked at the neighboring houses that were also dark.

"I don't think she can help. Looks like the power's out in a few of the houses around here."

He turned around, looking past her at...mostly nothing, since everything was dark. He looked at a loss for the first time since she'd met him.

Andie sighed.

"Go get what you need for the night. You can come home with me."

Trevor wasn't sure exactly why he'd agreed. Well, part of it was because his place was dark and cold, and he didn't have a car here, but he hadn't thought through all that when he'd agreed and gone back to pack a bag. He'd been curious. What was Andie's place like? What was her family like?

This was his chance to understand her better and see how much trust he could place with her.

Andie didn't say much as they drove to her place. She was focused on the drive, and though her big truck gripped the road, he didn't want to distract her.

He remembered she'd said she lived out of town, back when they'd met at the pub and he hadn't known who she was. He'd heard her calls that day and while on-site and when she talked to her brother, so he knew she lived at home with her family.

He did wonder why but had never been able to ask. He might find out now.

Just outside the town limits, they pulled into the driveway of a bigger house than he'd expected. There was a large garage and work shed, a big sign, and some oversize equipment in the shadows of the yard. This was obviously headquarters for Kozak Construction.

Andie pulled her truck into the garage. She handled her vehicle competently. From what he'd observed so far, she was surprisingly capable at everything he'd seen her do.

Maybe he had more chauvinism in him than he'd realized. It was a disconcerting thought, and he set it aside for later consideration as he slid out of the truck with his duffle bag.

An older woman was peering out the door, watching as Andie led the way, striding over the snow-covered path to the house, leaving footsteps for him to follow.

"Andie! Was it slippery? Joey got back a while ago."

"Mom, it was fine." Andie's tone was patient. "I was in a meeting over at Abigail Carter's, and that ran a little longer than I'd expected. She had all the women over there, so you know how that goes. Then I drove Mr. Emerson home. Since his place doesn't have power, I brought him to spend the night. Trevor Emerson, this is my mom, Marion Kozak."

He hadn't seen much family resemblance between Joey and Andie, but there was a strong resemblance between Joey and his mother. Presumably, Andie took after her father.

He held out a hand to Andie's mother, who'd stepped outside as they approached. "It's a pleasure to meet you, Mrs. Kozak. I hope I'm not an imposition."

A smile broke through her worried expression. "No, not at all. There used to be seven of us in the house, and with only the three of us now, it feels empty. We have lots of room, and with this weather—"

She broke off to cast another worried look at the snow blowing through the yard.

"Let's go in, Mom. It's cold out. We're all home and fine. What am I smelling?"

There was an appetizing aroma in the air. Trevor felt his stomach attempting to grumble, and he pressed a hand to his midsection.

Mrs. Kozak moved ahead of them into the kitchen. Andie pulled off her hat and gloves and threw them into a basket by the door. She opened a closet door and pulled out a hanger.

"I can hang up your coat."

Trevor unbuttoned his and shrugged the coat off.

"Thank you." He passed the coat over and carefully bent to undo his boots.

The entrance was roomy, leaving space for several people to don or remove their outerwear. He carefully stepped out of his boots and set them on a plastic mat already holding several pairs. Andie hung up her own jacket, removed her boots and led the way past a shabby living room with worn couches around a TV.

"Mom, I'm going to show Trevor to the spare room."

"Okay, Andie. I'll start serving soon." Her mother's voice echoed back.

Andie led the way down a hallway. She opened a door and flicked on the ceiling light.

The room wasn't as crowded as the rest of the house. It appeared to be a mostly unused guest room with a queen-size bed, a dresser and end tables.

Andie read the surprise on his face.

"Growing up, my sister and I shared this room. As you can see, it's a guest room now for when my siblings come back. Joey has the boys' room, and I have the other bedroom to myself.

"Why don't you drop your bag, and we'll get to the table. Mom is a great cook, but she likes to get dinner done before her game shows come on."

Trevor dropped his duffle and followed her back to the kitchen.

Joey was already seated at one end of the table, and Mrs. Kozak at the other. Andie headed to what was obviously her usual chair, and Trevor sat at the remaining place setting.

"This looks delicious, Mrs. Kozak."

He wasn't just saying that. The meal was homemade and emitting an aroma that was about to make his stomach embarrass him, with quantities beyond what four of them could possibly consume.

He felt welcomed but not overpowered.

Mrs. Kozak passed him a bowl to start.

"It's my *bigos*. The kids need a good meal after working all day." The "kids" certainly wouldn't be hungry after this.

"You're new to Carter's Crossing, Mr. Emerson?"

Trevor almost whimpered at the aroma wafting from his plate. His own cooking was healthy and basic. This was something else. "Yes. I'm here to work on the mill. I'm the architect."

Mrs. Kozak's eyes widened. "Oh, really? Andie, love, perhaps Mr. Emerson could talk to you, give you some advice."

Surprised, he looked at Andie. Her cheeks were flushed.

"Mom, let me take care of it. Mr. Emerson is busy, and so am I."

"Oh, come on now, Andie. All we ever hear is how much you sacrifice instead of going to study, so go ahead and talk to him." Joey jerked his head at Trevor. "Then you can escape Carter's Crossing and leave Mom and I here."

Andie's eyes widened, and her mouth turned down. "I'm not escaping. Can we just let this go? Trevor didn't ask to find himself in the middle of our family drama. Were there any problems on the site after I left, Joey?"

Trevor didn't want to be in the middle of family drama, but he was extremely curious about the issue he was supposed to offer advice on. And what sacrifices Andie had made. He was also very interested in whether there'd been a problem on-site. He was allowed to be curious about that.

Joey promised there'd been no problems. "Do you need a play-by-play of everything we did, or can you just accept that?"

Andie bit her lip just as their mother broke in. "Joey, I'm sure you did everything just fine, but Andie's a worrier."

"Wonder where she gets that?" Joey grumbled under his breath.

"Let's pass the food. So, Mr. Emerson, where is it you're staying?"

Trevor answered, and Mrs. Kozak commented on the place and what she knew of the people on the street, none of whom he knew. He kept a polite smile on his face and indulged in the best meal he'd enjoyed in weeks.

Mrs. Kozak asked where he was from and what it was like to grow up in a city. From her responses, she obviously didn't believe that a childhood in the city could in any way compare to growing up in this small town. She didn't probe into his family, and he was relieved. She mentioned where her other children were living. Andie had three siblings who'd moved to other places. One was in Albany, one had gone to Boston and the farthest one appeared to be in Chicago.

They were all younger than Andie. Trevor wondered why everyone had left, but Andie had stayed. He wondered what had happened to Mr. Kozak, who was never mentioned. And he wondered why she had chosen to stay in this town and be a contractor, when her siblings had all gone to college.

But he didn't ask. Not when these were the issues that had sparked the drama at the beginning of the meal. Not when Andie had looked upset. For some reason, he didn't want to upset her. Not more than he already had.

He offered to clear up, but Mrs. Kozak refused. She shooed him away while she carried the serving dishes into the kitchen, and despite an urge to follow that delicious food, he let her go. Joey went to the living room and turned on the television. Trevor asked for the restroom and escaped from there to his room. He didn't want to intrude, but he'd forgotten his phone charger, and he needed Wi-Fi if he was going to do anything more than stare at the walls.

He could see the access point, but he needed a password, obviously. He hooked his laptop up to his phone data, but after fifteen minutes, it was almost dead.

He brought his laptop out to the living room where Joey and his mother were watching television. Andie worked on her own laptop at the dining room table.

"Um, can I use your Wi-Fi?"

Andie gave him a polite smile. "Sure." She scratched a random-looking code on a scrap of paper and passed it over to him.

He should return to his room, but he was tired of lonely nights with the internet, and he was curious.

He sat down across from Andie and typed in the password. Since the other two were immersed in a loud game show, he leaned over the table, seeming to catch Andie by surprise.

"What advice did you want me to give you?"

Her cheeks flushed again. She frowned and shot a glance over at her relatives.

"I have no plans to trouble you, don't worry."

Her reluctance made him push. There was something about her that made him prickly and juvenile. "I'm here, and you're not troubling me now."

As her mouth firmed in an upcoming denial, he added, "Or I could ask your mother."

Now she was frowning harder, forehead creasing. She glanced to the side and then back.

"Fine. Just remember that you insisted, I didn't ask." She waited for his nod. "I had planned to study architecture."

He blinked.

She had her head down and was facing her screen again, carefully avoiding his glance.

Oh, he wasn't letting that go. "So, why didn't you?"

This wasn't irrelevant; he knew it.

Andie sighed, as if hard done by, and stood.

Trevor stood, unsure of where they were going, hoping it wasn't someplace difficult.

"Mom, I'm going to the office with Trevor."

Her mother nodded, gaze never leaving the TV screen.

Andie headed toward the door they'd used to enter the house, but instead of pulling on her outdoor gear, she turned down a short hallway and opened the door there.

She flicked on the overhead light, and he saw they were now in the offices of Kozak Construction. Not only was it recognizably a business office but it had Kozak Construction painted on the walls. And photographs.

There were black-and-white photos of a man he didn't recognize but who bore more than a passing resemblance to Andie. Color photos of presumably the same man with a younger version of himself. A couple of Andie on job sites. A lot of pictures of projects presumably completed by Kozak Construction. None of them were basement renovations.

Andie sat behind what must be her desk and waved for Trevor to sit across from her.

"We grew up working for Kozak Construction, all of us kids." She pointed to the photos. "My grandfather and my dad. I loved the buildings, so I applied to Pratt when I was a high school senior. I got in. I was pretty excited, and my dad was so proud.

"I was working with my dad on a job one New Year's Eve fourteen years ago, and after we closed up, my dad and I stopped at the Goat and Barley to have a celebratory drink. I couldn't have alcohol, so I had a soda, and we talked about my going to school and what the new year would be like. I was gonna be the first kid in the family to go to college. He said that someday he'd make a building I designed."

She paused, straightened some papers on the desk. "I headed out to a party with friends."

Trevor's muscles tensed in a futile effort to help. He remembered the soda she had stared into at the Goat and Barley on New Year's Eve. An anniversary, she'd told him. Something bad was coming.

"Mom called me at the party. Dad had a heart attack as he was driving home, went off the road, and that was it. He was gone."

Trevor opened his mouth to offer sympathy, but she held up her hand. He could see her throat working.

Now he understood the drink at the bar. He wondered if she'd just happened to be there this past year or if she went every year.

"Anyway, the company was how this family survived financially. Dad's foreman, Sid, tried to keep the business running, but he wasn't that kind of guy. He needed someone to direct him. I had worked the most with Dad, so Sid and I did our best to stay on top of things till I was done with high school.

"Then I took over. I couldn't leave to go to school, or Mom would have had to sell the company, and then how would she support us all? I learned the business. Each of my siblings went to college. Joey graduated in December. I was going to apply, to go somewhere this fall, but Abigail told me about her plans for the mill renovation. This is a big job for us, and Joey isn't ready yet."

Her head shot up, and her expression stilled. It was like she'd just remembered who she was talking to and regretted sharing with him.

He regretted it, too.

He didn't want to know that she was someone who'd put others first. That she cared for her family and sacrificed for them. That when you were in her inner circle, she would be there for you.

He didn't want to feel the urge to reach out to comfort her. To be in that circle. Because this story didn't give him any more confidence in her abilities. It made him remember how Geoff Compton had taken over from his father and how that had changed his life.

She'd learned by necessity on the job. Did she have any training? Did she know what she was doing? Did the crew do the work, leaving her as a figurehead? Did she keep people on her crew because they were old friends?

Would she be willing to take shortcuts like Geoff, to try to keep things afloat in that crisis? Probably not. She'd been the head of the company for a long time. But he'd trusted Geoff, too. He just couldn't shake his suspicions.

"Don't worry. I'm not going to ask you for anything. I won't impose. If my mother says anything, just let it slide."

He nodded and rose to his feet. "I should probably..." His voice trailed off, and he had no idea how to end the sentence.

He wanted to get away to someplace he could think. He had no advice to give her on a career. She was starting late. If she hadn't been in school for the past fourteen years, would she be able to handle it? Would her brother be able to take over?

That wouldn't be Trevor's problem, since he'd be gone by then. *But* she was planning to leave. How invested would she be in this job?

He hated that he was this paranoid, but the need to protect himself came from a place deep, deep inside.

Even when people meant the best, they could still hurt you. Badly.

CHAPTER NINE

ANDIE SHOOK HER head at how fast Trevor left.

Why had she blurted all that out?

Part of it had been because she knew her family was going to spill the news of her academic dreams anyway. The guy was so spooked, any new information was evaluated as if it were going to blow up in his face. It was better that she told him than have her mother ask him to talk to her and put him in an embarrassing position. But if she was honest, part of it was because she wanted to show him they had something in common, a bond.

She wanted the guy from the bar back.

Andie leaned back in her chair and sighed. Somewhere in that stuffy package Trevor presented was the guy who'd helped her get through New Year's Eve. He'd made her laugh, made her feel seen and appreciated. She had no idea where that guy had gone, or why.

Andie didn't date a lot. Part of it was the lack of potential partners in Carter's Crossing. Since her construction company was one of the few employers in town, some of the single guys worked for her, and dating any of them was out.

She'd tried that once, and the repercussions had dogged her for most of a year. It was too hard to earn respect in this field to jeopardize it for a few dates. Honestly, none of her current staff tempted her.

Some guys also didn't like the way she looked. She had calloused hands, unpainted nails and muscles. She wore dirty jeans and work boots most of the time, often wearing orange for safety, and she knew orange was not a flattering color for her.

She spent long hours keeping the company going, and she lived at home. It didn't all add up to a totally appealing package. But for that one afternoon, Trevor had made her feel attractive and witty. He'd talked to her about things she loved.

She needed to acknowledge that whoever he had been that afternoon, he didn't feel the same way about her now that he knew more about her. And yes, that was a depressing thought. It would be better for her to shove that afternoon away and forget about it, because there wasn't going to be a repeat.

Maybe she should have planned to go away to school this fall. She wasn't sure staying was worth it.

She didn't sleep well but woke up at her usual time the next morning. Her mother was up making coffee and breakfast.

Living at home when you passed your thirtieth birthday might sound depressing, but there were perks beyond the fact that her business was here within walking distance. Her mother making a big breakfast before a long morning of hard work was one of them.

"Morning, Mom." Andie got her coffee cup, filled it and added sugar and milk. At least her job meant she didn't have to count calories.

"Morning, Andie. Will your friend want breakfast?"

Andie's lips twisted. "Friend" was a stretch. She wasn't sure he'd even admit to being her coworker.

"Don't know, Mom. I didn't ask him last night."

By the time Andie had come back from the office, Trevor had been hidden in the spare room, their conversation over.

Her mother began to twist her fingers. "Would you ask him? I don't want to make something that he doesn't want or that he doesn't eat, but it doesn't seem right not to offer and—"

Andie held up her free hand. "It's okay, Mom, I'll ask him. I'll take him a cup of coffee and ask if he's hungry."

She set her cup down and took a clean one from the cabinet, filled it with coffee, milk and the tiniest bit of sugar she'd seen him add to his coffee in the trailer. As if taking a full spoonful was somehow an admission of weakness.

She hadn't heard any movements behind his door when she'd passed, so maybe he needed a caffeine jolt to get started. She tapped lightly on the door but got no response.

She checked the bathroom. Joey was in there, grumbling as he fussed with his hair. She'd been hearing him do that for years.

She returned to Trevor's door and knocked a little harder. Still no answer.

Had he left somehow? Called someone for a lift and snuck away? Was he that determined to get to the site before her? She wouldn't put it past him.

She twisted the handle of the door quietly and slowly pushed it open.

The early light coming through the curtains showed her enough to make out shapes. There was a person-shaped lump in the bed, a duffle on the floor beside it and a prosthetic leg...

She gasped, and the figure on the bed shot up, revealing a male head and torso.

"What?" he asked in a sleepy voice.

"Sorry!" she squeaked, her cheeks hot. "Um, we're heading out in about twenty minutes, if you can be ready then. And my mom asked if you want breakfast, and I, um, coffee." She held out the cup in her hand as if it would vouch for her.

He ran a hand through his hair. It was tousled in a way she was sure he never allowed anyone to see. He reached to the side table. "Phone died. I'll just..."

Andie realized she was staring at him, the messy hair, the bare chest, the...leg on the floor.

She finally managed to close her mouth and left him, closing the door firmly behind her. She stood for a moment, not ready to go back to her mother.

It was a good thing she would never be in a position to see a newly awakened Trevor again, because he looked too much like the man from the bar, and it was way too appealing. She was dealing with the architect now, not him. Without glasses, his eyes looked vulnerable, and without that prickly air, he looked younger and approachable. And annoyingly appealing.

Gah!

And he had a prosthetic?

She wanted to ask him what had happened. Did if affect him day-to-day? Did he need help sometimes? That was undoubtedly why he didn't tell people about it.

It was none of her business what had happened or how it affected his life. It didn't mean any adjustments to the work they were doing, and she needed to proceed now as if she hadn't seen anything.

She was embarrassed. She shouldn't have opened the door. If she'd thought he was gone, she should have asked Joey to check the room.

She straightened and headed back to the kitchen, still carrying the coffee. She told her mom their guest had just gotten up, so he probably wouldn't have enough time to eat. Andie did her best to eat most of her own breakfast, with Joey showing up not long after.

She heard the sound of a door opening down the hallway and then another closing. She expected their guest was making use of the bathroom now that Joey was done. By the time Trevor showed up with his bag, she and Joey were finished with their food, and her mother had prepared a takeaway container for Trevor.

Andie was tempted to offer to help carry something but restrained herself.

She wasn't surprised when Trevor ended up getting a lift to the site with Joey. Having him spend the night at the house had just made things more uncomfortable between them.

Coffee. He definitely needed coffee.

Trevor never slept in. He had his phone alarm, and he was used to getting up when he needed to. Even last night, when he'd realized his phone was almost out of battery and that he'd forgotten his charger, he'd been sure he'd wake up.

This was the worst morning for him to sleep in.

It had been a strange, strange night. After leaving Andie, he'd gone to his room and done his best to immerse himself in work, but instead, he'd found his thoughts circling around the Kozaks.

Andie had lost her dream so young. It had been brave to take over the company and support her family when her dad died. He'd wanted to go back in time and offer her help. Support. Had she gotten that from someone? Was she lonely?

He understood lonely. He'd been lonely growing up. Even during his relationship with Violet, he'd felt like he was on the fringes, not the center.

That had reminded him that if anything went wrong, he was the one on the outside here in Cupid's Crossing. Being isolated had been why he'd been blamed last time.

Again, he wondered if Andie was counting down till it was time to leave, and if that meant she really cared about this job. Could he have confidence in Joey as the head of the company? Her crew appeared to respect her, but he wasn't sure they felt the same about her brother.

His only concern was how it touched the job. He had no other reason to dwell on it, but he hadn't gotten to sleep for a long time with more thoughts of Andie than of the mill in his head. Despite being in a strange bed, he'd slept in until Andie had woken him up.

And now, she knew about his leg. She'd seen it.

He was braced for questions. For a change in how she looked at him and how she treated him. He didn't want that. He'd leaped at the opportunity to drive to the mill with Joey.

The storm had passed overnight, and now, with the rising temps, the snow was melting, leaving the roads bare and wet. Joey was quiet on the drive, listening to the radio and drinking from his travel mug. Trevor had been given a mug, as well, by Mrs. Kozak. The coffee inside was exactly the way he liked it.

Either Mrs. Kozak was clairvoyant, or one of her children knew how he liked his coffee. Since he drank it in the trailer and since he thought Andie had been carrying a mug when she opened his door, he knew which Kozak he'd bet on.

His thoughts circled back to Andie and how they were going to get along after last night. It wasn't as if they'd had an easy relationship before.

Andie had arrived on-site just before them. She was unlocking the office trailer as Joey parked his car beside her truck. Trevor thanked him for the lift. Joey nodded and headed into the mill. Trevor dropped his overnight bag in his car and then braced himself before opening the door to the trailer.

Andie was on the phone, so he was able to make his way to his desk and pull out his laptop, finally getting his phone on a charger before he had to face her.

Someone had called in sick, and Andie was dealing with it as Trevor passed her again on his way to walk through the mill.

He checked over everything each morning and again in the evening before he left. So far, everything was going well, and he'd like to think it was because Kozak did a good job rather than because he was checking, but he couldn't take the risk.

He lingered in the mill, spending time staring around the open space where work hadn't yet begun. He crossed to one of the windows and pushed up to watch the stream burbling past. The days had warmed enough that the ice was mostly gone. The weather yesterday was probably the last bite of winter.

He was avoiding Andie. He needed to stop that.

He made his way back to the trailer. Andie was frowning at her laptop. She looked up as the door opened.

"I have a question for you."

Trevor's stomach clenched, and he was glad he hadn't yet eaten any of the food Mrs. Kozak had sent with him. He continued to his desk, wanting the security of some space between them before she asked questions. Questions he hated answering. Questions he was tired of. Questions about his leg.

She looked up and met his gaze. He saw a flicker in her eyes and knew it was coming. He didn't have to answer. Could he be rude enough to say that to her?

"Our supplier in Albany has a problem sourcing the fire-suppression hoods you requested. They're offering us a couple of substitute options."

It took a minute for his brain to catch up. That wasn't what he'd been expecting.

"Ah… Can you send me information on the substitutes?"

Suddenly, everything was fine. It was a typical workday with no talk of family dramas or artificial limbs. He was relieved. But for some bizarre reason, he was also disappointed.

Why didn't she ask about his leg?

Andie didn't bring it up, not that morning or in the weeks that passed. Winter turned into the ugly part of spring, and she'd still never mentioned it. He spent too much time trying to decipher if she'd seen his prosthetic and decided to ignore it or if she hadn't noticed.

If she had seen it, had she understood that he didn't want to talk about it? Could he trust that? It was a lot like trusting her.

And that was scary.

Still, he stepped back from reviewing every invoice that came into the trailer. He'd been taking copies at first, double-checking prices, quantities, looking for any possible scam he could think of. He could no longer justify doing that. He hoped he wasn't being a fool.

The snow was gone, leaving dirt and debris behind. There were indicators that green things were about to sprout and make things better. For now, there were crocuses and scilla promising what was to come. The mill was proceeding on budget and on schedule. Trevor knew his stuff, and that definitely helped.

Andie hadn't asked Trevor about his leg, and he hadn't offered any information. They spoke about work and never touched on personal matters, which was fine. Really. She didn't expect anything else. But she found the slow march of spring to be frustrating. She was restless, as if she were waiting for something and it was so slow in coming, she wasn't sure if it was going to arrive in time.

A call from Denise was perfect timing.

They had been waiting on an inspection for two days now, and the inspector was finally scheduled for tomorrow. Since everything was on track here at the mill, Joey had taken the crew to a couple of the homes that needed to be renovated for the B and B business. Trevor had gone to watch them, as well, leaving Andie with some quiet time to process payroll and pay some invoices.

"Denise! How are things going?"

Denise told her husband to run away for a bit, and Andie heard her settle down for a talk.

"Things are going…well. Actually, there's a lot going on. You got a minute?"

Andie sat back and propped her boots on a handy waste bin.

"You couldn't have timed it better. I was about to pay vendors, so I'm happy to put that off for a bit."

Denise laughed. "Anything better than accounting, right? Okay, first, thanks for not telling anyone I'm pregnant."

"I promised." Andie didn't normally see much of Denise's family now that Denise was gone.

Andi knew her own mother would like to know about the pregnancy, but telling her that Denise's parents were about to become grandparents would only make her mom talk about the grandchildren she was missing. Or how Andie should find a nice boy.

Andie hadn't found any nice boys here in Carter's—no, Cupid's—Crossing. Well, maybe one, but that wasn't going to go anywhere. She'd decided to wait till she was finally away and following her own dream before considering a relationship. She didn't need any more ties to keep her here.

"Well, we have some more news on the pregnancy front, and I've told my mom."

That meant it would no longer be a secret.

"Are you going to tell me, or should I ask your mom about this news?"

"We're having twins!"

Whoa.

"Do I offer congratulations or condolences?" Andie was only partly joking.

Denise had a moment of silence. Oh, maybe that wasn't a great joke for an expecting mom.

"It's kinda both. I mean, twins are going to be a challenge, obviously. But Mom and Dad have decided to move down here. Like, I told her yesterday, and today, she told me they're going to list the house."

Andie's feet dropped to the floor. "What? That's crazy."

"Totally. So you can offer both congratulations on the babies and condolences on their move."

Andie knew Denise's mom was difficult.

"Is it going to be that bad?"

Denise sighed. "I hope not. I mean, having help with the babies will be great. But you know Mom."

Denise's mother was a person who seemed to enjoy not being happy. She always found the glass half-empty. And she complained about it.

"I'm dealing with that. And now Dave is mad because he thinks Mom just wants an excuse to avoid his wedding."

Andie didn't know the story firsthand, because she didn't hang out with Jaycee and Dave, but Denise had told her that their mom had made Jaycee feel unwelcome. As a result, her brother Dave had put his foot down with her not long before the Valentine's Day party to celebrate his engagement to Jaycee.

The skating party at the mill. It had been an incredible event, but there wouldn't be any more events like that till the mill was done. Currently, they were hoping for an October finish, if they could keep on deadline.

"Maybe it will be nicer for Jaycee if your mom isn't there."

"Well, whether it would be or not, we won't know. That's the other news I have for you. Dave and Jaycee are getting married on the Fourth of July, and we're coming up for it. It'll be the last chance I have to travel before the babies arrive."

Andie sat upright.

"You're coming back? This summer? That's great!"

"I know. I need to go a little crazy once more before I have to become a responsible mom."

Finally, Denise was sounding like the happy woman Andie was familiar with.

Andie snorted. "I have so many stories to tell your kids about you, O responsible mom."

Denise giggled. "I know. It seems impossible that I'm going to be a mom, let alone to two unfortunate kids."

"Hey, you're going to be a fantastic mother. Those kids are lucky. I'll make sure I can take some time off while you're here. We'll have fun like you're still single."

Denise groaned. "I'm going to be as big as a whale. There are two babies being incubated in here. And I can't drink, and there's food I can't eat... I'm not sure how much fun I'll be."

"Hey, Dee. You are plenty fun. I'd love to see you on the rope swing at Weyman's Creek."

Denise snorted and then laughed. "Oh, we will have to go there. But I won't try the swing. I'll likely break it."

"I promise to take pictures if you do."

For the rest of the call, Andie was happy to reminisce and make plans. In just under three months, her best friend would be here. It would be great.

After they hung up with promises to talk again soon, Andie turned back to her invoices. That call had been just what she needed. Talking with her best friend, getting good news and having something to look forward to.

She needed something to look forward to, something that wasn't work. She still had months before the mill was done and she could plan for something beyond Kozak Construction for herself.

As she went through the paperwork, she wondered what was going on with Dave and Jaycee's wedding. It wasn't happening at the mill, obviously. Over the summer, they'd be taking out part of the wall to open up to the stream, and there'd be no place for a wedding. Not like the party they'd had here in February.

Andie had to banish those thoughts and concentrate on her paperwork. She was down to the last invoice, but there was a packing slip missing from a month ago. She remembered working on it yesterday. There'd been a discrepancy in the amounts shipped, and she'd planned to send all the details back to get the invoice corrected.

She went through her papers again. No packing slip.

It had to be here. Had some breeze from the door opening blown it somewhere? But she always put a paperweight on her stuff because of that. Still, she got up and began to look farther from her desk.

She looked under the desk. In the garbage, which fortunately hadn't been emptied. Under the table with the coffee maker.

She even checked through the paper they recycled to use for printing internal documents. And when she did, she found a copy of another packing slip. It was covered with notes in Trevor's careful handwriting. She found herself reading them before she thought about whether she should. Suddenly, she was gloriously angry.

CHAPTER TEN

THE CREWS HAD done well at the two Victorians they were converting to B and Bs.

Abigail Carter wanted Cupid's Crossing to be a first-choice destination for people looking for a romantic getaway, not a cut-rate, nothing-else-is-available one. So while it would have been easy to add a couple of bathrooms to the homes and call it done, they were making sure the walls were soundproof, the electrical systems were upgraded to handle a larger load, and the walls and windows well insulated. They'd added air conditioning, extra outlets and made sure there was lots of water pressure.

He hadn't worked on small projects like this for a while, but he enjoyed it. Partly because he was working for himself and partly because he kind of enjoyed the seniors of Cupid's Crossing.

They plied him with tea and cookies and wanted to know if he was single because they knew someone. He politely turned down the dating offers, but their easy acceptance of him was flattering.

It was possible they were trying to soften him up to cut corners or do something to harm his reputation, but that was difficult to believe. They were too open and honest, or maybe he just didn't want to suspect nice old ladies.

They were all too happy to tell him about every renovation or change in wallpaper that had happened in the home's lifetime. Some of those changes had been unfortunate, but the homes mostly spoke of the elegance and craftsmanship of a previous time. He enjoyed them. These people were practically adopting him.

He truly hated being suspicious and guarded all the time, but he couldn't risk something happening at the mill, so he maintained a distance with the construction crew. That meant he was cut off from nonbusiness, human contact.

Except for Mavis's overly friendly Great Dane, who wanted to get to know him and lick all the places that had been covered up when he changed her tire, it had been a lovely afternoon. He was going to head back to the mill, check that nothing had changed and then maybe risk going to the diner on his own tonight. To get away from his own cooking and to see some faces that weren't digital.

He pulled into the parking lot at the mill and noted Andie's truck was still there. She'd often left by this time. She had the office at the family home, so she didn't need to be on-site, especially when they hadn't done any work to the place today.

Maybe she'd lost track of time. Maybe she had a question for him. Maybe he should ask if she wanted to join him at the diner.

Not like a date, but they could talk about buildings. Or work. Yeah, not a date, but it would be a change. Maybe he should try to warm up the relationship. So far, there'd been no signs of anything suspect going on. Maybe she was totally legit and so was Abigail Carter.

Maybe he could risk being friendly with his contractor again and not have everything blow up on him.

Or maybe those cookies Mavis gave him were spiked.

In any case, he was in a good mood until he opened the door of the trailer and met Andie's gaze.

Her furious, laser-like gaze.

He took a quick look over his shoulder to make sure she was looking at him. Since he'd been gone most of the day, it seemed unreasonable that she'd be this angry with him. He hadn't been around to do anything.

"I didn't expect you to still be here."

Her lips moved upward, but with enough tension that he didn't consider that it was a real smile.

"Did you come back to double-check the vendor order? Maybe go and count everything we received, see if we were keeping some back, trying to cheat? Or wait." She pulled out the copy he'd made of the packing slip that had been short shipped and the notes he'd made. "Perhaps you want to check if we're conspiring with the vendor, either to cheat Abigail or to substitute inferior product?"

He didn't have an answer to her accusations, because she had his words, written on the paper, asking those very questions.

The delivery was from a month ago. He'd stepped back since, after finding everything going well. Hadn't he thrown that paperwork out? Obviously not. How had he been so careless?

"Were you snooping through my papers?" Pivot and deflect was all that occurred to him.

"It was in the recycling. Maybe I should have checked that more carefully. How long have you been doing this?"

His cheeks warmed. He apparently wasn't as good at espionage as he'd hoped. He didn't think telling Andie he'd stopped checking things a few weeks ago was going to help.

"You've been doing it since the beginning, haven't you? I thought I was confused, because sometimes the papers would be out of order. I assumed things had fallen off the desk, and someone put them back wrong. Maybe Joey had been looking for things. But it's been you.

"What are you trying to do here? Are you trying to destroy my reputation, or are you looking for some way to cheat things yourself?"

Trevor's temper spiked. He wasn't going to be called the bad guy again, not when he was the one trying to make sure things went right.

"What's the matter, Ms. Kozak? Hiding something? Afraid of a little scrutiny?"

Andie stood, matching anger on her face. "I've spent years building my reputation. You have no idea what I've gone through, heading this company as a woman. And you are not going to destroy our company by bad-mouthing me to my vendors and clients. I've had it."

She grabbed her bag, threw on her jacket and pushed past him, heading to her truck. Trevor watched her go, his fury ebbing.

She'd left his notes on her desk. Everything else was locked up. Maybe she'd done that because she had nothing to hide and was angry that he'd been through her files. He had access to digital copies on a shared folder, but they could be changed, reworked. After all, everything came to Andie first.

Her anger could be because she had planned something, and now he'd thwarted her. He remembered the expression on her face. She'd been angry but also...hurt?

No, she wasn't upset because he'd stopped her in an evil plan. She was upset because this showed his lack of trust in her.

He'd thought he was mostly over it. That he could just take a few precautions, watch over things, and he'd be fine. But he wasn't. His first response to her anger was to wonder what she'd been hiding.

That had hurt Andie.

He had to fix this, if he could.

Andie pulled into Abigail's driveway, fueled by righteous anger.

She'd cried many a night when she'd started, out of fear and grief and frustration. She didn't cry now. She took care of things.

If this guy, fancy architect Trevor Emerson, was going to call around, asking questions to double-check on everything she did, it was going to sow doubt in people's minds. No smoke without fire. This was a small community, and they relied on trust. She'd earned that trust the hard way, with men second-guessing her every step of the way. She couldn't let him do that to her, or to her family business.

She was hurt, too. She'd thought she'd shown Trevor that she was good. Trustworthy. She'd thought they were past his initial doubts.

She was wrong.

She couldn't work like this. She wouldn't. And she was going to tell Abigail that.

She knocked on the door and stepped back. Looking down, she saw her boots were dirty, but before she could worry about it, the door opened, and Abigail was there, a question on her face.

"Andie. Is something wrong?"

"Can we talk?"

Abigail gave her an assessing look and then stepped back. Andie hesitated.

"I'll just take off my boots out here."

"Don't bother. Having some mud to clean up will be the high-light of Rebeccah's day tomorrow. Come on in and tell me what the problem is."

Abigail held a hand out for Andie's jacket, and after passing it over, Andie unlaced her boots, flinching as the mud flaked on the floor.

Abigail led the way to a front room and waved Andie into a seat.

"Can I get you anything?"

Andie shook her head. Her anger was cooling, but her determination was not.

Abigail sat. "What's the problem?"

"Trevor Emerson."

Abigail cocked her head. "How so? Mavis was very happy with him today."

Andie frowned. Trying to get into their clients' good graces? What did he have planned? His suspicious nature was wearing off on her.

"Today, I found out he's been going through my paperwork, trying to find ways we might be cheating either our vendors or you. He double-checks everything we do, apparently convinced we're all in on some kind of scam. If he starts calling people to ask them to verify the information I'm providing him, it's going to hurt Kozak Construction. I can't have that. I can't work with him."

Andie sat back. She hadn't planned to give an ultimatum, but there it was. She couldn't risk her company's future, not for any single job.

Any personal hurt was beside the point.

Abigail stared at the coffee table, her lips pursed.

"I see. I guess it makes sense."

Andie shot to her feet. Did Abigail suspect her? "Do you think—? Could you possibly suspect—?"

"Andie."

Andie wasn't sure what it was about Abigail, but she stopped her outburst and drew in a breath. She sat back down in her seat.

"Andie, I know you. I don't suspect anything, or I wouldn't work with you. I'm not a fool."

Andie swallowed.

"Would you let me talk to Trevor before we get to the stage of ultimatums? He is gifted at his job, but I appreciate that you are, as well, and that you need to protect your family and your company."

Andie nodded. "I'm not sure what you can do, but I know not to underestimate you. Thanks for listening, I don't want to be difficult, but this is a major problem."

Andie rose, calmly this time, and Abigail followed.

"I'm very glad you came to talk to me." A smile touched her lips. "I do understand the difficulties of a woman leading a company in a masculine industry."

Andie nodded.

"Tell your mother hello from me. I hope she's doing well."

Andie shoved her feet into her boots, not bothering to tie them up.

"She is. Thanks for asking. I'll wait to hear from you."

Abigail smiled. "Dealing with people is the most difficult part of the job, isn't it?"

Andie paused, wondering if Abigail was implying that Andie was failing with this particular skill. Trevor's lack of trust was infecting her. That was something she couldn't put up with.

Abigail rested a hand on her arm. "I forget sometimes that meddling can stir things up."

Andie didn't think she'd done any meddling, so Abigail must be talking about her own actions. She didn't know what meddling Abigail had done, but the drama had exhausted Andie. She wanted to go home, have a quiet dinner, call Denise to complain and then maybe find out what Abigail had been able to do.

Trevor answered the call from Abigail. It was an hour after Andie had left, so he was confident he knew why his client had requested they meet. She asked him to join her for dinner.

She hung up after his acceptance, so he didn't know what to expect. If she was going to fire him, he wouldn't stay for the meal. He'd head back to his place to pack up.

He locked the trailer up carefully, making sure all his own belongings were in his bag. There wasn't much. He didn't want to have to return for anything. The thought of Andie smugly watching him pack up his stuff was more than he was prepared for.

It was ironic that he was in trouble for his lack of trust when he'd finally begun to show some.

The roads were clear, making it a smooth drive to Abigail's house. He paused for a moment to admire the lines of the building before he mounted the steps to the front door.

Abigail answered, dressed as elegantly as always. She invited him in and led him into her parlor, where a tray of cheese and olives was set out. She offered him a drink, and he decided the condemned was allowed that much.

Once they were seated, he waited, letting her start the conversation.

"Trevor, I looked into your story before I asked you to come to Cupid's Crossing. The friend that recommended you told me I had the opportunity to get a gifted architect who would normally not consider working here, because you were in the process of re-establishing your reputation."

Trevor nodded.

"We didn't go into details when we first met, but I wouldn't have offered you this job if I didn't know you weren't at fault for the accident in New York. I understand the owner and contractor blamed you for their own misdeeds and being cleared so long after the fact meant that there was a mark on your reputation, and I took full advantage of it."

He nodded again. She'd summed it up well. She pinned him with her gaze.

"It must have been difficult when people judged you based on lies."

Difficult was one way to put it.

"And it must be very frustrating when people judge you now based on the misdeeds of someone else."

Trevor nodded. He was trying to figure out where Abigail was going with this conversation. Andie must have complained to her, and because this was a small, tightly knit town, he'd expected he'd be let go.

How was Abigail going to terminate his contract?

She paused long enough to ensure he was paying attention.

"I did not expect, Trevor, that you would do the same thing to someone else."

His jaw dropped. He wanted to argue, but he had to catch his breath. It took him a minute to understand her point.

"Pardon?"

"I appreciate that you're cautious and skeptical. But you've been here for more than two months now. I expect you've carefully monitored everything that's going on with the work at the mill. Have you found any issues of concern?"

He narrowed his eyes. "No."

"So are you judging Andie based on the actions of your last contractor?"

And there it was, the hit coming under his guard with the skill of a master.

He struggled to regroup. "I needed to ensure that the job is being done properly."

"True." Abigail smiled at him, but there was little warmth in it. "There's due diligence, and then there's...paranoia. As you probably guessed, Andie spoke to me. She feels that your, shall we say, concerns have moved beyond the normal due diligence?"

His cheeks warmed.

It was like Abigail had seen him looking through the papers, watching over shoulders, going online back at his rental to double- and triple-check everything that was going on. He'd even kept his own time sheets of the crew that first month.

Yeah, that was well beyond due diligence. He'd been at offices being audited, and he'd surpassed that level of inspection.

He rubbed his forehead. "I lost a lot in that accident."

Abigail nodded. "All the reports I read indicated it was a serious event. And you were injured quite seriously."

He had been. Without thinking, he rubbed his leg. The one that wasn't really his. Her words sank in. She was wasted in this small town.

"You make a good point, Abigail. I was too trusting, too naive on that job, and I paid. I've..." He took a breath. "I've overreacted here. I know that. I did stop some of the checking. What Andie found was from the first month. Still, I might...no, I have...gone too far."

She held back a smile. "A smidge."

He felt the corner of his own mouth tilt up. "Maybe more than a smidge. So am I fired?" She'd made her point first, but if it was just to support her decision to fire him, he wanted to know.

She raised her eyebrows. "Oh, I hope not. I haven't gone through this much trouble for no payoff. Do you think you could speak to Andie? I would, but I feel the two of you need to find some common ground here, and I don't want to be your intermediary the whole time you're working together."

That was fair. But it wasn't going to be an easy talk. Andie was angry and hurt, and she had every right to be.

He was going to have to explain things to her. He would rather do almost anything else. But the alternative was to leave like a child who couldn't handle cleaning up his own messes.

That was not the man he wanted to be.

"If she doesn't take a hammer to me, I'll try to explain."

Abigail smiled at him approvingly. "If it turns out you do need my help, I'll do what I can, but I have confidence the two of you can work things out. Are you ready to eat now that we have this cleared up?"

"I would be happy to."

CHAPTER ELEVEN

THREE HOURS LATER, Trevor sat at home, replete after excellent food and wine. He'd also enjoyed the conversation. Abigail was well-read and intelligent. She'd led him to a discussion of buildings in New York, a topic he could speak on for hours, and she'd seemed to enjoy it.

He was home now, and it was time to deal with his problem. His contractor might not be coming to work tomorrow if he didn't reach out.

It was his fault. And he hated that he'd hurt her.

He debated calling but wasn't sure she'd pick up the phone. He needed to get her attention and convince her to listen to him before she had a chance to delete his message or hang up. He carefully selected the subject of his email, hoping it would be sufficient.

I owe you an apology and an explanation.

With any luck, the apology part would make her consider listening, and the explanation would make her curious enough to meet him.

Would you meet me at the diner for lunch so I can provide both?

He could work from home for the morning and let her have the trailer to herself. It was a struggle, but he'd let her meet with the inspector without him. It was a token of trust.

He had to step back, at least a bit. He would still do his due diligence, and it might be more than anyone else's normal due diligence, but he had to step back from the paranoia. It was a line he'd crossed.

He hoped it wasn't too late.

Andie waved the inspector off, trusting that his promise of a positive report coming to her email once he was back at the office would hold. Tomorrow, the crew could get back to construction on the mill. They were almost wrapped at Mavis's house now.

She went back to the trailer and sat at her desk. The place felt... odd without Trevor at the other end. It should be a good *odd*, and she should get used to it, since she wasn't spending time with him ever again. But the email was there, flagging her attention.

She'd wavered over that email from Trevor for longer than she'd admit to. She'd been tempted to call Denise to parse it out, like they used to with messages from boys, but this wasn't a social question, this was her business. She should be able to handle a business decision without depending on her best friend.

That she'd even considered doing that meant there was more than a business hurt happening, and that was a problem. She didn't need Denise to recognize that.

Abigail had spoken to Trevor, as she'd said she would. He must want to save his job, which meant he had to apologize to her. She was grateful that Abigail was backing her up, but that didn't mean she was going to accept a half-hearted apology from Trevor.

If his apology included anything along the lines of "I'm sorry *if* you took my behavior the wrong way," she was out. She was not working with a jerk, and she was not risking her company's reputation.

She couldn't imagine an explanation that would change her mind, but she couldn't go back to Abigail and say she wouldn't listen to Trevor. She'd listen to what he had to say, assuming he got through the apology without messing up, and then she'd calmly and collectedly tell him they couldn't work together.

Her crew would be able to keep on with the plans at the mill until Abigail found a solution. Another architect. They knew what they were doing at the mill and could handle it till Abigail found someone else.

She sighed and slammed her computer shut before heading out to Bertha. She had taken longer than she should to get ready this morning. She pretended that she'd wanted to look good for the inspector, but she was glad Joey was working on the houses this morning and hadn't seen her wearing nice jeans and some lipstick.

She told herself she was just preparing herself for battle. She didn't want to admit that the battle wasn't with the inspector.

Her stomach was churning as she pulled open the door of the diner. Trevor was sitting in the same booth as before. Probably not a good sign. But she held her head high and crossed to the table, sliding in opposite him.

She scanned his face, looking for anger, resentment or false cheer. Instead, he looked resigned, and tired. She didn't need to soften just because of that.

Jean came over with her coffeepot. Andie flipped her mug and placed her order. Trevor already had his coffee in front of him. Jean walked away, and Andie waited. He'd asked for the meeting. She wasn't speaking first.

He met her gaze. "I'm sorry."

She still waited.

Trevor moved his cutlery over an inch and then back again. "I should not have done what I did. I do have a reason I was so… paranoid. It's not an excuse, though. I crossed a line."

Andie put creamer and sugar in her cup and stirred. Then she picked up her cup and took a sip. Trevor cast a glance up at her.

She put down the cup and lifted an eyebrow. "The explanation?"

His eyes dropped. He moved the cutlery again. He took off his glasses and polished the lens with a napkin. He looked younger, more vulnerable.

"Two years ago, I was in charge of my first major, solo project. I'd set up my own firm. It was in New York, and I had big dreams."

Andie knew it wasn't going to be a happy story. No one behaved like Trevor because something good had happened. The journey from his own business in New York to doing bed-and-breakfasts in Carter's Crossing was one with a downward trajectory.

She resisted an urge to put her hand on his. He was apologizing and explaining his bad behavior, and it wasn't her job to make him feel better.

"I believed the contractor and owner were good people. The contractor's father had recently resigned, and he'd taken over. Their reputation was excellent. I thought we had a relationship. Friendly. Close.

"I double-checked things at the beginning. It was going well, and I trusted them. So while I didn't shirk on anything, I didn't look any deeper than I needed to."

Andie's hands clenched, and she dropped them onto her lap. She could see where this was going.

"There was an accident on-site. I was there. I was hurt."

Her eyes dropped of their own volition to the tabletop, the section above where his legs were. When she looked back at him, he nodded.

"Yes, I was in hospital for a while. I lost part of my leg. And once I was able to pay attention to things going on outside the hospital, I found out that the owner and contractor had blamed the accident on me.

"There was an investigation, of course, and I was exonerated. But by the time that happened and I was able to work again, people remembered the initial claims, not the truth."

Trevor stopped there. He put his glasses back on, Jean arrived with their meals and, after checking on their coffee, left again.

Trevor was breathing carefully, staring at his food. He lifted his sandwich to his mouth. Andie grabbed a French fry, waiting for what else he had to say.

That appeared to be it. What was she supposed to do with that?

"You were screwed over by a crooked contractor and owner. So now you plan to micromanage the job at the mill to make sure Abigail and I don't do the same thing."

He set his sandwich down and swallowed. "I need to take precautions, yes. I went too far, but I hope you understand why I'm not willing to accept things at face value."

It wasn't a pretty story that he'd shared. But if you'd been in a relationship where your partner cheated, you were not allowed to put a tracking device on your next date. As tempting as the thought might be.

Andie grabbed another French fry. "You didn't ask for more access to what we were doing because you thought we might just hide things better."

Trevor nodded. "What you saw, that paper with those notes, was from the first few weeks we worked together. I haven't been going through things like that lately, but it was something I shouldn't have done behind your back."

Andie considered. Yes, she understood why he was so worried. But he had to consider other people, as well. He wasn't the only one who'd had a difficult past.

"When my father died, and I had to take over Kozak Construction because there was no one else, I was eighteen and female. I had, and still have, men insisting they have to double- and triple-check everything I do, simply because of my gender. It's insulting, sexist, and it bogs down my schedule."

Trevor had paused in his eating, watching her. "I'm sorry if you thought I was questioning you because of your gender. Or age or experience."

Andie raised her brows. "Instead of just questioning me because you thought I was crooked."

The corner of his mouth lifted up. "But I didn't think you couldn't successfully fool me just because you're a young woman."

Andie couldn't resist smiling in return. "So I should thank you for questioning my ethics the same as you would an older man's?"

His shoulders sagged. "I don't think thanks are in order."

Andie took a bite of her burger while she considered the situation. They couldn't continue working the way they had, but she was at least willing to consider working with him. And that was something she hadn't thought possible before their conversation.

Because, after all, if you'd dated a cheater, you might not put a tracking device on your next partner, but you'd be much more careful of what he was doing. You might be tempted to look at a text message popping up on his screen.

"Can we find a way to work together that won't drive me crazy and will give you more confidence that nothing improper is going on? Something that doesn't involve you being my shadow all the time or going through my paperwork?"

Trevor finished his sandwich and used a napkin to wipe his mouth. "They fudged the invoices on that job."

"I can ask vendors to copy you on all emails. You'll end up with a lot of stuff to go through, but if that makes you happier, I'll do it. I just ask that you don't malign me and my company's reputation while you try to reassure yourself."

"How so?"

"If you ask them to independently verify every piece of paper you get, it will imply that you think I'm doing something wrong. I have earned my good reputation with most of the suppliers in this area, but if a rumor starts, it'll be almost impossible to fight."

Trevor started shifting his empty coffee mug around. Andie wondered if that was his tell. As well as playing with his glasses and the cutlery.

She liked that this situation made him nervous. She was out of her depth and didn't want to be the only one.

"You could be using a separate email account or chain to get different invoices."

Andie raised her brows. "I hadn't even thought of that possibility."

His smile was mocking. "There's a lot you consider after you've lost what I have."

Andie understood, but she also couldn't spend all her time reassuring him or risk her reputation by having him independently verify everything she did. The man had more ideas about how to cheat on the job than she'd ever considered. Maybe she had been too trusting with him.

"What about an audit?"

"When the project is done?"

Andie shrugged. "I'm not that familiar with all the possibilities, but perhaps someone could randomly verify transactions. Abigail would probably know how to set it up. But then you don't trust her, either. Or is it only me?"

Trevor shrugged.

"Why don't I ask Abigail if there's a way we can do that and then, perhaps, agree on an auditor? Because you might take advantage of us."

Trevor sat back. He blinked at her and then nodded. "I get it. Trust goes both ways."

He moved his coffee cup again.

"Let's start with sharing emails. Since I don't have a lot of projects going on here, I'll spend time at the mill site and let you know if I have questions. If I feel unsure of how things are going, we can explore a midterm audit."

Andie nodded. "I can live with that."

Trevor smiled, an honest smile, and Andie couldn't hold back her own smile in response.

She'd been sure nothing he could say would reconcile her to working with him. And now here they were with a way to move forward.

In theory.

He might not be able to keep to this. She understood that he'd been betrayed, and the results had been catastrophic for him.

But her first commitment was to her family and her company, the people who depended on her to support their families. They trusted her, so she needed to watch who she trusted, as well.

Trevor might have a smile she found hard to resist, but that didn't mean he was going to follow this plan. They'd have to wait and see.

Trevor felt lighter after their conversation.

He hadn't enjoyed repeating the story of that last job, but everything was out there on the internet if someone was going to look. Andie didn't sound like she'd heard the story before, but as much as he might wish it, it wasn't that easy to get over his suspicions.

Still, if he was going to see the emails with the suppliers, he should be able to track the materials, which was where things had gone wrong on that last job.

Maybe, if he could trust the information, he could relax and get to know the people he was working with. Maybe he'd even hang out with people. It had been getting very lonely in his rental with no one to talk to.

He had family back in the city. Maybe even a few friends. But he'd been so bitter after the accident, after he'd let Violet out of their engagement, that he'd lost touch with most of their friends. He'd been reluctant to reach out. He and Violet had been together for three years, so his friends were their friends. He'd lost his confidence along with his trust.

With the warmer weather, they were about to start the major renovations on the mill. Now came the big test on the project. They were opening the back wall to bring in that view through new doors, windows, skylights. They were doing all this while maintaining the structural integrity of the building and its complex history.

They needed to finish up the commercial kitchen and get fixtures in the newly designed bathrooms. And everything needed to be right, before they added the final finishes that would cover up the skeleton of the building.

He couldn't relax. He wouldn't till the job was done and all inspections had been passed…and maybe not until they'd had years of use behind it. He couldn't undo what that accident had done to change him, but he could *try* not to be paranoid.

He could keep a close eye on things and ask questions before he rushed to conclusions. Like the packing slip Andie had found his notes on. After he'd written that down, he'd worked out that every item had been reconciled. There had been nothing wrong. So far, everything Andie had done should have earned her his trust.

He was first on-site the next morning, and he had Andie's mug of coffee ready for her when she arrived, full and filled with enough milk and sugar to make him cringe. She smiled and thanked him, and that was surprisingly rewarding.

The crew showed up, ready to get started on this next phase. This time, as he followed Andie through the building, her shoulders weren't hunched up in discomfort. He'd thought it was how she did her walk-through. Now he realized he'd caused that.

When one of the crew had a question, she turned to let him answer. She was smiling instead of pinching her mouth up in frustration. Now that he wasn't pushing, he was being invited and she was treating him as one of them, not an outsider.

It was almost enough to make him relax. He hadn't felt part of a group like this since before the accident. Back when he'd had

a full life. His new company had been busy and he'd had an un-
limited future. Violet was making wedding plans, and they had
their friends to hang out with. He'd never realized how tenuous
his life had been.

It still was.

He reminded himself to be wary, but a couple of weeks later,
when he was invited to the Goat and Barley for trivia night by
the Kozak crew, he agreed to go. It didn't mean he was giving
up his due diligence. Mostly, he was tired of his own company
every night.

He knew where the Goat—as locals called it—was, but he
hadn't been there since New Year's Eve. He'd planned to check
it out, to try to find the woman with the soda once he was settled
into the town.

Instead, he'd found her at the mill.

He could almost imagine it was a different place, with spring
warming the air and the winter snow gone. He recognized some
of the vehicles in the parking lot, including Andie's truck. He
opened the pub door and blinked to adjust to the dimmer lighting.

He looked to the bar first, pausing as he saw the place he'd sat
with Andie at New Year's, but he didn't recognize any faces. He
looked around the room and spotted the people he knew. Andie,
Joey and a couple of other guys from her crew were at a table at
the other side of the restaurant from the bar. They'd saved him a
seat, and he felt warmed. Wanted.

Something he wasn't used to any longer.

The others already had their beverages, so Joey got the attention of one of the waitstaff and ordered a beer for Trevor.

Andie leaned over and asked, "Is this your blind-date beer?"

She was smiling and relaxed, and he recognized the woman
from the bar more than he had in any of their encounters since.

He bit back a snort of laughter. "No, that relationship wasn't
meant to be. But I'm hoping for good things from this one."

Joey had the papers for the quiz in his hand.

"So, Trev, what do you know?"

Trevor hadn't heard that diminutive nickname for a long time.
He swallowed his first taste of beer. "Um, buildings?"

Joey rolled his eyes. "Andie's already good at that. What else?"

Trevor searched his memory banks. "Sports? At least, up till fifteen years ago."

His family was sports crazy. He'd joined in as a kid, hoping to feel more like an essential part of the family. He'd always been different and done his best to try to fit in with them. Fifteen years ago, he'd realized it wasn't going to happen, and he'd stopped forcing it.

"We've got hockey and baseball covered. Know basketball or soccer?"

"Some."

Joey turned to another teammate, and Trevor took another sip of his drink. He wondered, for the first time, just how serious these people were about their quizzes and if he was going to look stupid.

Andie nudged him. "Don't worry." Apparently, he didn't have a poker face. "These aren't super difficult," she said. "Sports questions that aren't related to hockey tend to be more about what team won whatever was the final trophy."

He smiled at her. "That much I can handle."

"So why did you give up on sports fifteen years ago? That wasn't because…" Her glance dropped to his legs.

He stiffened.

"I'm sorry. Foot in mouth."

She wrapped her hand over her mouth. Her cheeks were bright red. She dropped her hands and closed her eyes. "I had no idea I could be that offensive, totally by accident, I mean, without meaning to. I'll just shut up and not speak anymore. I'm so sorry."

He stifled his amusement at her embarrassment. "No, not because of the accident and prosthetic leg. That was only a couple of years ago. My family was crazy about sports, and I…wasn't."

He saw her watching him and hoped nothing much was showing on his face.

She grimaced. "Family… Yeah, that can be complicated."

He was relieved that she let it go, but also disappointed. He didn't want to talk about it normally. But he'd like to get her perspective. Did she ever feel like she was on the outside with her family?

Was that why he felt a connection with her?

* * *

Team Kozak didn't win. But they weren't the worst team, either. And Trevor wasn't the weakest link on the team.

There weren't any questions on architecture, but there were some history questions he'd helped with. It turned out having studied buildings in previous eras helped him with some history knowledge. He'd known a question about when New York last won a basketball title. His dad brought that up every postseason.

After the points were tallied and the winning teams won vouchers, the Kozak team stayed at the table, sharing some surprisingly good onion rings, drinking responsibly—Andie was the designated driver—and talked. For a while, he was peppered with questions about working on big job sites in NYC. Before he'd been out on his own, he'd worked on some jobs using the biggest cranes, and everyone was interested. Trevor wasn't comfortable being the center of attention, though, and he was relieved when the conversation veered to stories of the jobs Kozak Construction had done.

Trevor listened and did his best not to piece out details to check for mistakes or accidents. He needed to rein in his suspicions. But the only accidents they mentioned were small ones, mistakes that tended to be embarrassing rather than dangerous.

When they stood up to leave, not too late since they rose early in the morning, Trevor was disappointed. Not the disappointment of having wasted an evening or not having his expectations met— he hadn't had expectations—but disappointment that the evening was ending. It had been the best evening he'd spent in Cupid's Crossing since that first night when he'd met Andie. When he was asked if he would join again, he was happy to agree.

He wasn't sure who was more surprised by that. Joey, who'd extended the offer, or Trevor himself.

Trevor even volunteered to drop one of the crew at his home to save Andie some time on her trip back. The smile she gave him was worth the extra mile.

He hadn't wanted to share what had happened on that last project with anyone, but now that he'd told Andie and promised to stop his secret investigation into her work, a load of tension had vanished.

He might even enjoy the remainder of his time in Cupid's Crossing.

CHAPTER TWELVE

ANDIE CONSIDERED THAT night at the Goat to be a turning point. It marked a change in the workplace dynamic that had been troubling her more than she'd realized.

She didn't wake up the next morning stressed about getting to the job site. She hadn't been worried about work that way since the early days when she first took over. She didn't feel judged and micromanaged every minute of the day.

In the following weeks, she tested Trevor to see if he was keeping to his word. She left some paperwork around with notes on it that could trigger questions or further snooping on his part. She felt like James Bond trying to entrap him, but apparently, he was no longer checking her stuff.

The work was still demanding and often physically challenging, but more than just things with Trevor improved. The change of season helped. With the increasing warmth, as spring aimed for summer, the whole crew could gather outside the mill for lunch.

Before that first trivia night, Trevor always ate lunch in the trailer. Now, as they gathered by the stream, sitting on rocks or makeshift seats made of construction materials, Trevor joined them, but always on the edge. Not totally one of the group. Andie didn't know if he preferred the distance or was reluctant to intrude without an invitation. She decided it was time to find out.

She grabbed her thermos and her sandwiches and moved to sit near him. "I hear you helped the team last night."

Andie had missed trivia night last night. There'd been a meeting of the local business owners at Abigail's. The new B and B owners had been there representing new businesses in town, and that had dragged the meeting on a lot longer than usual. They were just so keen and wanted to discuss everything in detail.

Trevor smiled in response to her comment, and when he did, he was…attractive. Very attractive. Warm ribbons curled inside her, and she gave herself a mental swat.

"Apparently, there aren't a lot of classical music fans at your pub on trivia night."

Andie wasn't surprised Trevor knew classical music or that he was the only one of the team that did. He was different from most of the guys in town. More like Nelson, Abigail's grandson, than her brothers and their friends.

She was more like those guys. Not that she was upset by that. Not at all.

"Glad my absence wasn't missed." Andie didn't know classical music, either.

Trevor glanced away. "I didn't say that."

Andie was embarrassingly aware of her heart thudding and the chill running down her arms.

He'd missed her? But—

"How was your meeting?"

She shook off the strange feeling to answer him. "It was…long. I should send Joey next time so he knows what it's like."

She should, she decided. Next month, he could attend the meeting for business owners in Cupid's Crossing business while she went to trivia night.

Trevor looked over at Joey, who was joking with some of the other young guys on the crew. Guys who were his friends. They played hockey in the winter, and baseball had just started up again for the summer.

"I have a difficult time picturing Joey sitting at Abigail's, talking business."

Andie did, too. She wrapped up the remains of her lunch. "It's not a fun part of the job, but he's got to be able to handle it when he's in charge."

Trevor looked back at her. "When's that?"

Andie shrugged. "That partly depends on how the mill project goes. We're doing well now and are on time, but if it drags into the new year... It's probably better if I don't plan on going anywhere until next fall."

"That's more than a year away."

Andie smiled at him. "Nice to see you didn't waste your time at college."

He didn't smile back. "You don't mind waiting another year?"

She shrugged and looked away. Her fingers tightened on the lunch wrappings. "I made my decision when my dad died. I'm not second-guessing it now."

She'd done that enough over the years. Smiling at college graduations for her siblings without having one of her own. Waving them off as they left Carter's Crossing while she stayed. She couldn't change the past, and she wouldn't begrudge her siblings achieving what they wanted.

"Was it difficult? Making that decision?"

Andie glanced over at him. He narrowed his eyes like he did when he was frowning at his computer.

Apparently, she had noticed that.

She normally glossed over how difficult that time had been after her dad died, but for some reason, she didn't now. Not when Trevor appeared...invested in what she'd done.

She cleared her throat. "Yeah, it was difficult. It wasn't like there was one moment when I just decided I had to do this. It was more...a series of small decisions that built up until it was either my family or me.

"I couldn't do that to Dad, his memory and all the work he'd done to make Kozak Construction what it was. I couldn't let it all fall apart. That first tuition deadline I had... I told my mom I'd wait another year to get things settled."

The relief on her mother's face had been overwhelming. It had soothed her when she'd felt so unsure of what she was doing.

Trevor put his lunch containers back into his bag. "A year?"

She nodded. "At first, it was just a decision to wait another year.

And then just one more. Then Arlie was supposed to go to college, and two of us studying at the same time was too expensive. I was getting good at running the place, so it made sense to wait."

"And you're still waiting."

Andie couldn't read his expression, but the words weighed on her.

She was still waiting. And maybe going now was a little scary. But that wasn't something to dwell on, not now, and not with this man. She'd shared enough. She stood up, dusting off the back of her pants.

"Hey, guys, let's get back at it."

Everyone slowly got to their feet, picking up scraps and papers and complaining good-naturedly. Trevor stood, too, still watching her.

She flashed a stilted smile. "No rest for the wicked."

She went back into the mill, all too aware of Trevor standing in place. He must think she was silly. Small. Lacking in ambition.

She'd had big dreams and lots of ambition, but she'd had to channel it into her family, the family business and being strong for everyone.

She wasn't sure if she'd lost her dreams and used up all that ambition. She'd spent a long time shoving all that down until it was her turn. It was hard to get excited about school now.

Maybe she'd missed her chance.

Trevor found life more pleasant after he and Andie declared a... détente? He wasn't sure how to word it, but they were cooperating. And maybe just a bit more.

He was welcome on trivia nights. He wasn't the best player on the team, but he wasn't the worst. And he was greeted warmly even though he didn't have a lot in common with the rest of the team. He wasn't from Cupid's Crossing, but he'd been asked if he played baseball. No one minded that he was quiet or asked him if something was wrong because he didn't talk a lot. Thursday nights had become the highlight of his week.

He'd been working on some ideas for the next round of B and Bs and had questions about what materials were available locally.

He took advantage of the warmer relations with Andie to ask if she'd grab a drink with him while he picked her brains.

That was a Tuesday, and Tuesdays at the Goat was darts night. Darts was something Trevor was good at. He convinced Andie to pair up with him, and they won.

Afterward, Andie introduced him to the two men they'd played against. Their names were Dave and Nelson. Nelson was Abigail Carter's grandson and Mariah's fiancé. They sat at a table together and talked, and it was a fun evening. Trevor was invited back next week for darts, and it seemed he now had, if not friends, people to spend time with outside of work.

Now that he wasn't doing an audit on the job every day, he had more free time. He didn't want to spend that time isolated in his rental, alone and lonely. He felt that he was getting to know the real people in town.

He hadn't planned on trying to fit in, not when he was going to be here for only a year. But the job was going well, and he was growing tired of the isolation he'd imposed on himself since the accident.

Since he and Andie hadn't talked about the B and Bs on darts night, they stayed the next night in the trailer, bouncing ideas back and forth. When it got a little late, Andie's mother messaged about dinner, and Trevor ended up invited and spending the rest of the evening there.

It wasn't awkward, like the last time, and he didn't take refuge in the spare room. That would have been weird, since he wasn't staying over. Instead, Andie showed him around the construction yard. It wasn't exactly the way he would set things up, but nothing looked problematic. He imagined this was the way Andie's father had arranged things, and she wouldn't want to change what he'd done.

By the end of May, the work on the mill was progressing without a hiccup. Trevor was checking things but staying on the side of due diligence. He had a life in Cupid's Crossing, complete with friends and regular plans.

Mariah stopped by to see them on-site one day. She'd texted Andie and Trevor to let them know she was coming. Once she'd arrived, Andie offered to show her around the mill, and after carefully donning a hard hat, Mariah got the tour. Trevor let Andie take the lead, interested in hearing Mariah's opinion.

"I'm so glad you're opening up that wall to the stream. It's going to make this venue stunning. It's not going to get too hot in summer with all that glass?"

Andie let Trevor explain how he'd dealt with that concern. Finally, Mariah asked if there was a place they could sit and talk.

Andie offered the trailer. Mariah had been appreciative of the work they'd done, but Trevor was leery about why she was here. He suspected Mariah hadn't come here to get a tour.

Trevor braced for last-minute design requests or demands to shorten the timeline. Mariah wouldn't have any say on the budget, so at least that wasn't going to be the topic of discussion, but any alterations would have financial repercussions.

He'd come across clients who wanted to switch things up once it was no longer possible to make changes. Abigail was the owner, but Mariah wasn't just engaged to Abigail's grandson, she was also in charge of the romance business the town was setting up. She had clout with Abigail and with this project. She was definitely in a position to have a say in how things went.

Andie offered coffee, which Mariah accepted. Once they'd gone through that social obligation, they settled behind their desks with Mariah on a chair in front of them.

Mariah took a sip of coffee and then set the cup down by her feet. "I have a reason for this visit, as you've probably guessed. I wouldn't stop by and interrupt your work out of simple curiosity." She grinned. "But I *was* curious. I got a walk-through last fall, and what you're doing is impressive.

"The real reason I'm here isn't about the mill, at least not directly. Well, it is, but I should explain.

"I want Cupid's Crossing to be a place people think of for romantic events. We made a start on that in February, and we've got the website up now so that people can actually find this place. Thanks to you two and your work, we have a few of the B and Bs now open and getting reservations. That's all great."

Trevor had been in meetings like this before. There was a *but* coming. Mariah looked at Andie and then at Trevor.

Here it was.

"But we need the mill before we can really get under way."

He knew it. Trevor opened his mouth to explain the timeline, but Mariah put up her hand.

"I know that's going to take time. I warned the committee from the beginning about that. This is a big project, and big projects can't be rushed, not if they're done right.

"It's now May. February is long gone. We've got Dave and Jaycee's wedding happening in six weeks in the park, so that will be more buzz for the town, but I want to keep online interest going. That means we need content on our website, and one wedding isn't sufficient."

Trevor suspected what Mariah wanted. He knew that the mill had been used for an engagement party on Valentine's Day preconstruction. They couldn't host any kind of event till the job was done. There was too much going on now that the mill was a construction site rather than an empty building. It wasn't safe for a crowd. They could block off the areas currently being worked on, but in his experience, signs and fencing didn't keep the curious away, and at a party?

He couldn't allow something like that. He leaned forward, ready to present his objections once Mariah paused.

"This is my idea. I'd like to have ongoing videos about the transformation of the mill."

Mariah stopped then, giving them time to come to terms with the idea. Trevor had been about to launch into a list of reasons why they couldn't have people at the mill, and it took him a moment to switch gears.

Trevor's eyes met Andie's. She had her brows pulled together, looking as unsure as he was about what Mariah wanted.

"What exactly are you asking for, Mariah?"

Mariah glanced at both of them and then held up her hands. "I should have thought of this from the beginning, but I was a little distracted before the events in February."

Which included her own engagement.

"I thought the two of you might have taken photos or video as the job went along."

Trevor saw Andie nodding just as he did.

Mariah smiled. "I thought it was something you would do. Are you planning to continue doing it?"

They both agreed.

"Good. I don't have a video crew, and I'm not sure if I could put one together here."

Trevor saw Andie's expression. Yeah, they didn't think she'd be stopped by that.

"Once a month, we could put together a video showing how the renovation is progressing. I'll add my plans for events, and hopefully, it can keep us in the public eye till we can really get our romance initiative under way."

Trevor thought that between Abigail and Mariah, there was no way they wouldn't succeed. It pleased him that his building would be used and admired in future.

But...

The photos and videos that he'd taken were for his own purposes. They focused a lot on structural things that would have no appeal to the general public. Did he really want to share them?

"I'm afraid, Mariah, that what I have isn't something to post on your website. There's not been any editing, and most people would find a lot of it boring. I don't have any skills at making video."

He turned to Andie, wondering if she had some previously undetected talent in that direction.

Andie shook her head. "Same here, Mariah. It's boring stuff for the general public."

Mariah was unfazed. "If you provide me with rough footage, I can take it from there."

Of course she could.

"Oh, right," Andie said. "You've done wedding videos, right?"

Mariah shook her head. "Oh, not me personally. Definitely not something I'm good at. I don't do everything. I just arrange it."

Trevor was curious, but he didn't know the town and most of the residents, so he stayed quiet. Andie, however, asked his question.

"Will you send the photos away to someone?"

Mariah smiled. "We actually have someone here in Cupid's Crossing who makes videos of his repairs all the time for his YouTube channel. I thought this would be right up his alley. Can you send whatever you have to me and to Benny Gifford? Here are our email addresses, and we'll make sure you get copies of the finished files to use for yourself. If you can add an explanation of what's happening in the videos or photos, that will help."

Mariah finished her coffee and then left. Andie looked at Trevor after she was gone. Had they actually agreed to that?

"That was...unexpected."

He nodded. "I was sure she was going to pressure us to move up the timeline. Or ask us to allow them to use the parts of the mill we aren't actively working on."

Andie frowned. "First, Abigail would be the one to do that, if anyone did. And Abigail is smart enough to know better than to pressure us."

Trevor didn't respond, but Andie kept her gaze on him, so he finally nodded.

"And Mariah is also smart enough not to ask us for something impossible."

Trevor didn't like being suspicious all the time, but he'd paid too much for his previous complacency. Time to change the subject.

"Have you been taking videos or just photos?"

He'd seen Andie using her phone around the site. She'd never shared with him what she was doing.

And neither had he.

"A few videos. A walk-through at the beginning and some show-ing the major and interesting things we've done. You?"

Trevor had a digital camera. He brought it with him every day.

"I did a walk-through when I first checked out the place with Abigail last fall, and I've taken a lot of photos and videos as we go. Maybe we should compare before we swamp this guy Benny with everything? And we can make sure we don't send anything we don't want in the public domain."

Trevor knew he'd documented almost everything they'd done. Last time, that had helped exonerate him. Late, but still, he'd been cleared of any wrongdoing or neglect. He reminded himself that sharing the material didn't mean he'd lose it.

Andie cocked her head, and the corner of her mouth kicked up. "You have a lot, don't you?"

He nodded.

company did some renovations here. The rest of the house hasn't changed much, but these cupboards weren't green."

Trevor looked around as if he hadn't noticed the color. "Kozak Construction worked on this?"

Andie nodded. "We updated the kitchen, added a bath, opened up the dining room and living room into one space."

Would this freak him out?

Trevor looked around the room and then back at her. "I guess you know this place as well as I do."

Andie paused. "It's been fifteen years—more could have changed. I didn't mean to make you feel uncomfortable."

He shook his head. "The small-town thing still surprises me."

Right. He was used to the city. This must seem...gauche to him.

"I guess I'm used to it."

Trevor blinked and then smiled again, like it didn't bother him. "I hope you like pasta carbonara. I'm only a so-so cook."

She would have bet money he was understating his abilities.

"Mom never lets me in the kitchen, so you're better than me."

Trevor grabbed potholders and drained some of the water into a bowl. The rest he tossed into the colander, spaghetti tumbling with it.

"If you'd take the salad to the table, this will be ready in a few minutes."

Five minutes later, they were sitting across the table from each other, a plate of warm pasta in front of each of them.

"Thank you." Andie found herself fiddling with her fork. "This is really nice."

Trevor shrugged. "I hope you think so after you eat."

The food was good, exactly as she'd expected. He relaxed after she reassured him it was. There was a silence, and she searched for something to say.

"Do you cook a lot?"

"I've been on my own for a while. It was a survival thing. I have a limited repertoire of easy meals, but I've gotten pretty good at them."

"I've never been on my own," Andie confessed.

"No?" She didn't hear judgment in his voice, and by now, she knew exactly how he sounded when he didn't approve of something. It was enough to encourage her to keep talking.

"You know that when my dad died, I took over the company. With four younger siblings, I was busy doing a lot of the things he used to do, things my mom hadn't done and didn't want to handle. It made sense to live at home with the office right there. I could focus on work and not worry about the domestic stuff."

"So no time spent learning to cook."

That would have to change.

"After the mill is done, maybe I'll have my chance. I'll have my own place. I'll ask you for some of your recipes. Mom tends to make complicated dishes without precise measurements."

Trevor swirled the spaghetti with his fork. "Not to pry, but why didn't you ever find your own place here?"

Andie set her fork down. It was an obvious question, but she'd never found an obvious answer.

"At first, we all leaned on each other after dad died. My mom kind of fell apart and worried about us kids all the time, so living together worked. I think if one of us had moved out, she wouldn't have been able to function.

"Then it was a money thing, since there was a lot of tuition to cover. I had so much to learn, and living at home meant I could focus totally on the company."

She risked a glance at Trevor, worried that she might see pity or contempt on his face, but he showed only interest.

"Mom still worries. After my oldest brother moved out, I had my own room, so that was an improvement. And it seemed like if I moved into my own place here in Carter's, I was telling everyone that I was staying here. That I was giving up on my own dreams. And I wasn't ready to do that."

He was watching her intently. "Do you have regrets about giving up your plans?"

Andie shook her head, fingers pushing her plate around.

"Well, for what it's worth, I think it was an admirable thing you did."

Andie's chest warmed, surprised by the compliment.

"And I hope you get to achieve what you want."

Embarrassed, she searched for a change of topic. "Did you always want to be an architect?"

A smile tugged at the corner of his mouth. "From my first Lego set, I wanted to build things. It grew from there."

He moved the base of his wineglass in a precise clockwise circle. "What about you?"

She put her hands in her lap to hide the nervous fidgeting. The two of them fiddling with their place settings showed just how ill at ease they were. "After working on so many buildings while I was growing up, I wanted to be the one designing them. I guess I always wanted to be the boss."

They exchanged a glance, sharing something together. And it made Andie feel...restless. She grasped for another question. "Your family supported you?"

Trevor's face closed up, and Andie remembered how he'd done the same back in the bar when she'd mentioned brothers.

She remembered a lot about Trevor. More than she should for someone leaving at the end of the project.

He still had walls, ones that didn't allow anyone across. She didn't know if she'd ever see the real man.

CHAPTER THIRTEEN

TREVOR TOOK A bite of his meal, and Andie tried to think of a way to retract the question.

"My parents have always supported me."

He spoke carefully and deliberately. Had they been overprotective, the way her mother had become? Had they been cold and remote?

Somehow, the latter seemed more possible.

"I'm sorry, I didn't mean to pry. If you're uncomfortable talking about your family, that's fine."

Trevor set down his fork on his plate. "I'm adopted."

Andie didn't know what to say to that. She'd had no idea. She wondered how old he was when that happened. Maybe there had been some tragedy, and he was reserved and quiet as a result.

Trevor stared at his plate. "It was the usual story—teenagers not ready to be parents. I've known about it for as long as I can remember. I was adopted by a lovely couple who couldn't have their own child. And then, right after the papers were signed, she discovered she was pregnant."

"They gave you back?"

Andie couldn't imagine that.

Trevor shook his head. "No, they kept me. I have a brother. He's ten months younger than me."

It all sounded...nice? But Trevor was holding himself stiffly, still staring down at the table, so there was something happening here.

"Do you get along with your brother?"

His mouth kicked up, but it didn't look like a smile. "Yes, we all 'get along.'"

Andie narrowed her eyes. "Then, what's the problem?"

He finally looked up at her, drew a breath and then focused his gaze out the window.

"My parents kept me, kept their promise. They wanted to treat us the same. Every Christmas, birthday, graduation, everything was equal and fair. I'm pretty sure they kept a spreadsheet to make sure that they treated me exactly as well as they did the son that shares their DNA."

That sounded very rigid. And it didn't explain what was setting him on edge. Or did it?

"But?" Andie asked.

His gaze swung to her again. "But some things don't fit on a spreadsheet. The things you can't force, or measure, or distribute fairly."

Andie put her fork down, appetite gone. "Feelings?"

Trevor shrugged. "It took me a while to figure it out, because I was just a kid. I knew something was…different. Somehow, I always felt like I'd done something wrong. They couldn't help how they felt. And they bonded more tightly with my brother." He was playing with the wineglass again.

"The three of them are extroverts, happy in big crowds of people. My dad sells cars, and my brother will take over for him. They are all like each other, and I'm the oddball, so obviously we aren't as close, but—"

He was trusting her with a secret. But she couldn't let him accept thinking it was right that they never fully brought him in to their circle.

"No." Andie said. Her voice was a little loud.

He stopped in the middle of whatever excuses he was making up.

"No. It's not obvious. You're not supposed to love someone like that—in levels. Blood kin here and adopted relatives one step down. I've known people who were adopted. They had parents who loved them just as much as ours loved us. Sometimes I thought more. My friend Liv was adopted, but when she got sick, her parents were devastated."

"But if they'd had their own kids—"

"Trevor, you're saying that once a child is orphaned, they'll never be loved the same as children who are with their biological parents. And that's just…wrong. So wrong.

"Do you know Ryker Slade? The guy who's designing the town website? He grew up here with six siblings, and his dad…was terrible. He didn't love those kids. He couldn't, not the way he treated them. And they were his DNA. He wasn't a fraction of the parent that Liv's were. The biological bond didn't do anything for those kids."

Trevor focused on her face, watching her closely. She couldn't imagine growing up thinking you were always second-best. What that would do to a child, and how that would shape the person they grew up into… If you couldn't trust the people who raised you, how could you trust anyone?

She absolutely knew that it had shaped Trevor. And what had happened in that accident had built on that lack of trust.

"Family is not limited by blood connections. Your value, your lovableness is not based on having blood relatives raising you. And to suggest otherwise is horrible for kids who are adopted. I'm sorry that happened to you. They did you a disservice. People can love you, even if you don't feel like your parents do."

There was silence then. Andie wondered if she'd crossed some line, and if the friendship she'd thought had been growing between them was damaged.

Trevor cleared his throat. "Thank you."

Andie blinked, her eyes watering.

"No one has ever said that. I somehow felt that I shouldn't have expected more. That it was my mistake."

Andie twisted her hands, gripping them tightly together in her lap. "No. It's never the kid's fault."

Trevor cleared his throat and picked up his fork again.

She unclenched her fingers and tried to lighten the tensions. "Unless we're talking about Joey."

Trevor looked up and flashed her a smile. She smiled back. "It's always Joey's fault."

Trevor wasn't sure which surprised him more—that he'd told all this to Andie, or that she'd defended him. Passionately and in a way that made him believe that there really wasn't something wrong with him.

Intellectually, he knew that. But as a kid, always coming up short of his brother when it came to his parents' affections, it had taken root in a way that went deeper than intellect. Andie's passionate defense reached down to those levels. He'd felt warmed inside, like he'd been given a hug.

Trevor refused Andie's offer of help with the dishes, insisting the dishwasher would handle most of them, and he'd be happy to deal with the remainder. They had work to do, and he suggested they start on that.

He appreciated what she'd said, but now he had to put that behind him. They were working together, and he needed to maintain that level of relationship. He could trust that, more than something emotional.

They sat on the couch in the living room. Trevor had gone through the photos and videos he'd taken and thinned out the number considerably. There was still a lot to share. Andie had just as many.

Most of his shots were better, since he'd used his camera rather than his phone, but Andie had some things he'd never seen. She'd taken pictures while her crew was working. She'd also taken some with him in them, photos he'd been unaware of. That was...

He wasn't sure how to define how that made him feel. Surprised. Wary. And maybe...pleased?

Trevor shook his head. "No one wants those."

Andie disagreed. "You insisted we send some of the ones I'm in. Fair is fair."

He had taken additional shots of Andie, ones he hadn't included in this file of photos to share. She was the contractor, so of course, she was there when he took his photos. She was in a lot of them.

Of course.

Had she taken more of him, as well? He banished those thoughts before he could dwell on them.

"I doubt the man who edits these will want pictures of me, so it doesn't matter."

"Why not?"

Trevor paused. Why would he?

"I'm not someone local."

"The videos on the website for Cupid's Crossing aren't meant for the local people. This is supposed to bring in strangers, people who wouldn't come here otherwise."

True, but...

"After the accident... I was blamed for what went wrong. People remember that more than that I was cleared of any responsibility later."

Andie snorted. "Are you so important that everyone remembers you and what happened? I mean, here in Carter's—Cupid's Crossing, everyone would know and remember the story, but they'd also know you were cleared. We keep track of what happens here. I thought in a big city that would be different, that people would have forgotten or ignored it."

"Maybe, but other architects and contractors..."

"Would they examine a tourist website? Are there that many people who remember your accident? I don't mean to be cruel, but are you that well-known?"

He opened his mouth, but he didn't know what to say. Truthfully, he wasn't.

He'd been living a small life since he got out of the hospital. Part of that had been dealing with his broken engagement and adapting to life with a prosthetic. But part of it had been fear of what he might see in someone's eyes, seeing they believed he'd risked lives for money.

But did anyone remember him? Anyone who didn't know him, or the building and the people involved with that job?

"You must think I'm very conceited."

Andie shook her head. "No, I didn't think that the first time I met you at the Goat, and not even working on the site when we were... Well, I never thought you were conceited when we were having some issues."

He risked a glance at her. "Should I ask what you did think of me then?"

"On-site? Probably not."

She paused and bit her lip. Did she fear he'd take that to heart? Hold it against her? He needed to reassure her.

"I won't ask. I won't even ask how I compare to Joey."

A smile crossed her face, and he felt his own in return.

Then her phone buzzed. Her smile vanished, and her brow creased.

She sighed. "That's my mom, worried about me making it home. I should get back. I need to be on-site early."

He remembered that first meeting at the pub. Her mom had called then, too. She would call frequently before Andie left for home at the end of their workdays.

"She worries about you?"

Andie's lips tightened. "She worries about everything. Excessively. But I went to the sites with Dad the day he died. He died on the way home, and ever since...it's like... I don't even know. I think she's somehow connected me to Dad and that day, or something? Sometimes it feels like I'm still a fifteen-year-old kid in her eyes."

Andie stood. "I didn't mean to bore you with my problems."

"It's not a bore. And I asked."

He didn't find her or these details about her at all boring.

"Still, my mom worrying so much is not your problem, and there's nothing you can do."

She had a point. He didn't want to push. He didn't like to be pushed himself, so he respected her boundaries.

He stood and followed her to the door. "You're right. There's nothing I can do. But I do understand worrying, perhaps to the point of paranoia."

She smiled again, and it loosened something in his chest.

"I seem to inspire worry in everyone around me."

Trevor wanted to deny it. He didn't want to burden her. But he was worried about her. Just like her mom.

No, probably not just like her mom.

"I'm sorry, Andie. I'll try to do better."

Andie was startled when Jaycee interrupted her on darts night.

Tuesday nights had been darts night at the Goat and Barley for a long time, but those nights tended to include more male patrons than female. Andie, working mostly with men, was comfortable being outnumbered, but she also knew none of the guys she played with or against were interested in her romantically.

There had been one memorable Tuesday last fall when Jaycee had come to play. She'd brought Mariah with her. That wasn't long after Mariah had come to Carter's Crossing to set up the romance initiative Abigail had come up with to bring the town business opportunities. Mariah, who'd grown up sailing the world with her family, was a darts champion. She said it was popular in many places around the globe, so she'd had plenty of opportunity to practice.

People still remembered that night. She'd beaten all comers, handily.

Mariah was with Jaycee tonight, but they turned down invitations to play. Instead, they wanted to talk to Andie.

Andie didn't know Jaycee that well. They had been in different grades in school, and Jaycee had no connection to anything related to Kozak Construction. Their only connection was that Jaycee was marrying Dave, Andie's best friend's brother.

The pub was a little loud, so they went outside to talk. They were into the month of June now, so the days were long, and there was still light enough for Andie to see the other women clearly. The weather was warm, even at dusk. It was a beautiful time of the year, and one where Andie was grateful to be working outdoors so often. She didn't feel that way in January.

"What's up?"

Jaycee looked at Mariah, and Mariah nodded.

Curiouser and curiouser.

Jaycee took a breath and blurted out, "Andie, will you be one of my bridesmaids?"

Andie blinked at Jaycee, not sure she'd heard her correctly.

"I'm sorry, this is so late, and it's rude, but Dave's mom…"

Andie knew very well what Deirdre was like. Andie put up a hand to stop Jaycee's apology.

"I understand, Jaycee. What's she done?"

"She's insisting Don, Dave's brother-in-law, has to be one of the groomsmen, and that means I'm short a bridesmaid. I know she's just causing trouble, but I'm trying to keep her happy so she doesn't skip the wedding and make Dave angry on our day. The guys are renting suits to wear, so they'll be fine, but for the women..."

"And you think I can help?" Andie wasn't sure how.

Mariah answered this one. "I've done some research. We have a bridesmaid dress, a sample dress that works with the other brides-maid dresses, that should fit you. You're good friends with both the groom's sister and husband, so having you as a member of the wedding party isn't strange. I hope you aren't offended that we didn't ask you at first."

Andie rushed to assure them, "Don't worry, honestly. I'm not upset. I know exactly what Deirdre is like, and I've heard all about how stressed she's been making you and Dave. I'm happy to help anyway I can.

"Do you just need me to stand up there on the day, or are there other things I can do to help?"

Jaycee's relief was almost comical, except that Andie knew the woman Jaycee was dealing with.

"We can pay for the dress, if you'll just go and get it fitted. You don't have to do anything else, but you're welcome to come to the bachelorette party. And thank you, thank you so, so much."

The woman was seriously wound up. Andie could only imag-ine how Deirdre was behaving. Andie wrapped her arms around Jaycee, who collapsed against her in obvious relief.

"I can pay for my dress, unless it's so ugly I'll never wear it again?"

Jaycee gave a shaky laugh, and Mariah raised her brows.

"The dresses are not ugly. And I say that not as the bride but as someone who's seen some truly horrible dresses."

Andie gave Jaycee another squeeze and let her go. "Jaycee, you've got a lot on your plate dealing with your future mother-in-law. Don't worry about this. I'm glad for the chance to spend more time with Denise while she's here. I've missed her."

Jaycee sniffed. "Thanks, Andie. I swear, I can't wait for this wedding to be over."

"Hey, I lived through Denise's wedding. I know what it's like."

Mariah mouthed a thank-you to Andie, and then after more reas-surances on Andie's part, Mariah dragged Jaycee away, and Andie returned to the pub. The crew was still sitting at the table, and other teams were busy at the dart board. Andie dropped into her seat.

"What was that about?" Joey asked.

"I'm going to be one of Jaycee's bridesmaids. Dave's mom insisted on including Don as well as Denise, so it unbalanced the number of male and female attendants."

Joey frowned. "Wait, isn't the wedding in just a couple of weeks?"

Andie nodded. "It's on the Fourth of July. The whole town is invited."

Trevor looked at them as if surprised by the information. Hadn't he been invited? Or was he just surprised that people would come without specific invites?

Joey grabbed a French fry and leaned back in his seat. He had that troublemaking look on his face, so Andie braced herself.

"So, sis, who's gonna be your plus-one?"

Andie blinked. "What plus-one?"

"For the wedding."

Andie shook her head. "I don't need a plus-one."

"Sure you do. Who else is in the wedding party? Nelson Carter and the wedding planner, right? Your buddy, Denise, and her husband. Jonas over there has a girlfriend, so you really should have someone."

Andie decided to humor him. "You can be my plus-one, then."

"Uh-uh." Joey finished his beer. "I've got a date. Jonas asked me to take his girlfriend's sister."

Andie paused for a moment to work through who else was in the wedding party, wanting to prove there was no need for a date to an event the whole town was invited to.

Rachel. Rachel was Jaycee's best friend, so she was definitely part of the wedding. She wasn't seeing anyone, was she?

"You should take Trevor," Joey said, smirking.

Andie felt her face heating up. Sure, she and Trevor weren't in opposition the way they had been in the beginning, but they weren't dating. She kicked out her foot, catching Joey's shin.

"What was that for?"

"For being an idiot. Don't put Trevor on the spot like that. I don't need a plus-one, and if I did, I could find someone for myself."

CHAPTER FOURTEEN

TREVOR PACKED UP his laptop and notebook. The trailer was quiet. Normally, he enjoyed this quiet part of the day after the crew left. He and Andie would wrap up paperwork. They'd talk. They were becoming friends.

He couldn't forget to be watchful, but he thought they had a connection.

Today, Andie had gone out with Mariah. Trevor was on his own. No darts, no trivia.

He stepped out of the trailer and locked it up. He did his usual walk-through of the site. Everything looked good.

The idea of going home to his lonely house was not appealing. After making sure the mill was closed up, he wandered to the back.

The little valley that the mill was placed in looked very different in late June than it had last fall when he'd first come here or during the winter when they'd started work.

The leaves were out, showing shades of green patterned like a quilt over the hillside. The creek, burbling through stones as it passed the mill, no longer looked forbiddingly cold.

In fact, with the temperature increasing as summer took hold, the creek was tempting.

Trevor looked around, but he was alone. Totally alone. He put his bag down on a stone and sat to peel off his socks and shoes. He then rolled up his pants.

The prosthetic leg stood out as jarring as it always did. He couldn't look at it without remembering Violet.

She'd been at his bedside for those first terrible days in the hospital. But as the weeks went by, her visits grew shorter. She was fidgety when she came by. It took him a little while to realize she couldn't look at his legs.

Leg. He had only one complete leg.

She was uncomfortable with him and with his injuries, but she couldn't admit to herself that this made a difference to her. To their relationship.

He'd been the one to suggest they end their engagement. The relief on her face had been blatant, even though she'd protested. Weakly. She'd promised they'd still be friends. But her visits grew further and further apart. It was a relief when she stopped coming by altogether.

Trevor stood and made his way carefully down to the stream. He put his right foot in the water and felt the shocking coolness of the water. Then he moved his left foot in for balance. The temperature wasn't an issue for that foot.

He didn't wear shorts, not anymore. He'd stopped swimming. After Violet, he hadn't wanted to show his prosthetic leg to anyone.

Andie had seen it that morning at her house when he'd slept in. She hadn't treated him any differently since. But then, they didn't have that kind of relationship. They weren't dating.

Would it bother Andie?

He stepped out of the stream and sat down, letting his feet, flesh and plastic, dry before putting his socks and shoes back on.

Maybe, someday, he'd find someone who wasn't bothered by his leg. Someone who hadn't known him before, and who wouldn't compare him to who he'd been. That made him think of Andie, and he was more optimistic.

Mariah didn't waste any time getting Andie to the bridal salon to try on the dress she'd found for her last-minute bridesmaid. Mariah ensured the process was as streamlined as possible. The dress and a seamstress were at the ready when they walked in the door.

Andie was all too aware of her jeans, boots and grimy nails, since she'd come straight from the mill.

The dress was waiting in the change room for her. It was a vivid shade of blue, cocktail length, with broad straps and a heart-shaped neckline. Andie loved it on sight.

Mariah helped her into it with practiced ease. It was wide at the waist, which Andie found all too common when she tried to get dresses to fit her chest and shoulders. That didn't faze Mariah.

Andie stood on a raised platform in the salon while the seamstress and Mariah got to work. The waist was pinned, and the hem shortened. Andie watched herself in the mirror and stood straighter as she saw herself in the reflection.

Her hair was pulled back and messy, and she didn't have a bit of makeup on, but she looked good. The dress, once fitted, accentuated her curves in all the right ways. She hadn't realized how small her waist looked when properly set off.

Mariah walked around Andie, still on the platform. "Perfect. You can have that ready in a week?"

The seamstress nodded. "This is a straightforward job. I'll call you when it's ready."

Andie stood for a moment, until she realized they were waiting for her to move.

"Oh, right. I'll change."

She was reluctant to take the dress off. It made her look…different. She liked that, but she stepped down and into the change room. She removed the pinned dress carefully and passed it to Mariah before changing back into her work clothes. The dress would be useless on a job site, but she was going to enjoy wearing it to the wedding. And she was definitely going to find another time to show it off.

Mariah was waiting for her when she stepped out of the change room.

"It's a beautiful dress, Mariah. I'll find a way to wear it again."

Mariah smiled. "I'm glad you feel that way. There wasn't another option. One thing about this rushed wedding is that Jaycee hasn't been able to fixate on her perfect wedding plan, so she's gone with what we can do in the time frame. More stress in one way, less in another."

"I'd never have thought Jaycee was the bridezilla type."

Mariah sighed. "If she was marrying anyone else, she probably wouldn't be, but Dave's mother—"

Andie nodded. She had no problems understanding what Jaycee was going through. "I know. Denise and I were best friends all through school, and she much preferred being at my place than at hers."

"You really understand why Jaycee needed a last-minute brides-maid?"

"Totally. But I should maybe have warned you that Deirdre is not one of my fans. Not after I took over the construction company. She's big on traditional gender roles."

Mariah grinned. "Rachel mentioned that. Deirdre can't really complain when her daughter's best friend is in the wedding party, but she might want to."

Andie laughed. "I can't believe Rachel said anything that un-charitable."

"Rachel is changing."

Andie thought of the quiet woman, a pastor's daughter and always the first to help when trouble struck.

"It's probably time. People have taken advantage of her. So, are we good now?"

Mariah raised a finger. "One question. Shoes."

Andie grimaced. "I can check what I've got, but I'll probably need to buy something."

"The other bridesmaids are wearing flat sandals. Want to go get some now?"

Mariah wasn't leaving anything to chance. Andie was happy not to have to make another trip to find sandals, so she was willing to deal with everything now.

"Lead the way."

They found sandals without much difficulty. Andie appreciated that they wouldn't be too hot for an outdoor, afternoon wedding in July. It wouldn't be too difficult to walk on the grass in them, since the wedding was taking place in the park in the middle of town.

When Mariah suggested they grab something to eat before heading back to Cupid's Crossing, Andie was happy to agree to that, as well. She hadn't thought she and Mariah would have much in common, but she was enjoying the time they spent together.

Andie had felt alone after Denise moved away. She hadn't found another girlfriend and had resigned herself to being lonely till she left town for school.

She was going to spend some time with Denise at the wedding, and also Jaycee and Rachel and Mariah. Maybe she didn't need to feel lonely. Maybe she didn't need to put off her life. She just needed to make an effort.

"I'm really putting a downer on your bachelorette, Jaycee, aren't I?" Denise sighed as she lowered herself into a chair.

Abigail Carter had offered the use of her home for Jaycee's party, though everyone knew who had engineered the event. Mariah lived in the house and was taking care of everything connected to the wedding.

The party had been designed with Denise's pregnancy in mind. There were no strippers, little alcohol and no going out. Instead, Mariah had arranged for a spa to come to them.

Jaycee was currently getting a massage while Rachel and Mariah were getting pedicures. Andie couldn't see the details of what was going on, since it was her turn for a facial and she had something over her eyes.

Didn't matter. This was bliss.

Jaycee's voice was languid and slurring. "Shut up, Denise. This is awesome."

"We needed to get this all done for tomorrow anyway." That was Mariah. "There isn't going to be a lot of time on the day, since the ceremony starts at two. And I really don't need a bunch of hungover attendants when we're having an outdoor, summer wedding."

Andie wanted to shudder at the thought of a hangover and the bright afternoon sun, but she'd already gotten in trouble for moving while she was being worked on.

"What about the guys? Are they going to be in trouble tomorrow?" Denise was invested, since this was her brother's wedding.

"If they are, the hangover will be the least of their problems."

Now that Andie had seen Mariah in action, she had no doubts about it. Since Joey wasn't in the wedding party, there was a good chance Nelson would be able to keep them in line.

Andie was content to lean back, eyes closed, while the conversation moved around her.

"Can I ask you guys something?" said Denise.

Andie knew Denise. They'd been friends all their lives. That was her troublemaking voice.

"Sure, ask whatever you want." Rachel had been mostly quiet, which surprised Andie. Not that Rachel was someone to take over a room, but she had circles under her eyes, and her smiles looked forced.

Andie had asked Mariah if anything was wrong with Rachel, and Mariah had explained Rachel and Ryker Slade had fallen out. That shocked Andie. She'd heard Ryker was back, but she'd never dreamed he and Rachel would ever spend time together. Ryker must've changed.

She'd never imagined Rachel with him. She hadn't had time to get the details, but she hoped she'd get a chance at some point. There had to be a story there.

"Someone tell me about Andie's architect, because she won't."

It was good for Andie that she had a mask drying on her face, or her heated cheeks would have been visible to all. And good for Denise that Andie had to keep still, or she'd have gone over and muzzled her friend.

That, or strangled her.

"He's not mine" she growled and was shushed by her attendant.

"Well, Andie's working with him. Closely. Every day."

Denise made that sound like something must be going on. Andie worked with a lot of men, closely and every day. Andie started to growl again, and suddenly a cloth was laid over her mouth.

"And he's going to the wedding with her."

"Ooh." Rachel was awfully interested in Andie's affairs for someone who had her own problems.

"He's good-looking, in a slightly nerdy way. Messy hair, glasses, lean, like he's a runner." Jaycee ticked off his attributes, and Andie wondered why she was checking him out so carefully when she was getting married tomorrow.

"Is he nice?" Denise wasn't giving up.

"Do we have to call people nice?" That was unexpected, coming from Rachel.

"He's quiet," Mariah said. "He and Andie put some video and photos together for the website, so that's how I've got to know him. He's very good at his job, doesn't talk a lot, doesn't seem to think he's God's gift, and he's kind of reserved."

As the mask was gently removed from Andie's face, she agreed with Mariah's assessment. Mariah didn't know his story, not like Andie did, but she'd described Trevor well.

Andie could have added *paranoid* and *suspicious*, but he hadn't been, not lately. And that made her feel better than it should.

"And he's from New York City, right? Is that one of the places you're going to apply to study, Andie?"

Andie was happy for the need to keep quiet while her face was done.

"Andie's leaving?" Rachel asked.

Denise grimaced. "I'm sorry, Andie. Was that a secret? You get your turn to go to school now that your siblings are all taken care of, right?"

With a final swipe, Andie's technician cleaned her face and left for the kitchen, so Andie had no excuse not to answer. She saw four faces, women she would call friends now, as well as a couple of the estheticians all watching for her to answer.

She sighed. "In theory, yes, but I've got to wait till the mill is done, and honestly, I'm not sure Joey is ready. I'm not sure he'll ever be ready."

Suddenly, she had a whole team of women ready to talk, suggest, condole and stand by her. It was wonderful.

Rachel had made plans to leave Cupid's Crossing before her uncle's recent accident. Andie was slow to put the pieces together. Ryker had been on his motorcycle when he'd been hit and seriously injured by Rachel's uncle. Rachel was her uncle's paralegal. Ryker was out of the hospital but still on crutches. With Rachel's uncle in rehab, Rachel had put her plans to leave on hold to try to help sort out the mess this left for his law practice.

Rachel was on Team Leave.

"You've done so much for your family. You deserve your own chance," Rachel told Andie.

"I know," Andie said. "But after putting everyone else through school, there's not much of a buffer left in the company's bank account. If Joey messes up, I'm worried about how Mom will survive."

"No one else has worried about that for the last fourteen years. It's time one of your siblings stepped up," Denise countered.

Denise had argued for this frequently. She was also on Team Leave, the unelected captain.

"Well, do I really want to start college now? If I want to be an architect, there's years of school, plus apprenticing... It's going to take a while."

"You should ask Trevor about that. He'd know."

Andie wanted to move the whole conversation away from Trevor. Her future plans and what would happen to Kozak Construction were a big problem, but she knew all the variables connected with that. She knew the problems, the possible solutions... but Trevor was an unknown.

She wasn't sure how she felt about him, she wasn't sure how he felt about her, and she had no idea what he was doing once the mill was done. None of that should have any impact on her planning process.

They had a truce, a tentative trust. She enjoyed spending time with him. She wanted to know what his plans were and what he thought of hers. Sometimes, she let herself imagine that their plans could overlap. She was more attracted to him than she wanted to admit, and it was going to hurt when he left.

She didn't need to get closer to him.

Everyone was looking at her. Everyone thought that asking Trevor was a perfect solution. It wasn't, but she didn't feel like it was appropriate to share all the gory details of Trevor's story with them.

How could she explain that he knew her plans but hadn't offered to help? She thought it was because he wanted to maintain boundaries, hoped that was why he hadn't said anything further.

She didn't want to push, didn't want to bring back that suspicious, cold person she'd first worked with. She'd do a lot to maintain the warmer relationship they had now, even if it meant missing out on something that would help her plan her future.

They were staring at her, so she'd have to give them some reason. Or with her luck, they'd ask him themselves and trigger his paranoia.

"He was injured on the last big project he worked on when the contractor messed up. They purposely cut corners, used cheaper materials, stuff like that. Trevor is…wary about whether Kozak might do something similar. I'm trying to maintain a professional boundary so he doesn't think I'm… I don't know, distracting him so he doesn't notice me doing the same kind of thing."

"You'd never do that." Denise was a loyal supporter.

"I know, but it's not like I can just tell him that and he'll stop worrying."

"That is a problem." Mariah was frowning.

"But if you're trying to just be professional, how come he's going to the wedding with you?"

Andie felt her cheeks warm again. "That's because of Joey. And it's not a date. It's more, um, he didn't want to go alone when he doesn't know very many people."

Denise got it. "How did Joey involve himself?"

"On darts night, after you asked me to be a bridesmaid, Jaycee, Joey told me Trevor should be my plus-one…in front of Trevor."

Everyone groaned.

"You were at darts night together?" Denise asked.

She knew that look on Denise's face. Troublemaker. Mind you, Andie had been just as bad back before she had to take over the family business.

"Yes, I was there with Trevor, Joey and a bunch of other guys from the crew. It was *not* a date."

And now the idea of a date was in her head. *Thanks, Denise.* Andie had to change the focus of the conversation.

"So, have you told Deirdre whether you're having boys or girls or one of each, Denise?"

Jaycee swung around to look at Denise. "You know? And you haven't told her?"

Denise shot Andie a glare, but Andie grinned back. What were friends for?

Trevor stood at the edge of the park.

It was a glorious summer day. The sky was bright and clear, but there was enough of a breeze to keep people cool without causing damage to the decorations.

There were a lot of decorations.

The colors were red, white and blue. Fitting for the Fourth of July. Yet somehow, through whatever magic Mariah employed, the patriotic color scheme still looked…romantic. Appropriate for a wedding.

He was sure he wasn't seeing all of what Mariah had done for this wedding. There were too many bodies in the way. The park was packed. He wouldn't be at all surprised to learn that everyone in Cupid's Crossing was here.

He searched vainly to find Andie among the crowd. Since she was in the wedding party, she had told him she'd be busy taking pictures and other wedding-related things before the ceremony. He wouldn't see her, at least as her plus-one, until after.

He'd see her during the ceremony, since she was part of it.

Maybe. There were a lot of people here.

"Trevor!"

He turned, happy to find someone he knew. It was Joey, wearing a button-up shirt over khakis. Trevor looked down at his dress pants and jacket. He must have overdressed.

Joey slapped his shoulder. He was flanked by some of the other guys who worked for Kozak Construction.

"Come on. You get a seat since you're connected to the wedding party."

Trevor wanted to protest, but Joey was crowding him, and it seemed easier to let himself be shepherded to wherever Joey was taking him than argue with him.

There were chairs in rows in front of the gazebo. A central aisle led to the steps. If the park had looked prepared for a wedding, the gazebo was even more so. This close, he could hear strains of music underscoring the murmur of voices.

It looked like something out of a wedding brochure. Trevor had seen a lot of those—with Violet.

About half the seats were occupied. He didn't know what the protocol was, but he would have been happy to stand or slip into a seat at the back. Joey, however, headed to a row in the middle. There were two women sitting there.

"Hey, Rose, Amelia, this is Trevor. He's with Andie, so you guys are together—dates of the wedding party."

This wasn't supposed to be a date. Was it? Andie said they were going as friends. That was fine. He shouldn't want it to be a date.

The two women looked up and smiled politely.

"Go on, sit, Trevor. They're with Micah and Jordan, the guys who are standing up with Dave."

"Hello."

They echoed his greeting. He sat beside them, and with unexpected dismay, he watched Joey leave.

Rose and Amelia continued their conversation. He had no desire to interrupt or vie for their attention, so he sat back and watched the people around him. Some greeted him or waved. He smiled or waved in return. It was…nice. Nice to know people. Even if he wasn't officially with Andie for this event, he wouldn't have been alone.

The seats rapidly filled up, leaving room only in the front row. The mothers were led down the aisle, and then the groom and his groomsmen climbed the steps to the gazebo to wait.

The music changed. Everyone turned to face the rear, waiting for the bridal party. Trevor was a half-second behind. He looked in the same direction as everyone else, ready to see the first bridesmaid walk down the aisle. His mouth dropped open when he saw her.

CHAPTER FIFTEEN

IT TOOK TREVOR a moment to recognize Andie. She didn't look anything like the contractor he knew. Her hair was up, and she was wearing makeup. That was one change. The other was the dress.

He'd thought her pretty when he first saw her at the Goat and Barley. She was more than just pretty now. She looked beautiful. It did strange things to his insides.

She was smiling as she walked down the aisle, familiar with the people watching her and making their own greetings. Then her gaze caught on him, and for a fraction of a second, she froze.

He was already still, watching her with who-knew-what expression on his face. He hoped he wasn't drooling. He felt his cheeks flush.

Andie recovered and looked to another part of the crowd, and his eyes followed her helplessly as she finished her trip down the aisle. One of the groomsmen met her, and together they climbed the shallow steps to the gazebo.

He was scarcely aware of the rest of the bridesmaids passing him. He stood when everyone else did, and the bride walked slowly down the grass aisle, holding the arm of a man who must be her father.

The rest of the ceremony passed in a blur. He tried to focus on what was happening, but he kept stealing glances at Andie.

Andie in a blue dress that lit up her face. Andie exchanging grins with the groomsman she was partnered with. Trevor didn't like him.

The service was short, the groom soon kissed his bride and the party retreated down the aisle. People stood, and Trevor stood with them, unsure of what to do next.

Rose took pity on him and led him around the back of the gazebo where photos were being taken of the wedding party. Andie and her groomsman had been joined by another bridesmaid, one who was conspicuously pregnant.

Andie looked over and smiled when she caught sight of him. He couldn't resist responding. She said something to her companions, and the three of them walked toward him.

Rose and Amelia left him to find their dates. Trevor barely registered their departure.

His eyes were on Andie.

She stood in front of him, a small smile crossing her face.

"Trevor, this is my friend, Denise, sister to the groom, and her husband, Don."

He relaxed once he knew this man Andie had been partnered with was married to the pregnant woman. Andie shook her head slightly as Denise stepped forward. Denise ignored Andie to give Trevor a wide smile.

"It's so nice to meet you, Trevor. I've heard so much about you."

Trevor shot a glance at Andie. Her cheeks were pink.

"Denise!"

Denise widened her eyes. "We're all pretty excited to see how the mill looks after you two are done."

Don took Denise's elbow in his hand. "Weren't you telling me you had to find a bathroom?"

Denise hesitated, then shrugged. "Hazards of pregnancy. I hope I see you later. I have *lots* of questions."

Andie poked her.

"About architecture, of course."

Don dragged her away while Andie shook her head.

"I'm sorry. We've been best friends since we were kids, and she's suffering from pregnancy hormones."

Trevor was curious. About what Denise would have said had

she not left and what Andie had told her friend to inspire those comments.

"I should just ignore whatever she's been hearing about me?"

Andie flushed and bit her lip. "You do understand small towns are gossipy, right?"

Flushed Andie was doing strange things to him. His palms were sweating, and his pulse quickened. What had she said? Right, small towns.

"It's become apparent since I've been here. I haven't seen Denise around before."

"No, she and her husband moved to Florida about a year and a half ago."

"I see."

There was an awkward pause. He swallowed.

"Um, you look very nice." Internally, he groaned. Why couldn't he tell her she looked beautiful?

Andie met his gaze. "Thank you. Bridesmaid dresses can be a bit of a crapshoot, but I love this one. Denise's dresses were... Well, I love Denise, but I will never wear the dress from her wedding again."

That sounded familiar. Violet had discussed the subject extensively. Without thinking, he spoke. "I remember there being a lot of debate about that."

He froze. He hadn't planned to say that. Of course Andie didn't miss it. Her eyebrows lifted.

"You've been through a discussion about bridesmaid dresses?"

He shrugged. "I was engaged."

Her mouth dropped open. She obviously hadn't expected to hear that. He braced himself, waiting for her next question. He understood he wasn't his best self anymore, so why would she think someone had wanted to marry him? Violet *had* changed her mind, after all.

"Married?"

He shook his head. He heard her exhale.

"Something you prefer not to talk about?"

"Exactly."

Andie glanced around, and a frown pulled down her eyebrows. "Is being here today a problem? I'm sorry, I didn't know."

That wasn't the response he'd prepared for. He'd prepared for curiosity and questions, not concern. He put his hand on her arm, wanting to reassure her. The tingle in his fingers when he touched her skin was not what he was expecting, or honestly, wanting. He drew back.

"It's fine, Andie. I could have made an excuse. I'm not bothered by weddings. I just prefer not to talk about why my engagement ended."

She grimaced. "She didn't leave you at the altar, did she? Sorry. I wasn't supposed to ask."

It hadn't been *that* embarrassing. "No, we never got that far."

"Good. I mean, I'm glad that didn't happen to you. It happened to Nelson, and it would be a little freaky if it had happened to you, too."

He almost turned to look for Nelson. He couldn't imagine the man waiting at the altar for a bride who didn't show.

"Nelson? And Mariah?"

"No, this was a few years ago. Someone else, not from here. I don't know all the details, just that it happened, and Nelson came back to Carter's after."

Andie turned and led the way toward the tables where food was being set out. Trevor quickened his step to keep pace with her, careful on the uneven ground. He was annoyed by how curious he was about what had happened with Nelson. The town was wearing off on him.

She considered. "I don't think Mariah would do that, leave someone at the altar. If nothing else, she wouldn't jeopardize all the work she put into planning something like this."

He glanced around. "She has worked hard. Everything's beautiful."

"It's way beyond any other wedding we've had here. We just might be able to pull off this romance-center thing." Andie sounded like she'd had doubts.

Trevor had been focused on his job, on getting the mill done, but he hadn't connected it to the whole concept of the town's survival. He wasn't pleased with himself. He wasn't the only person who'd had problems. He had no business being so self-centered.

"I think people would be willing to travel to have an event like this."

"I hope so. The whole town has united behind this idea. They've worked hard to make this look good. I mean, I've never seen Mr. Lawrence in anything but sweatpants for years."

Trevor had no idea who Mr. Lawrence was, but he'd seen a few older men in sweatpants around town. Not today. Today, it did look like the town was doing its best to shine.

"I was afraid I'd overdressed."

Andie's gaze traveled over him, and his cheeks flushed again. He hadn't been looking for a compliment, but her gaze was warm and admiring. He wasn't used to that, but despite his embarrassment, he liked it.

"You look good, Trevor. You're not more dressed up than the wedding party, so I don't think you need to worry. If you're comparing yourself to Joey, on the other hand, you'll always be overdressed, which probably means you're doing it right."

She grinned at him, the two of them sharing an inside joke, and he returned the smile before he was aware of it. His cheeks were feeling the effects of this much smiling, and a warmth that had nothing to do with the summer sun spread through him.

Denise and Don joined them again, which was good. He didn't think grinning at Andie was going to help his situation.

"Trevor, I'm very sorry if I embarrassed you earlier." Denise shot a glance at her husband.

Don shook his head. "Adding that '*if* I embarrassed you' negates most of the apology."

"No, don't worry about it. I'm fine." Trevor didn't want more attention or to upset someone so conspicuously pregnant.

Don tried to glare at his wife, but their obvious affection reduced the effectiveness of his stare. "Sorry, Trevor, but when these two get together, there's no telling what might happen."

Andie poked his arm. "Don, don't you dare tell stories."

Trevor was very interested in the stories Andie wanted silenced, and he couldn't even tell himself it was to better understand his contractor. He wanted to know her as a person. An attractive, interesting woman.

The four of them moved in a group to get some of the food

spread out under tents. Andie and Denise and Don knew everyone. Trevor recognized only a few of the people, but Andie gave him a low-voiced bio of each person before they met.

"That's Mr. G, retired high school computer teacher with his son, Benny. Benny may be in a wheelchair, but he can fix almost anything."

Trevor remembered Benny was the person they'd sent their photos and videos to. It was nice to finally put a face to the name.

"That couple—Gord and Gladys. She's fussing over him now because he broke his hip this winter, right before their fiftieth wedding anniversary."

Gord looked pretty grumpy.

"And that's Judy, who works at the vet clinic, and her husband, Harvey. Just don't mention zombies to them."

Trevor couldn't imagine any circumstance in which he would.

He recognized Mavis Grisham, who was accompanied by her Great Dane, Tiny, who was wearing a tuxedo T-shirt.

"Don't ask," Andie advised, so he didn't.

He recognized some people from meetings and some who were working on the mill. Everyone was friendly and obviously enjoying themselves. The food was good, and he was startled to find that he was enjoying himself, as well.

This was the first big social event he'd attended since his accident. No one asked him about it or how he was doing. He was just one of many people at a party. A weight rolled off his shoulders.

It seemed like no time had passed before Mariah announced it was time for the throwing of the bouquet and the garter.

Andie groaned.

"I'm just going to hide behind you. Don't move, and if anyone asks, you haven't seen me."

Trevor didn't think her chances of hiding behind him, even this late in the afternoon, were very good. "I'm not sure that's going to work."

"Don! Cover me."

Denise chuckled. "You should hide behind me. I'm as big as a house."

Don held up a warning hand. "Don't agree with that, Andie. It's a trap."

Trevor allowed himself another smile.

Andie's maneuvering was in vain, since Mariah came up behind them, beckoning for Andie.

"Mariah, this is such a silly thing to do. It's embarrassing and—"

Mariah took hold of Andie's arm. "Don't worry. Jaycee has something planned for the bouquet, and it doesn't involve you catching it. You won't want to miss what's coming. Nothing embarrassing for *you*."

Andie allowed herself to be dragged away, and Trevor followed with Don and Denise. They were all curious.

Jaycee, glowing in her white dress, took her time getting ready. She fidgeted with the bouquet and looked over her shoulder, then she turned to where a man was making his way on crutches to the center of the park where everyone was gathered.

"Is that Ryker Slade?" Denise asked. "I heard he was back."

"Are you asking me?" Don rubbed her back where she'd placed her own hand. "I didn't grow up here. Never seen the man before."

Trevor had heard the name. Something to do with the website for the town? Right. Andie had mentioned him. Big family, terrible dad.

Jaycee threw the bouquet to the man they thought was Ryker who struggled to catch it, and Mariah pushed Rachel to walk over to him. He dropped one of his crutches and fell on one knee. Trevor didn't catch everything, but it was clearly a proposal, and Denise was squeeing with pleasure. The whole park burst into applause as the couple kissed.

Andie came back to them. She had a dreamy smile on her face. Trevor would never have imagined his prickly contractor could look like that. Something else that would mess with his concentration at work.

"That was so romantic."

Denise was almost vibrating in place. "Was that Ryker Slade?"

Andie nodded. "Yes. He came back. He's changed, and he and Rachel are a thing. I had no idea, but that's so sweet. Not what I thought I'd ever say about a Slade."

Trevor didn't say anything. That proposal hit a little too close to home. The memories weren't welcome. He excused himself, pretending he needed to find the portable toilets.

He hadn't thought much about Violet for weeks, months even, but the wedding and the proposal were all bringing it back. At the last wedding he'd been at, he'd proposed to Violet. He'd thought his future was settled then. Everything had been planned out. The accident had upset not just his career.

He needed some time and space to get rid of this unsettled feeling. He found a bench at the edge of the park, away from the crowds, and watched from a safe distance.

The sun was setting when he roused himself to find his date. It wasn't fair to leave her hanging. He needed to behave like an adult, not a hurt child. Andie deserved to know why he'd vanished. His muscles tightened at the thought of exposing himself like that, but he trusted her.

He really did.

CHAPTER SIXTEEN

ANDIE WAS AWARE of Trevor's absence, and she fended off questions from her friends. Denise had to leave. The long day was trying on her ankles, which she swore were swollen to the size of watermelons. As soon as the newly married couple were sent off on their honeymoon, Don took Denise back to her parents' place.

Andie stopped to talk to her mother, avoided Joey and wondered if Trevor had gone. Wouldn't he have said something? Had something here reminded him of his broken engagement and caused him to leave? She wished she'd had some way to carry her phone, but since the dress had no pockets, she'd left it locked up in the truck.

If Trevor was gone, she might just leave, as well. People were staying to see the traditional fireworks display, but Andie had seen many over the years, and she could give this one a miss.

She took one final glance around. Then she spotted Trevor returning from wherever he'd been. He was scanning the crowd, and when he saw her, he smiled.

It was the smile she'd seen that first night at the Goat. When they'd been two people sharing an interlude, not adversaries on a job together.

She couldn't resist a smile in return.

"You okay?" He'd been gone a while, and she didn't want to pry, but she was concerned about him.

He glanced away. "I think so. Would you like to take a walk?"

"Sure." She asked Mavis to let her mother know she would be home later and followed Trevor past the tents and chairs that had helped turn the park into a wedding venue for the day.

The town was quiet once they left the park, where the crowd still enjoyed the food and music. They walked in companionable silence. She felt no urge to break it, and Trevor didn't speak, not till they'd covered two blocks.

"I'm sorry I left like that."

"Not a problem." That was true. She'd missed him, but she knew everyone in this town. She was used to attending things solo and enjoying herself. "This event was so informal, I'm not sure many people knew you were with me."

He made a grunty noise in his throat, whether of agreement or something else, she wasn't sure.

"I'm not a party person. I tend to be quiet. And this..." He waved his hand, indicating the wedding event. "It brought back some memories."

Andie wanted to slap Joey. Trevor could have avoided this if it hadn't been for her brother's big mouth.

"You should have made an excuse. It would have been fine. I've gone solo to lots of things here in Carter's—I mean, Cupid's—Crossing, and I'm good on my own."

Trevor shook his head with a jerk. "No, honestly. I don't dread or hate weddings. But that proposal threw me. It brought things back, things I don't think I've dealt with. I guess that's obvious since it hit me like that today."

Andie had never been in a serious relationship. She hadn't wanted to be tied down to Carter's Crossing when she'd been counting down the days till she could leave.

No. She was leaving. Still. She thrust that sense of confusion down. This was Trevor's moment to process things, not hers. She didn't have anything to process. Enough!

She turned to him. "Everyone gets to deal with things the way they need to."

She noticed the corner of his mouth quirk up. "Probably better to choose a healthy way. I've mostly been pretending it never happened. That hasn't been completely effective."

"I can understand the appeal." Sometimes, though, pretending wasn't an option.

"I wish the easy way worked. I proposed to Violet after her sister's wedding. I didn't really plan it, but we were at the reception, talking about the wedding, and she said what she would like for *her* wedding, and I agreed with what she'd suggested, and… We knew we were ready. It was what we wanted. It was the next logical step, so…"

Ryker's proposal had been much more romantic. Andie pushed that thought aside.

"We got a ring the next week and told her family. I asked her again then so that her sister wouldn't think we'd tried to take any attention away from her wedding."

Andie didn't like the way her hands were fisting. This was not her story. She had no stakes in it, so there was no reason to feel upset. Except something had gone wrong, and it had hurt Trevor.

Trevor didn't speak for a few minutes, and Andie had to clench her jaw shut to restrain herself from asking what had happened. She had no right. Anything Trevor offered was a gift. Trust came to him with difficulty.

"We were going to get married the next winter. Violet wanted a winter wedding, and that worked with my schedule. I was busy getting the firm going, so she did most of the planning. I hadn't worried about the day itself. I was focused on what would come after. The two of us, living together, making our own family.

"The accident at the site happened about six months before the wedding was scheduled. After the accident, I was out of it most of the time. I wasn't in good shape. Violet had to cancel everything related to the wedding, because we had no idea when I was going to be able to walk again. It was a disaster.

"She came by every day, just like a good fiancée should. But once I wasn't lost in a world of painkillers all the time, I could see that she wasn't comfortable."

He rubbed his leg, the one with his prosthetic device. Andie wondered if it bothered him, or if it was a reaction to talking about the accident.

"When it was time to get the prosthetic, she couldn't look at it or the leg that was only partly there. I asked her if there was a problem, but she said there wasn't."

Andie wished she could somehow stop the end she saw coming.

"She was lying. She couldn't deal with it, couldn't handle that I was...damaged, but she was also afraid what everyone would think of her if she broke our engagement after what I'd been through. I couldn't imagine seeing that...repugnance for the rest of my life. So I broke it off."

Andie's hands were fists again. She wanted to hurt that shallow woman who'd not been able to look past a surface injury. She wanted to hurt her for hurting Trevor.

She could read between the lines. He'd trusted the people he'd worked with, and they'd betrayed him. He'd trusted his fiancée, and she'd abandoned him, even if he'd been the one to end things. No wonder trust was such an issue for him. Even his family had allowed him to feel less wanted.

"I could see the relief on her face. She said if I felt that way, it would be best if she returned the ring. She stopped coming by soon after that."

Trevor paused. Andie didn't want him to regret telling her. She wanted him to know that he'd done nothing wrong.

"Please tell me she went for a facial that went badly and scarred her, and she finally asked your forgiveness for being so shallow."

Trevor stopped. Andie paused, as well, wishing she could see his face in the dark.

"Andie, she isn't a bad person. It wasn't all on her. She tried. She really tried, but she couldn't help the way she felt."

He was so forgiving, just like with his parents. Andie drew a breath, trying to be fair.

"She couldn't help the way she felt, sure, but when you agree to marry someone, you should care for the whole person, not just the superficial parts."

Trevor didn't respond for a moment. "You think 'real' love would accept something like that, like this?"

He pulled up his pant leg, his prosthetic showing in the pale light of the streetlamps. His skepticism came through loud and clear.

Andie let her gaze rest on his leg, neither flinching nor gawking. It didn't freak her out the way he obviously expected. She tried to choose her words carefully. "As far as your leg… It doesn't bother me. I work in the construction industry. We try to be safe, but accidents happen. My grandfather lost a couple of fingers, and my grandmother didn't leave him. In the same accident, my uncle lost his arm. He ended up moving to Arizona and is still there with his wife.

"Things happen in life. Bad things as well as good. You can be hurt or lose your money… And even if you're lucky, if you make it through life without major tragedies like bankruptcy or cancer or an accident on a building site, time is going to happen. Would you have felt differently about her when her hair turned gray or she got wrinkles or had to walk with a cane?

"If you can't handle those things, that's not love. If you love someone, the surface is that, the top layer. But you love the whole person, all the layers. If the surface changes, or one of those inner layers does, the love is still there."

"What if all the layers change? How can you trust that the person will still love them?"

She wasn't sure exactly what he meant. "I… I don't know. To be honest, I've lost track of the metaphor."

She heard him chuckle. It was a quiet sound, but it pleased her. She'd brought him something good after he'd been dwelling on something bad.

"I think you're using the onion metaphor. Only not saying that everyone has so many layers, but that a person needs to love all the layers."

"That's a good thought. Maybe Violet and I never showed each other all those layers. Maybe I never trusted her enough to show her."

Andie thought he'd just shown her more than one, layers he didn't share with many people. Maybe not with anyone. Her chest felt like something was turning over, expanding at the thought that he was trusting her with this.

She wouldn't betray that trust. She wouldn't be another person on the list of people who'd made Trevor feel like he was less, insufficient.

Her mouth opened, ready to say something reassuring, when

suddenly, a whistle sounded and light shot through the sky. The fireworks had started.

They stood there, close but not touching, while the bright lights shot through the sky, punctuated with booms, crackles and more whistles. Abigail always put on a good show for the Fourth.

The finale firework lit up the sky, imprinting images on their retinas. They blinked, and their eyes started to grow accustomed to the dark again. Andie drew in a breath, feeling peaceful. Content. Ready to stay here for a long time yet.

"It's getting late," Trevor said.

Andie swallowed. Apparently, she was the only one having a moment. Or maybe Trevor was retreating after sharing with her. She needed to let him take the lead here, on whatever he was comfortable with.

"Let me walk you back to your truck."

Andie didn't want Trevor to feel obligated. If he didn't want to be with her, she'd rather be alone.

"It's not necessary. This is a safe town."

She knew almost everyone, and everyone knew her. Trevor didn't argue, he just waited till she started to move. He didn't speak till they arrived at Bertha.

Andie wasn't sure how to end the evening. Slamming the door and roaring away wasn't a good option.

"Would you like a lift?"

"No, it's only a couple of blocks. Good night, Andie."

"Good night, Trevor."

And that was it. She climbed into Bertha, turned the key, and the engine started immediately. Trevor nodded and headed toward his own place.

As she pulled the truck into the street, she glanced back at the figure almost swallowed up by the dark. He'd opened up to her, and she wasn't going to force anything more. She didn't want him to regret having shared with her.

She also needed to remind herself that he was not her project, not her concern...possibly not even her friend. They'd spent time at the wedding together, but Joey had forced that. They were co-workers, nothing more.

He trusted her now and she wouldn't abuse that trust. The reminder didn't make her feel any better.

The next morning was busy for Kozak Construction. They'd helped set up the park for the wedding, and now everything needed to be torn down, cleaned up and either tossed or put into storage for another event. None of that required Trevor's assistance, and that was good. Really.

Andie picked up Denise later that afternoon. Denise had kicked Don out to spend time with the guys at the Goat. Nelson was there along with a few other people in town for the holiday and the wedding. Denise told him to go be manly while she had her girl time.

Andie drove Denise to what had been a make-out spot in their high school days. At Andie's home, her mother would hover, and at Denise's, her mother would be Deirdre. They wanted somewhere they could be alone and be themselves without worry or disapproval.

Andie pulled a couple of lawn chairs and a cooler out of the back of her truck. They sat in the shade, watching the creek flow by. In daylight, this place didn't attract a lot of attention.

"So Dave is married. My mom is torn between pride at the wedding and disappointment that Dave didn't marry Delaney."

Andie spit out her drink. "What? Dave and Delaney? Delaney Carter? Were they ever even together?"

"Nah, not since that week in high school. But my mom really got her hopes up. She would have been happy for me to go out with Nelson, but that was never going to happen. He and Dave spent too much time together. Nelson is like another brother."

Andie leaned her head back, staring up at the leaves above her. "I remember that now. You were never interested in Nelson?"

Denise shook her head. "What's up with you and Trevor?"

"Nothing." Unfortunately.

"Oh, come on. I heard the two of you disappeared together after we left."

The town was full of busybodies.

"How did you hear that if you were gone?"

"Andie, this is still Carter's Crossing, no matter what they change the name to."

"The joy of small towns. Everyone gossips."

Denise reached her soda can out to touch Andie's. "Not like where we live now. We could die in our bed, and no one would know for days."

"Here, someone would know exactly the last time your door opened and be knocking to see if you'd fallen in the tub."

"Not the worst thing. Well, depending on what you were doing when they knocked. But that still doesn't tell me anything about Trevor."

Andie might as well talk. This was her best friend. "I'm not sure about him myself. We might be friends now."

"Friends?" Denise's eyebrows were inching up to her hairline.

Andie nodded. "We talked last night. He's had some things happen to him. He doesn't trust people much. And I understand. But it makes working with him difficult."

"Hmm." Denise took a drink of soda and let the silence settle.

There was rustling from the leaves and gurgling as the stream ran over stones. Sounds of people were distant. Andie soaked it in and realized she'd miss quiet like this.

"What about school?"

"Dunno." The day was peaceful, and Andie was reluctant to bring up any drama.

"Andie, you need to think about what *you* want for a change. You've been good to your family. All your brothers and your sister have had their chances. You need to take yours now."

Denise was right. Andie knew that. But…

"I know. But my mom still worries all the time and Joey isn't ready to take over."

"Maybe he can't be ready when you're here and everyone knows you're the boss."

Andie had wrestled with that idea. "But what if he makes a mistake?"

"What if he does? You made mistakes, didn't you? That's how you learned."

True. But when she'd been learning, she'd been burdened by the responsibility of her family. She didn't take risks, and she never relaxed. When she'd taken over, she'd been years younger than Joey was now, but he was much less mature than she'd been.

"He seems so immature. And he doesn't push to take over."

"Again, it would be difficult for him to do that when you're around. Maybe he doesn't want to try only to be told he's doing everything wrong."

Andie looked over at her friend. "Have you been eavesdropping on us?"

Denise smiled. "No, I just know you. No one else in your family could have taken over when your dad died. I know that. But you deserve some happiness, too. I'd like to see you find someone, but there's no one here in town, not if we're taking your architect out of the picture, is there?"

"I know. I just… I mean, I wanted to be an architect back in high school, but I'm not sure if I want to start that now. It takes years, and I may be too old."

Denise reached out a lazy hand to swat her. "Don't you dare say you're too old, because I'm just as old as you are, and I'm still only twenty-two."

Andie snorted. "I think I'm too old to start school now. At least, not something that requires postgraduate work and apprenticing. I don't think I could relax enough to be a student and do nothing else."

"Maybe you should give it a try before you write it off. Spend a year at college. See what it's like. You could even choose a school in Florida… And if you have too much time on your hands, come and babysit."

Andie laughed. "This is all a ploy to get free babysitting?"

Denise reached out a hand for Andie's. "No, it's a ploy to get my best friend the life she deserves. You deserve to do something you want. If you weren't here in Carter's Crossing—"

"Cupid's Crossing now."

Denise rolled her eyes. "Fine, if you weren't here in Cupid's Crossing, your mom couldn't obsess over where you are all the time. You wouldn't have the burden of your family suffocating you. Don't argue. I know you'd rather have your own place. And I will nag you till you get what you want."

"I know. And thanks. I just have to figure out what it is that I want."

"When is this big project with the mill done?"

Andie huffed a breath. "If all goes well, before the end of the year."

"Then, I want you to make some plans for then. If nothing else, take a vacation. When was the last time you left Cart—this place?"

For any amount of time? Years. "I have thought about taking a holiday."

"Does it involve beaches, sunshine and men without shirts to drool over? Don't mind me, I'm not going to have that for a long time once these babies arrive."

Andie smiled at her friend. "It might, if you're having boys. You don't have to bundle them up with shirts down in Florida, right? Though they might be the ones drooling, not me. I thought I'd come down and see you in the fall, maybe help with the new babies?"

Denise sat up. "Are you sure? I mean, I'd love to have you, and I'm panicking about how I'm going to handle two kids, but that doesn't sound like a great vacation."

Andie was serious. She turned in her chair to be sure Denise got what she was saying.

"I can't picture myself taking a solo vacation. If I visited you, I could spend some time thinking about what I want, and maybe if I help with the babies a bit, I can talk it over with you as well as help you out. And you're in Florida. Beaches and sun all the time, right?"

"Totally. They close the borders when clouds roll in."

"I could give Joey a chance to step up, and we can see how he does while I'm away. And you could make sure I don't fuss too much."

Denise cackled. "Oh, I'll keep you busy enough that you won't fuss. But after the mill is done, you need a real break."

"Maybe I can look at schools in Florida while I'm there. Get some ideas."

Denise held out her soda can again, and they clinked. "Good. It's time you did something for yourself, Andie."

It was. If she could just figure out what she really wanted. And she pushed a picture of Trevor out of her head.

CHAPTER SEVENTEEN

TREVOR WASN'T SURE what things were going to be like when they returned to work after the wedding. He had no idea what had gotten into him, sharing intimate details with Andie. For that matter, why had he even agreed to be her plus-one?

He needed to remember that she was his contractor. He didn't need to be her friend. In fact, being her friend made it more difficult to retain that distance required. Friendship assumed trust. He couldn't let down his guard. Except, he already had.

He was trying not to be too overzealous, like he'd promised Abigail, but he needed to be cautious. It wasn't just about Andie. There were other people involved. Any one of them could jeopardize the project, if they wished and weren't monitored.

He was assuming she was totally on the level because he liked her. He'd liked the contractor that screwed him over, as well. Though that contractor had never worn a dress like Andie's blue one.

He didn't sleep well that night, but he made sure to arrive early on Tuesday morning when work on the mill resumed. He was safely behind his desk with his laptop open when Andie came in. He didn't look up right away, afraid she might think...

Might think he'd enjoyed spending time with her. That they were more than coworkers. More than friends.

When he finally looked up, ready to say good morning, Andie was about to head out.

"Sorry, Trevor, I just got a message that Pastern's is delaying the next shipment, so I'll have to deal with them. You must have gotten the message, too."

He'd been so anxious about seeing Andie that he hadn't read his email. "Right. Yes. Let me know how it goes."

Andie left the trailer, and Trevor wanted to bang his head on the desk. It was all too obvious that the problem wasn't Andie.

By the end of the week, Trevor had managed to settle their working relationship. At least, he thought so. He'd almost skipped darts night, but Joey had insisted they needed his skill. He'd planned to sit away from Andie and talk to the others as much as possible.

He hadn't needed to worry. Andie had been sidetracked by Mariah, who was there with Nelson. Since Jaycee and Dave were on their honeymoon, Mariah was there to take Dave's place.

Mariah was the strongest competition Trevor had faced thus far, and she defeated him. Nelson beamed as if he'd had some impact on the win. Mariah didn't want to keep playing after the first round. Instead, she and Andie started a conversation that kept them busy.

On Thursday, they all went to trivia night, and he was no longer worried that Andie might assume too much after their time at the wedding together. It was like it had never happened. She'd been busy, and they hadn't discussed anything that wasn't related to the mill. That was good, he reminded himself. He found himself a little too aware of where she was all the time, but he threw himself into work to squash that.

Despite the Pastern's delay, construction had gone well this week. They were about to open up the wall on the river side of the mill. It was a big event, and the crew had been let go early on Friday afternoon. Andie was finishing up some payroll stuff in the trailer while Trevor was going through the plan for the wall removal again when they heard a car pull into the lot.

The door was open, and fans were spinning to dissipate the heat.

Mariah climbed the steps and stuck her head in. "Can I talk to you two for a minute?"

Andie looked up with a smile. "Sure, Mariah. Want to take a seat?"

Trevor shut his laptop. He'd gone over this process more times than he needed to already. He should have left when the crew did, and he didn't try to decipher why he'd stayed.

"Thanks for all you've done with the photos and video on the mill renovation. It's been great. You saw the first couple of videos I sent you, right?"

Andie nodded. "We're opening up the back wall next week, so we'll be sure to get good coverage of that."

Mariah made a note on her phone. "That's all great, but it's not the main reason I'm here. I have a business thing to ask you, but it's not mill or town business."

Andie pulled out a notebook. Trevor wasn't sure if he was supposed to take notes, as well.

Mariah sighed. "Nelson lost one of his horses yesterday."

Andie looked sympathetic while Trevor wondered how he'd misplaced something that large.

Andie shot him a glance. "Nelson has a farm where he has rescue horses." She looked back at Mariah. "Which one?"

"Sparky."

Andie shook her head. "That was the first one he rescued, right? What happened?"

Mariah blinked rapidly. "Nelson has the medical terms, but mostly, Sparky was just old."

Ah, that kind of lost.

"He's in a bit of a funk about it, so I was wondering if you wouldn't mind going out to the farm."

Trevor froze. He'd never been close to a horse in his life. What was he supposed to do on a farm?

"Does he need company?" Andie looked surprised, as well.

"He needs a distraction. I'd like the two of you to look at the house and tell us if we have to tear the place down and start from scratch or if we should try to salvage it. I know what I think, but I won't try to influence you."

Andie's blinked. "You two plan to live out there?"

"Once we're married." Mariah nodded. "Which reminds me. Do you have an idea when the mill will be done? I know you can't promise, but if nothing unexpected happens, when might we reasonably expect it to be ready?"

Andie turned to him. "I thought maybe the end of October, beginning of November. What do you think, Trevor?"

He frowned. He reviewed the schedule every day and adjusted it for any variables he could possibly imagine impacting their work.

They'd soon be mostly working indoors, and then there was less chance of delays since weather wouldn't be a factor.

"Why don't we say mid-November, just to allow for contingencies?"

Andie nodded. She had undoubtedly been working on her own projected schedule.

"Are you planning your wedding already, Mariah?" Andie teased.

Mariah shook her head. "No, I'm not going to have a big wedding."

Andie raised her eyebrows, and Trevor thought he must show as much surprise on his face as Andie did. After what Mariah had accomplished with Dave and Jaycee's wedding, he'd thought she'd be planning something even more attention grabbing for herself.

"I've seen enough big weddings, and Nelson doesn't like them. We'll do something small when the time comes. I did have an idea for a Christmas wedding for someone else, so it sounds like I can explore that idea."

Andie slid a finger over her lips, and Trevor watched too closely.

"I won't say anything. After all, there are only so many couples in town."

Mariah held in a smile. "I can neither confirm nor deny, but I appreciate your discretion. I need to talk to the couple involved if I decide it'll work. So can you take a look at the house? Then I can bother Nelson about it, and he'll have less time to mope."

Trevor wasn't sure he approved of Mariah's plan, but he was curious to see the place now.

"Are you in, Trevor?" Andie asked.

He nodded. "When would you want to go?"

Andie looked at the papers on her desk. "I can finish this up later if you're free now."

He was just doing busywork. "Probably good to go in daylight. Are you available, Mariah?"

"Oh, I'm not going."

Andie shot Trevor a perplexed glance, and they both looked over at Mariah.

"Don't you want to tell us what you've got planned?"

"Nope. I'm not going to make plans till I know if we're restoring or starting over. I've got other ideas to distract Nelson with for now, then when I hear from you, I'll have that option in hand for when I need it."

Andie had risen to her feet, so Trevor stood. "Are you really planning to do something with the house, or is this just a diversion scheme?"

Mariah's eyes widened. "Oh, we're absolutely going to be moving on to the farm. Nelson won't want to leave the carriage house until Abigail has settled her plans, but if you weren't tied up with the mill right now, we'd already be working on the place."

Trevor was glad to know this wasn't just a distraction, and he was glad of a break. Something new would be good for him.

Mariah waved goodbye and left, having ticked something off on her list.

Trevor rode out with Andie since she knew where they were going.

"Nelson bought the old Abbott place when he returned to Carter's Crossing and keeps some rescue horses there. The place was falling down, but he got us to help put the barn in shape. He lives in the old carriage house next to Abigail's house right now, but I get why Mariah would like her own place, especially if Abigail makes the house an inn."

"Do you have any idea what condition the house on the farm is in? What was it like when you worked on the barn?"

Andie scrunched up her nose. "It was pretty bad, if I remember correctly. My guess is that it isn't reclaimable, but we'll see what you think."

Andie slowed to turn onto a smaller county road. The countryside was pretty in the afternoon sun. It was hot enough that Andie was wearing shorts, but Trevor still wore long khakis. Both were wearing T-shirts. The road was shaded by green trees that almost met overhead in some places. Behind the trees were fields. Most had some kind of crop growing, but he'd spotted cattle in one field. Andie signaled and pulled into a driveway.

It had been a gravel drive at some point, but it was mostly dirt now. The weather had been dry, so the drive was rutted and slightly dusty. Ahead, he saw a barn in good condition and a few horses in the field.

On the other side of the driveway was a house. At least, he assumed it had been once upon a time. Andie came to a stop and turned off the truck. Neither said anything.

Trevor had no idea what made Mariah think anything could be renovated here. He turned to Andie and saw she was biting back a grin.

"Shall we get out and take a look so we have a full report for Mariah?"

Trevor stretched a hand toward the house. "There's no way to restore this. You had to know that."

Andie let the grin escape. "It's gotten a lot worse since we were working on the barn. But it's a beautiful day, and I was ready for a break. Maybe we can reclaim some of the timber or something, if they want to try that."

Trevor shrugged, unclipped his seat belt and opened the truck door.

Once out of the truck, he took a moment to look around and drew in a deep breath. The air was fresh and warm, and some kind of insect sounded in the background. A slight breeze moved the leaves of the trees, many of which were now growing close enough to the house to make work there a difficult prospect.

Andie led the way to the building. There had apparently been a verandah out front and two stories, both of which had now fallen into the basement.

Trevor walked carefully over the uneven ground. Around back, the house was even worse. A sapling was growing in the rearmost room, a branch jutting out over what had been a backyard.

"I think this is a demolition job for you, not a renovation for me," Trevor said.

Andie looked at the remains of the farmhouse. "But once we

remove the debris, you can start with a blank slate, plan any kind of house here."

He moved in a circle, looking not at the house, but at the surroundings, imagining what he might design. It was only speculation, of course. Mariah and Nelson would have their own ideas as to what the house should look like.

Andie slid to a sitting position under a huge old oak growing in what would have been the home's front yard. Trevor walked around the house, getting an understanding of its size and what it must have looked like previously.

He came back to Andie, who patted the ground beside her. "Sit."

He did, still slightly awkward with his prosthesis.

"Have you designed a lot of houses?"

"I'm always designing houses. Not always for clients. But I need to know the budget and what the owners want before I can start a project."

"But if Nelson and Mariah asked you for suggestions, what would you say?"

He relaxed his head against the tree trunk, enjoying the place, the quiet and the company.

"There are constraints, of course. I doubt Nelson and Mariah want a massive place. If they do, they'll have to overcome some of the landscape. Materials would need to be suitable for this climate."

"Of course, but within reasonable parameters, what would you suggest?"

He let his imagination free. "A mudroom, for coming in from the barn. A big kitchen. An informal place. Bedrooms on the second floor, maybe an attic."

Andie paused, as if imagining what he'd suggested. "What would you do the exterior in?"

"Stone is too heavy for what I'm picturing here."

"Brick?"

He shook his head. "Wood siding. A muted shade that would fit with the trees. Maybe even white."

Silence fell. "Not very progressive or avant-garde."

"This isn't the place for it. There aren't any breathtaking views, and no one is coming here to be impressed. You said Mariah grew up on a boat, and now she wants to stay put. I think she'd want something that looks like home, like you'd see in a movie. Something to match what she'd dreamed of."

Andie nodded. "I think you're right."

"I don't know Nelson, so maybe I'm wrong..."

"I don't think the guy who rescues horses here is looking for a showplace. Right now, what he wants is to make Mariah happy."

Trevor grew up in the city. This sense of space and quiet, of time passing slowly, and of peace was not something he was used to. His first instinct was usually to compare places to the city and note how the city was superior. Sitting here, that idea took too much effort. He enjoyed just...being.

After a comfortable silence, Andie looked over at him. "Have you ever imagined your dream home? The one you'd want for yourself?"

The corner of his mouth hitched up. "Of course. I'm sure you have, as well."

Andie gave a noncommittal shrug. Didn't matter. He knew he was right.

She shot a glance his way. "What's yours like?"

He stared up into the leafy bower overhead. "When I was a kid, I imagined castles and mansions where I'd have rooms for toys and books. I'm pretty sure I used to have rooms for candy, as well. When I got older, I always focused on the interior, because there's not a lot of space for exteriors in the city. Everything was sleek and smooth and modern, maximizing the space and feeling bigger than it was."

He heard Andie sigh. "I'm going to have to get used to the city, I expect."

He looked over at her. She was gazing up at the leaves, as well.

"Do you want to live in the city?"

She shrugged. "I always thought so. I imagined a place of my own. Not too big, but something I didn't have to share. Our house was always full of people, and during the day, clients and the crew were often there. Now it's hard to imagine giving up space and quiet." Andie paused, as if she'd surprised herself with what she'd just said.

"Not every city is like New York. You might find another place where you can live outside the city but still be close enough for school and work."

"I guess. If you weren't in New York and had space, what kind of place would you design for yourself?"

Trevor knew there were other things he could be doing, though not necessarily should be doing right now, but he was content sitting under a tree talking about dream homes. It didn't matter what had happened on that last job in New York or what Violet had felt.

His time here in Cupid's Crossing was limited, but if it wasn't...

"I'd first want a lot with a view. A river, a ravine, something. And I'd want to open up part of the house to invite that in."

"Open space, inside and out."

"Mmm-hmm," Andie murmured. "That sounds like more of a showplace."

Trevor pursed his lips. "No, that's not what I want. Think un-painted wood, warm colors—a place that welcomes in people as well as the outdoors."

"Really?" There was no missing the skepticism in her voice. He held in a smile. She was right.

"Okay, I wouldn't want that many people. But I'd want a place that could be comfortably lived in." There was a pause. It was time to flip the script. "What about you?"

He watched her face as she puzzled it out. Her brow creased and then smoothed. There was a ghost of a smile, and she bit her lip.

"Peaceful. That's what I'd like. A creek, maybe, instead of a river. But the open spaces, if they aren't cold and empty, sound good. We're all squished in small rooms at our place."

Trevor felt a warm flutter in his chest. It was silly. They were talking about a home that would never exist. He wasn't building a place here, and Andie wasn't, either. But he liked that she embraced his vision.

Quiet and peaceful. That sounded like a great base for a home. Not that there wouldn't be noise from people living in it, but it would be an oasis from the rest of the world. That was it. A safe place to recharge to face the world again.

Something inside clicked. That's what he wanted. When he got his life back together, he needed that kind of space. But not an oasis for one.

For so long after Violet, he hadn't opened his mind to the possibility of having someone again. Surely there was someone out there who would be interested in an introvert who could play darts and had a prosthetic leg.

The sun was warm on his face as the trees rustled overhead. This town, where he'd come because he didn't have other options, was providing him with a safe haven while he finished healing.

This year in a small town was helping more than his reputation.

CHAPTER EIGHTEEN

ANDIE HAD BEEN counting down till her vacation in Florida, date set now that Denise had given birth to twin girls. Work on the mill was going smoothly. With Trevor looking over everything, making her more careful, things were going almost scarily well.

There were occasional hiccups. Supplies that came late. Inspections that lagged. But she'd built a buffer into her time budget, and they were still on track. They might finish just before the end of October, but she and Trevor had agreed not to mention it to Mariah again in case she planned a Halloween event that might need to be delayed.

The biggest challenge had been opening up the back wall so that the large event space was lit up and offered a view over the stream and hillside. Again, they'd planned and checked things over and over, and it had gone off without a hitch. The big glass doors and new larger windows were installed with shutters for protection and to shut out the exterior as needed.

Andie thought that even Trevor was almost relaxed. They'd worked together on the trickiest part of the whole renovation and it had gone perfectly.

Perfectly enough that she was willing to leave Joey in charge while she went away. All the supplies were ordered, the plans of what needed to be done while she was away were laid out, simple and easy. It was a perfect opportunity for Joey to step up and show he could lead the company.

Maybe she should knock on wood, in case it was too perfect.

Now, just before Andie left on her vacation, Abigail and Mariah were standing in front of the new glass doors in the mill, obviously impressed. Andie showed them how the doors opened.

The exterior area in front of the doors, where they planned a patio, wasn't finished yet, but that was a fairly simple project, especially compared to the work involved in installing the doors.

"You've done an incredible job," Abigail said.

"This is even better than I'd pictured." Mariah had accepted the verdict on the farmhouse without a flinch. Andie wasn't sure exactly what she'd said to Nelson, but Trevor would be meeting with them while she was away to discuss designing a new place for the two of them.

"What is the crew doing while you're in Florida, Andie?"

Abigail might not micromanage the project, but she kept up on everything.

"There's the patio here and out back behind the kitchen. We also want to get the portico done before there's any chance of bad or cold weather, and the exterior cladding."

Abigail smiled. "Yes, the unpredictable autumn weather."

"Then we can wrap up the finishes inside and should be done about when we'd hoped."

Abigail nodded. "Give Denise my congratulations when you see her. And try to enjoy yourself, as well. You've worked hard and deserve a vacation."

It was true. She did deserve a break. But while she was looking forward to seeing Denise and spending some time in a bathing suit rather than a hard hat, she was also looking forward to coming back.

She didn't want to consider all the reasons why that might be. Why she was reluctant to go. But she couldn't banish the image of the man she'd been working with.

Abigail and Mariah left, which left just her and Trevor.

"Are you worried about leaving Joey in charge?" he asked.

He must have picked up on something.

"It's stupid, I know. He's overseen most of the work on the

B and Bs and the demolition of the house at Nelson's farm. But I've always been close by."

The corner of Trevor's mouth quirked. "You know I'll still be here."

"True." It was an indication of how far they'd come that they could joke about this.

They'd become…friends since that day out at the farm. They worked together weekdays and played together at darts night and trivia night with the rest of the crew. They had fallen into a routine of working on photos and video of the mill renovation together, and on the weekends, Andie showed Trevor some of the area, especially any interesting buildings.

He watched her, eyes keen behind his glasses.

"I thought you'd be a little more excited about taking a vacation."

She was, really. "I am. I mean, Florida, my best friend, not wearing a hard hat…"

"Those are all good things."

She nodded. "It's just…when Denise was here, we talked about what I was going to do after the mill is done. Soon it'll be time for Joey to take over Kozak, and for me to finally do what I want to do. I'm supposed to make plans for college."

She should be more excited about it. Instead, it felt like one more chore.

"Are you having second thoughts?"

She parsed his response for meaning. Was he judging her? Doubting her?

"I don't know. It's been so long, it's like I've forgotten how to be excited about it."

Trevor stood in front of her. "Is this a temporary, distracted loss of excitement, or is the excitement completely gone?"

She blinked at him. "How could it be gone? It's my dream. Those first years, when it was so difficult to keep the company going, I imagined attending classes and learning how to design beautiful buildings. I had sketches I worked on when I had free time. That got me through."

Trevor was still watching her, eyes intent behind the glasses. "I don't know if your dream is gone, but maybe it's…changed?"

"Yours hasn't."

He nodded. "That's true, but not everyone wants to be the person they imagined themselves being back when they were eighteen."

Andie paused. Those words hit something inside. She'd grown a lot in the last decade, almost fifteen years. Had her dreams changed? Really? Or was she just giving up? She couldn't imagine being a quitter. She'd never backed down from a challenge.

"Do the dreams really change, or do those people just give up?"

Trevor shrugged. "Some may give up. Some may have to acknowledge their dreams aren't realistic. Some may achieve their dreams and find they aren't what they wanted. And some people change, and their dreams don't fit them anymore."

The last sentence had a trace of bitterness. Was he thinking of his dream of his own architecture firm? Or of the fiancée who couldn't accept how he'd changed?

"How do you know if you've changed or just given up?"

"Maybe that doesn't really matter. Maybe the important thing is that you find what the dream is for the person you are now."

The conversation was approaching deep waters, and Andie wasn't sure she was ready to swim. She forced a smile.

"So you're telling me I should reconsider getting that Oscar?"

"I'm sorry." Trevor stepped back. "This isn't my business."

Andie hadn't meant to offend him. She'd wanted to change the subject because of her own fear, not because she didn't appreciate and value what he was saying. Those words of his would have an impact on what she would decide to do.

She reached out and grasped his wrist. "No, I'm sorry. I appreciate what you said. It's just a little scary to think about big changes like that. I've had a plan for most of my life, and suddenly, I may have the rest of my life in front of me with no idea what to do with it."

He didn't break her hold. "It can be scary. But maybe it can be a little freeing? You don't have those limits anymore. Imagine doing anything you want."

Andie wasn't sure how they'd wound up so close. She could see the flecks of color in his irises, a bit of stubble he'd missed while shaving and that his lips were slightly parted. He was staring at her, and his words, *anything you want*, were circling in her brain. Suddenly, she was kissing him.

And he was kissing her back.

Andie had no idea why they were doing this, but her hands were gripping his T-shirt. She was tightly pressed against him, his arms around her waist, pulling her closer. He turned his head, and the angle was better, and she went up on tiptoe because she'd never had a kiss that felt like this. Like her center was burning while her skin pebbled with a chill that had nothing to do with the temperature.

She didn't know how long they spent kissing, pausing only for breath before meeting lips again. But eventually, they pulled apart, chests heaving, eyes wide, and reality slipped back in.

Trevor stepped back, clearing his throat. His hair was mussed, his shirt showing creases from where she'd gripped it. And his lips— No, she couldn't look at his lips, swollen with their kisses, without wanting to launch herself at him again. Andie dropped her gaze.

"I'm sorry—" she started. What had come over her?

He was staring at her, his brow furrowed. "We can't... We can't do this. Not when we work together."

Heat rolled over her cheeks, spreading down her neck. "I know. I won't do it again. I'm sorry."

Trevor was in front of her somehow, hand on her chin, tilting her head up. "It was incredible, but we can't be involved, not when we're working the way we are."

Could he not let this go? She was mortified.

"I understand, Trevor. I don't know what happened, but I won't kiss you again."

Her eyes dropped, unable to meet his.

"As long as we know this will never be repeated..." His breath hitched, and suddenly his lips were on hers again, and she wrapped herself tightly against him, determined to enjoy it while she could.

Everything had to end sometime. Even incredible kisses. When they finally pulled away, Andie could feel her lips, swollen, and her legs, shaking as they supported her.

Dusk settled as they left the mill. They didn't break the silence, because there was nothing to say. Andie let Trevor lock the doors, and they each went to their own vehicle.

She didn't know how to speak to him, what to say. The good part was that she was leaving the day after tomorrow. Tomorrow wasn't a workday, so she didn't have to face him.

Hopefully, by the time she came back from Florida, she'd have a better idea of how she felt, and what she might want to do about it.

She remembered his words about dreams, that facing a new one could be freeing. Would Trevor be part of a new dream? The mill would be done in a couple more months.

What happened after that?

"I'm sorry. can you repeat that?"

Trevor found himself using that phrase more often than he ought. He couldn't concentrate like he normally did.

All because of Andie and those kisses.

At first, he'd thought it a good thing that she was in Florida. They needed time and space to get back to their working relationship. He refused to work with someone he was involved with. The risk of trouble was too great. It was just a terrible idea. And yet he couldn't forget the kisses.

It shouldn't have been a problem. It wasn't like he'd never kissed a woman before. He hadn't dated that many women—he was somewhat shy—but he had gone out with women, and he'd been engaged to Violet.

Undoubtedly, it was some combination of forbidden fruit and the friendship he and Andie had developed that made it so...

No, he wasn't thinking about it again.

His phone ringing gave him an excuse to pull his attention from his desperate attempt to follow what Joey was saying about something they were going to do with the portico.

That *something* was exactly what he should be focusing on, since it was part of his job, something that kissing Joey's sister was not.

"Trevor Emerson."

Joey waved and left the trailer, giving him some privacy.

"Trevor, it's Howard. How are things going out in the woods there?"

Trevor relaxed in his seat. A call from Howard was just what he needed. "Things are going well."

Incredibly well.

"Good to hear. Nothing like the last job?"

Trevor's thoughts wandered to Andie again, but he shook it off. "No, this contractor is honest and doing good work."

"But you're keeping an eye on him, right?"

"It's a *her*, not a *him*, and I am."

Howard whistled. "Let me guess, fifty and able to bench-press you if she wanted."

There was silence as Trevor tried to find words to explain Andie. "Um, not fifty."

Howard cleared his throat. "So, she's pretty?"

Trevor was defensive. "Yes, but she knows her job."

"Just don't take anything for granted."

"Thank you, but I of all people understand the importance of keeping on top of what my contractor is doing."

Howard sighed. "I'm just worried about you."

Trevor rubbed his eyes under his glasses. "I know. I'm sorry. I hope with some time people can see me without that accident being the first thing they think of."

"You're right. And I actually called you about a job."

Trevor's mood lifted. He was hoping the finished mill would be good for his reputation, but it wasn't done yet. He hadn't had a good prospect in ages. There were some projects here in Cupid's Crossing, and he'd wondered if he should stay a little longer. Going back to New York City was a little daunting.

"My boss has a buddy who's moving to the East Coast and is looking to build a place—big and splashy. He wants to impress everyone. I talked you up, and they want your number."

The light feeling grew.

"I'm not done here for almost two months."

"Guy still has to close on this lot he wants to buy, but he's excited to start, and I've told him you're someone who can design his house and that you'll be a new discovery. Impress his friends that way."

"Then, give him my number."

This was absolutely what he needed, wanted.

"He's going to be in New York next week. Can you meet him there?"

Trevor quickly scanned his calendar.

The portico was going up next week. Joey should be able to handle that. It wasn't as tricky a thing as opening the wall had been.

Trevor had been watching Andie and Joey closely, and everything had been fine. He could miss a few days.

"Sure. I'll be there."

Trevor relaxed in his hotel room. The tension eased out of his shoulders as the day replayed in his head.

The interview with the lead Harold had gotten him had gone well. It wasn't a done deal, but the man, Oscar, had expressed admiration for some of the work he'd done and found the mill project to be quite interesting.

They'd discussed what the property Oscar and his partner were purchasing was like and what they wanted in their home.

They were talking to other architects, but they'd talked to him as if they were already working together, so there was a fair chance he'd get this job. It would be a good one. It would put him back in the middle of things.

He should be a lot happier about it, but New York City felt more busy, noisy and smelly than usual. He'd grown up here, lived here all his life, and now he didn't feel a part of it.

He'd grown accustomed to Cupid's Crossing. The quiet and the space had been new to him, but it had all been a relief. He was slow to make friends, but in Cupid's Crossing, people knew him. They didn't wait for him to reach out. They drew him in. It made him feel a part of the place.

He considered calling someone he knew, maybe even his family, to let them know he was here for the evening. Instead, he sat and watched the dark shadow the room. The person he wanted to talk to was Andie, but that was wrong.

He'd talked to Andie about her dreams and what she might want in the future, but he was at a crossroads, as well. He wanted to keep his own firm. To have the chance to design and implement his vision. He'd never thought about doing that outside New York.

He'd considered the job in Cupid's Crossing a detour. A temporary diversion that he would accept because it would bring him back to where he'd started, to where he belonged.

Now, when he had a chance to return, he wasn't sure he belonged here in the city anymore.

Was it the location? Was he more suited for a quiet place? Or were Andie and those kisses messing up his perceptions? How did he feel about her?

He wouldn't change his future for her, would he?

He shook his head. No, Andie was nice enough. She was one of the best contractors he'd worked with. She took care of her family, sacrificed herself for others, was kind, pretty, could kiss like—

His phone rang, disturbing his train of thought. He was grateful for that until he answered the call and heard what had happened while he was gone.

"Go spend some time at the beach, girl."

Denise had bags under her eyes, mysterious substances all over her shirt, and her hair was partly braided, partly in a ponytail and all a disaster.

"Nope. I've seen what some of those women look like in bikinis, and I can't compete. I'm better off here." Andie leaned over and carefully picked up Twin One from her friend's arms.

"You go have a shower and a nap until these two need you again."

Denise sighed and then shrugged. "I should argue, but I can't. Bless you."

The twins were cute, and when they were asleep, they were totally adorable, but they didn't sleep all the time and not often at the same time. Denise and Don had looked exhausted when Andie arrived a week ago, and despite her assistance, they still did.

Don stumbled in from the kitchen with Twin Two, also mercifully asleep in the baby carrier.

Andie kept her voice low. "Don, I just sent Denise to shower and sleep. Why don't you leave Two with me, and you do the same?"

He shot a glance at Twin Two and gave a longing look at the hallway to the bedrooms.

"I shouldn't leave you."

"Come on. I know these are the two most precious humans on the face of the planet, but I can handle them while they're sleeping.

I can even change diapers. You guys won't let me help at night, and you need to sleep or you're going to fall over."

The torn look in his eyes was almost funny. Then she saw him lose the battle with his manners.

"Thanks, Andie. But call if you need me."

Andie nodded, determined to let them sleep for as long as she could. She was glad she'd come, not because she was getting a beach vacation, but because her friend needed the help.

Denise's mom, Deirdre, had moved from Cupid's Crossing to Florida to be near her grandbabies. Despite that, she was too busy to help much, so the two parents were running themselves ragged.

Twin Two stirred in the carrier. Andie set Twin One down carefully and picked Two up. She rocked her slowly the way Denise and Don did.

"Hey there, cutie. You're not going to cry now, are you? You wouldn't do that to your mom and dad. They need some sleep."

The bleary eyes turned her way. Over the past week, the twins had become accustomed to her voice, and they now accepted her.

Andie stood up and jiggled Two as she walked around the living room. After getting #One and #Two cloth pins and tags to identify each twin, they were now being called by the numbers. Once Denise and Don got sleep, Andie knew they'd be able to decide on names.

"So, Two, can you help me here? I was supposed to talk with your mom, but you've made her too tired. Since that's your fault, you owe me."

Twin Two made faces. Andie sniffed to see if the baby needed another diaper change, but when that was clear, she continued her chat.

"I have a bit of a problem, Two. I don't know what I'm going to do with myself. Now, you're not worried about your future yet, but the time will come. If you help me, I promise I'll help you."

The baby blinked.

"I'm taking that as a yes. So do I finally get those applications in to school to be an architect? Huh?"

She paused, but Two just stared back at her.

"Or should I consider something different?"

The baby blanket was flopping over the baby's face, so Andie used a finger to push it back. Two gripped Andie's finger in a tight hold.

"You think I need to look at other options, right? I think you're on to something. But what should I do? Go to school and see if there's something else I want to do?"

The baby blew bubbles.

"You're right again. That's wasting money. But what else? Should I just keep doing what I'm doing?"

The tiny arms thrashed.

"I'm sorry, Two, but you need to do better than that. I don't know if you're disagreeing or agreeing with me on that one."

The baby yawned.

"Oh, I'm boring you, am I? Nice."

The tiny eyes closed, and the baby drifted off to sleep again.

Andie kept walking.

What if she did keep doing what she'd been doing? Would that be a good life?

She couldn't keep on exactly as she was. If she was staying in Cupid's Crossing and taking on the responsibility of Kozak Construction permanently, she had to find her own place to live. Somewhere totally separate from where her mom and brother lived.

There were a lot of projects being discussed for the new and improved Cupid's Crossing. There would plenty of work for the company. But what about Joey? If she stayed, what would he do? Could they share being in control of Kozak Construction?

Would he want to?

She suspected he might like to be free of that. But this was supposed to be her turn to go. Her turn to chase her dream.

Walking around this house, chaotic as it was, made it obvious to Andie that her dream included this—a home, a spouse, children. She might have to sacrifice that to become an architect if she was starting at this late date.

Did she want to return to school, to start over, to go back to books and classes after having been in charge of her own business for so long?

When she'd stepped up to replace her father, she'd hated it.

Hated not knowing the answers to questions, hated making mistakes, hated the responsibilities.

But that had changed. She knew most of the answers now, and she didn't make mistakes. Responsibility was a burden, but she also didn't have to listen to someone she didn't agree with and do what they told her to do. Being the person making the decisions was part of her now.

She wasn't happy with her life as it was, but that wasn't because of her job. She didn't dread going to work in the mornings, and she didn't escape home the first chance she had.

The part she didn't like was her personal life. She'd been reluctant to move out, since it signified that she was giving up on school. But if she did, if she had her own place, then Cupid's Crossing was a good place to live.

Trevor.

There was a different issue.

She wasn't sure what they were to each other now. Not after the kisses. She couldn't deny she had feelings for him.

Would he be part of her future? With a pang, she realized he wouldn't be. Whether she stayed in Cupid's Crossing or not, she didn't see a future for them. He would go back to New York City, and she couldn't picture herself there. She was used to space, and there wasn't a lot of that in a big city.

If people came to Cupid's Crossing, maybe she could find someone else. Someone who'd like a contractor with an overdeveloped sense of responsibility and a mother who worried too much.

She decided to let the idea percolate, and if she had a chance to talk to Denise before she left, they'd discuss it.

The idea felt good. Cupid's Crossing was going to come back to life, and being part of it held a lot of appeal.

She carefully set down Twin Two, relaxing when the baby stayed sleeping. Andie picked up her phone to check what was going on in the world while the babies slept. Right now, her goal was to give her friends their own time to rest. Nothing she saw was that interesting.

She was starting to doze when the ring of her phone woke her and Twin One. She answered, hoping for a quick call and a chance to settle One down so that Denise and Don could sleep a little longer.

When her mom told her Joey was in the hospital, she knew that wasn't going to happen.

CHAPTER NINETEEN

TREVOR STOOD IN front of the disaster that had been the portico on the mill.

It had collapsed, with Joey Kozak underneath it. Joey was in the hospital. The mill had been taped off while they figured out what had gone wrong.

It was all too familiar.

Accidents happened on work sites. Workers slipped, cut themselves, fell, knocked things over. Since construction sites were full of large materials and tools, those little accidents had consequences. That stuff happened.

A building, or part of it, collapsing? That was different. That meant something had gone wrong with the design or the materials or the process.

It was a small accident in a small town, but something had collapsed with a human underneath, and Trevor had to shove his hands in his jacket pockets to prevent them from shaking.

He couldn't believe it had happened again. He'd been so careful.

He'd been less vigilant lately because of Andie. He'd been thinking too much about her and not enough about the job. Obviously. The evidence was in front of him.

He couldn't give up his dream for her. No matter what she'd done, deliberately or not, the result was another of his projects had a structural problem, and there'd been another serious injury. Thank goodness it hadn't been worse.

There would still be an inquiry. Last time, he'd been in the hospital and hadn't been able to give his side, and he'd been blamed. He wasn't taking the blame this time.

His phone rang. He was sure it would be Andie, and he had no idea what to say to her. But when he checked the name, it was Harold.

He hoped Harold hadn't heard about this. If it got through to these potential new clients... His stomach dropped.

He almost missed the call, between his hesitation and the shaking in his hands, but he managed to say hello before it went to voicemail.

"Trevor, you okay?"

That jolted him. If Harold was asking how he was, then somehow the information was out there. With Trevor's name attached.

"I'm fine. Why are you asking?"

"My boss saw something about a wall collapsing on a construction site in a place called Cupid's Crossing. That's where you are, right?"

Trevor nodded and said yes.

"Is it your site? Who got hurt? My boss is asking, worried about that referral he gave you."

No. Trevor couldn't have this happening again.

"Harold, it's my site, yes. But it's not me. It's something the contractor did. I don't know what. I was in New York meeting those clients, but you can tell them it was a contractor issue."

"Are you serious? How can that happen to you again?"

For a moment, Trevor wondered if it was him. Had he done something?

No. He hadn't done anything in New York, and he hadn't here. He'd gone through those plans over and over again.

This wasn't his fault.

"The contractor is the only local outfit, and the owner insisted on them. The head of the company is out of town, and her brother is in charge. He must have been the one to mess up. He's also the one who was hurt."

"Will he be okay? Was anyone else hurt?"

Trevor's hand clenched the phone. "Word is he's going to make a full recovery, and no one else was involved."

"That's a relief. I'll talk to my boss. Reassure him. Small-town contractor, didn't know their stuff, and you won't work with them again. That should cover it."

Trevor opened his mouth. He was about to say that it wasn't Andie's fault and that he'd happily work with her again. But she wasn't going to stay to run the company, so it didn't matter. He was going back to New York City, and she wasn't.

Harold and his boss wouldn't have any impact on Andie and Kozak Construction here in Cupid's Crossing. He let it go. Right now, he needed to protect his own future.

This wouldn't do any real damage to Andie. And the chances were good that it was Joey's fault. Something obviously had gone wrong, but not on Trevor's watch.

The blame would fall on Joey, not Andie. Andie hadn't taken shortcuts, but she had left Joey in charge. When it was your company, the buck stopped with you. That's what she'd said.

He didn't want to do anything to hurt her. If he'd only stayed here instead of going to New York.

If word of this got back to his client, if they heard it might be his fault, he'd lose that job. He might not ever get another.

And Kozak Construction?

This town would take care of them. It was probably Joey's fault, and that would have some impact, but Andie would be okay. People here loved and trusted her. They didn't feel that way about him.

He filed the necessary reports and met the investigator. He did his best to start the investigation with Joey, what he'd been doing and how.

This time, no one was blaming Trevor first. Of course, that meant they were blaming Joey instead.

Andie was relieved to find a flight home leaving only a few hours after she received the phone call. She didn't know the whole story, but her mother had told her there'd been an accident at the mill, and Joey was in surgery.

Fortunately, the flight was short. Once she landed, her mother assured her that Joey was in recovery. Andie met her at the hospital where she was still waiting for Joey to wake up.

He regained consciousness the next day, and Andie was finally able to get her mother to go home with her.

After some sleep, she managed to pull her focus from worried sister to contractor. That was when she got the details.

Reports needed to be filed within twenty-four hours of the accident. With Joey being hospitalized, that was Andie's job. Since she'd been in Florida, on her way home and then in the hospital waiting to find out if Joey would be alright, Trevor had filed the report.

Trevor had met with the OSHA investigator. At first, she'd felt only relief that her inaction while she was dealing with her family hadn't led to any delays in procedure, but as members of the crew stopped by or called for word on Joey, they also shared what had happened with Trevor and the investigator.

Trevor had immediately placed the blame on Kozak Construction. It was inevitable and understandable, but it still hurt her deeply.

There were a limited number of things that could have caused this, but Trevor had immediately steered the investigator to Kozak Construction.

She understood that he wanted to protect himself after last time. But still. The materials from the supplier could have been defective. That wouldn't have put the blame on either of them, but because of what had happened to him, he'd immediately blamed her company.

She remembered how suspicious and defensive he'd been when he first arrived. But she'd thought they'd learned to trust each other since then. They'd talked to each other, become friends. And then…those kisses. Those kisses hadn't meant that much, it seemed.

He'd told her they couldn't do that, be like that. She wondered how long it had taken before he'd decided she'd kissed him to get away with something. She hoped she was wrong, but she was too afraid that she was right.

She didn't see or talk to Trevor for the first couple of days. She had to deal with work-related things, and she was spending the rest of her time in the hospital. She was there when the investigators came to talk to Joey.

There was a man and woman with laptops and serious expressions. They struggled with how to handle Andie and Joey. Normally, they preferred to interview witnesses without the employer being present. But Andie was the sister of the person injured, and Joey had been the employer at the time he was hurt.

Andie got to stay, but she had to promise to be quiet.

Joey had been alone when the portico collapsed. He explained that he'd gone to look at how it was holding up. There'd been some strong winds. He'd heard a crack, and he didn't remember much after that.

The investigators had already done a lot of work. Undoubtedly, Trevor had helped them find the paperwork relating to the building of the portico.

It was supposed to be a simple job, but… Joey had messed up. It was all too heartbreakingly obvious. There'd been a shortage of what they needed. Joey had decided to get what he could from a vendor Andie had stopped dealing with. They had promised they had an equivalent product, and Joey had accepted their word. The "equivalent" product hadn't met specs, but waiting for more materials would mean the project would fall behind. Since they were starting to nudge at the top of their budget, he thought it would save there, as well.

Andie bit her lip, but it was hard. She was angry at Joey and disappointed. She didn't understand why he hadn't realized what an obviously bad idea it was.

Joey was pale, but he answered the questions unflinchingly. Andie was just grateful her mother wasn't present. Andie had relieved her of watch duty and sent her to catch up on some sleep.

The investigators finished by asking Andie questions. She had some documents to send through to them, but the conclusion was foregone at this point.

The investigators had just left when their mother returned. Andie couldn't hold her tongue any longer.

"Joey, I'm sorry, but what made you think you could ignore the specs we had?"

"He's in no condition for you to grill him like this, Andie."

Her mother put a hand on his shoulder, standing between her two children.

"Mom, if he could talk to the investigators, he can talk to me."

"He needs his rest. You're upsetting him."

Andie counted to ten. "He made a stupid decision, one that put him in the hospital, and one that messed up our biggest job and damaged our company's reputation."

"He's too young for this."

"I took over the company when I was younger than him. He's never going to grow up if you don't let him accept some responsibility for what he does."

"I almost lost him."

"And I want to make sure he understands so that he doesn't do anything like this again."

They were arguing in whispers.

"Of course he won't."

"Yes, well, I didn't think he'd be that idiotic to begin with, but here we are."

"It's not his fault."

"Mom, the investigators were just here. It is *totally* his fault."

Her mother burst into tears, and Andie walked out before she said anything more. She leaned against the wall just outside the room, struggling to control her temper.

"She's right, Mom," she heard Joey say.

Sniffles. "You just rest. Forget about that."

"Jeez. I'm telling you she's right. I thought, I dunno, thought I'd impress everyone by finding a shortcut. It's my fault it happened."

"Shush, now. You probably hit your head and didn't know it."

"I didn't hurt my head. Andie's right. I made a mistake. I don't think I'm cut out for this. When I get out... I'm going to leave."

"What? You can't leave." Her mother's voice was shocked.

"Why would I stay? Everyone is gonna know it was my fault. Smitty was saying he could get me a job in Syracuse. Maybe I'll go there."

"You can't leave me, Joey!"

"I'm not *leaving* you. I'm just finding a job somewhere else. There's nothing else to do in Cupid's Crossing."

"But what if something happens?"

"Something just did happen, Mom. And it's my fault. You need to get your own life, you know?"

"You're my life. You and your siblings."

"We're adults now. You have to let go."

Andie stepped back into the room. "You're upsetting Mom, Joey."

Her brother was sitting up in his bed, eyes flashing, cheeks flushed. Their mother was on the verge of more tears. For the first time since the investigators had shown up, he met Andie's gaze.

"I'm done tiptoeing around everything because we can't upset Mom. I want to live my life, and I can't do it here. I'm sorry, Andie, but I'm not you. I can't run the company, and I'm tired of trying. It's not what I want. It's never been what I wanted."

The words resonated. It was what she'd suspected.

"Mom, I think we should let Joey rest. You're right, we're upsetting him."

Andie managed to lead their mother away.

"It's just the accident, Andie. He'll be back to himself soon."

Andie would normally agree with her to protect her. But denying what was obvious hadn't helped with Joey, and she needed to prepare her mother. She wouldn't be surprised if Joey did what he'd said.

He needed to find himself, and he wasn't going to in Cupid's Crossing.

"Mom, you need to be ready in case he does leave."

"He can't! You're leaving, and I'll have no one."

Andie sat her down in a seat in the waiting room. "Whether we move out of town or not, you still have us. We're still your children. But Joey is right that you need to have your own life. I may not go away to school, but if I stay in Cupid's Crossing, I'm going to get my own place. I need my own life, too."

Her mother's mouth was open, eyes blinking back tears. "You'd move out? But how will I know if you're safe?"

Andie grabbed her mother's hand. "Mom, you need to see someone. A counselor or a therapist. You worry too much. After Dad died, you said you could handle things on your own, but you're not.

"I understand that you were worried about us after Dad, but it's been a long time. We're grown up now, and you should have your own things to worry about, your own life to live. Maybe you just need a bit of help so you can let Joey and me go."

Her mother was still crying when they got home. Andie desperately needed to talk to someone, but she didn't know anyone to call. Denise was overwhelmed with the twins. Her siblings were all far away, except for Joey in the hospital.

She couldn't talk to Trevor, because he was one of the problems. She had no idea what she was going to face in the morning when she got to work. She was so anxious about what would happen tomorrow that she couldn't settle down to do anything.

She got in her truck, drove out of the yard and found herself at the mill. She stopped just inside the driveway.

There was a pile of rubble in front of the mill—the remains of the portico. They'd have to clear that away. They'd be behind schedule and over budget.

Her mind started scheduling, budgeting, seeing how they'd get things done. They'd have to restock on materials, and they'd need to do it fast.

She needed to talk to Abigail. Abigail was a smart businesswoman, and Andie was sure she'd give Kozak a chance to make up for this. Abigail knew the company was important to the town, and Abigail knew Joey. Kozak would bear the additional costs, and Andie would commit to finishing the project as they'd planned.

Joey was not going to take over the company. Andie would need to remain here if the company was to stay alive, and she was okay with that.

More than okay. She wanted this.

She'd find her own place here in Cupid's Crossing instead of waiting to start her life when she left for school. She was used to being the boss, and she enjoyed her job. She'd embrace that now and start making the life she had the life she wanted. The essentials were all here—work she enjoyed, people she knew, space and community.

It wouldn't include Trevor, and that brought a stab of pain. But the incident with the investigation had proven that he wasn't a part of her community. He'd put himself first. He needed his reputation untainted so he could return to New York City and live his dream life.

Despite the kisses, they didn't have any bond, not like she'd hoped. No feelings, no connection, no relationship. No future.

How could she be disappointed? She'd built up castles out of sand. But somehow, it still gutted her.

She hoped Trevor didn't think she was going to make any presumptions based on their kisses. No, they were business associates, and that was all. She'd make sure to act in such a way that he knew that. It was bad enough that she had to apologize for her brother's behavior. She didn't need any "talk" where he explained to her that they were only coworkers.

She might be ready to make Kozak her career now, but these next few weeks were going to be bad.

Trevor got to the site while it was still dark, an hour before there was a chance anyone else would show up. He wanted to be inside, behind his desk, laptop shielding him, before he saw Andie.

He owed her an apology. He'd been too quick to jump to conclusions. He'd been right but also wrong.

It *was* Joey.

Trevor had carefully listed the specs for all the materials for the mill, including the portico. The supplier had been short on what they needed, and Joey had accepted an inferior product from another supplier.

Trevor looked at the paperwork and was horrified at the laxity. It was obvious to him that the substitution would never have worked. He was sure Andie would have known, as well.

It all came out when the results of the investigation were announced. This time, Trevor wasn't blamed. There'd be no blot on his record.

He should be relieved. He'd done nothing wrong, but there was a lot of guilt behind the relief. He had lashed out and blamed Kozak Construction before any of this was known. He hadn't said anything that was wrong. He'd been justified and correct in assessing the problem. Harold told him his boss had passed on word to the prospective clients.

He shouldn't feel guilty. But he did. He'd left Cupid's Crossing to see a potential new client after he'd told Andie he'd be here with Joey. If he had stayed, this wouldn't have happened.

His job wasn't to babysit Joey, but he'd known Joey wasn't reliable the way Andie was. Then he'd blamed Joey first thing. That kept him awake at night and away from the people he'd come to know here in Cupid's Crossing.

He hadn't heard a word from Andie or any of the Kozaks. Work on the site was halted, so he didn't need to go to the mill. He didn't want to be with anyone. He was afraid to see blame coming from the people around town, people he'd come to know and like. Last time, even those who knew him well had turned away from him. What could he expect in this small town?

He wasn't one of their own.

The site had been cleared, so they could resume work. He had to face the crew he'd been working with. And Andie. Joey wasn't out of the hospital yet, so it would be Andie.

He hadn't tried to reach her, and she hadn't tried to reach him. That said it all.

He pretended to bury himself in work, but he was listening for the sound of her truck. When he finally heard the rumble of tires, he found his hands clenching, his palms sweaty.

Her truck door slammed shut. He knew that heavy thump. He heard footsteps heading to the front of the mill.

More vehicles pulled in, and greetings were exchanged. He couldn't hear the words, but he could imagine there were questions about Joey and how he was doing. Questions about the mill and the job. He heard her voice, and he imagined she was assigning responsibilities.

Was she avoiding him?

There were footsteps on the steps to the trailer. He woke his laptop and focused his gaze on his screen. The door opened. His posturing was in vain, because he couldn't resist looking up.

For a moment, he just looked at her, at the direct gaze he was used to, the hair mussed by the helmet, the familiar work garb. But there was no warmth in her gaze today, and he shivered.

Right. He'd done that.

He opened his mouth, but she was quicker than he was.

"I apologize for what Joey did. Kozak will bear the cost of redoing the work, and it will be done right. I've told the crew you'll want to oversee everything they do, and they understand. They're putting in some extra hours, so you may want to hang around to make sure they do it correctly."

Trevor knew how inviting someone in to micromanage the work she was doing would cost her. And surprisingly, he didn't feel the obsession to do so. Joey might have taken a shortcut, but he knew Andie wouldn't. He trusted her. He knew that now, too late.

He interrupted before she could continue. "I owe you an apology, as well. I'm sorry, I shouldn't have immediately blamed Kozak. I'm a little wary after the last time, but that was wrong of me."

Her expression didn't soften. "You *were* right. We failed to do our job. I'll make sure we don't make any additional mistakes."

"I know—"

Andie turned and left the trailer, heading outside. When he stood and looked out a window, she was working with her crew, making up for what her brother did.

He had the urge to go out and pitch in, as well. But he stopped himself.

He could picture too well the rejection, being told he wasn't needed. Wasn't wanted. He wasn't part of this company or this town.

Somehow, even though he'd not been at fault this time, he was still on the outside. That appeared to be his destiny.

He left at noon. He couldn't stand being alone in the trailer, sure Andie wouldn't do the work she needed to do in there if he was around.

No one said anything to him.

The next day, Andie did stay in the trailer to work, but she didn't talk, and she gave monosyllabic replies to his attempts to speak to her. He overheard her tell someone on the crew that she wouldn't be at darts night because she was going to see her brother. He stayed in the trailer until everyone was gone, and he didn't go to darts night, either.

He was at home, washing the dishes from his lonely meal when he heard a knock on his door. For a moment, he felt his heart lift. Maybe it was Andie. Maybe they could talk and somehow work this out.

He opened the door eagerly.

His smile fell. It wasn't Andie. It was Abigail Carter. There was no warmth in her expression, so it obviously wasn't a social call. She was going to fire him, even though he'd done nothing wrong. The unfairness burned inside him, and his voice was tight as he invited her in.

"Would you like a drink?"

Abigail shook her head. "Let's get to the point of this visit."

Trevor indicated a seat and was somewhat surprised when Abigail sat down. She folded her hands in her lap and looked at him with a frown. He was reminded of how his high school English teacher had looked at him when he'd gotten the theme of Macbeth wrong.

"Why do you think I'm renovating the mill?"

Just like in school, he attempted to work out why she was asking such an obvious question. "For the romance initiative. You need an event venue."

"And what is the purpose of all this effort? In case you wondered, I do *not* need the money."

He hadn't thought she did.

"As a family legacy?"

She snorted, a sound he hadn't expected from her.

"I've changed the name of the town from Carter's Crossing to Cupid's Crossing. It's not for my family name.

"The legacy I want for this town is for it to be alive. Growing and vibrant. And that's what this romance initiative is all about."

She paused, as if to make sure he understood. He nodded.

"We're a small town. We know each other, and we look out for each other. We may seem gossipy or nosy, but it comes from a place of caring. Well, most of it. Like everywhere else, we have people here who aren't good people. We know who they are, and we work around them, and if we can encourage them to change, we do it. And possibly overdo it."

There was another pause and another nod from Trevor.

"I know you had a problem on your last job. Your reputation was damaged, through no fault of your own. This project was a chance for you to reestablish yourself. I was happy to provide that opportunity, because you are an excellent architect and would never otherwise consider working here. I thought—no, I *hoped*—

you would appreciate that this community is more like a family than a band of cutthroats.

"You were unjustly accused of something when you were unable to defend yourself. I presumed that would make you more understanding of others who might find themselves in trouble. I was wrong."

Trevor wanted to argue. To defend himself again. After all, Joey *had* been responsible, not Trevor.

But Trevor hadn't known that when he first reacted. He'd wanted to protect himself, and he hadn't considered the harm he'd do someone else. He understood that now. He just wanted to know how badly he'd messed things up.

"Are you firing me, or would you rather I resign?"

Abigail frowned at him. "I certainly don't want to fire you, and I didn't think you were a quitter."

Trevor wasn't sure what she wanted. She was a couple of steps ahead of him, and he was tired of being flat-footed.

"I'm happy to finish my obligations here." He spoke carefully. "Did you come here only to express your displeasure, since you don't wish to end my involvement with the mill?"

Abigail sighed, and her expression was sad. "It seemed to me that you were finding your footing in this community. I spoke to you about turning my home into an inn, and there are other growth opportunities here. I'd hoped you might consider staying for a while."

For a moment, Trevor thought the ground had tilted under his feet, and he checked that nothing had fallen. But it wasn't a physical jolt.

Stay in Cupid's Crossing? Why did that thought suddenly excite him more than this big home he had a chance of designing back in the city? But Abigail was talking about hope in the past tense.

"You've changed your mind." His voice was flat. The tilting was gone. The ground was stable, and his future…was exactly as it had been.

"Honestly, I don't think Andie would work with you again after the mill job is done."

He held back from saying he'd been right, that Joey had screwed up. Because the problem now wasn't about blame.

He understood that. This was about community. About working together. Finding out what was the truth and what was the best thing to do rather than immediately saying it wasn't his fault, as if he were a child being accused of misbehaving.

"You're right about that." Andie had been doing her best to avoid him while they were still working on the mill together.

Abigail stood. "It's unfortunate. Lately, we've been reclaiming people in this town, letting them show that they've grown and matured. You are, of course, welcome to stay through the end of the year, even after the mill is done, but I'll understand if you wish to leave earlier."

Trevor stood, followed her to the door and closed it after her. He hadn't been fired, not officially, but he felt just as bad as if he had been.

CHAPTER TWENTY

ANDIE WAS DOING her best to avoid Trevor. The first day back at work, she stayed out with the crew, helping to remove the rubble of the former portico. She had to be in the trailer the next day to track down materials to redo the work, but she'd done her best to ignore the man at the other end of the on-site office.

The trailer had never felt so small.

On the third day, he surprised her by joining her and the crew as they unloaded some of the new materials she'd managed to track down and expedite delivery on.

"Excuse me."

His voice wasn't loud, but as the nearest workers to him turned, the next looked to see what was going on. There was eventually silence as they all watched him.

He cleared his throat. "I wanted to apologize to you. On my last job, there was an accident and an injury. I was blamed by the contractor, though my work was cleared later. Because of that, I was too quick to react to what happened here. Before that happened, this job had gone as smoothly as any project I've worked on, and that's down to Andie and your hard work.

"I had some concerns that this project might be too much of a challenge for you, and I was wrong. I appreciate how you've pulled together to make up for the lost time. I have every confidence we'll finish up the project, and it will be great. So, um, thanks and sorry."

Trevor turned and almost fled to the trailer. The crew looked at each other and at Andie.

She shrugged. "We have a job to finish up, so let's get it done."

It was nice what he'd done. She knew the crew felt betrayed, just like she did. But she refused to let herself soften. The apology was one thing. That didn't mean he'd trust her or her company again.

She needed to keep that wall between them up, because there would be no more kisses, no more cozy discussions. She didn't need to get any more attached to Trevor. She was already more attached than was wise.

The next day, Mariah arrived. For a moment, Andie shot a look at Trevor, but he looked as surprised as she felt. Then she remembered they weren't a team now, and she needed to ignore him.

"Andie, Trevor, do you have a minute?"

Andie nodded, and Trevor shoved his laptop aside. "What is it, Mariah?"

"This is probably the worst time to ask, but do you have any idea when the mill will be done?"

Andie stilled, hating that Mariah had broached the topic that sat between Trevor and her, a landmine they couldn't discuss.

"The crew has been working hard to redo the portico." Trevor filled the momentary silence. "The last projections I saw had the mill ready about the third or fourth week in November, but that does include a lot of variables."

Andie had kept posting paperwork to their shared drive. She'd shot photos and video and posted them there, as well. Things they would have discussed in person prior were now all handled digitally. Trevor had been keeping up.

Of course he had.

Mariah turned to look at Andie, and she nodded. She was determined that the job would be done, no matter what, by the end of November, if she had to work 24/7 herself. Trevor could be back to his real life before Christmas.

"I don't want to pressure you, and I have a plan B if something comes up, but it sounds like I could tentatively plan something for mid-December in the mill?"

"That should work. Knock on wood. Dare I ask what you're planning?"

"Remember I'd mentioned a possible wedding? A Christmas wedding? And no, it's still not mine."

Andie could imagine what a great job Mariah would do. The mill would look beautiful, and since this town was now Cupid's Crossing, what better event than a wedding to kick off the new event center?

"Should I ask who's getting married then?"

Mariah grinned at her. "I need to tell the happy couple first."

Andie laughed, for the first time since her return from Florida. "That's probably a good idea. It's someone local then?"

Mariah held a finger to her lips. "Thanks, guys. That's all I wanted to know. Like I said, I have a backup plan, but I'd like to have the first event here be something the town can all be part of, and something that will look really good on the website."

She turned with a wave and left.

Andie knew whose wedding Mariah was planning. There were only two engaged couples in town, and one of those was Mariah and Nelson.

She wondered if Rachel and Ryker knew what was coming their way.

Andie was surprised when Abigail stopped by the house one evening. Andie welcomed her in, since her mother was flustered. The Carters didn't normally visit with the Kozaks.

"You're looking good, Marion," Abigail said.

Abigail was right. After the argument with Joey, her mother had finally started talking to a therapist. She hadn't been going that long, but Andie was getting fewer frantic requests for her location. Her mother had also joined a committee at church. It was the first time she'd been involved outside the family since her husband died. They were small steps, but they were having a big impact.

When Andie told her mother she was looking for a place of her own after Christmas, her mother had fled to her room. After, though, she'd come out and promised to help Andie furnish the new place.

Joey would be home from the hospital soon, and her mother would have him to care for, but Andie wasn't sure Joey would be staying long. At least her mom should be able to handle it better now.

"Marion, I was hoping to tempt you into helping out on the romance committee after everything is settled with Joey."

Considering that Joey had caused the accident, Andie thought Abigail was being more than generous.

Her mother's eyes were wide. "I'd be happy to help."

"I'm pleased to hear that. But for now, I'd like to talk to Andie."

Andie nodded and led the way to the construction office. She'd known at some point that she was going to need to talk to Abigail.

Andie had called her, but Abigail had promised to speak to her later. Later was now.

She didn't think Abigail would fire them from the mill project, but she might not wish to work with Kozak again, and that would make it difficult for the company. Abigail carried a lot of influence in this community.

"This has nothing to do with the accident. Or at least, nothing directly." Abigail opened the discussion after settling herself in a chair.

"We're absorbing all the additional—"

Abigail held up a hand, so Andie stopped.

"I know. I also understand what happened, and as long as Joey will be supervised until such time as he's able to take this kind of responsibility again, I have no qualms about working with Kozak Construction in the future. But perhaps I need to ask if Kozak Construction will still be operating here in Cupid's Crossing."

Andie gripped the arms of her chair. Abigail wasn't following the script she'd expected, but unsurprisingly, she was going directly to the heart of the matter.

"It wasn't much of a secret that you'd hoped to go to school after the mill is done."

Andie nodded but remained silent.

"You've certainly earned the opportunity to fly the nest and stretch your wings."

For the first time, Andie tried to put her feelings into words. "My wings have been pretty well stretched here, heading up this company."

A slight smile tugged at Abigail's mouth. "Was it enough of a stretch to change your plans?"

Andie pulled in a breath. "It was. Mom has been getting some help, and I'm going to move to my own place in the new year. I want to stay here and run the company. Permanently. If you haven't lost confidence in us, that is my plan."

Now the smile on Abigail's face was complete. "I'm very pleased to hear that. There's going to be a lot of work in the immediate future here, and I'm pleased to have Kozak Construction available."

That feeling fluttering in Andie's stomach was relief. Joey's irresponsibility hadn't harmed the company, and she could continue a job she'd grown to love. One that gave her satisfaction, not just by doing good work but by helping to keep the community thriving.

"I had a meeting with Mr. Emerson."

Suddenly, Andie wasn't feeling so light anymore. Her feelings about Trevor were many and confused.

He'd hurt her, hurt more than just her professional pride. She understood that he'd be defensive after what he'd been through. Lashing out without proof had been bad, but he had apologized to the crew for that.

This hurt was personal.

She'd thought he trusted her. That they'd become friends. She'd thought their kisses had promised there was potential for something more in the future when they weren't working together.

But he hadn't trusted her. He hadn't even talked to her before he'd placed all the blame on Kozak. And as the head of Kozak, on her. She'd put up a reserved wall of politeness and wariness between them. She wasn't opening herself up to any more hurt.

She suspected that when he left, it was going to hurt badly anyway. Still, she braced herself for whatever Abigail was going to say.

"I let him know that there's no chance of him continuing to work here on future projects if he can't work with our local construction company."

Future projects? What was Abigail talking about? "But he's going back to New York anyway, isn't he?"

Andie was counting the days until he left. She'd told herself she wasn't counting with regret.

Abigail shrugged. "We have projects coming up. I know he's been talking to Mariah and Nelson about the house on the farm. We've also talked to him about converting my house, and Gerry's project. Realistically, I don't think you'll want to work with him again, and Kozak Construction is more essential to Cupid's Crossing than Trevor Emerson. We'll find someone else. Hopefully, someone more congenial."

Andie bit her lip before she said anything about being quite happy with how congenial Trevor was. That had been before.

She rose to her feet when Abigail did and followed her back to the door.

Abigail left, inviting her mother to a planning meeting next week on her way out, and Andie closed the door behind her.

"What did she want?" her mother asked. Abigail had never come to their office before.

"To let me know there's going to be work coming up for the company. She wanted to know if I was staying to keep things going."

Her mother's smile wavered at the corners. "I'm glad you are. Your father would be very proud."

She pulled her mother into a hug. "You're sure Joey won't mind?"

Her mother sighed. "I don't know. But he's not ready."

Andie was. She was ready to claim her life now. She wasn't waiting anymore. She was living it. Now she needed to take the necessary step to make it what she wanted.

Unfortunately, it was going to be a single life for a while.

The Mill looked gorgeous.

Snow had fallen the night before, dusting the ground, and everything was white and fresh, as if the weather had been specially ordered for this day.

Rachel and Ryker's wedding day.

Rachel had been the town's good girl, Ryker the bad boy. He'd come back after serving in the Air Force and had become a town asset.

Rachel had learned to stand up for herself with his help while learning to ride a motorcycle. It was a story Andie would never have believed. But after that proposal at the wedding in July, it was all too real.

There was greenery and lots of red, candles and mistletoe. Mariah had managed to hit winter and romance without detouring too much into Christmas.

The wedding service had been held at the church where Rachel's father was pastor, and the reception was at the Mill, as it was now officially called. And like Dave and Jaycee's wedding, it was a town-wide event.

Mariah had arranged transportation for guests from the town park, since the parking lot at the Mill wasn't large enough to hold every vehicle in town. Andie hadn't been at the service. She'd come straight to the Mill, parked at the rear and walked through the building again, just to enjoy the results of a successful job. This building represented a future for Cupid's Crossing. It was a visible symbol of its new life.

The kitchen was busy. There were professional caterers from Oak Hill as well as offerings from the town. It wasn't a sit-down meal, but the smells Andie encountered as she passed the doorway made her stomach growl, and she placed a hand on her tummy to calm it.

The bathrooms were spotless. In the main space, long tables near the back were waiting for food, while high tops were scattered through the rest of the room so that people could mingle while enjoying the food and beverages.

A large cloakroom near the doors already had some high school students waiting to handle the coat check. There was a grouping of photos of Rachel and Ryker in one corner and a place for presents to be set next to it.

The shutters were open on the glass doors they'd installed, and the hillside above looked like a Christmas card, with trees and outcrops dusted with snow.

Cupid's Crossing was open for business.

Three hours later, the official part of the reception was winding down. Rachel and Ryker were leaving for a weeklong honeymoon and would return for the holidays. Andie ducked away from the bouquet toss, and later, she saw Mariah carrying the bride's bouquet.

The town saw Rachel and Ryker off and then settled in to celebrate until they were kicked out.

Abigail was present, with Mariah's grandfather keeping close to her. Mariah had been busy coordinating all the activity, but somehow she never looked flustered or upset. If this was an indication of how events would go in the future, the town would be a success.

Andie was reluctant to leave. Joey was home, and her mother was helping him while keeping up with her new venture on the town romance committee. Joey's friends were often there, and Andie was unsettled. She blamed it on the fact that she was moving out so soon.

There was nowhere else to go tonight. Families with small children had made their exits, but everyone else was here. The diner was closed. Moonstone's was closed. Everyone was either home or at the Mill.

Andie didn't want to admit she was hesitant to leave the party because of Trevor, but she'd been aware of him all day. He'd never come close to her, but he'd still pinged her radar constantly. Enough that she knew where he was and was careful to keep some distance.

Word was he was leaving after today's party. That Abigail had insisted he stay for this first event, to see the culmination of his— no, *their*—work.

She'd assumed too much and felt too much after a few conversations and some kisses. She had to get over him, and it would be easier to do when he wasn't around.

She was not going to regret his departure. She wasn't. And the only way to keep that promise to herself was if she didn't interact with him.

Enough of this. It was time to go. She'd received kudos from everyone on the work they'd done on the Mill. Couples were dancing, and romance was in the air. There was no reason to stay. Not for her.

She reached into her purse to get her coat-check tag. She turned, and this time it wasn't her radar pinging. Trevor was right there. She shivered and gripped her tag tightly.

"Uh, hi," she said.

She'd prepared a speech before she got here, in case she had the opportunity to talk to him. It was dignified and professional.

But he hadn't come near, and now it was forgotten. Instead, she scanned him, checking his appearance. Did he look tired? Thinner?

She'd never seen him dressed in a suit, and it flattered him. Did he think she looked good, as well? What did it matter, if he was leaving? When he couldn't trust her?

He swallowed. "I hoped to have a word with you."

He'd had lots of time today if he'd really wanted that. She didn't need to listen to any words he had, since she'd forgotten all the ones she had prepared for him. But she couldn't keep up her indignation. This would be the last time she saw him.

She clenched her fingers into her palms so that she didn't reach for him. Despite everything, she didn't want him to hate or resent her. She was obviously stupid.

"Uh, now?"

She wasn't getting any smarter or more literate.

"If you don't mind? We could go upstairs?"

Rachel had changed out of her gown up there, in the rooms set up for that purpose, but they were empty now.

He wanted to talk in private.

She really didn't need to be nervous. There was nothing he could say to throw her off-balance. Not now. The job was done, and he was leaving.

Andie forced her feet to move toward the stairs. Her dress was cocktail length, so there was no problem climbing the steps. She looked over her shoulder, and no one on the main floor appeared to pay them any attention. She heard Trevor following her.

She led the way to the office in the back corner. It had been Abigail's old office, but after the renovations, it was now a smaller room. Just big enough for someone like Mariah to meet clients who wanted to plan events at the Mill. Instead of a desk, there were a couple of chairs and a loveseat with a coffee table in between.

Andie sat in one of the chairs. Her knees were a little shaky. Trevor followed her in and sat on the edge of the loveseat across from her.

She was torn between the urge to fill the silence and another urge to keep her mouth firmly closed. She couldn't say anything stupid if she didn't speak, right?

"I'm sorry, Andie."

Her gaze shot to his. He looked serious. His eyes focused on her from behind his glasses.

She opened her mouth to speak, to tell him he'd already apologized, but he kept going.

"I'm obviously still not over everything that happened back in the city. But you didn't deserve to be hit by my issues. I did to you exactly what was done to me, and I'm embarrassed by that."

"But you were right in the end. It was Joey's fault." She hadn't planned to blurt that out.

"If I'd waited for that to be proven, I wouldn't feel like I betrayed you, betrayed the trust we'd built up. And he didn't do it maliciously or even to benefit himself at my expense. I knew you were out of town, but I didn't stay to be available if a problem came up. That's on me. Joey made a mistake, and he paid for it."

Andie swallowed. "Thank you. I appreciate that."

She did. That acknowledgement helped to soothe her professional pride.

He smiled, but it was a polite lacquer. She hurt, because the real smile was no longer on offer for her. He'd hurt more than her pride. He'd hurt her heart.

He rubbed his hands on his thighs, clearly restless. "I wanted to tell you that before I left. I wasn't sure you'd want to talk to me, so I hope you don't mind I tracked you down here."

No, she didn't mind.

"I don't hate you, Trevor. I was hurt, though. I thought we'd built up trust, and that's not easy. When you reacted like that, it felt personal." She needed to stop talking before she revealed too much.

"I'm sorry I broke that trust. That's why I'm leaving."

Andie frowned. "What?"

He shrugged. "Abigail told me she has to find someone else for the new projects around here."

"But you don't want to stay, not here in Cupid's Crossing? You have everything back in the city."

He lifted a hand, then dropped it. He shook his head. "Not everything. There's more here than I'd realized. But there's no future for an architect when the area's top contractor won't work with him."

Andie wanted to hit a replay button. He couldn't be saying what it sounded like he was saying, right?

"You want to stay? If we could work together, you'd want to stay?"

She tensed, scarcely able to draw a breath. He'd never mentioned staying. Why would he want to?

He didn't speak for a moment, and she felt her cheeks warm.

"I've been considering my options. Whether there's enough opportunities for me here, either, in Cupid's Crossing itself or in the general area around the town. It seems I'm more of a country mouse than I realized. But no one will want to partner with me after what I did."

Really? He'd considered staying here? What could that have meant for them? What could it mean now? Was she brave enough to find out?

"I guess it would depend on whether you would do something like that again. Everyone makes mistakes."

He leaned forward, staring at her intently. "I mean, I forgave Joey, so…"

Wait, she needed to think before saying anything more. Trevor was talking about cooperating on projects together. Nothing more.

"I didn't think you'd even consider that we could get past what I did."

Could she? Would she want to work with Trevor again? She thought of those weeks after they'd gotten past their initial problems, and things had been… Things had been great, actually.

"If I could be sure you trusted me." She couldn't go through that again.

Trevor shook his head. "I've learned my lesson from that. We were a team, and I hurt everyone by only considering myself. I'd felt alone for a long time, so I didn't understand that at first."

She tried to picture a professional future with Trevor going forward. Would they be able to make it a success? Could they get back to where things had been before she left for her vacation?

"Would you want to try? You always talked like the city was where you belonged."

"I did. It's true I never considered anything else. It's an adjustment, going from there to a small town. But I'm not good at getting to know people, and here, people get to know you whether you want them to or not."

A smile briefly warmed her lips. "You have a point there."

"I had no idea that I'd find a place that could accept me, all of me, just as I was. People that would accept me. Maybe a particular person that would."

He examined her face, and she waited. Had he just been talking to make her feel good? Had he made up his mind about his future?

"There's one other thing I damaged, something that doesn't involve Kozak Construction directly. I hurt you. I broke the trust you placed in me. Not as someone you worked with, but personally."

Her breath caught. It sounded like he had made some kind of decision.

"I think I would find it difficult to be here and not have that connection with you anymore."

He was still watching her. There was tension in his neck and shoulders and an anxious expression on his face.

"I, um, I mean, I would...find it hard, too."

"Would you? But is it possible to have it again?"

Andie tried to picture it in her head. Trevor staying here. Working here. Being with her here.

She felt her pulse beating slowly and thickly through her veins. She was aware of every breath, as if time had slowed.

"I think it is possible." Her voice was small.

"You think so? Just think so?"

"I—" She swallowed. "I'd be willing to try."

He jerked as if his body wanted to move but had been stopped. "Can we work together and have something personally going on, as well?"

She raised her brows. "I can handle that, but I don't know if you can."

She watched the expressions play over his face. Worry, confusion, and then...he looked at her and smiled. Not just any smile. A warm, promising smile.

"Maybe you could give me some tips."

Andie stood and walked over to Trevor, reaching her hand

down. He gripped it, and she felt warmth move through her. She tugged and brought him to his feet.

"Here's one," she said and kissed him.

Back in the driveway of the Carter house, Gerald came around the limo and opened the door for Abigail. She let him help her to her feet and led the way to the front door of her home.

Once inside, Gerry took her coat and hung it with his in the hall closet, then he followed her into the living room.

"I'd say the launch of your romance initiative was a success."

Abigail smiled. She raised the decanter, and he nodded.

"I think you're right."

"Mariah tells me that you're going to turn this place into an inn."

Abigail passed him a glass and indicated that he should sit. She picked up her own glass and sat across from him. "I'm fairly certain I will."

His brows lowered. "I bought that property outside of town, the Slade place, for an inn and spa. Are we going to be competitors?"

Abigail smiled. "The town will need both places. We've already got a couple of weddings booked for this summer, and not everyone is willing to stay in a B and B."

Gerry leaned back, looking at her. "Are you going to be an innkeeper then?"

Abigail sat straight and shook her head. "No, I don't think I'm suited for that."

"I don't think you are, either. What are you going to do if your home becomes a commercial enterprise?"

She shrugged elegant shoulders. "I think I've done my part for Cupid's Crossing. With Mariah taking over, the town is in good hands."

"Don't think I've forgotten that you poached her. She was supposed to be here for just a year before she came and worked for me."

Abigail upturned a hand. "But that was her decision."

"Abigail, you may fool many people, but you don't fool me."

"She and Nelson are in love. He'd never be happy in a city, and I think Mariah is quite content here."

He snorted. "Yes, she is. What are you going to do? Last winter at the Valentine's events, you talked about leaving."

She looked into the distance, staring more through than at the painting on the wall. "I think I'd like to travel."

"Travel?"

"I've worked hard. I'm ready to enjoy myself now, to be free of responsibilities."

He quirked up his mouth. "That sounds nice."

"Of course, I'd prefer doing it with a companion."

Gerry put his drink on the table. He leaned forward. "And do you have someone in mind?"

"Let's not be coy, Gerry. You haven't been coming to town just to check up on Mariah. It's time for you to give yourself a break, as well."

He grinned. "People don't tell me what to do, Abigail."

"I'm not people. And it's time you don't get your way on everything."

"I should just pack my bags and run away with you?"

Abigail raised elegant eyebrows. "Don't be silly, Gerry. I'm sure it will be about a year before either of us is ready to go. I've got this house to deal with, and you have your businesses. But I think I'd like to spend next winter somewhere warm."

"How long have you had this planned?"

She shook her head. "I'm not the devious planner you think I am. I'm just looking at our situation and being practical."

Gerry stood up and moved till he was in front of Abigail. "You know, the way I feel about you has never been practical."

Abigail stood up, allowing him to take her hand. "I should hope not."

EPILOGUE

IT HAD BEEN a great year.

Andie had used her college fund to put a down payment on a small home in drastic need of updating, and she spent her free time renovating the house while living in it. It had been a challenge, but Trevor helped, both with the design and with the hands-on work. When the kitchen was being renovated, Andie almost lived at Trevor's. The proximity hadn't been a problem.

The Mill was a resounding success. There had been five weddings there over the summer. Mariah and Nelson were married, but not at the Mill. They'd had a small service in the park on Valentine's Day. Andie thought Nelson was happy about that.

Mariah and Nelson had just moved into the house on the farm that Trevor had designed for them, and that Kozak Construction had built.

Nelson had been concerned that the noise of the construction would bother the horses, but the crew had enjoyed spending time with the animals. One of Nelson's more recent rescues was now the property of—or more accurately, the pet of—one of the Kozak Construction crew.

Abigail was well into the process of converting her home into an inn, and Mariah's grandfather was building a small inn and spa on the old Slade property. Both projects were being handled by Trevor and Andie. They'd decided that when there was trust between them, working together while dating was not actually a problem.

Andie's mom was much better. She'd adapted to Andie moving to her own place, and even to Joey moving out of town. She'd become involved in the planning committees and taken on the bookkeeping for Kozak Construction again, freeing up time for Andie.

The first New Year's after Joey's accident, the family had gathered together one last time. They'd said a final farewell to their father. Andie's mom wasn't going to be attending any New Year's Eve parties, but this year, Andie wasn't spending the night with her family. She was at the Goat with Trevor.

For the first time in years, Andie was looking forward to the night. This past year had been the best she could remember, and she expected more of the same in this new year.

With Trevor.

Her house was almost ready to sell. They'd been discussing another project together but hadn't decided on one yet. Andie was leaning toward a family home. If all went well, maybe it would be one they could stay in. Together. And start a family.

It would be a big step for Trevor. She'd met his family, and they'd been polite, but they would never be close. Andie could see the difference in how they reacted to their two sons. With Trevor living in Cupid's Crossing, they could have a friendly relationship, though Andie did a lot of teeth gritting when they were around.

Trevor had found his true home in a small town well outside New York City. Her mother had practically adopted him anyway.

Trevor was in a strange mood today, though. He'd insisted on bringing his computer bag to the bar, which made no sense. They weren't supposed to be working. Maybe he had a new client he thought he might bump into.

He now ran his firm out of the Kozak Construction office, and while they didn't do every project together, they collaborated on most of them.

The bartender stopped in front of her with a soda for her and a beer for Trevor. Andie frowned. She didn't need to keep up that tradition, not now. The bartender moved on to another customer, and she sighed. She could drink one glass of soda and then get a beer. It was time to start something new.

She picked up the glass and turned to Trevor, but he was digging something out of his bag. She wished he could forget work for one day. She wanted to make this New Year's Eve something new, something happy, something to overshadow the previous ones.

A new start.

He pulled out a roll of paper and laid it on the bar top. She recognized the blue ink. These were blueprints. Another project to work on? Was this something they could do together?

If that was all this was, they could have discussed it at the office. She set down her drink, a little ticked now. This was supposed to be a special night. The anniversary of the first time they met.

He rolled off the elastic and carefully flattened the paper. She leaned over, curious in spite of herself, to see what he'd created, to see the vision in his head traced here so that she could build it in wood and stone and concrete.

It was a house. She scanned the lines, noting things like the elevation and the size. She ran a tentative finger over the letters and numbers he'd carefully inscribed, picturing in her mind what the finished structure would look like.

Two stories, four bedrooms. A fireplace of stone. Gorgeous. She couldn't imagine who in their small town could be building this home.

Oh.

Maybe it wasn't going to be built here. Somewhere else. Maybe this beautiful home, his next project, wasn't one she'd be working on. Was that why he hadn't showed it to her till now? How soon would he have to leave? And why did he have to do this now? This day had been a bad day for so many years. Did he think she wouldn't mind if he added more disappointment to it?

She'd hoped he'd be here in Cupid's Crossing to work on flipping a house with her.

She kept her face tilted downward, determined not to show any feelings, any hurt.

"It's beautiful. You've done an excellent job."

Her voice was steady, right? She wasn't revealing anything.

She heard his hand on the paper before she saw it. He was sliding something toward her, something that scratched across the paper. With an indrawn breath, she pulled together her tattered control and let her gaze move to where his hand rested.

He'd stopped on the kitchen, the heart of the home, and in his hand was a ring.

Her gaze shot up, meeting his. He wasn't smiling, and his fingers trembled.

"I love you, Andie. I wanted... I hoped, um, maybe we can build this place together? For us?"

Bubbles fizzier than any champagne moved through her body. She flung herself at him, wrapping her arms around his neck and almost knocking him off the stool.

"Yes, yes. There's nothing I want more."

She grabbed his cheeks, meeting the smile creasing his face. She pulled that face toward her, not caring who was watching, and kissed him.

Whistles around them finally brought her to her senses, and she pulled back, still ignoring the crowd. She had eyes for no one but him.

He grabbed her hand and slid the ring on. "It's not a big stone or very fancy. I didn't want it to be a hazard while you're working."

Andie didn't care about the size. "It's perfect. You're perfect."

"No, I'm not. But hang on to that thought as long as you can. We might argue a bit on this." He tapped the blueprints.

She rubbed her thumbs over his cheeks. "Doesn't matter. As long as we do it together."

He rested his forehead on hers. "I was so nervous. I hoped this would make the day better for you."

"It has. But I'll warn you, Mariah is going to be annoyed that you didn't make a big deal of it to put on the website."

His cheeks turned pink. "Um..." His gaze moved past her, and she turned her head to see what he was looking at.

A cheer went up from the crowd. Her mother, some of her siblings, most of her crew, Rachel and Ryker, Jaycee and Dave, Mariah and Nelson... Almost everyone she knew was here to celebrate with her, making this a day of happiness, no longer one of regret.

She gripped Trevor's hand in hers. "Have I told you I love you?"

"No, but I'll forgive you if you kiss me at midnight."

"It's a date."

* * * * *

Keep reading for an excerpt of
The Troublemaker
by Maisey Yates.
Find it in
The Troublemaker anthology,
out now!

CHAPTER ONE

HE WAS THE very image of the Wild West, backlit by the setting sun, walking across the field that led directly to her house. He was wearing a black cowboy hat and a T-shirt that emphasized his broad shoulders; waist narrow and hips lean. His jaw square, his nose straight like a blade and his mouth set in a firm, uncompromising manner.

Lachlan McCloud was the epitome of a cowboy. She was proud to call him her best friend. He was loyal; he was—in spite of questionable behavior at times—an extremely good man, even if sometimes you had to look down deep to see it.

He was…

He was bleeding.

Charity sighed.

She had lost track of the amount of times that she had stitched Lachlan McCloud back together.

"I'll just get my kit, then," she muttered, digging around for it.

Not that there was any other reason Lachlan would be coming by unannounced. Usually now she went to his house for cards or for dinner; he didn't come here. Not since her dad had died.

She found her medical bag and opened up the front door, propping her hip against the door frame, holding the bag aloft.

He stopped. "How did you know?"

"I recognize your *I cut myself open and need to be sewn back together* walk."

"I have a…*need to be sewn back together* walk?"

"You do," she said, nodding.

"Thank you kindly."

She lived just on the other side of the property line from McCloud's Landing. One of the ranches that made up the vast spread that was Four Corners Ranch.

Thirty thousand acres, divided by four, amongst the original founding families.

Her father had been the large-animal vet in town and for the surrounding areas for years. With a mobile unit and all the supplies—granted, they were antiquated.

Charity had taken over a couple of years ago.

Her dad had always understood animals better than he did people. He'd told her people simply didn't speak his language, or he didn't speak theirs, but it didn't really matter which.

Charity had known how to speak her dad's language. He liked chamomile tea and *All Creatures Great and Small. Masterpiece Theatre* and movies made in the 1950s. Argyle socks—which she also loved—and cardigans. Again, something she loved, too.

He'd smoked a pipe and read from the paper every morning. He liked to do the crossword.

And just last month, he'd died. Without him the house seemed colder, emptier and just a whole lot less.

It was another reason she was thankful for Lachlan.

But then they'd both had a lot of changes recently. It wasn't just her. It wasn't just the loss of her father.

Lachlan was the last McCloud standing.

His brothers, resolute bachelors all—at least at one time— were now settled and having children. His brother Brody was an instant father, since he had just married Elizabeth, a single mother who had come to work at the equestrian center on McCloud's Landing a couple of months back.

But Lachlan was Lachlan. And if the changes had thrown him off, he certainly didn't show it.

He was still his hard-drinking, risk-taking, womanizing self.

But he'd always been that way. It was one reason she'd been so immediately drawn to him when they'd first met. He was nothing like her.

He was something so separate from her, something so different than she could ever be, that sometimes being friends with him was like being friends with someone from a totally different culture.

Sometimes she went with him and observed his native customs. She'd gone to Smokey's Tavern with the group of McClouds quite a few times, but she'd always found it noisy and the booze smelled bad. It gave her a headache.

And she didn't dance.

Lachlan had women fighting to dance with him, and she thought it was such a funny thing. Watching those women compete for his attention, for just a few moments of his time. They would probably never see him again.

She would see him again the next day and the day after that, and the day after that.

"What did you do?" she asked, looking at the nasty gash.

"I had a little run-in with some barbed wire."

He was at the door now, filling up the space. He did that. He wasn't the kind of person you could ignore. And given that she was the kind of person *all too* easy to ignore, she admired that about him.

"We've gotta stop meeting like this," he said, grinning.

She'd seen him turn that grin on women in the bar and they fell apart. She'd always been proud of herself for not behaving that way.

"I wish we could, Lachlan. But you insist on choosing violence."

"Every day."

"You could stop being in a fight with the world," she pointed out.

"I could. But you know the thing about that is it sounds boring."

"Well... A bored Lachlan McCloud is not anything I want to see." She jerked her head back toward the living room. "Come on in."

He did, and the air seemed to rush right out of her lungs as he entered the small, homey sitting room in her little house.

She still had everything of her father's sitting out, like he might come back any day.

His science-fiction novels and his medical journals. His field guides to different animals and the crocheted afghan that he had sat with, draped over his lap, in his burnt orange recliner, when at the end of his days he hadn't been able to do much.

She had been a very late-in-life surprise for her father.

She'd been born when he was in his fifties. And he had raised her alone, because that had been the agreement, so the story went. Amicable and easy. Which made sense. Because her father had been like that. Steady and calm. A nice man. Old-fashioned. But then... He had been in his eighties when he'd passed. He wasn't really old-fashioned so much as of his time.

He'd homeschooled her, brought her on all his veterinary calls. Her life had been simple. And it had been good.

She'd had her dad. And then... She'd had Lachlan.

And there was no reason at all that suddenly this room should feel tiny with Lachlan standing in it. Because he had been in here any number of times.

Especially in the end, visiting her dad and talking to him about baseball.

She sometimes thought her dad was the closest thing that Lachlan had to a father figure. His own dad had been a monster.

Of course, the unfairness of that was that Lachlan's dad was still alive out there somewhere. While her sweet dad was gone.

"It's quiet in here," Lachlan said, picking up on her train of thought.

"It would've been quiet in here if Dad was alive. Until you two started shouting about sports." She grinned just thinking about it. "You do know how to get him riled up." Then her smile fell slightly. "*Did.* You did know."

"I could still rile him up, I bet. But I don't know that we want séance levels of trouble."

She laughed, because she knew the joke came from a place of affection, and that was something she prized about her relationship with Lachlan. They just *knew* each other.

She hadn't really known anyone but adults before she'd met Lachlan. She'd known the people they'd done veterinary work for; she'd known the old men her dad had sat outside and smoked pipes with on summer evenings.

Lachlan had been her first friend.

He was her only friend. Still.

He'd taught her sarcasm. He'd introduced her to pop culture. He'd once given her a sip of beer when she'd been eighteen. He'd laughed at the face she'd made.

"I do not want that level of trouble. I also don't want *your* level of trouble," she said. "But here you are. Sit down and bite on something."

"I don't need to bite on anything to get a few stitches, Charity. Settle down. I know what I'm about."

"You can't flinch, Lachlan, and sometimes you're a bad patient. So brace yourself."

"You could numb me."

"I could," she said. "But I'm not just letting you use all my supplies. I'm stitching you for no cost."

"Considering you normally stitch up horses, you should pay me to let you do this."

"Please. Working on animals is more complicated than working on people. People all have the same set of organs right in the same places. Animals… It's all arranged differently. I have to know way more to take care of animals."

"Yes. I've heard the lecture before."

"But you've never taken it on board."

"All right," he said, resting his hand on the coffee table in front of her and revealing the big gash in his forearm.

She winced.

"Hardass doctor, wincing at this old thing," he said.

"It's different when it's on a person," she said.

Except it really was different when it was on him. Because he was hers.

He was special.

Seeing him injured in any capacity made her heart feel raw, even if she'd seen it a hundred times.

"All right, Doc."

"Okay," she said.

She took her curved needle out of her kit, along with the thread, and she poked it right through his skin.

He growled.

"I told you," she said.

She thought back to how they'd met. He'd been bruised and battered, and in bad need of medical attention.

His had been the first set of stitches she'd ever given.

She swallowed hard.

He winced and shifted when she pushed her needle through his skin again.

"I can't guarantee you that you're not going to have a scar," she said, her tone filled with warning.

"Just one to add to my collection of many."

"Yes. You're very tough."

"Oh, hell, sweetheart, I know that."

"Don't *sweetheart* me." He called every woman sweetheart. And she didn't like being lumped together with all that. She liked *their* things. Baseball and jokes about séances and *Doc*.

"How is everything going at the facility?"

She had a hands-on role in the veterinary care of the animals at the new therapy center on McCloud's Landing. But everything had taken a backseat when her dad had declined, then passed. She was working her way back up to it all, but it was slow.

"It's going well. Of course, I am tripping over all the happy couples. Tag and Nelly, Alaina and Gus, Hunter and Elsie, Brody and Elizabeth. It's ridiculous. It's like a Disney cartoon where it's spring and all the animals are hooking up and having babies."

"The domesticity must appall you," she said. But she wasn't even really joking.

She continued to work slowly on the stitches, taking her time and trying to get them small and straight to leave the least amount of damage, because whatever he said about scars, she was determined to stitch her friend back together as neatly as possible.

"I'm glad they're happy," she said.

"Yeah. Me, too. It's a good thing. It's a damn good thing."

But he sounded a bit gruff and a bit not like himself. She had to wonder if all the changes were getting to him. It was tough to tell with Lachlan, because his whole thing was to put on a brave face and pretend that things were all right.

He'd tried that when they'd first met.

She had been playing in the woods. By herself. She was always by herself. Even though she'd been fifteen, she'd been a young fifteen. She'd never really gotten to be around other children. So she was both vastly older and vastly younger in many different ways. She liked to wander the woods and imagine herself in a fairy tale. That she might encounter Prince Charming out there.

Then one day she'd been walking down a path, and there he'd been. Tall and rangy—even at sixteen—with messy brown hair and bright blue eyes.

But he'd been hurt.

Suddenly, he'd put his hand on his ribs and gone down onto his knees.

She could still remember the way she'd run over to him.

"ARE YOU ALL RIGHT?"

"Fine," he said, looking up at her, his lip split, a cut over his eye bleeding profusely.

"That's a lie," she said.

"Yeah." He wheezed out a cough. "No shit."

She'd never heard anyone say that word in real life before. Just overheard in movies and read in books.

Her father was against swearing. He thought that it was vulgar and common. He said that people ought to have more imagination than that.

"That is shocking language," she said.

"Shocking language... Okay. Look, you can just... Head on out. Don't worry about me. This is hardly the first time I've had my ribs broken."

He winced again.

"You need stitches," she said, looking at his forehead.

"I'm not going to be able to get them."

"Why not?"

"No insurance. Anyway, my dad's not gonna pay for me to go to the doctor."

"I... I can help," she said.

She could only hope that her dad was still at home.

He had a call to go out on later, but there was a chance he hadn't left yet.

"Can you stand up?"

"I can try."

She found herself taking hold of his hand, which was big and rough and masculine in comparison to hers.

Like he was a different thing altogether.

She'd seen the boys on the ranch from a distance before, but she'd never met one of them.

He might even be a *man*, he was so tall already.

He made her feel very small. Suddenly, her heart gave a great jump, like she'd been frightened. He made her feel like a rabbit, standing in front of a fox, and she couldn't say why.

But he wasn't a fox. And she wasn't a rabbit.

He was just a boy who needed help.

"Lean on me," she said.

He looked down at her. "I don't want to hurt you. You're a tiny little thing."

"I'm sturdy," she said. "Come on."

"All right."

He put his arm around her, and the two of them walked back to the house. Her father was gone. But his bag was still there.

"I've watched my dad do this a lot of times. I think I can do it."

"Your dad's a doctor?"

The best thing would be to lie. It was to make him feel better, not for nefarious reasons. It wasn't *really* a lie. But of course what this boy meant was a doctor for humans…and she was going to let him believe it.

"Yes. I've been on lots of calls with him. I can do this."

"Good."

She found a topical numbing cream in the bag and gingerly applied it around the wound on his forehead.

His breath hissed through his teeth.

She waited a few minutes before taking out a needle and thread. Beads of sweat formed on his forehead, his teeth gritted.

But when she finished, he looked up at her and smiled.

"Thanks, Doc."

SHE LOOKED DOWN at the stitches she was giving now.

"That ought to do it," she said.

"Thanks. Hey, Doc," he said and he lifted his head up so that they were practically sharing the same air.

His face was so close to hers; close enough she could see the bristles of his stubble, the blue of his eyes, that they were a darker ring of blue around the outside, and lighter toward the center.

What is happening?

Her throat felt scratchy, and her heart felt…sore.

"Yes?" It came out a near whisper.

"I need a favor."

"What?"

"I need you to reform me."